together

Also by Julie Cohen

Dear Thing
Where Love Lies
Falling

together

Julie Cohen

First published in Great Britain in 2017 by Orion Books,
an imprint of The Orion Publishing Group Ltd
Carmelite House, 50 Victoria Embankment,
London EC4Y 0DZ

An Hachette UK company

1 3 5 7 9 10 8 6 4 2

Copyright © Julie Cohen 2017

A CIP catalogue record for this book is
available from the British Library.

ISBN (Hardback) 978 1 4091 7174 4
ISBN (Export Trade Paperback) 978 1 4091 7175 1

Typeset by Input Data Services Ltd, Somerset

Printed and bound by CPI Group (UK) Ltd, Croydon, CR0 4YY

MIX
Paper from
responsible sources
FSC® C104740

www.orionbooks.co.uk

To Teresa
and
To Harriet

'It is, in short, music which observes neither end nor beginning, music with neither real climax nor real resolution, music which, like Baudelaire's lovers, "rests lightly on the wings of the unchecked wind."'

Glenn Gould, on Bach's *The Goldberg Variations*, 1956

PART ONE

2016

Chapter One

September 2016
Clyde Bay, Maine

Robbie woke up when it was still dark outside. They'd slept with the windows open and he could hear the surf on the rocks. It was such a constant sound that he rarely heard it any more, but this morning he did. He could hear Emily's breathing, too. He lay there in his bed for a few moments, listening to her breath and the water, both steady and familiar, as if both of them could go on forever.

Emily's face was turned away from him but her body touched his, her backside snug against his hip, her ankle curled around his so her toes rested against the sole of his foot. Most mornings he would roll over on to his side and put his arm around her waist, and she would nestle back against him in her sleep, and they would stay there for a little while, long enough so that when he got up, leaving her asleep in their bed, he would still feel the warmth of her pressed against him and he would go about his morning routine, recalling the scent of her hair.

If things stayed as they were, if they progressed as they would, he knew this would be the one thing that would never change. Not the rhythm of their sleep or the pattern of their touching. They had slept together this way on their first night together, fifty-four years ago, and every night since then that they hadn't slept in the same bed was a wasted night as far as he was concerned. Robbie knew his body would remember Emily's even if he allowed himself to live long enough for his mind to forget her.

It would be enough, to live for these moments of touching. For himself, it would be enough. But he had to think of Emily.

Since the day he had met her, over fifty years ago, everything he had done was for Emily, and this was the last thing he needed to do for her. Now, while he could still do it.

Robbie eased himself away from Emily without disturbing her. He sat up on his side of the bed. He was eighty years old, and aside from a twinge from the old wound in his thigh in the rainy weather, he was in pretty good shape, physically. He still more or less recognised himself in the mirror these days, though his hair was almost entirely gone to grey and he had the leathery, ageless skin of a man who had spent most of his time outdoors. His body probably had ten, fifteen more years in it. Preserved by the salt: that was what they said about old sailors.

Without thinking too much, he got dressed in the near-darkness, as he did almost every morning except for some Sundays. He went downstairs trailing his hand over the banister railing he'd carved himself out of a single piece of oak. He'd had to take the front door frame out to get the railing in the house. Back in 1986 – Adam had been ten.

He tested himself on dates like this now, reiterating the facts, so maybe they would stick. *Adam married Shelley in 2003. We moved to Clyde Bay in 1977. I met Emily in 1962. I was born in 1936, during the Great Depression. I retired in 19 . . . No, I was seventy, or was I . . . where are we now?*

Robbie looked up. He was in the kitchen, where he'd built the cabinets with his own hands. He was filling the pot for coffee. Every morning he did the same thing, while Emily slept upstairs, and soon Adam would come downstairs, yawning, to do his paper round before he went to school.

A dog nudged his leg. 'Just one minute, Bella,' he said easily, and he looked down and it wasn't Bella. This dog had a white patch on his chest, and it wasn't Bella because Bella was pure black, it was ... it was Bella's son, it was ...

Another dog yawned noisily and got up stiffly from the dog bed in the corner of the kitchen, a black dog with grey on his muzzle and a white patch on his chest. Robbie looked from the old dog to the young dog and the young one nudged his hand and wagged his tail and he was Rocco. It came back to him in a rush. This was Rocco, and the old one was his father, Tybalt, and Bella was Tybalt's mother and had been dead for thirteen years.

Robbie's hand shook when he opened the door to let the two dogs out.

It was like the fog that came in silently and out of nowhere, and socked you in so solid you couldn't see a single thing, not even your own sails. In a fog like that you could only navigate from instruments, not from sight – but with this fog, none of the instruments worked. You were in waters you knew like the back of your hand, but you couldn't tell where you were. You could strike a rock that you'd avoided a million times before; that you knew like an old friend. Or you could head in completely the wrong direction and never find your way back.

He didn't finish making the coffee. He found a piece of paper and a pen and he sat right down at the kitchen table and he wrote Emily the letter he had been composing in his head for days now. He wrote it quickly, before the fog came back and stopped him. The words weren't exactly as eloquent as he wanted them to be. There was so much left unsaid. But then again, he'd always told Emily that he was no poet.

I love you, he wrote. *You're my beginning and my ending, Emily, and every day in between.*

And really, that was everything he meant anyway. That summed it all up.

He folded the letter carefully and wrote *Emily* on the outside of it. The letter safe in his hand, he went out the kitchen door to the yard, where the dogs greeted him with wagging tails and tongues.

It was the grey light before dawn. Tybalt and Rocco followed him as he walked around the house that he had built for Emily and himself. He checked the windows, the porch steps, the doors, the shingles; he peered up at the roof with its three gables, and the chimney. He'd spent the summer doing repairs. Planning ahead, for this day.

There was nothing left to be done here. It was all sound; she should be fine for the winter, when it came. And after that, Adam would help her. Maybe William would come back and help her, too.

A wild rose bush grew against the cedar shingles on the side of the house. Last month the bush had been ablaze with blossoms; now there were only a few left to face the end of summer. Avoiding the thorns, he picked a rose off the bush. It was bright pink, with a yellow centre. The petals were tender and perfect.

He whistled for the dogs and they came into the house with him. He tipped some food into their dishes and refreshed their water bowls. He stroked their heads and scratched behind their ears.

Then he went upstairs to their bedroom, carrying the letter and the rose.

She was still asleep. She hadn't moved. He gazed down at her. Her hair had threads of silver and sunshine, her skin was soft in sleep. She was the girl he'd met in 1962; the girl he felt like he'd waited his whole life up till then to meet. He thought about waking her up to see her eyes again. They were the same colour that the sea had been the first time he'd ever seen it, back in 1952, a shade of blue that up till then he had never even been able to imagine.

But if he woke her up to see her eyes for the last time it wouldn't be the last time, because she would never let him go.

And if he put this off and put this off, one day the fog would surround him. It came in stealthily, but all at once. One minute you could see clear – and the next moment you were blind. And more than blind: you couldn't even remember what it was like to see.

He placed the letter on her bedside table, next to the glass of water she kept there. It would be the first thing she saw when she woke up. He put the wild rose on top of it. Then he bent and kissed her, gently, on her cheek. He breathed in a lungful of her scent.

'I'd never have forgotten you,' he whispered to her, more quietly than the sound of the ocean outside.

He made himself stand up straight and leave her there, sleeping. He'd thought it would be hard but there had been a harder time, once, walking away from her. That first time they had said goodbye.

This time was easier than that. Now, they had so many good years behind them. Every one of the years they'd spent together had been good. It had been worth it, every single bit.

Robbie went through the front door so he didn't have to see the dogs again. He walked down the porch steps and down the sloping path to the end of their yard. Across the road and along the little path cleared in the brush, the twigs snagging his trousers till he was standing on the rocks on the shore. Grey Maine granite, darkening to black, and when you looked at it closely there were little shining chips of mica like diamonds in it.

He took off his shoes and socks and left them on a high rock, untouched by spray. He left his shirt and trousers folded up beside them. Then, barefoot, he stepped on to the furthest rock, which was wet with surf and slippery with seaweed.

He'd thought it might be foggy today, but it wasn't. It was all clear ahead of him and the sun was beginning to rise. It was gold and pink, not far off the colours of that wild rose he'd left beside Emily. It was going to be a good day, the kind of day where you could see Monhegan Island on the horizon. Lobster pots bobbed on the water, blue and white and red. He knew who owned all of them and knew what time they'd be coming in their boats to haul them up. Not for a little while, yet.

He had enough time.

Robbie jumped into the water. His body made barely a splash into the waves.

He had always been a strong swimmer. It was easy for him. Part fish, Emily called him. He kicked through the waves. Even after being warmed all the summer long, the water was cold enough to take your breath away, but if you kept moving you would be all right, for a while, at least until the current took you. Pieces of a boat that was wrecked on Marshall Point, a quarter mile from here to the north, had been found all the way up in Newfoundland.

He swam and he kept his eyes on the horizon. It took him a long time to tire out. Long enough so that he saw the top curve of the sun rising up from the water in front of him, a brilliant light, shining all the way along the water to him. It would shine through the window of the room where Emily slept and it would touch her cheek and her hair.

Robbie kept swimming until he couldn't swim any more and then he let the water carry him away, into something bigger than himself, more vast than memory.

Chapter Two

July 2016
Clyde Bay, Maine

The cake was eaten, the iced tea drunk; Emily sat in the afternoon sunshine at the picnic table in their garden, holding Robbie's hand. A breeze came off the ocean and kept it from being too hot.

'I wasn't expecting a cake,' she said to Adam and Shelley, 'but it was delicious. Thank you.'

'We couldn't let your anniversary go by with just ice cream,' said her son. 'Forty-three years is nothing to sneeze at.'

'Only seven more years till you make it to fifty,' said Shelley, their daughter-in-law.

Robbie squeezed her hand under the table. Francie, their youngest grandchild at four, wiped a blob of buttercream off her cheek and said, 'What's an anniservary?'

'Anni*versary*. It's a celebration of the date that two people got married,' her father, Adam, told her. Francie had Adam's blonde hair and Shelley's dark eyes and freckles. The two elder ones, Chloe and Bryan, were pure redheads, unlike anyone else in the family. Sometimes Adam made a joke about recessive genes and the postman, which always ended in Shelley swatting him.

Rocco dropped a ball at Bryan's feet and the boy was up, throwing it across the lawn for the Labrador to chase. Tybalt, the elder dog, lay panting in the shade of a tree. Chloe, who at twelve preferred to stay with the adults, drew faces on the table with spilled iced tea and said, 'Where are your wedding pictures, Grandma? I've never seen your wedding dress.'

Emily smiled. 'That's because I didn't have one. We eloped, your grandfather and I.'

'Because I'm a born romantic,' declared Robbie. 'I swept your grandmother off her feet and she couldn't rest until I put a ring on her finger.'

'I seem to recall that you were the one who insisted on giving me a ring.' She touched it with her thumb: a gold band in the shape of two clasped hands.

'Can I see it?' asked Chloe, and Emily twisted it off her finger. It wasn't easy; her knuckles had swollen with age. She dropped it into Chloe's waiting palm and watched her granddaughter turning it over, admiring it. 'It's like it doesn't end,' she said. 'One hand turns into another one and then they hold on to each other.'

'That's exactly why I chose it,' said Robbie. He took it back from Chloe and presented it to Emily, who took it and slipped it back on, smiling.

'Was it love at first sight?'

Chloe was quite interested in love at first sight, Emily knew. The girl read book after book of young adult romance, most of it involving horrible illnesses, terrifying alternative futures, or vampires. Emily had read a few of them herself, on her granddaughter's recommendation. She enjoyed them very much.

'Absolutely at first sight,' said Robbie. 'The minute I saw your grandmother, I knew she was the only girl for me. And you knew the same, didn't you, Emily?'

'I knew you were very handsome. I can't say marriage was on my mind right at that exact moment.'

'You knew I was the most handsome man you'd ever seen,' corrected Robbie.

'Yes.' She smiled, looking at his silver hair, still a full head of it. His dark eyes still had their twinkle, and his mouth quirked with good humour and confidence. 'The most handsome man I'd ever seen. Also the most full of himself.'

'With good reason.'

'With very good reason.'

'Where were you?' asked Chloe.

'In a train station,' said Robbie. 'I saw her across a crowded room.'

Emily squeezed his hand again, quickly. 'No, darling,' she said. 'It was in an airport.'

He blinked at her, his face clouding and then clearing almost instantaneously, fast enough so that no one else but her would notice. 'Oh, yes, that's right. An airport, in 1972.'

'In Florida,' said Adam, 'where I was born. We'll have to go down there, one day. I don't remember anything about it.'

'Disney?' suggested Francie immediately, climbing on to her father's lap.

'Maybe.' He kissed her blonde head. 'Or we could go to England, where your Grandma was born.'

'So you eloped and moved from England to America?' Chloe pursued. 'You didn't have a dress or flowers or anything?'

'We just sailed off into the sunset together,' said Emily.

'In the same boat you have now?'

'It was a different boat, back then.'

'You got your feet wet,' said Robbie. 'But I rescued you.'

'We rescued *each other*,' said Emily. 'And we've never been apart since, except for a night or two here or there.'

'That's so romantic,' sighed Chloe. Emily swallowed hard, seeing across years the echo of another twelve-year-old: this one with dark hair instead of red. That was exactly something that Polly would have said, all those years ago. She glanced at Robbie, to see if he had caught it as well, but he was just smiling at his granddaughter.

'Actually,' Emily said, 'romance is quite exhausting. I like everyday life much better.'

'Not me,' said Chloe.

'Your parents have just as romantic a story,' said Robbie. 'They met over the photocopier.'

'Your father,' said Shelley, 'was never prepared for his morning

American History class and always got to school early to copy worksheets, just at the time when I was trying to photocopy poems for Honours English.'

'It took her half a semester to figure out I was doing it on purpose,' Adam said.

'Ugh,' said Chloe. 'Nothing romantic ever happens in a *school*.'

Emily saw Adam and Shelley exchange a look – the complicity of married couples, communicating without words.

Bryan, aged eight, ran up. He was breathing hard. 'Grandpa, Rocco wants to go for a swim. Can I take him?'

'Not here,' said Adam. 'The current's too strong in front of the house.'

Robbie stood up. 'I'll walk you down to the bay,' he said. 'You can throw a ball all you want for him there down by the landing. You won't all fit in the dinghy but I can borrow Little Sterling's launch and give you a ride if you want. Want to come, William?'

'I'm Francie,' said Francie.

'Well then, do you want to come, Francie?'

The little girl hopped off her daddy's lap and put her hand in her grandfather's. 'Can I have an ice cream at the store?'

'You just had ice cream,' said Shelley, but Robbie winked at the little girl and said, 'Shh, don't tell your mother.'

'I'll come too,' said Chloe. 'Mom, can I borrow your phone?'

Shelley rolled her eyes, but handed over the phone.

'Are you coming, Em?' asked Robbie. 'I'll buy you an ice cream too. The biggest ice cream you ever saw, for my sweetheart.'

'Adam will come with you, won't you, Adam?' Adam nodded, and Emily kissed Robbie's cheek. 'I'll stay here and do the dishes. Dry the dogs and kids off before you let them back into the house.'

He kissed her and she watched him go, accompanied by their son, surrounded by grandchildren and dogs. Other than the grey of his hair, from the back he could still be the man she'd first met all those years ago, before they'd imagined any of this was possible.

12

He'd called Francie 'William'.

In the kitchen the two women filled the dishwasher, working in an easy rhythm. Some of Emily's friends had problems with their daughters-in-law, but Emily knew she was blessed. Shelley told her about their plans for the rest of the Fourth of July holiday weekend, taking the kids up to Rangeley where Shelley's family had a camp on the lake. They'd stay up there a couple of weeks, so the kids could play with their cousins and Shelley could catch up with her extended family. 'It's the best part of being a teacher,' she said, wrapping up the remainder of the cake. 'The summer holiday.'

'I don't believe that for a minute,' said Emily. 'You love your students.'

'You could join us. You and Robbie would be really welcome, and we've got an extra bedroom. You could bring the dogs; they'd love the lake. My brother has a little sailboat he doesn't even know how to use.'

'I'd like that. I'll have to ask Robbie. He's doing some work around the house this summer.'

'Adam said that, from the looks of it, he's got about six projects going at once. He was complaining because Robbie had always told him to finish one job before starting the next.'

'Is that so?' said Emily vaguely. 'Well, he must have a lot of repairs to do. It was a hard winter. Have you heard from William lately, by the way? He hasn't called since last month.'

'He sent an email last week with some photos of the kids. I'll forward it to you, if you haven't got it.' Shelley opened the refrigerator to replace the jug of milk, and paused. 'Er . . . what's this?'

'What's what?'

Shelley took something out of the refrigerator and held it up. It was Robbie's wallet.

'He's going to have trouble buying ice cream without this,' said Shelley, beginning to laugh.

Emily turned away quickly, back to the dishes, before her daughter-in-law could see her face. 'One of the kids must have put it there as a joke,' she said, indistinctly, rinsing a glass. Though she knew it had not been one of the kids.

Fireworks exploded in the distance, over Clyde Bay, around the point a quarter mile from their house. Some years they watched them from the boat, with a view of the lights on the shore and the fireworks reflected on the water. This year the kids had left too late and Emily had been too tired to bother with getting the boat off their mooring. The main problem with being older: being tired. And this afternoon, happy though it had been, had been a strain, too, with watching Robbie and watching Adam and Shelley to see if they noticed, if they understood.

William had called late in the afternoon to wish them a happy anniversary. It was only three o'clock where he was in Alaska. He'd called her phone instead of the house phone and from the look that Adam and Shelley exchanged when she answered the call, she knew that one of them had sent him a text to prompt him to ring. She pretended not to know as she chatted with him, told him about the cake and the sunshine and how the dogs and kids had tracked half the beach into the house with them. William's laughter, a continent away, sounded just like Robbie's.

'Your father would love to speak with you,' she said, and passed the phone to Robbie. 'It's William.'

She watched as Robbie took the phone. 'Hello, son. Yes, thank you. All good there? Good, good.' A silence, and Emily tried to hear if William was speaking on the other end.

'You probably want to talk with your brother.' Robbie handed the phone to Adam, and Emily drew the familiar sigh.

Now, from the spare bedroom they used as an office, Emily could see flashes through the window, though she couldn't see the fireworks themselves. Wrapped in a dressing gown she sat at the desk and checked her email. As promised, Shelley had forwarded her William's email as soon as she'd got home. Emily opened it and gazed with pleasure at the photographs of William's two children. It was tough for him, splitting custody with their mother; but he only lived a couple of miles from her and saw them almost every day.

The girl, Brianna, most resembled what William had looked like as a child: gap-toothed, dark-haired – even a haircut much like William had had in the 1970s. Emily supposed everything came back into style, eventually. Brianna posed with her older brother John in front of a lake and pine trees, with fishing rods in their hands. Alaska looked a lot like Maine, though William said that they had even more vicious black flies there.

She was about to call Robbie to come in and look when she saw that she had another email as well, from someone called Lucy Knight. The subject was *Christopher*.

Dear Emily,
I hope you don't mind my emailing you out of the blue like this.

I thought you would probably want to know that Christopher passed away last month. I would have told you sooner, but everything seems to take so much more time for me since he's been gone. He didn't suffer; he died in bed, suddenly, of a heart attack. I woke up and he was gone.

I know we never met bar the once, but Christopher often spoke of you, as a colleague and a friend. He regarded his time in South America as – he never said in so many words that it was the happiest, because, as you know, he could never be anything but kind – but he spoke of it as one of the most productive times in his life, as the time he felt he did the most good. He was a fine man and I was very lucky to have him. I miss him very much.

Yours sincerely,
Lucy Norris Knight

She put her hand over her mouth. Christopher.

'Sweetheart?' Robbie came in and rested his hand on the back of her chair. 'Coming to bed?'

'I . . . was looking at a photo of Brianna and John and I just got this. About Christopher.' She swivelled the chair so that Robbie could read the email over her shoulder.

'Oh, Em, I'm sorry.' He pulled up a second chair and put his arm around her shoulders.

She had tears in her eyes. 'Sometimes I think of him. I often wondered how he . . . but I didn't ask. I don't know how Lucy got my email address. That's his wife, Lucy. She must have looked it up somewhere.'

'Polly?'

'I doubt it. I don't think Polly knows it. It must have been a search engine or something.'

'Maybe Christopher had it.'

'He never emailed me. I saw him for the last time at my mother's funeral.' She shook her head. 'I think of him now and I just picture him the way I knew him at Cambridge. I can't picture him an old man, or even as he was when we were – when we were in Bolivia together. I see him skinny, with that hairstyle he had, so neat, and those horn-rimmed glasses he used to wear. There's been a whole lifetime since then. Isn't that funny?'

'He was your best friend.'

'For a very, very long time, yes, he was. Until you.' She put her palm on Robbie's cheek and he turned into it and kissed it.

'I'm sorry,' he said. 'That's sad news.'

'I knew him so well. I knew everything about him, once.' She scrolled down the email, but there was nothing else. Just the fact of Christopher's death, and the kind words from his wife, who was obligated to send her nothing but had anyway.

'He knew,' she said. 'He knew . . . that . . .'

Robbie frowned slightly. 'He did?'

'I told him, once. Or he half figured it out. When we were still at Cambridge, doing our exams. We only spoke about it once and

16

he never mentioned it again. Not even when you and I . . . when I left him.'

'Do you think he told his wife?'

'I don't think so. Christopher was a gentleman. I told him to keep it a secret and he would have done. He was a good man.'

Robbie gazed at her. 'That means,' he said, slowly, 'that no one else knows, now.'

She nodded.

'Not Polly?' he said.

'I don't even know if Polly is still alive. But I don't think she knew. She didn't want to know. Not Marie?'

'I never told Marie.'

'So no one knows.'

'Only you and me,' said Robbie. 'We're the only people left alive who know it.'

'Yes,' she said. 'Yes. Just you and me.'

'Then we're free,' he said. 'Finally, you and I are free.'

Chapter Three

When Emily woke up, Robbie was gone. She put her hand out to touch his pillow and it was still warm, still bearing the imprint of his head. The sun had risen and was shining through their bedroom window.

When they'd first moved to Maine, they could only afford seafront property by buying a lot with a near-derelict house on it: a boxy, strict Victorian farmhouse, weathered and sagging, with holes in the roof. Robbie had renovated the house so extensively that little of the original footprint remained. It was a three-gabled, cedar-shingled house with a wide porch on the side facing the ocean, white trim on all the doors and windows, and a garage workshop on the side. But sometimes, when Emily looked up at the house, she could see the ghost of that old nineteenth-century building standing there, too.

The original master bedroom had been at the back of the house, facing the woods, but Robbie had moved it to the front, facing east and the water. He wanted to hear the ocean as they slept, and he wanted to see the sun rise.

In practice, he was usually awake before sunrise, even since he'd retired.

Emily smiled and listened for him around the house. He whistled, sometimes, moving from room to room. He always listened to rock music, but he whistled Bach. She didn't even think he consciously realised he was doing it. It was a thread of sound that tied their years together: along with the dogs' toenails on the floor, children's footsteps, the radio in his workshop, the constant susurration of the sea.

She didn't hear him this morning, but she kept listening anyway.

The phone rang; she let it go for a couple of rings to see if Robbie would pick it up downstairs, since at this hour it was bound to be for him, not her. When he didn't, she reached over for the extension on his bedside table.

'Dr Brandon?'

She recognised the voice at once: he'd never quite lost his Quebec accent. 'Good morning, Pierre.'

'I wondered if maybe you wanted to come down to the boatyard? It's not a problem, we're always glad to see Bob, but—'

She sat up straight. 'What's he done? Is he all right?'

'Oh, nothing to worry about. He's fine. But maybe you want to come down, you know?'

She dressed in a hurry and left in her own car, noticing that Robbie's truck was gone.

Pierre hadn't changed the name of the boatyard when he bought it from Robbie on his retirement; the sign was still painted blue on white, Brandon's Boatyard. Pierre had had it repainted recently, from the looks of it. When she got there, Pierre was waiting for her near the entrance to one of the work bays, standing next to Little Sterling, both with Dunkin' Donuts coffee cups in their hands. Pierre was small and scrappy, descended from generations of woodsmen; Little Sterling, despite his name, was a mountain of a man descended from generations of lobstermen. The two of them made a Laurel and Hardy silhouette together, though this morning Emily didn't find them comical at all.

'He was here when I got here this morning,' Pierre said to her. 'And he's been working steady, won't have coffee or nothing. Says he's got to get the ketch done by the weekend, but you know, there's no deadline on her, she just come in yesterday.'

They all looked down to the water, where Robbie worked on

19

one of the boats in the slips. His back was turned to them.

'Did he . . .' She swallowed. 'Did he know who you were?'

'Oh yeah, he did. He told me I'd never finish my apprenticeship if I stood around drinking coffee all day.'

'Is he all right, doc?' asked Little Sterling.

'I'm sure he's absolutely fine,' she said, firmly, and walked down to the slips. Her footsteps on the wooden pontoons announced her presence and Robbie looked up from his work on the white-hulled boat and smiled at her.

With that smile she could tell that he knew her. She didn't know how afraid she'd been until she felt the relief.

'Robbie? Are you all right, love?'

He put down his wire brush. 'Never better.'

'Why are you here?'

'I'm working on this ketch. She's . . .' He faded off, and for a moment he looked confused.

'It's not your boatyard any more,' she said to him, gently, touching his wrist. 'You sold it to Pierre, remember?'

'Pierre?'

'Pierre L'Allier. You said he was the best person to take it on when you retired and you let him have it at a ridiculously good price.'

'Oh. Oh, yes, I did. Daylight robbery.' Robbie looked around at the boats in slips, the boats in the yard, the white-painted workshop. Pierre and Little Sterling had disappeared into the building, presumably to give them some privacy.

'Why am I here?' he asked Emily.

Her heart wrenched in her chest. 'I . . . you don't remember?'

'Maybe I wanted to do some work on *Goldberg Variations*?' He looked around again. 'But she's on the mooring, isn't she?'

'We could take her out today.'

Robbie nodded, seemingly relieved. 'I'd like that. Let me . . . let me put away these tools.'

'I'll go ask Pierre if we can use his dinghy to get out there so we don't have to go into town.' She kissed him on the forehead, and went up to the workshop. Pierre and Little Sterling were standing by a mobile hydraulic lift, talking quietly. They looked up when she entered.

'It's all fine,' she said. 'Thanks for calling me. We're going to go out on the sailboat; I wonder if we could borrow a dinghy?'

'Fourth will give you a lift,' Little Sterling said. 'You just call him when you want to come back.' He reached into his pocket for his cell phone. 'I could have sworn Bob thought he was still working here, when I saw him this morning.'

'It's all OK,' Pierre said quickly. 'He's welcome here any time. Far as I'm concerned, it's still his place. He built it up from scratch.'

Emily nodded, and swallowed, and tried to ignore the burning, sick feeling of shame in her stomach.

Fourth – real name Sterling Ames, the Fourth, the son of Little Sterling who was the third of that name – drove his motor dinghy up to the end of the slip with the careless competence of a person who has been piloting boats since childhood. Robbie hopped in and helped Emily. He still had that look on his face: that lost look, almost helpless, almost as if he were desperately searching for some meaning.

It was not an expression that sat well on his face. Robbie had always been able to do anything. This expression made him appear almost a stranger.

Their sloop was on a private mooring in Clyde Bay proper; Fourth steered them to it without having to ask where they were going. People around here knew each other's boats as well as they knew each other's children. She watched Robbie's face as they approached their boat and saw his lost look gradually being replaced by pleasure. He'd made that boat with his own hands: shaped it and sanded it, rigged it, varnished the teak, painted its decks white and its hull a deep green, lettered the name on the stern himself. It was countless weekends and afternoons and mornings, this boat: time and memory made visible.

'That's a fine boat,' said Robbie.

'Pops says there's no better wooden sloop in the state of Maine,' said Fourth.

'There isn't,' Emily said. 'She takes a lot of care, but she's worth it.'

'Like a woman,' said Robbie, automatically, and she smiled and squeezed his hand.

'I always meant to ask,' Fourth said, 'is Goldberg your maiden name, doc? Is that why you called her *Goldberg Variations*?'

'No,' said Robbie. 'It's ... it's a ...' He snapped his fingers. 'Goldberg, it's a ...'

'It's a piece of classical music,' said Emily, to Fourth rather than to Robbie, though she was saying it for him. 'By Bach. It's an aria, followed by a series of variations in different tempos and moods, which ends with the same aria. Sort of like a circle.'

'That's it,' said Robbie, reaching out for the railing on the stern. 'I knew I'd remember.'

'Have you talked about it with him?' asked Sarah. She and Emily were sitting at her kitchen table, having lunch. Most Wednesdays they had lunch, sometimes out, sometimes at one of their houses. Sarah had made a chicken salad and iced coffee. Her eldest daughter, Dottie, was bringing a pecan pie later on, from the Clyde Bay General Store where she worked.

'No. Not yet.'

'Isn't that sort of strange, in itself?'

'But ...' Emily stirred her coffee. 'There's a lot we don't talk about.'

'You two are always talking. You talk all the time.'

'Yes, but there are things ... we've known each other so long, we've been with each other constantly. There are things we don't need to talk about, because we know.'

'I can see why none of my marriages ever lasted,' joked Sarah. 'I'm always asking the questions. Where were you last night? How many beers did you drink? When did you get home? Whose perfume is that on you?'

Emily laughed despite herself. By any logic, she and Sarah shouldn't be friends; they were entirely different, from completely different backgrounds. There were nearly thirty years between them. Emily was a retired obstetrician and Sarah worked as a cashier in the supermarket up in Thomaston. Sarah was a native Mainer, and Emily, even after forty years in Maine, was what they called 'from Away'. They had become friends, purely by chance, and then over the years their roots had intertwined. For a while, she'd been Emily's daughter-in-law, though that hadn't lasted long.

Sarah was the only person she could talk to about this. She couldn't mention it to their family, not until it was something to actually worry about.

'People are noticing,' she said. 'Pierre and Little Sterling, after what happened at the boatyard the other day. And Joyce at the pharmacy said he'd come into pick up my prescriptions twice in one day.'

'That's the thing about a small town. People notice. But they look out for you, too.'

'Robbie's such a proud man. He's so self-sufficient. If he thinks that people are pitying him . . .'

She trailed off.

'Or if they're pitying you?' said Sarah. 'Are you worried about that, too?'

'Of course not. This isn't about me.'

'I know you pretty well by now, Em. And I know you like helping people. It's your role around here. How many people in Port Clyde have you delivered as babies?'

'About eighty per cent of the population between forty and ten years old. There are quite a few families here where I brought both the parents into the world, and then I've delivered their children.'

'You brought Dottie into the world. I wish you'd deliver her baby, too. She's about ready to drop.'

Emily smiled. 'Retired.'

'Robbie has helped people too. He's given people jobs, fixed people's boats. He did all of that for William. I know he's done a few jobs for people who couldn't afford it. He did a lot of rebuilding after Hurricane Sandy came through here. You don't need to feel bad about people noticing, or wanting to do something.'

Once upon a time, Sarah had taken help from her, and Emily had wanted to give it. They'd done each other many kindnesses over the years. But Sarah didn't know everything. She didn't know why Robbie and she needed to be self-sufficient, a completeness of two. No one knew now, except for her and Robbie.

'My father,' Emily said, 'was the town doctor. Everyone respected him. He'd helped everyone in the village, at some point or another. All I ever wanted was to be like him.'

'And what happened when he needed help? Because I'm sure he did, at some point.'

'I . . . don't know. We'd lost touch by then.'

Sarah touched her hand across the table. 'It's not a failure. It's an illness. That's what you kept on telling me, that time when you helped me.'

'We don't even know that it's an illness yet.'

'What if it is?'

'Then, if it is, we'll do what we always do. We'll get through it, Robbie and I, together.'

Sarah got up and brought the bowl of chicken salad to the table, and spooned more on to their plates. 'How's Adam and the kids?'

'They're wonderful, as always.'

'And William?'

'He's all right. You know what he's like. He and Robbie are too alike to talk with each other, but he calls me, and he's in touch with Adam.'

'Same here. He called Dottie last week on her birthday. Not a word to me.'

'I'm sorry, Sarah.'

Sarah shrugged. 'He's a better dad to her than her real dad was. How are his kids?'

'He sent some pictures.' She took out her phone and showed Sarah the photos of Brianna and John.

'That girl is the spit of her father,' said Sarah.

'Yes, the Brandon genes are strong. Adam is more like me.' It was an automatic response.

'Is he back together with their mother?'

Emily shook her head. 'He's happier as a father than as a husband. As you know.'

'Family is what's important,' said Sarah. 'And we can find family in our friends, too. That's what you taught me back then. You'll let us all help you. All of us who you've helped. That's what it's about, being part of a place. And you're part of this place now, whether you like it or not.'

'I know,' said Emily. And as good a friend as Sarah was, Emily didn't add that being part of a place was one of the things that worried her the most. Because that was fragile, too.

A pattern is harder to break than almost anything, Robbie thought. Once you started it going, it had its own inevitability, its own momentum. You might as well try to stop the wind.

But Emily knew something was wrong. And he knew, too. It had been months, now. Maybe even years. There was a fog clouding a part of his life: a different part every day. It moved in without warning and left him lost. And she knew that he knew, and he knew that she knew, and yet neither one of them had said anything.

It was a pattern they had laid down at the start of their relationship: not right at the start, but later, when they had discovered that their love could only last if silence held it together in certain places.

Friday was always his night to make dinner and he usually made chilli or phoned out for pizza. Tonight he did neither. He waited until six o'clock and then he went outside to where she was digging weeds in the garden, her head shaded by a broad-brimmed straw hat. He knelt beside her on the grass.

'Oh,' she said in surprise. 'Are you helping me?'

Her voice was pleasant: she was happy to see him, she loved him and she was the same, but there was a small wariness in her eyes. Because any variation from the pattern was cause for concern, now. The variations were what was wrong.

'It's Friday,' he said, 'but I haven't cooked dinner. Do you know why I'm saying this?'

'So that I know we're having pizza?'

'So that you know that I know what day it is, and what time it is. Because I don't always, do I?'

She didn't reply.

'This is something we have to talk about. It won't go away if we ignore it.'

'Nothing goes away,' she said.

'Are you frightened, sweetheart?'

She nodded. He put his arm around her shoulders, kneeling beside her in the grass.

Chapter Four

August 2016
Portland, Maine

The hospital in Portland was bigger and more specialised than Pen Bay Hospital where Emily had worked all those years, but she knew one or two of the people working there. Sometimes when she went up to Portland she arranged to meet them for lunch, or coffee.

Today she sat in the waiting room with Robbie among other patients and their families, waiting to see the neurologist. In her hospital career she had seen mainly pregnant women and young mothers; it was slightly shocking to see so many elderly people in this waiting room, and even more shocking to realise that she and Robbie were also elderly.

'I always picture us as young lovers,' whispered Robbie to her. 'I still see you as you were when we first met. Does that mean I have a memory problem?'

He had good days, and he had bad days. Today was a good day. He'd got ready, taken care of the dogs, talked about their mutual friends, joked about where they were going, chatted about what restaurant they should go to in the Old Port for lunch after his appointment. He'd let her drive, but that was normal when they took Emily's car. He didn't misplace his keys or his wallet or forget to tie his shoes.

Emily had worried about it being a good day: what if the neurologist failed to spot the symptoms that had become apparent to her?

But she would have worried if it had been a bad day, too.

He called it a fog. Fog was a part of daily life in coastal Maine. The chill of the water met the warm southerly wind and produced condensation. You could be inland, in a clear blue summer day, and as soon as you came within half a mile of the coast, maybe even a mile, the fog would billow in around you. Some summers they had fog every single day. She could look out of the windows of their house and think that she was floating in a cloud.

'That's not a memory problem,' she whispered back to him. 'That's being a softy romantic.'

The neurologist, Dr Calvin, was reassuringly aged. He had no hair on his head but a surprising amount growing from eyebrows, nostrils and ears. Emily had researched, of course, and knew what to expect; she'd asked Robbie if he wanted her to explain the tests to him, but Robbie had said he didn't want to know.

What is today's date? What day of the week is it? What is the season? What state are we in? What city? What building are we in? What floor are we on? I'm going to name three objects and I want you to repeat them back to me: street, banana, hammer. I'd like you to count backwards from one hundred, by sevens.

She sat in the spare chair and watched and listened to the doctor and the man she had loved for most of her life. She listened to the answers he gave. She watched him trying to draw a simple clock.

It was a good day. A *good* day, today.

But as he drew, horror crept over her, cold and insidious as fog.

Chapter Five

Afterwards, they didn't go for lunch at the restaurant they'd chosen. They didn't have to say anything to know they agreed; Emily drove them back up the coast and back to Clyde Bay, where she didn't go home, but parked in town, instead. They took the dinghy out to the boat and wordlessly climbed aboard and got her ready to sail.

They'd done this so many times together. They each had their allotted tasks and their bodies performed them automatically. It was like a piece of music, the notes the same every time even though the performance was slightly different. It was a pattern that ran its own way.

They could be silent about this new knowledge if they chose. He knew they could. They had ignored bigger things.

The bay was calm and when Emily was poised at the mooring line, ready to cast it off, he switched on the motor so that they could get more quickly out into open water. He enjoyed it more when they sailed off the mooring and the wind was light, and they could just about do it today, if they wanted. But the engine made noise. It put off the point of conversation for a little while longer.

He cut the engine when they rounded the point past Marshall Lighthouse and they raised the mainsail together. Emily unwound the jib. It was her boat; he'd built it for her. A twenty-four foot sloop, small enough to handle easily alone, big enough for the two of them to take out for overnight trips. But she'd named it for something that had significance for both of them, and out of habit he generally took the helm when they were together.

This time he gestured for her to take it. He sat on the side of the cockpit, on the bench where Emily usually sat.

'So,' he said, once they were well under way and there was no other sound except for the snapping of the sail and the crying of the gulls. 'Tell me what you know, doc.'

'I'm an obstetrician, not a neurologist,' she said, her eyes on the horizon.

'But you know anyway, don't you?'

'You know too.' Her voice held so much barely concealed pain that he was tempted to let it go, to talk of something else. But that wasn't why they'd come out here on the water. The place where they were the most truly alone together.

'I want your opinion. The doctor wouldn't tell us anything. He said to come back next week.'

'He wants to wait for the results of the blood tests.'

'But we don't need to, do we?'

'The tests he gave you showed that you have impairment of short-term memory. You have some aphasia – that's difficulty in re-calling or understanding words – and some psychomotor difficulty.'

'I messed up drawing that damn clock, didn't I?'

She nodded. He hadn't really been frightened, but now he felt something cold touch him. Because he'd thought he'd drawn that clock fine. Just fine.

'There's no sign of a stroke on the scans,' said Emily. 'And it's come on gradually, not all at once. It could be vitamin deficiency, or an infection.'

'But you don't think that's what it is.'

'No. I think it's most likely Alzheimer's.'

She was brave. Her voice didn't waver at all when she said it. It made him proud of her.

'I think we'd better tack,' he said. 'If we want to avoid Mosquito Island.'

The wind was stronger at this point of sail. Robbie secured the main sheet and leaned back against the side of the cockpit, which was tilted at nearly a forty-degree angle.

'So tell me what to expect,' he said. 'Alzheimer's works backwards, doesn't it? It erases the most recent memories first?'

'I don't think it's so methodical,' she said. 'I think it takes what it damn well wants.'

'But in general, the newer the memories, the sooner they go. Like Perry. Before he had to go into that home, he used to sit in the general store and insist it was 1953.'

'You won't go in a home,' said Emily. 'You will stay right in our house with me. We'll live together as we always have, no matter what happens.'

'I don't want you to have to take care of me, Emily.'

'Too bad. Because I will.' She said it fiercely, and he was proud of her for that, too. 'I'll take care of you, and you'll take care of me, for the rest of our lives. That's what it's all about.'

He watched the water rushing by. 'There's more to it than that, and you know it.'

'I don't know that there is.'

'What about if there's a time when I think it's 1962?'

'1962 was a fine year.'

'You're deliberately misunderstanding me.'

She went quiet for a few moments. Finally, she said, 'You won't.'

'I most likely will, Emily. And it won't matter to me, by that time. But it will matter a great deal to you, won't it?'

'We're going too fast. Can you loosen that sail?'

He loosened it.

'It doesn't have to matter,' he said. 'We've been here in Maine for a long time. We raised our family here, and we worked here. Everyone here has only known us as we are now. They don't judge us. And everyone who ever did or would, is gone.'

'We said we'd never talk about this.'

'Things have changed. We could let people know, in a way that

we controlled. Then we could deal with it, together, while I'm still
. . . while I'm still myself.'

'What about Adam?'

'Adam is old enough. He's happy. He could handle it. He'd
understand.'

'No. I won't put him through that. One of the things I've always
loved best about Adam is that he's sure of himself. He knows who
he is. He's like you, that way.' *He's like the way you used to be, before
this.* She didn't say that. 'Telling him would take that certainty
away from him. He'll question everything he thinks he knows
about his life.'

'It wouldn't have to. Think about it. I know you don't want to,
but think about it. We wouldn't have any secrets any more. There
wouldn't be anything to be afraid of. We'd be free.'

'You said we were free now. After Christopher died.'

'Isn't it a better freedom if everyone knows, than if no one does?'

She didn't answer. He didn't press her. He knew her well enough
to be sure that she'd heard him.

They didn't have any particular destination. They sailed where
the wind took them. It was Robbie's favourite kind of sailing, if
he were honest: without aim, without schedule, meandering back
and forth where the wind took them, sometimes fast, sometimes
slow. This was the kind of sailing they had done their first time
together, when Emily hadn't known port from starboard. Back
in 1962. On the water, all their time merged together. It was one
time, and their love was always as fresh as it had been the day they
had met.

He looked up, surprised to see they were passing Mosquito
Island again, on their way back to Clyde Bay. He recognised all
the landmarks: the cluster of buildings around the general store,
the town dock, the big white house owned by summer people
on the point. He hadn't thought about . . . what was it they were
thinking about? Something awful. Something terrifying.

'Are you all right?' Emily asked him, and he nodded.

'I understand what you're saying, Robbie,' she said. 'But I can't do it. I can't do it to Adam.'

He frowned, and was about to ask, *What can't you do to Adam*, when he saw the launch heading towards them. 'That's Little Sterling,' he said.

Little Sterling was waving his big arm at them. Emily altered their course to come alongside.

'Doc!' he called as soon as they were within hailing distance. 'We'd call it a favour if you could come ashore with me right now.'

'What's wrong?' Robbie asked.

'Dottie Philbrick, at the general store. She's about to have her baby. We're waiting for the ambulance, but you looked closer.'

Robbie took the helm. Emily scrambled over the side of the boat and into the launch. 'Meet me there!' she called to him, and then Little Sterling was motoring away, towards the town dock.

'You let the guy who forgets everything take care of the boat?' Robbie said, but without urgency. He didn't need any memory to wrap up the sails, to catch the mooring line, make everything fast, jump into the dinghy. He followed the launch, arriving not long after Little Sterling and Emily disappeared into the general store.

When he got inside, everything was already happening. Dottie Philbrick was standing behind the deli counter, leaning on it, bent over at the waist. Her skirt was pushed up and Emily was examining her. She moaned loudly, and Emily smoothed her back. Several people were standing around, watching in shock. Fortunately most of what was going on was hidden by the high glass case filled with cold cuts and cheese.

'She was about to make me a tuna melt,' said Susan Woodruff, clutching her handbag, 'and she suddenly looked all surprised. And then she shouted that the baby was coming, and George offered to take her up to Pen Bay in his car, and she shouted that the baby was really coming so I called 911, but then Little Sterling saw you coming in.'

'I told you, everyone,' said Emily, hurrying to the sink at the back of the deli counter to wash her hands, 'get the hell out of here and let this woman have her baby in peace. When the ambulance arrives, send them in.'

'You heard what the lady said,' said Robbie. 'C'mon outside. The doctor will holler for us if she needs us.' He began to shepherd the bystanders out of the store.

'Not you,' said Emily. 'I need you, Robbie. Do they sell beach towels out at the back? I could use a couple.'

'By the sunglasses,' said Dottie, and groaned loudly as a contraction hit her.

'Hurry,' Emily told him, and Robbie went to grab some beach towels off the shelf. He handed them over the deli counter to Emily and stood back a little, keeping his eyes trained on a shelf of home-made preserves, a lot of them made by Dottie and her mom Sarah. He listened as Emily reassured Dottie and coached her along.

Remember this, he told himself. *Remember how proud of her you are right now. Remember how everyone here trusts her. Remember how you would do anything for her. Don't forget.*

'That's it,' said Emily. 'That's it, you're doing exactly right, the baby's nearly here, Dottie. She's coming much more easily than you did, if I recall. One more push, and—'

He heard a liquid sound that he didn't want to think too much about, and a baby's cry.

The sound did something to him. Hooked him in the gut. Outside, he heard applause. When he glanced over the deli counter, Dottie was on the floor and Emily was handing her the baby, wrapped in a blue and yellow beach towel. The look on Dottie's face. He'd seen that exact same look on Emily's, when she first held Adam.

Don't forget don't forget don't forget.

He wanted to grab Emily and hold her as tightly as he could. He wanted to seize this moment, this *now*, before the fog rolled in, and make it last forever. He wanted to feel the weight of all their shared past, everything they had done and felt and told the truth about and lied.

All the lies had only been to preserve the truth. He had to remember that as well.

There was a noise from the doorway: the paramedics. Emily spoke a few quick words to them and then she came round to Robbie. 'Wasn't that amazing?' she said. 'A healthy baby girl in eleven minutes flat.' She had a wild, exhilarated look on her face and Robbie pulled her into his arms.

'I'm all covered with blood and amniotic fluid,' she protested, but she wrapped her arms around his waist and leaned her head against his chest.

'It always begins again, doesn't it?' he murmured to her. 'New babies. New life.'

'Adam,' she whispered. 'Adam, and his children. We need to protect them, Robbie.'

He smoothed his hands over her hair. *Remember this. Don't forget.*

'You can be my memory,' he said.

Emily drove. Emily did most of the driving, now, and when he drove himself, he knew she was worrying about him, that he'd forget where he was going, or forget to look both ways before pulling out into a junction, and although he thought it would be some time before he forgot how to drive a good old-fashioned truck, it was a real possibility that he could get lost, even in this area where they'd lived for so many years. He kept misplacing things in his workshop: reaching for a hammer that wasn't there, or finding an awl where he expected a screwdriver. Sometimes he thought he was back at the boatyard in Miami and he'd stand in the middle of the garage, staring at unfamiliar objects, wondering how the big work bay had become so small.

He thought for now, though, that he would be all right to drive around here. But Emily worried, and so he let her drive him, even

35

to the store, and definitely further afield like to Adam's house in Thomaston. His brain was misfiring and it was better to be safe. It was as dangerous as being drunk. Even more.

He'd had a dream in the early hours of this morning. A full-bodied, immersive dream: he was hot, awash with sweat and dirt and other people's fear, and his ears were filled with the motor of the patrol boat as it churned up the Mekong River. The water was a sheet of flat brown, the jungle every colour of green. An insect alighted on his cheek and he swiped it off with his shoulder. Fear, and cordite, and defoliant, and cigarette smoke, and the taste in his mouth that never went away, never enough no matter how much alcohol he sipped and downed, and the familiar breathing of Benny and Ace on either side of him, and there was a flash and then a pause, a long pause like the end of the world, and then the crash and the screams.

He woke up with the scream silent and digging into his throat and he was in the darkness and he thought he must be in the hospital with his eyes covered and then he felt that Emily's arm was around his waist. It was Emily and she was here. She wasn't lost, and he wasn't torn.

He'd wiped the sweat from his forehead on the sheet and held her closer to him until his heartbeat calmed. In the morning he still remembered the dream as vividly as when he'd had it, and his hands shook as he poured the coffee, but she didn't notice, or if she did, she didn't ask.

The past was a double-edged sword. It inflicted wounds, and the wounds you didn't talk about festered. They grew inside you and they waited to spill out.

Adam barbecued chicken on the grill and Shelley had made a pasta salad and the younger couple drank beer and he and Emily drank iced tea. The kids played some sort of complicated game involving a ball, a Hula hoop, and a dozen flags until the sun went down and Adam got the two younger ones to bed, and Chloe went upstairs with her laptop to do whatever pre-teens did with their laptops. It was so peaceful and so normal and Robbie found himself doing what he kept doing these days: pressing his lips together and telling himself to remember, to remember, to keep it all inside and never let it go.

Telling himself he had to do whatever it took to keep this alive.

And then Shelley made coffee, and Adam opened two more bottles of beer, and they sat in the living room and Adam said, 'What is it, Mom and Dad?'

He let Emily do the talking, as she'd done the driving. She held his hand. He watched Adam's gaze go from Emily to him and back to Emily, the way he'd looked at them both when he'd been a child and there was a storm coming and he wanted reassurance that the lightning wouldn't hit them.

'But we've got years, yet,' Emily was saying. 'There are things we can do to try to slow it, and you know your father is a fighter. And we are going to do everything together.'

'We'll help,' said Shelley immediately.

'But Dad,' said Adam, and it was funny how you could see the past in the faces of your children, how their younger selves were overlaid on their older selves so you were both surprised and not surprised to see them grown.

Emily had been right, the other day. Adam was sure in his skin. He was one of those kids who carried the fact that he was loved with him everywhere he went, and it protected him. That was the gift he and Emily had given him, he supposed. And Robbie could see that gift more clearly now, because Adam's face was blank with grief in a way that it had never been before.

And he saw what Emily had meant. If they took away Adam's sense of himself, they might end up taking that gift back from him, too. He might learn to doubt their love for him. And with that gone, Adam might start to doubt everything.

'I'll be fine, son,' he said. 'I don't mind relying on your mother. I've been relying on her since the day I met her. She's a good person to rely on.'

He meant what he said, but he heard the ring of untruth in his own voice as he spoke it. You could talk and talk and talk sometimes, and speak the truth the whole time, and never get to the truth at all.

Robbie wasn't sure when he'd made the decision: only that it was sometime in the bright spaces between forgetting. Maybe it was this morning, waking up from the dream of fear and death; maybe it was here, right now, in the safety of his family.

He thought, though, that he'd made it before. Maybe he'd made the decision and forgotten it and made it all over again.

He almost hoped that was it, because if he decided the same thing over and over again, then it had to be the right decision. Like Emily's hand in his.

'You can rely on all of us,' said Shelley firmly. 'We'll all do whatever we can. Do you want us to let William know?'

'We'll tell him,' said Emily.

'Dad,' said Adam again. Robbie stood up and Adam stood up too and they hugged. Adam was a little taller than he was. Robbie closed his eyes. *Remember, remember.*

'You'll need to take care of her for me,' he murmured into his son's ear. He felt his son nod and he felt Emily behind them, watching them, and without looking he knew she had tears in her eyes.

Without looking, he knew he had made the right decision.

Remember. It never ends.

Chapter Six

September 2016
Clyde Bay, Maine

Emily was dreaming about a crowd. She was rushing through it, pulling a heavy, clumsy suitcase behind her, bumping into people. She had to get a train, it was about to leave and she was going to miss it and she couldn't find the platform, she'd forgotten the tickets. Heavy voices boomed from the tannoy, announcing departures and arrivals in words she couldn't understand. It sounded like English, but all the words were blurred together.

She felt lips on her cheek. The scent of roses. A gentle kiss. Robbie's voice.

'I'd never have forgotten you.'

There he was, standing on the platform, wearing his denim jacket, rucksack over his shoulder, a smile on his face. And everything was starting from here. From right now, this moment, and it was all going to be all right.

She reached out her hand for him and he was gone.

Emily opened her eyes. The first thing she saw was the rose, pink and yellow. There was a note underneath.

She smiled and sat up. He said he was no poet, but she had all the letters he'd written her since they'd been together. Birthday cards, Valentines, little notes he left on her bedside table for her to find when she woke up.

And then there were the letters from before: the letters he wrote to her from Italy and on board the *Nora Mae*. That first note he'd ever written her, left on the bedside table in the hotel in

Lowestoft. She'd destroyed all of those, but she still remembered every word in them.

Emily opened the letter. She read it, stock-still in bed, the dawn light filtering pink and gold through the open window.

Then she pushed herself out of bed and ran, barefoot and stumbling in her nightgown, through their house, down the stairs, out the front door and across the wet lawn, seeing his footprints in the dew. Left minutes ago. Across the road and on to the black and grey rocks, pain lancing up from her feet. She slipped and fell and barked her knee and forced herself up again, old legs frustrating and slow, because she saw his shoes on a high rock. His shoes and his shirt and his trousers, carefully folded and dry.

Not like this, not all at once, not forever. Please, no.

And the sun was up now and the sea was empty and vast before her and kept on crashing, landing and splashing on the shore as she called out his name, over and over again, without stopping.

PART TWO

1990

Chapter Seven

She had been looking for it for so long that when it arrived, she hardly realised it was there. It had slipped between the pages of *DownEast* magazine, and when she was walking back from collecting the post from their mailbox at the end of the drive, hurrying because it was cold and she hadn't put a coat on, her boots crunching on the ice and salt, the envelope slipped out and fell to the ground. She scooped it up without looking at it, automatically turned it over, and stopped dead still in the drive.

The card was heavy, good quality, and the address was written in fountain pen. The name on it was *Dr Emily Greaves*, and even if she hadn't recognised the handwriting, she would have known by the fact of her maiden name.

A flake of snow fluttered down and landed on the envelope, and then another. Emily's breath came out in clouds and she stared at the envelope. The handwriting had a shake to it. The person who wrote it would be nearly eighty: retired, spending his time in the garden and with his books, walking around the village as he always had, speaking to everyone he met, asking about their health and their families.

Emily felt a wave of homesickness so strong that she nearly slipped on the ice underfoot.

She tucked the other mail underneath her arm and carried the envelope into the house. Belladonna, their black Lab, met her at the door with her lead in her mouth.

'Not now, Bella,' she said, dropping an absent caress on the top of her head and taking the envelope into the kitchen. Adam was at soccer practice, due back any time now; he'd left a peanut-butter smeared knife and crumbs on the counter from his snack this morning. Robbie was in his workshop in the garage. The sound of the radio reached her faintly.

She sat at the table and opened the letter. The handwriting alone took her back to afternoons visiting the surgery as a little girl. Looking at the notes he wrote to himself, things to remember to do, lists of patients, his signature on the prescription pad. The surgery always smelled of antiseptic and the roll of flimsy paper they used to cover the examination table, which he kept behind a silk screen embroidered with nightingales. It smelled of his pipe tobacco and his receptionist, Hilda's, perfume. Emily lifted the letter to her nose to try to catch the scent of tobacco, but there was none there. Perhaps he didn't smoke a pipe any more. Most people had given up smoking.

Eighteen years. A lot could happen in eighteen years.

Dear Emily, began the letter, and Emily's eyes filled with tears, to see her own name next to the word 'dear'.

'Mom? Are you all right?'

Adam was in the doorway, wearing his soccer kit. His dark blond hair fell in a fringe straight into his eyes. Emily liked it best this way, when it was too long and it needed a haircut, though it drove Adam crazy.

'I've had a letter,' she said. For a second she considered hiding the letter, but then she put it on the kitchen table in front of her. 'It's from your grandfather.'

He put down his sports bag. 'The one in England?'

'Yes.'

'I didn't know he writes to you.'

'He doesn't.'

'Is that why you never talk about him?'

She bit her lip. 'I didn't ... I thought you assumed that you didn't have any grandparents.'

Adam pulled out the chair next to hers. 'Everyone has grandparents. I thought maybe they were dead, like Dad's mom and dad.'

He said it in a matter-of-fact way and Emily swallowed. 'Sometimes I don't talk about things that hurt,' she said. 'It's easier not to think about them.'

'But if they're not dead, why does it hurt? And why haven't we ever seen them?'

Adam's eyes were blue, sometimes bright enough blue to dazzle her when she caught a glimpse of them. At fourteen, he was a bundle of potential: quick, bright, fast on his feet, with a temper that melted away as soon as it was roused. Everyone said how much he was like his parents: clever like his mother, cheerful like his father, with Emily's light hair and eyes and Robbie's manner of feeling comfortable in himself.

'I write to them every year,' she told him. 'That's why they knew where to write to me now.'

'So they know about me?' Adam frowned, and Emily reached over and hugged him.

'Sometimes people just have to stay distant,' she said. 'It has nothing to do with you, sweetheart. Nothing at all.'

'Don't they want to meet me?'

'If they knew you, they would love you. Nearly as much as I do.' She held him tight. She knew, one day, that her son would be too old to be held and squeezed. Her friends' children had mostly grown out of it by now; they flinched when their parents tried to kiss them at the school gates. But Adam had always been a cuddler. Even now, in the evenings, a newly minted teenager, he would fold up his long skinny limbs and curl up on her lap to watch television with her.

'Anyone would love you,' she told him.

'Do they have any other grandchildren?'

'I don't know. My sister may have had children by now.'

'I could have cousins that I don't even know.'

'How . . . would you feel about that?' she asked him carefully.

She watched him think about it. 'It would be weird?' he said at last. 'But maybe nice? If I got to meet them one day.'

'I don't know, Adam.'

'What's the letter about?'

'Aren't you hungry after your practice? I can make you a sandwich.'

'I'd rather know what the letter is about.'

She nodded, but she let him go and turned her chair slightly so that Adam could not see the writing in the letter. She picked it up again and read.

Dear Emily,

It has been many years, but I think it is only fair that I should tell you.

'Oh,' she said.

'What is it, Mom? Is it good news? Are they going to come and visit us?'

'No,' she said. 'No, nothing like that. My mother has died.'

'He doesn't say how,' she said to Robbie, later, in front of the wood stove in the living room. She had a glass of red wine, and he had a glass of iced water. Even in the dead of winter, he liked his drinks very cold. 'He's a doctor. You'd think he'd say how my mother died.'

Robbie had been reading over the letter. 'He doesn't say much at all. Then again, you can't pack that much information in three lines.'

'Eighteen years,' she said. 'I still remember the last time I saw him and my mother.'

Robbie had been there. She didn't need to explain. He took her hand and squeezed it.

'You tried,' he said. 'But they might have made the best decision. Considering everything. I don't know if we could have been as happy together if there hadn't been a clean break – some things are better forgotten.'

'But I never saw her again, and now she's dead. When I said goodbye, I didn't think it was going to be forever.'

'I'm sorry, sweetheart.'

She sighed and leaned against him. 'You said your own good-byes too. We both made the choice. But I didn't . . . she was only sixty-eight.'

'Your father must be in his seventies.'

She nodded. 'And Polly is forty-two. My little sister.'

'And Adam is fourteen.'

'He wanted to know if he had cousins. He said he would like to meet them.'

Robbie exhaled, slow and long.

'Remember when he was six and had an imaginary brother?' Emily said. 'And called him William?'

'I didn't think he actually minded, though. Being, for all practical purposes, an only child.'

'I used to imagine I had a little sister, before Polly came along. Every child has an imaginary sibling at some point or another. Even if his wasn't entirely imaginary.'

'I didn't have one,' said Robbie. 'But he's got a better imagination than I ever did.'

'He's thought about my family in England. He's wondered about them. Maybe I should have told him something.'

'What could you have told him?'

'I don't know. Something.' She took the letter from Robbie's lap and smoothed it between her fingers. 'Why do you think my father told me? He didn't have to.'

'He says he thought you should know.'

'But why?' She turned over the letter, as if looking for more writing on the back of it, more than the three scanty lines on the front. 'Does he want to see me again? Does he want to connect in some way?'

'He doesn't say that.'

'But does he?'

'I think,' Robbie said carefully, 'that you shouldn't read more into the letter than is there.'

She traced over the signature with her finger. *Yours sincerely, James Greaves.* 'He would have thought about how he signed it. About how distant to be. You met my father; he's one of the most courteous and social men I've ever known. But he would have been careful. He'd say less than he meant, not more.'

'So you'll write back?'

'I'll try to call him, tomorrow after work. I don't know if he'll speak to me. I don't even know if they have the same phone number as they used to.' She leaned her head against Robbie's shoulder and twisted her ring around her finger. Two clasped hands, a circle complete with only two. Round and round in a circle, self-contained, forever.

Self-contained and complete. But how many people did that circle exclude?

Her last appointment of the day was an antenatal patient, a young woman, with her first baby. She was a single mother – one of the things that had changed the most in Emily's practice since the 1970s was how routine it had become to see single mothers. The shame was gone – and thank God for that.

Delivery had been tricky; the baby had come too quickly and there had been some tearing. She examined her patient while the baby fretted in a carrier on the floor.

'How are you feeling in yourself?' she asked, already writing her notes in her head: healing as expected, all normal, advised to finish the course of antibiotics and painkillers, no reason for follow-up visit.

'I'm all right,' said the woman. Her name was Sarah. Emily smiled at her, a practised smile of professional reassurance, and left her to put her clothes back on. She checked the clock: it was three, which was eight in the evening in England. Her father would be making a cup of tea, reading a book. Maybe he had the radio on to keep him company. Radio 4, voices, so the house would not seem so empty.

Her parents had been married for forty-seven years. What would it be like to live a lifetime with a person and then, suddenly, to find they had gone?

There would be a space in the house. A blank where that person should have been. You would look up to say something, something normal and boring, an offer of tea or a comment on the weather, and that person would not be there to hear.

The baby grizzled. Her patient emerged from behind the screen and sat gingerly in the chair, rocking the carrier with her foot.

'Are you getting any sleep?' Emily asked, finishing up her notes. They'd put in a new computer system for patient records and as far as she could tell, it was about three hundred per cent less efficient than old-fashioned paper. She pressed 'Save' and an hourglass appeared on the screen.

'Not much.'

'Well, that's normal I'd say.' She smiled again at Sarah, and Sarah smiled back. There were dark circles under her eyes. Emily glanced at her records to try to see Sarah's family circumstances, but the screen had gone blank while the system tried its best to save a few simple lines of text. If it went down again, tomorrow was going to be a nightmare. She clicked the mouse in irritation, and the baby wailed, and Sarah rocked her more quickly with her foot.

'Don't try to do too much during the day,' Emily said. 'Sleep when the baby sleeps, that's the trick. Is there anyone who can come and sit with her while you get a nap?'

Sarah shook her head. 'No, I'll be OK.'

'Don't be afraid to accept help. You're a new mother, and you're healing. You should take all the help that's offered, and if none is offered, don't be afraid to ask. What about your mother, is she close?'

It was the standard advice she offered, but Sarah flinched at it and for the first time Emily noticed how thin the other woman was. Her belly was still slightly distended from the pregnancy, but her arms were skinny, poking out of the sleeves of her woollen sweater.

'My mom died last year,' Sarah said.

'Oh.'

Emily must have looked stricken, because Sarah's eyes widened. 'It's OK,' she said quickly, 'it's all right; it's just that she loved babies. She was wicked good with babies. People called her the baby whisperer. She could take any baby, and make it stop crying within like a second.'

The baby was full-out crying now, red-faced. Sarah stood and took the carrier in her arms, rocking it back and forth.

'Well, that sounds like a very useful talent to have,' said Emily.

'Especially in the middle of the night, right?' Sarah laughed nervously over the sound of the infant. 'Anyway, is that all?'

'Just keep taking your antibiotics until they're all gone, and if you think you're not healing properly, don't hesitate to make another appointment.'

'OK. I will. Thanks, doctor.' She picked up the baby and left, and Emily turned back to her computer, stabbing the 'return' key. The machine started to make a whirring sound.

There were times, in the middle of the night, when Emily had wanted her own mother. Adam had been an easy baby, on the whole, but every baby had wakeful nights; every baby got a fever. She recalled one night when he had been hot, inconsolable. Robbie and she had taken turns walking him around the house, holding him, crooning, rocking, soothing. Nothing had worked. His hands were little fists, his face a constant scream. Finally, she had sent Robbie to bed to catch some sleep before work while she circled the house singing every lullaby she could remember. He'd stopped crying as the sun came up. When she touched his face it was cool. Adam fell asleep in her arms and outside the windows the sun was coming up over the bay. Over the ocean that stretched eastward all the way to the country where her own mother was at that very moment. The water that separated them and connected them.

She'd thought of the photographs of herself as an infant in her mother's arms. There was one in a silver frame in her parents' house, on a table with several other photographs of Emily as a young child, her sister Polly as a baby and toddler. In the photograph, her mother's hair was swept up into a chignon; she wore a white blouse with a lace-edged collar, and she held the sleeping Emily wrapped in a crocheted blanket. Emily remembered the blanket. It had been pink. She somehow remembered the texture and scent of her mother's blouse in that photograph, too, though that was surely impossible and she had made it up because of the picture.

She'd hardly looked at that photo when she was living with her parents. It was part of the landscape, the million details of her childhood home that made it up and were too important to be noticed. But holding her own child in the same way her own mother had held her, she thought of that photograph and she wondered if it still stood on that polished mahogany table. Or if it had been taken away, put away. If all the photographs of her had been put away.

The PC beeped and shut itself off. Yvette, the receptionist, knocked and poked her head through the door, looking harried. 'Sorry, Dr Brandon, sorry, there's a system problem again, I'm about to get them on the phone.'

'Can you hold off for a little while, Yvette? I've got a call to make.'

'That's fine, it'll give me a chance to think up a list of really good swear words.' She disappeared.

Emily lifted the phone, pressed 9 for an outside line, and began to dial. 011 for overseas, 44 for England, and then the number she knew from when she'd been a child, a young woman, ringing from the payphone booth at the end of the corridor of her college in Cambridge. She didn't even have to think about it; her finger found the numbers by itself, even though she had not dialled them for eighteen years.

But she hesitated over the final button.

What if her father didn't answer? What if he did answer and immediately put the telephone down? What if she only got a snatch of his voice, and it sounded sad and alone and she could not speak with him?

Emily put down the phone. She sat for a moment, thinking. Then she took out the phone book from the drawer of her desk and looked up the number for International Information. Five minutes later, she had another number with the same beginning. The phone rang twice on the other end, and then was answered by a man with a voice she didn't recognise, but an accent so familiar it made her eyes water.

'Yes,' she said, 'I'm sorry to bother you so late at home, vicar, and I don't think we've met, but I wondered if you could tell me when the funeral will be for Mrs Charlotte Greaves?'

Chapter Eight

Robbie stopped off at the Clyde Bay General Store for a cup of coffee before he even got to the boatyard – the owner, Perry, made pretty bad coffee, but it was the only place open this time of morning, and besides, Robbie liked shooting the shit with the old guys who always hung around the store every morning eating home-made doughnuts from the tray on the counter. In the summer they sat on the bench outside, and as soon as it got cold they picked up the bench and put it inside, next to the old wood stove in the centre of the store. Retired lobstermen, all of them, who'd never got out of the habit of getting up before sunrise, even when they were too old to haul pots. They were good for a few minutes' banter about last night's Celtics game. In the summer, it was the Red Sox, and in the autumn, the Patriots. Time around here was measured by sports teams and the weather, everything in an endless cycle.

'What do you figure our chances for the playoff?' said Isaac Peck, before giving an exaggerated comic double take and adding, 'Oh that's right, Brandon, you're Cleveland Cavaliers. I forgot you're a flatlander.'

It was rendered *flatlandah*, in the broad Downeast accent.

'Isaac,' said Robbie, 'you've been forgetting I'm a flatlander every morning for the past ten years at least.'

'Not on Christmas or Thanksgiving,' Isaac said phlegmatically. 'On them days I stay home and look at my family instead of your ugly face.'

Perry filled his travel mug with coffee and Robbie drank half a cup, scalding hot, before holding it out for a refill.

'You need the buzz this morning?' Avery Lunt asked, shifting his skinny backside on the wooden stool.

'Drove Emily down to Boston last night for her plane. Didn't get back home till two and figured there was no point going to bed.' And he wouldn't have been able to sleep without her, anyway. The bed was too empty, her side too cold and smooth. He had not been apart from her at night for a very long time.

'Ayuh, she going back home to Limeyland for a visit?'

'*This* is home,' said Robbie. 'How long do we have to live here, anyway, before you stop calling me a flatlander and my wife a Limey?'

The lobstermen and Perry exchanged glances. 'Give it another thirty years,' said Avery at last.

'Are you going to be right here in thirty years, Avery?' Robbie guessed that Avery Lunt was seventy-five if he was a day, though as he had the leather face of someone who'd spent every day of his life on the ocean, he could be anything up to a hundred and ten.

'Plan to be.'

'Thirty years probably isn't long enough though,' said Isaac, considering. 'You still got that accent for a start. Your boy, he might make a real Mainer.'

Re-yul Mainah. They said it as if it was the pinnacle of achievement, and Robbie, to be honest, couldn't disagree. From the minute he'd set eyes on the Maine coast he'd felt it was his: the rocky shore with its intricate crenulations, the way the pine trees spiked up from the land. The islands crouching in the sea like hunched porcupines, countless – some of them inhabited, some no more than seal-strewn rocks. The old white lighthouses, the dead calm fog, the raw power of a Nor'easter. Right now, though the calendar said it was early spring, the water was still a slate grey, almost black at times, whipped into ice crystals, and the snow lay thick on the shore.

'I hope he will,' Robbie said. 'He already refuses to believe that any team exists except for the Red Sox.'

'Good boy.'

Sterling Ames put down his half-chewed doughnut and spoke for the first time. He had powdered sugar on his grey moustache. 'Where you from again, Bob?'

'Ohio, with a detour via the south as far up as Maryland.'

'Ever see the ocean before you grew up?'

'Not until I was sixteen, and then I was hooked. I fell in love at first sight twice in my life, and that was the first time.'

'You got any relatives in these parts?'

'No.'

'Because Little was down Camden on the weekend, got talking to some fella called Brandon in the Rusty Scupper.'

Robbie's hand tightened on his plastic mug. 'Yeah?'

'Said he looked just like you, 'cept twenty-five years younger. Little came back with a head on him like a sore grizzly, 'cording to his father.' Sterling took another bite of doughnut, scattering powdered sugar.

'There are a lot of Brandons around,' said Robbie.

'Boat builder, this one. He's been working over there for Harkers.'

'Huh,' said Robbie, his heart pounding as if he'd just sprinted a mile at full pelt. 'Well, got to get to work. It's been a pleasure being abused by you guys, as always.'

'Get the hell to work,' said Avery. 'Stop bothering us old folk, we got stuff to take care of.'

Brandon's Boatyard was only about five miles from Clyde Bay General Store, off Route 1 and down a twisting access road to the coast, which was lined with snowbanks from October to April. Gravel crunched under the tyres of his truck but Robbie wasn't listening to that or to the 1960s oldies station that was pumping from the radio. He was thinking about how he wanted to go home and see Emily: to tell her about this, to try to work out what it might mean. To feel the touch of her hand on the back of his neck, see the furrow between her eyebrows as she thought.

But Emily was most of the way across the Atlantic by now. She was reading her book, or fast asleep, or most likely, looking out the window at the clouds over England and thinking about who she would meet there and what they would say. Maybe she was thinking about him, too. They hadn't been parted from each other for more than a night, for years.

Suddenly, fiercely, he wished he'd gone with her. Adam couldn't come, of course, but he could have stayed with a friend for a week – his best friend Luca's parents would have been glad to have him. Adam had been away from home that long this past summer for soccer camp and he'd been fine. They had missed him badly, him and Emily, but Adam had come home exhilarated from the freedom and the new friends he'd met.

'Separation is how they grow,' Emily had said, that night in bed, her hand seeking his, wanting not to be separate.

But Emily had left in such a hurry, to get to England in time for her mother's funeral that he'd had no time to think about how he'd feel when she was gone.

Surely this was a coincidence. Brandon was a common name. For all he knew, William wasn't even using his name. It was unlikely that he'd turn up in Maine. Emily would say all these things, if she were here. She'd also tell him to find out more.

He parked the truck in the lot. The lights in the workshop were already on and the sound of the radio came through. When he opened the door, the scents of diesel and bottom paint greeted him, wood shavings and pine tar. At the far end, he saw a figure in a flannel shirt and baseball cap bending over his work. Robbie put on a pot of coffee in the kitchenette near the office and poured two cups as soon as it was done. He added creamer and three sugars to one of them before bringing it over to Pierre L'Allier.

'Early start?'

The young man glanced up from the piece of cap rail he was fixing to the bulwarks of a wooden yacht. He'd been trying to grow a beard for the past few weeks; so far it was a bit of wispy hair on his chin and on the corners of his lip, which startled Robbie a little bit every time he saw it.

'Oh yeah, good morning,' Pierre said, his accent flavoured with Québécois. 'My brother dropped me off on his way to work. I hope it's OK to let myself in?'

'Course it is. Wouldn't have given you keys if it weren't.' Robbie nodded at the joint on the cap rail. 'That's a nice nibbed scarf.'

Pierre flushed. Despite the wisp on his chin, or maybe because of it, he only looked about sixteen. He'd been even scrappier and younger-looking when Robbie had taken him on as an apprentice, two years ago, straight out of school. Robbie hadn't been look-ing to take on anyone else – he already had three full-timers, five part-timers, and Pierre hadn't ever even worked on a boat before. His family were loggers – his father was the best tree surgeon Robbie had ever seen; he'd taken down that big spruce in front of the Methodist church as if he were dancing a ballet with chainsaw and ropes. But Pierre had walked into the boatyard and as Robbie had talked to him, Pierre had touched the cedar planks waiting to be riveted on to the oak frame Robbie had built. He touched them almost reverently. Almost as if his hands could see the shape that the wood should take. And Robbie had taken him on that very day.

'Tank you,' said Pierre. His French accent always came out more when he was embarrassed or excited.

Robbie sat beside him on the bench. 'Got a minute?'

'Of course.'

'Did you go down to Camden with Little Sterling last weekend?'

Pierre blushed again, more fiercely. He was a year short of drinking age, and his father Gill was notoriously strict with his sons.

'I don't really care what you got up to,' Robbie added. 'It's your own business. I just heard a story about someone that Little met there, who's got my name.'

'Yeah,' said Pierre slowly. 'Yeah, we were talking about that. I was saying he looked a lot like you, but younger. Little was saying maybe you had a cousin. You know how him and his cousins are all the spit of each other.'

Robbie was conscious of his heart pounding again. *Oh, Emily, please let it be, after all these years. Please.* 'What ... was his first name, do you know?'

'Charlie? No. Bill. William.' Pierre rubbed his forehead ruefully. 'We had a lot of beers.'

'William Brandon. You're certain.'

'Yeah, pretty sure.'

'And he was working for Harkers?'

'Yeah, definitely. Good boats, those, eh?'

'How old was he, do you think?'

'Dunno ... year or two older than me? He was a better drinker, anyway.'

Better, as in more accomplished. Robbie frowned into his coffee, and stood up. 'OK. Thanks, Pierre.' He put a hand on Pierre's narrow shoulder and went to the office to turn on the lights.

Inside, he closed the door behind him and stood looking out the window at the boatyard. Yachts shrink-wrapped for the winter in white plastic like fat-bellied ghosts. There was a man in his early twenties called William Brandon, a boatbuilder and a drinker, working not twenty miles from here.

'Oh God, Emily,' he whispered. 'What should I do?'

He knew the foreman at Harkers, had shared coffee and shop talk with him, and once had rafted up to his motorboat and done running repairs to his engine when they were both on their way to Matinicus Island. He found him overseeing work on a thirty-eight-foot sloop, every inch of it hand-built in this workshop. Harkers were among the finest vessels built in Maine, which meant they were among the finest built anywhere in the world: exquisitely crafted wooden boats made by men and women with rough hands and mostly bought by millionaires and billionaires as pretty toys.

Robbie paused in the doorway, looking around for a half-familiar figure, but he didn't see anyone new, so he strolled over to the boat to stand beside George and admire it.

'Wish I could afford one of these.' He touched the sloop.

'You don't need one. How's *Goldberg*?'

'She's fine. I need to recaulk her bottom before I put her back in the water.'

'Boats and women. Always more work than you think they're going to be.'

'Labour of love, though. How's Joyce?'

'The same. Emily?'

'The same,' he answered. She would be well on her way to Norfolk, now. On their trip down to Boston he had told her not to drive if she didn't get any sleep on the plane, but he suspected she'd ignore his advice if she felt she needed to. *Be careful*, he thought at her, across the ocean.

'Coffee?'

'I'm set, thanks. Listen, George, I'm sorry to bother you, but I'm looking for an employee of yours.'

'William?'

The promptness of the answer made Robbie's heart thump and his stomach sink. 'Yeah. Is he here?'

George shook his head. 'Sorry, buddy, but I had to let him go.'

Robbie's stomach sank further. 'Can I ask why?'

'He punched the head of the sales team in the nose.'

'Ah. So . . . so he's gone?'

'That was yesterday. I don't know how far he's got. Is he family?'

'He . . . might be.'

'He's a good boatbuilder, Bob. Very talented, and careful. When he's sober.'

59

'I understand. Where did he come from, do you know?'

'South. Charleston, I think. He didn't talk much about it. I get the feeling that he's moved around a lot, and I can see why. But he picked up some skills somewhere.'

In that small workshop, built out of leftover wood and corrugated iron, under the palm tree in their back yard in Coconut Grove. Curls of wood at his feet and sawdust in his hair, turning over a carved dolphin in his hands.

'Do you have his address?'

'I've got it in the office. But you'd have as good a chance going to the Scupper.'

He tried the Scupper first. It was three o'clock in the afternoon and Robbie had to pause at the door before he opened it. He had not seen the inside of a bar for years. Not a real bar, where beer stained the floor and the smell of alcohol had worn into the plaster of the walls. He tested himself: it was bad, but not too bad. It was the thought of William that was bothering him, not the thought of a glass pushed across the bar, cold and wet with bubbles crawling up from the bottom.

Well, that thought bothered him, too. But mostly it was the thought of William.

He opened the door and walked into the beery fug of the bar. Hockey played on the TV on the wall and the place was mostly deserted, except Robbie didn't notice any of that because sitting at the bar with his back to the door was his own self. Bent forward, shoulders shrugged down, dark hair mostly hidden by a baseball cap, feet in unlaced work boots propped on the rung of the stool. There was a duffel bag on the floor beside him. He was Robbie's own self, twenty years ago.

He had never seen William as an adult, but there was no doubt in his mind that it was him.

He watched himself drinking beer from a bottle with the grim efficiency of a man on a mission. At three o'clock in the

60

afternoon, William would have stopped keeping count of them already. Robbie would have lost count by now himself; the afternoon would have started to condense itself into mouthfuls taken, and lengthen itself into that no-time that started with the first drink and ended with forgetfulness.

Robbie swallowed hard, hung up his coat on a peg near the door, and walked up to the bar. He sat on a stool beside his son.

William was busy drinking. His eyes were on the hockey, but his concentration was on the beer in his hand. His profile was so familiar it hurt. Marie was in the tilt of his chin and the shape of his ears but the rest of him was like Robbie, down to the faint auburn in his unshaven beard. His hands had seen work and his clothes were the uniform of men all up and down the coast: plaid flannel shirt with the sleeves rolled up, worn jeans, untucked T-shirt. Robbie wore a version of it too, though his shirt was solid navy and he wore a sweater over it. The barman approached him, and he said, 'A Pepsi, please, with plenty of ice. And another Geary's for William here.'

At the sound of his name, William turned from the hockey and glanced at Robbie. The glance solidified into a stare. Robbie looked back at him.

It had been eighteen years. William had been a child of four. A child of four, and asleep. Now he had a man's face, unshaven chin, bloodshot eyes, a bruise on his cheekbone. He looked older than twenty-two. He looked like the stranger Robbie used to see in the mirror every day.

'Who are you?' William demanded.

'I'm the man who just bought you a beer.'

'But who the fuck are you?'

'My name's Robert Brandon.'

The look on William's face wasn't surprise, but anger. He narrowed his lips and his eyes and Robbie knew this was the expression he'd had right before he punched Harkers' sales manager in the nose.

'What are you doing here?' he demanded.

'I told you. I'm buying you a beer.'

The drinks appeared next to their elbows on the bar and Robbie picked his up and had a sip. Cold bite, not enough to quench the thirst, but good enough. It was all he needed. William didn't touch his.

'Is your mother Marie?' Robbie asked.

'Don't give me that,' William said. 'Not now, this is a fucking joke.'

'It is,' agreed Robbie. 'And I didn't expect it either. George told me to look for you here. He said you'd more likely be here than at your apartment.'

'My apartment.' William snorted. 'Why were you looking for me?'

'Because if Marie Doherty is your mother, then you're my son. I haven't seen you since you were four. And I didn't know where to find you until now.'

'You're an asshole, is what you are.'

'Yeah,' said Robbie. 'I probably am.'

'If you're my father, where have you been?'

'Right here for the past thirteen years. In Clyde Bay. Before that, I was in Florida, waiting for you.'

William's fist crashed down on the bar. 'I don't believe you.'

Robbie took his wallet out of his pocket. He put a bill on the bar to pay for the drinks, and he drew a photograph out of the back of it. It was creased, yellowed, and worn to the shape of his back pocket from being carried around in a succession of wallets over the years. He put it on the bar, next to William's fist.

The boy in the photograph smiled up at them both. He was missing one of his front teeth and his hair needed a cut, even by the standards of 1972.

'Get. The fuck. Out of here.' William's voice was wet and furious.

'This is my phone number.' Robbie grabbed a pen and a cocktail napkin and wrote it down. His writing was unsteady, and so were his words. 'I'd like to get to know you, William.'

'Get the fuck out of here! Get out!' William slid off the stool, knocking it over.

'Hey,' said the barman, 'whoa now, what's going on?'

'Get out!' William's hands clenched.

'I told you, Bill,' said the barman, 'it's your last chance. No more fighting.'

'I'm going,' said Robbie. 'Don't worry. I'm going. Call me if you want to. Please. Or find me. Brandon's Boatyard in Clyde Bay. I'll be there.' He stuffed his hands in his pockets and left the bar. The air outside was cold, colder than the drink he'd ordered, and he breathed great gulps of it to try to quench his thirst.

Chapter Nine

There were new houses on the outskirts of Blickley, crowded together behind cramped gardens; the tiny school where she and Polly had gone as children had a new, ugly extension on its side. But the church was the same, squat and grey, exactly as it had been for hundreds of years before Emily was born. After the dirty snow of a late Maine winter, the green of an English spring was almost shocking. Daffodils bobbed around the edges of the car park, which was full; she saw mourners, wearing suits and dresses, walking up the path into the church. Some of them she recognised, but she didn't see her father or Polly. Not yet.

She was late. After twenty years away, she had not expected the traffic in England to be so bad. The M25 had been stop and go, and she'd been stuck behind a tractor for half an hour on the A-road, pounding her hands on the steering wheel, trying not to look at the clock on the car dash. Her mouth tasted of awful airline coffee and she still wore the clothes she'd travelled in: a wrinkled shift dress, dark tights, a jumper, a winter coat that was more suited to Maine's icy temperatures than England. She turned the car around and found a space to park on the side of the road. Then she hurried up to the church, looking frantically for her father's slender build, her sister's curly hair.

The man she saw at the door of the church was not who she expected to see at all.

She came to an abrupt halt. 'Christopher.'

He was wearing a grey overcoat. His glasses were round, without frames. His sandy hair had receded, and although Emily was a parent, a doctor, and forty-eight years old, she was shocked for a moment that this person from her youth was a middle-aged grown-up.

Christopher's eyes widened. 'Emily?'

'I . . . didn't expect . . .' She stopped. 'Of course you're here. My mother loved you very much.'

'And I loved her. It's . . . good to see you again, Emily.'

She knew he was lying, or at least as close to lying as Christopher ever got, but this was typical Christopher, typical politeness. Because it wasn't good to see him again. It was strange, as if this person she knew so well had been dug up and replaced by someone else, someone nearly twenty years older whom she didn't know at all.

What was it going to be like to see her father?

'It's good to see you,' she said.

'This is Lucy,' he said, and for the first time she noticed that a woman was standing next to him. She also wore a grey coat, and glasses, though she couldn't take in many more details than that. 'My wife.'

'Oh. It's – it's nice to meet you.' She put her hand out to shake, because that seemed the right thing to do, and Lucy took it.

'It's nice to meet you too.' And Lucy actually sounded as if she meant it, so she couldn't possibly know who Emily was. Christopher couldn't have told her everything.

She stared at them both, with too much to say to be able to say anything safely.

'I think it's time to go in,' said Christopher.

'Yes.'

'I'm so sorry about your mother,' said Lucy.

'Thank you,' she said automatically, thinking that this was how both English people and New Englanders dealt with uncomfortable situations: falling back into polite truisms and a catechism of courtesy.

They both stood back to let Emily enter the church.

The pews were nearly full. The air smelled of damp stone and lilies. In the front of the church was the coffin, wreathed with flowers, containing her mother.

She had not understood, not truly understood, that her mother was dead until that moment. That her mother was dead and not coming back. Forever.

She felt her mother's hand in hers, as she had when she was a child and they used to walk to the shops. She smelled the scent of her mother's hair. She saw her mother one of the last times they had spent together, sitting near the beach on Key West with the orange sunset gleaming off the glass she held in her hand. How she smiled. How she laughed.

And now she was gone, and what did anything else matter at all? All the other things that had happened between them?

At the back of the church, Emily reached her hand out, touched open air, thought about touching the coffin's polished wood. She thought about her mother inside. Her mother was beyond her reach in a way that she had not been for the eighteen years that Emily had not seen her, nor heard her voice.

Once upon a time, it had only been the two of them. She was the first person Emily had ever known.

'Goodbye,' she whispered.

The vicar, a strange vicar who was not the voice of her childhood's Sundays, walked up to the pulpit and began to speak.

Leaning against the wall by the font, lost in memories of her mother, she hardly realised the service was over until the people in the front pew stood up and she saw her father. She watched, frozen, as he came out from the pew and began to walk up the central aisle towards her.

His hair was thinner and whiter. He wore glasses and a black suit and carried his overcoat over one arm. It was her father, after all these years, and the recognition nearly made her stumble backwards while at the same time she wanted to run forward into his familiar embrace.

She saw the exact moment he spotted her, because his expression changed from stoic calm to naked pain.

His footsteps quickened until he was almost running. God, he was thin – he'd always been slender but he was more than that, he was skinny, his features sharp and his suit too large. 'Dad,' she began, but at that same time he reached her and seized her elbow. He pulled her out of the church, around the side of the porch where they were alone.

'What are you doing here?' he demanded.

His eyes were hollowed, his cheekbones prominent. Something was missing in him, something she couldn't pinpoint but this was her father.

She had never seen this anger on his face before. She'd seen shock, dismay, sadness: never anger.

'I wanted to say good—'

'You don't get to say goodbye,' he said. 'You left your mother a very long time ago. Why did you come?'

'You wrote me a letter.'

'I wrote you a letter to be . . . to be polite. I thought it was my duty.' He nearly spat out the word. Her father, this gentle man, a doctor, friend of everyone. The guiding hands of her childhood. She shrank back.

He glanced over his shoulder. 'People are coming. You shouldn't be here; you shouldn't be seen. I don't know what you think you're doing but I don't care. Get out. Go away.'

'But Da—'

'Don't call me that! You gave up the right to call me that when you—' He glanced over his shoulder again. 'Go away, Emily. You don't belong here any more. Go away. Now. I don't want anyone to see you.'

She turned away from him. She couldn't see clearly from the tears in her eyes, but she heard the shuffle and murmur of people coming, and she ran away, into the churchyard.

She had played here as a child, after services while her parents talked with the old vicar. Her feet led her by themselves between the graves, along a listing flint wall and through an archway in it to a newer part of the cemetery, the part where the graves didn't lean and they were studded here and there with flowers, plastic and real. She leaned back against the wall, trying to gulp in air, holding her stomach in pain.

She thought of her father behind the camera and the photographs proudly displayed in their home, the photographs that documented her childhood, the person she had always thought she was. Birthdays, church fêtes, seaside holidays with her sister, her school photographs in pristine uniform, her graduation day outside the Senate House in her cap and gown. She was the good girl, the clever girl, the girl following in her father's footsteps into medicine, the girl who was going to deliver babies and save the world, Head Girl at school, first-class degree at Cambridge, the girl everyone in the village knew. *Your family must be so proud,* they had all said to this girl, Emily Greaves, the doctor's daughter.

I don't want anyone to see you.

She stuffed her fist into her mouth to stop from crying aloud.

The graves surrounded her, a community of the dead. Generations all buried in the same churchyard, side by side under their names and their dates. Her mother ... her mother was not from this village originally, but Emily knew where Charlotte Greaves would be buried, next to where Emily's grandfather and grandmother Greaves were buried. A collection of grey stones under a far-reaching arm of the yew. She'd used to play there as a child, too. The Greaves Graves, she'd used to call them, laughing. She had traced their inscriptions with her finger, all the way from John Greaves, 1784 to his however-many-greats-grandson, Emily's grandfather, Martin Greaves.

'Will I be buried here one day?' she had asked her father, aged eight or nine, and he had smiled and said, 'Perhaps. But wouldn't you rather get married and be buried with your husband?'

'I'm not going to get married, ever. I'm going to be a doctor, just like you.'

Emily sank down on to the damp, cold grass. The wet soaked through her tights in seconds but she didn't feel it. She listened hard for the sounds of her mother being interred in her grave, on the other side of the church, under the yew tree.

She heard footsteps instead: quick, hurrying footsteps, crunching on gravel. Approaching her. Emily stood, wiped her nose and eyes with the back of her hand, and was attempting to straighten her dress when the person appeared in the archway. She was tall and slender in a black coat buttoned up to her neck, a red scarf, curly hair pulled back into a clip and escaping in tendrils in the drizzle. The woman paused, dug in a black handbag and took out a packet of Marlboro Lights and a lighter. She lit her cigarette and sucked in the manner of a woman who needed nicotine in order to breathe.

'Polly?' said Emily.

The woman turned and spotted Emily, mid-drag. She started to cough.

'Polly.' Emily stepped toward her.

'Bloody hell.' Polly dropped her cigarette on the path. 'Emily? What are you doing here?'

'Same thing as you. Saying goodbye to Mum.'

'Has Dad seen you?'

'Yes.'

'Did he say it was all right for you to be here? Did he *invite* you?'

'No. I just came.'

Polly frowned. She was a pretty woman, stylish and poised, but to Emily's eyes she had aged possibly more than their father had: she had lines on her forehead and around her mouth. Her hair was dyed a shade darker than her natural one, which made her face appear sallow, despite the make-up she wore.

'You don't have any right to be here, after what you did,' Polly said.

'I haven't done anything that makes her any less my mother.'

'You killed her.'

Emily stepped forward, feeling, for the first time, a stirring of anger at her own family. It was easier to be angry with a younger sister, a sibling who had always looked up to Emily and hero-worshipped her. It was easier to feel that this drama was all manufactured and ridiculous.

'What? How can I have killed her? I haven't seen her in nearly twenty years, since we were on holiday in Florida together.'

'Do you even know how she died?'

'It didn't say in the letter.'

'It was cancer,' said Polly. 'Long and slow cancer. The kind that you get better from for a little while, but you never really get better. She got weak after you stayed in America, and we thought it was because you'd hurt her. Because you'd broken her heart. But finally she became so weak that Daddy persuaded her to go in for tests, and that's when they found it. She's been struggling with that every day for the past fifteen years, and where have you been?'

'I write every year,' said Emily. 'I've told Mum and Dad where I've been. Any of you could have reached me at any time. Any time you wanted to.'

'We didn't want to. We never spoke of you after that holiday. We were in Florida, and then suddenly we'd cancelled the rest of the holiday and we were going home, and it was if you never existed at all. I tried mentioning your name to Mummy more than once, and she acted as if she couldn't hear me.'

'But that couldn't kill her, Polly. And I'm as sorry she's gone as you are.'

'It killed her. *You* killed her.'

'Cancer killed her.'

'She died of a broken heart.'

'People don't die of broken hearts. I'm a doctor. That doesn't happen.'

'It happened to Mum!' Polly shouted it. 'After you left she was never the same. She kept it inside her for years without talking about it and it ate away at her. It caused something wrong with her. It caused something wrong with all of us.'

'She never talked about it? Not *ever*?'

'She wasn't herself after that. Not that you'd know.'

'You mean . . . you don't know what I did? They didn't tell you?'

Polly had been away, out with her new friends; not there for that horrible, final confrontation. The last time Emily had seen her father until now; the last time she had seen her mother at all.

'All I know is that you made me lie for you. I lied to Mum and Dad and Christopher, because I trusted you. I thought you knew what you were doing, that you'd always do the right thing.'

Polly snapped out another cigarette from the packet and lit it with shaking hands. Emily could see the ghost of the little girl that Polly had been, the smiling little girl who used to dance around the house.

'I loved you,' Polly said. 'I looked up to you. All my life, I wanted to be like my big sister Emily. And then suddenly you're gone. And everyone I love is heartbroken. And we never hear from you again.'

'I didn't want to leave you behind. I didn't have a choice. I tried calling you after you were back in England, but the person who answered said you'd moved out of the flat. I thought Mum and Dad would tell you where I was.'

'It hurt them too much to even think about you. You never even said goodbye. Just suddenly: gone.' Polly blinked hard and dragged on her cigarette. 'And Mum was different, and Daddy was different. And Christopher . . .'

'I'm sorry, Polly. This wasn't the way I wanted it to be. I never wanted to lose you, too.'

71

Her sister shook her head. 'I hope it was worth it for you. I hope you're happy.'

'I *am* happy,' Emily said. 'I have a little boy. Well, not so little now – fourteen. He … asked me the other day if he had any cousins.'

Polly laughed bitterly. 'Fat chance. What have my models for good relationships been? Yours and Christopher's? Mum's and Dad's? All that deception and silence? Nobody *ever* talking about *anything*? You think it was easy for me to trust someone after you left?'

'So you're not married?'

'Oh, I've been married,' said Polly through a cloud of smoke. 'Men are dicks.'

'I'm sorry.' The words seemed so empty for how she felt.

'No, you aren't.' She dropped this cigarette on the path, too, next to her last one, and ground it out beneath the pointed toe of her shoe. 'If you were sorry, you would never have come back. You would never have made my father look at your face and remind him of how you broke Mum's heart. He wouldn't be standing there right now beside her grave, looking like death himself, so bad that I couldn't stand it for another minute without a fag and had to miss my own mother's burial.' She kicked the filter, sending gravel flying. 'And I'm going to him now. I've had enough of you.'

'Please,' said Emily. 'Please tell him I love him. I … didn't get the chance before.'

'Too bad,' said Polly. 'Now you know how I felt when you left.'

'Polly, I'm sorry that I left. I'm sorry that you never knew why. I can tell you everything. I can tell you the whole story.'

'Too late.' She stuffed her cigarettes and her lighter into her bag and walked through the archway, leaving Emily behind.

She tried to ring Robbie from the phone box outside the post office but Pierre, who answered, said that he'd gone down to Camden. No one picked up at home, either. Adam would still be in school. She looked at her watch and tried to stem a fresh tide of tears.

This had once been home to her: this street with its row of shops, newsagent, baker, grocer; the Royal Oak on the corner, the path leading down to the river, the school, the bus stop, the house she'd grown up in. Now the shops were different, the pub had been repainted, the red phone box replaced by a metal half box on a post. The geography was the same, but everything else had changed and though she'd thought she'd feel like the same person when she came back, she knew she was a stranger. She had once belonged here in Blickley, and now she didn't. Her sister resented her, her father was ashamed of her, her mother was dead.

She put the phone back on the hook and wondered what to do next. She hadn't thought any further than getting to the funeral, though now that seemed silly: perhaps she'd had an idea that her father would let her stay at the house. She considered trying to get a room at the Royal Oak for the night, but it would be full of locals. If Polly didn't know what had happened to drive a wedge between her and her parents, the locals wouldn't know either, but they might have theories. She quailed at the thought of their questions and curiosity.

Uncertain of her reception, she'd only booked a single ticket to the UK, and even though it was only mid-afternoon, the thought of driving another five hours back to Heathrow was unappealing. She hadn't slept properly for nearly forty-eight hours. She needed time to rest, to lick her wounds. To try to work out whether she was truly the monster her family thought she was, or whether she was the person she'd felt like for the past eighteen years.

Emily got back into her rental car and drove south, to a place of happier memories.

Chapter Ten

'Your sister said *what* to you?'

'It's OK, Robbie,' she said, sounding bone-weary down the telephone. It was about nine o'clock there, and he doubted she had rested or slept. 'She can't help it. Polly has always been emotional. She's passionate by nature. She blames me for abandoning her, and I can't blame her for that.'

'But she never even tried to—'

'She took my parents' side. She had to; they never told her what happened.'

'You could tell her. If she knew, she might understand.'

'I offered to,' said Emily. 'But she didn't want to know. And I don't want her to know, either. I . . . don't want to give her any more reason to hate me.'

'You're not ashamed, are you?'

'I'm . . . sorry for causing them so much pain.'

He couldn't touch her, couldn't take her hand. 'I love you,' he told her.

'I know. I love you too.' He heard her sigh. He wondered where she was sitting: in a hotel room, but what did it look like? Was she on the bed, or in a chair?

'Anyway,' she said, 'tell me something cheerful. How is Adam?'

'Adam's out eating pizza with the soccer team. He sends his love.'

'How's your day been?'

He'd considered telling her about William. About that fetid bar, about the anger in William's face, the way booze and adulthood had not quite rubbed out all the traces of the little boy he had used to be. But Emily wanted to be cheered up. She'd been rejected by all that was left of her family and said goodbye to her mother forever.

'I went down to Camden,' he said. 'I'll tell you about it later. But right now, tell me where you are. What are you looking at?'

'I'm looking out the window.'

'Do you have a sea view from your room?'

'Yes, but it's dark. I can see some lights on the water.'

He picked up the phone and carried it across the room to the window. The water was slate-grey, the rocks black. 'I'm looking out the window at the sea, too. Can you see me?'

'Robbie, I'm on the east coast. I'm facing the wrong way for Maine, even if I could see three thousand miles.'

'Look anyway. Can you see me?'

She paused. He knew she was looking, even though it was impossible. Even though he was being silly.

'Yes,' she said. 'Yes, I can see you.'

'I can see you, too,' he said. 'Come home soon.'

After Adam went to bed, the house was very quiet. The absence of Emily was a tangible thing, as if the house had a hole in it that Robbie would fall through when he entered one of the rooms that had been familiar, but now seemed strange.

A second night without her, and tomorrow would be a third. Emily hadn't been able to get a flight home till Monday. He didn't go to bed, though he was tired and it was nearly eleven. He wanted to call her, but it was too late where she was. He ached to be with her. He wanted to be with her now. He wanted her home, safe, where she belonged, in this place they'd made theirs even though maybe they weren't supposed to.

When Robbie stepped out with Bella for a last time about

eleven thirty, he smelled snow on the air. After thirteen years here he might still be considered from 'away', but he could read the weather as well as anyone who'd been fishing the Maine coast all their life.

'Going to be a storm soon, Bella,' he said to the dog, who waved her tail, did her business and trotted back to be let in the house. For a dog born in Maine and supposedly bred for hunting, she hated the cold as much as a delicate Southern belle. In the summer, though, they could barely get her inside. He thought about the conversation he'd had with Emily last week about breeding her and maybe keeping one of the puppies. 'At least let's choose a father dog who isn't such a wimp,' he'd said, and she'd hit him with a rolled-up copy of the *Portland Press Herald*.

Smiling, he pushed open the kitchen door and was just unlacing his boots when the phone rang. He loped to the phone, one boot on, and snatched it up. 'Emily?'

'Yeah, no, this ain't Emily,' said the male voice on the other end, who sounded distinctly annoyed. 'Listen, you know Bill?'

'Bill?'

'Only we found this number in his pocket and we didn't know who else to call. He's pissed off everyone around here and I'm not prepared to have him sleep on one of my tables overnight.'

'William, you mean? William Brandon?'

'Yeah, that's right. Listen, will you come and get him or should I call the cops?'

'I'll come and get him.' Robbie was already reaching for his car keys. 'Where is he?'

'Rusty Scupper. I figure you know where it is because your number was on one of our napkins.'

'I know where it is.'

He hated leaving Adam alone in the house, especially with a storm coming, but he was fourteen and sensible and when Robbie woke him up to tell him he had to go out, he just nodded and said he'd go back to sleep anyway. It hadn't started snowing when he set out, though by the time he reached Camden there were flurries in his headlights. The outside lights on the bar were turned off and he had to knock on the door to be let in.

The guy who opened the door was different from the barman he'd seen earlier in the day. 'We're closed.'

'I'm here for William,' Robbie said. 'Bill.'

'Oh yeah.' The man held open the door for him. All the overhead lights were on, exposing exactly how grimy the walls were, how the chairs all had rips and stains on their vinyl upholstery. William was in a booth in the back, slumped over the table, asleep.

'Hey, buddy,' said the man. 'Hey, buddy, wake up. Your friend is here.'

William didn't move. Robbie, veteran of many drunken evenings and, if he were honest, afternoons – hell, sometimes even mornings – slid into the booth beside him.

'Come on,' he said loudly, right into William's ear. 'I'm going to take you home.' He picked up William's arm and put it round his shoulders, putting his own arm around William's waist. The smell of alcohol was overwhelming: beer, whiskey, and sweat. William stirred slightly as Robbie pulled him out of the booth, and made an incoherent sound when Robbie heaved him up on to his feet. He was heavy, but with the movement he woke up a little bit and took some of his own weight.

'We're not his babysitters, you know?' said the man, conversationally, not offering to help Robbie. 'And this ain't a hotel.'

'Doesn't he have any friends?'

'Not around here, not any more.'

'Does he have a coat? It's cold outside.'

'His stuff's in that bag, I guess.' The bag was on the floor next to the booth, the same duffel bag Robbie had seen him with earlier.

'Do you know where he lives?' He'd had the address from George, but it was in his other jacket, the lighter one he'd worn this afternoon before the storm.

'That apartment building on Penobscot Street? I've seen him

coming out of there before. Listen, I gotta close up.'

'OK. Lean on me, Will.' He was not quite a dead weight as Robbie hauled him across the bar, but nearly. The cold air and the snowflakes, falling faster now, on his face, roused him a little bit and he went into Robbie's truck with a few mumbled words. By the time Robbie got back with his bag, he was fast asleep again.

Robbie knew Camden, but not all that well, and he had to drive around a little while before he found Penobscot Street. The snow was settling and his tyres made tracks on the road. None of the houses were obviously apartments but he drove slowly, looking at front porches, until he found a house with several mailboxes.

Robbie shook William's shoulder. 'Which apartment do you live in?'

No answer. He snored. Robbie sighed and searched through his pockets for a key. The two front pockets yielded a wallet, very little loose change, half a pack of Marlboro reds and a lighter, a Leatherman knife which Robbie was heartily glad William hadn't seen fit to use in his fight with the Harker salesman. He had to push William forward to get to his back pocket and his keychain. It was attached to a promotional bottle opener shaped like a crab. Robbie saw a car key to a vehicle that was presumably still parked outside the Rusty Scupper, and a small key that could be to something like a locker. But no house keys.

He shook William harder. 'William! What number apartment do you live in?'

No answer. Robbie regarded him. Sleeping, in the passenger seat of his truck, lit by the streetlamp down the road, he didn't look much like the child he'd been. His mouth was open, his face rough with stubble, his eyebrows thick and dark. He'd lost his baseball cap somewhere between the stool and the booth. Robbie reached across him and opened the door to the truck, hoping the cold air would revive him again, enough for him to tell Robbie where he lived, but he didn't get much more than a grunt.

'Great,' said Robbie, and got out of the truck. He climbed the stairs to the front porch. One of the bottom windows had a light on inside; he took a guess which apartment it was and pressed the doorbell marked 'Apt 1.' He had to wait a while and was considering pressing it again before someone opened the heavy inside door, leaving the screen one closed. It was a woman, wearing a terrycloth bathrobe and bed hair.

'Sorry to disturb you,' said Robbie. 'I know it's late. I'm taking William Brandon home and I don't know which apartment he lives in, and I think he's lost his keys. Do you know anyone who has a spare one?'

The woman ran her hand through her hair. 'He doesn't live in any of them. Dean, that's the owner, evicted him ... I want to say last week? He said he hadn't paid the rent for a few months.'

'Where's he been sleeping, then?'

The woman shrugged.

'OK,' said Robbie. 'Thanks. Sorry for getting you up.'

Back in the truck, he turned up the heating, put on the windshield wipers to swipe away the snow, and looked at William. One duffel bag. He didn't even have a coat. Or anyone to call except for the unwelcome number Robbie had written on the back of a napkin.

He made a decision.

She didn't think she would sleep, but she did, dreamlessly and without moving, until six. For a moment when she woke up she didn't know where she was and she reached out her hand for Robbie, thinking sleepily that he'd got up to go to work already, and then she remembered and she sat up.

It wasn't the same hotel room in Lowestoft; it wasn't even the same hotel. She hadn't been back here since 1962, and she hadn't been sure she'd recognise the hotel where they'd stayed that one night, but when she'd parked her car in the seaside car park and walked along the esplanade, she'd known which building it was straight away. It was flats, now, with dirty windows and missing curtains.

The seafront had been nearly deserted, and many of the hotels were closed for the season. She'd found this one further up the street. The corridors were carpeted in patterned swirls of green and brown and she could smell all the ghosts of all the bacon and eggs that had been fried for all the breakfasts ever made here. But the room itself was clean and the owner, an auburn-haired woman with a strong Suffolk accent, had made her a sandwich and a cup of tea after Emily admitted she hadn't eaten all day.

She lay in bed and remembered a pink ruffled bedspread and a view of the sea. It was too early to ring Robbie, but she remembered what he'd said about looking across the ocean at her. Emily used the kettle in the corner of the room to make herself a cup of tea, proper strong tannic English tea, and poured in two little containers of milk. She didn't usually take sugar but today, she put in a packet. Back in bed, she listened to the seagulls arguing with each other outside. They sounded exactly the same as the ones on the other side of the world.

She missed Robbie and Adam so badly that her whole body ached.

Later, the landlady put an enormous plate of breakfast in front of her. Eggs and bacon and sausage and mushrooms and beans and tomatoes, a rack of toast, a metal pot of tea. Emily looked down at it. 'I haven't eaten this much for breakfast in years.'

'You get that down you,' said the landlady. Janie, she was called. 'You didn't have a proper tea last night, only a sandwich for supper.' She hung her tea towel over her forearm; Emily was the only guest in the dining room. 'Where's your accent from, anyway?'

'I'm from Blickley, in Norfolk.'

'Don't sound like it.'

'I've lived in America for nearly twenty years.'

'That's it. You sound American.'

'In America, they tell me I sound English.'

Janie laughed. 'You can't win, can you? I've always wanted to live in America. You're lucky.'

'Yes,' she said. 'I am.'

'Still, though, I imagine it must be hard sometimes. Like you don't know exactly where you belong. Accent not here nor there, past in one country and future in another. My gran came from Ireland and she said she never really fitted in here or back there. Never lost her accent, though.'

After breakfast, walking along the beach, she thought about her mother and her father and Polly, and about Robbie and Adam. She skirted the waves foaming on the pebbles and weighed up the two emptinesses in her heart. The two lonelinesses.

If she could have anyone with her right now, here on the beach where she had, for the first time, fallen in love, who would she choose: her new family, or her old one?

A gull swooped by her head, crying its plaintive cry, and she remembered that time in Old Orchard Beach in Maine when the gull had stolen Adam's slice of pier pizza and he had cried until Robbie bought him a new slice. She remembered the way she and Robbie had laughed and made a protective circle around Adam with their arms as he ate it, to keep the gulls away.

She smiled. There was nothing to weigh, nothing to wonder.

She wanted to go back home, to see her real family.

Chapter Eleven

'Who's in the guest bedroom?'

Adam's hair was wet from his shower and he reached into the fridge for the orange juice. He poured himself a big glass, drank it off, and refilled it.

Robbie was on his fourth cup of coffee. 'Did I wake you up when I came back?'

'No. I just heard the snoring. Whoever's in there is sawing logs. Want some toast?'

'No, thanks. It's your brother.'

Adam put down the slice of bread he was holding. 'It's . . . William?' A huge smile broke out on his face. 'He's here? He's really here? You found him?'

'He's really here. But—' Robbie saw the excitement of his younger son and he tempered what he had been going to say. 'He needs to sleep, so don't go running up there and bursting through his door.'

'When can I meet him? When do you think he'll get up?'

'I don't know.'

'I could stay home from school. We're not doing anything important today, there are no tests or anything, and it's snowing, maybe they'll cancel school anyway.'

'There aren't more than a couple of inches out there. School won't be cancelled.'

'Can I stay home?'

'No.'

'But he's my brother, and I've never met him. I've only ever seen that one picture. It's way more important than school.'

'Your mother would kill me if I let you stay home from school.'

'She doesn't need to know?'

'No. You can meet him after you get home.' *If he's still here.* 'Now have breakfast and get ready or you'll miss the bus.'

Adam dawdled over breakfast, deliberately burning the first piece of toast and having to make another one, pouring himself a glass of milk as well as orange juice, glancing up every now and then at the kitchen door as if he expected William to appear. 'How'd you find him?'

'Pierre and Little Sterling Avery met him in Camden. He was working for Harkers.'

'Nice,' said Adam automatically. 'You went out last night to get him?'

'That's right.'

'Did you tell him anything about me?'

'I didn't really get a chance. It was late.'

'Please can I stay home?'

'The bus is here in five minutes. Go brush your teeth, and don't go into William's room, OK?'

'Aw, Dad.' But Adam went. He was a good boy. He played by the rules, like Emily did. He wanted to please the people he loved. Their sunny, blond-haired boy.

Robbie wished he had Emily here to help him.

William didn't emerge till nearly noon. Robbie was outside, splitting wood, trying to let the rhythm of the task take the worry away from his mind. He saw movement from the corner of his eye and Bella bounded out on to the snow, followed by William. He didn't have a coat and his shoulders hunched immediately. It had warmed up, as it often did after snow, but it was still cold enough.

Robbie leaned his maul against the block. Bella ran up to him, panting and pressing her shoulder against his leg. He pulled off his glove and scratched her ear. 'Morning,' he called to William.

William was lighting a cigarette. 'Where's my truck?'

'I don't know,' said Robbie. 'Where did you leave it? Outside the bar?'

'It's got all my stuff in it.'

'We'll find it later.' He walked over. William looked pale, dark shadows under his eyes, stubble on his chin. He'd slept in his clothes; it had been too much trouble for Robbie to remove them and besides, he didn't think William would thank him for it. Robbie could smell the sour scent of hangover on him, the lingering booze seeping from his skin and into his breath, and he remembered the days he'd woken up like that and gone straight to the bathroom to shower and brush his teeth to hide the smell. It had never hidden very well. He wondered if William remembered smelling it on him, if he remembered Daddy's morning headaches.

'I'll make some coffee,' Robbie said.

The dog came in with him, but William didn't follow until he'd finished his cigarette. He stomped the snow off his boots and rubbed his arms with his hands.

'You can borrow a coat and gloves,' Robbie said. 'Mine will fit you.'

'Why am I here?'

'They found my number in your pocket at the Scupper. Apparently you didn't have many friends left to call. I tried to take you to your apartment but they told me you'd been kicked out.'

'I don't need your charity.'

'It's not charity. Do you remember who I am?'

'I remember.'

Robbie poured him a mug of coffee and put it on the table. William grudgingly left the mat near the back door and sat down at the table, his boots still on and dripping on the floor.

'Do you remember me from when you were a kid?' Robbie asked, pulling out the chair next to him.

'No,' he said, but it was too quick. He looked down at his coffee.

'I remember you very well. I remember teaching you how to use a hammer and throw a baseball.'

'I don't.'

William's headache and hostility were written all over him. Robbie shelved the questions for now.

'You're welcome to stay here as long as you like. Do you want some breakfast?' He glanced at the clock. 'Lunch?'

'I'm not hungry. I could do with a drink if you've got one.'

'Coffee and orange juice is all we've got. Milk, too, though I need to pick up some more. Emily has a big store of English Breakfast tea if you like that.'

'I meant a *drink* drink. Something to take the edge off.'

'Sorry.'

William glanced at him. 'You've been gone for my entire life and now's the time you pick to get fucking judgmental?'

'I'm not being judgmental. I don't have any alcohol in the house.'

'Oh man, you're not a religious freak too? I got out of all that.'

'I'm not religious. I've been sober since the seventies. I was drinking when I was with your mother. I drank a lot.'

William subsided into his coffee. 'Why am I here?'

'It looked like you didn't have anywhere else to go. George said he'd fired you, and your former neighbour was pretty sure you'd been sleeping in your truck.'

'You've been checking up on me?'

'Seems like you can be angry with me for not being part of your life, or angry with me for being too interested in your life, but it's not fair to be angry about both at the same time.' He said it sharply.

William dug his hand into his pocket. 'Give me some money. I don't have any.'

'No.'

'Why not?' He scowled. 'You owe me enough. I never saw a penny from you when I was growing up.'

Robbie opened his mouth, then thought better of it and took a sip of coffee instead.

'I didn't know where you and your mother were,' he said instead. 'Marie never answered my letters and your grandparents sent them all back.'

'Well, you can make up for it now. Give me some money, take me back to my truck, and we'll call it even. You've done your fatherly duty and you can feel good about yourself.'

'No.'

William swore. 'Why not?'

'Because if I give you money, you're going to go straight to the nearest bar and drink it all away.'

'I don't have a job or an apartment. I need money.'

'It's like I said. You can stay here for as long as you need to. I can find you work, too, if that's what you're looking for. George said you were good with your hands. But nobody wants a drunk boatbuilder.'

'It's my own business whether I'm drinking or not.'

'Maybe. But I'd just as soon you were sober when you met your brother.'

He straightened, looking a bit panicked. 'I've got a brother?'

Maybe it was perverse, but Robbie was glad to see something other than pure hostility on William's face. 'He'll be home in a couple of hours.'

'Shit.'

'He's dying to meet you. Do you . . . have any other siblings?'

William shook his head.

'How's your mother?'

'None of your business.'

'What did she tell you about me?'

'Nothing good. She told me once that you were a Vietnam vet but that you never talked about it, and for a while I thought you'd freaked out or something, like you hear about. But then I grew up and I realised that you just didn't give a shit.'

'She still with that church?'

'I told you: none of your business.' William shot him a look of pure hatred and stood up, scraping his chair back. 'I could do with a goddamn shower, and some aspirin.'

'The bathroom's upstairs next to the room you were sleeping in. There's Advil in the medicine cabinet.'

'All my clothes are in my truck.'

'You can borrow some of mine. I'm not taking you back to your truck until I know you're sober.'

'Who the fuck made you such an asshole?'

He watched his son storm out the room, anger and defensiveness in the line of his shoulders, the stiffness of his neck. His clothes would fit William. Physically, he was the spit of Robbie at that age.

Robbie had no illusions. He knew that he had caused William to be the man he was now. That Robbie's actions as well as his genes were responsible for this anger and this loss.

'I'm so sorry,' he said to the empty room, because he couldn't yet say it to his son.

William was outside smoking a cigarette when Adam came home. Robbie was at the stove, in the middle of cooking bacon. He recalled from his own experience that there was a time in a hangover when bacon transformed from something nauseating to the very thing that was the perfect cure. He didn't know if this was the right time for William, but there wasn't much else he could do. He saw the car pull up at the end of the drive and he took the pan off the heat. It was Luca's mom's car; Adam had asked for a lift instead of taking the bus, which was slower.

He got out of the car, backpack slung over his shoulder, and waved briefly at Mrs DiConzo before running up the driveway towards the house. Robbie saw the exact moment when he spotted his brother because he changed course and his strides got even faster, puppyish. William threw his cigarette butt on the ground and watched Adam as he almost skidded to a halt in front of him.

Adam was tall for his age, and he wasn't much shorter than William. He was fair to his brother's dark, and thinner, with a boy's build rather than a man's. Robbie couldn't hear from inside the house but he saw Adam's mouth moving, and he saw Adam stick out his hand for his brother to shake.

He didn't know what William would do. They'd had no more words since the ones they'd exchanged over coffee. He hoped that William wouldn't offer hostility to his brother, but he wouldn't be surprised if he did. He knew he couldn't go out there and mediate. Emily might have been able to say something to ease the introduction, but she wasn't there. It was between them: his two children.

Don't break his heart, he told his older son, silently, through the glass.

William took his hand out of the pocket of his borrowed coat and shook Adam's hand. Adam's face was wide-eyed and open, full of excitement and wonder. He was talking quickly, gesturing with his hands in the way he'd learned from Emily, and William was watching him. One son who had been protected from every possible care, who'd barely spent any time separated from his parents; and one son who'd been abandoned by his father at age four, moved around God knew where, who fought and drank and walked in loneliness.

How was William going to feel about this person, this happy person, being his brother?

Bella barked at the door to go out and meet Adam. Robbie swore that dogs had an innate sense of time; this one always knew when school was over. He let her out and she ran to Adam, jumping up on him and wagging her tail. Adam greeted her and said something to William, who shrugged. The two of them walked with the dog towards the woods at the side of the house, wading through snow, out of sight of the window. Robbie guessed they were looking for a stick for Bella to chase. Adam and chasing sticks were two of the only things that could keep that dog out in the cold.

He put the bacon in the oven to keep warm.

When they came back in, they both had rosy cheeks and the dog was caked with snow. 'Sunny side up, or over easy?' Robbie asked them.

'I'll have mine the same as William,' said Adam cheerfully, brushing snow off Bella.

'Over easy,' said William in the manner of someone who'd been trapped into accepting.

'Wash your hands, they'll be ten minutes.' Robbie got the eggs out of the fridge and watched the two of them out of the corner of his eye as they hung up coats, took off boots, washed hands in the kitchen sink.

'I'll show you my room after,' said Adam. 'I've got a load of pictures of Romário, who I was telling you about. Dad, William likes soccer too, isn't that a coincidence?'

'I've watched a couple of games.'

'I totally think Brazil is gonna win the World Cup. What do you think, William?'

William shrugged. Adam took out plates and cutlery and started setting the table for three. It had been his job since he was about eight years old. Robbie glanced over and saw William observing this easy domestic routine with the trace of a frown on his face.

'Where did you live before Maine?' Adam asked his brother.

'I was in Charleston for a couple of years. I grew up all over. Oregon, mostly.'

'Wow, all the way on the other side of the country. What's Oregon like?'

'It's sort of like here. A lot of trees and coastline.'

And nearly as far away as you could get within the continental United States from Florida. Marie had made a real effort to get away. Robbie wondered if Oregon was where William had picked up boatbuilding, but he didn't ask. It was safer to listen. He flipped the eggs carefully, not breaking the yolks, and after a few seconds slid them on to a plate.

'I want to travel some day,' said Adam. 'Dad travelled all over, didn't you, Dad? All over the world. And Mom's from England. But I've only ever been to Florida, which was where I was born, and Maine and New Hampshire and Massachusetts and Vermont and New York once. The soccer team might go to France next year on an exchange and if I make Varsity I can go.'

'I was born in Florida too.'

'You were?' Adam grinned as he tackled his bacon and eggs. 'I don't remember anything about it at all; we came up here when I was a baby. What was it like?'

'I don't remember much of it, except it was hot and there were lizards.'

'I'd like to see the lizards.'

'They were fast.'

William used to chase them in the back yard and he could never catch them. As soon as they saw him coming the lizards darted out of sight under rocks, fast as thought. Robbie put toast on the table, poured orange juice and coffee, and sat down with them to eat. He kept his mouth shut and listened to the conversation. Adam kept up a steady stream of comments and questions, which William answered with as few words as he could. The meal got eaten, the coffee got drunk. William looked less grey. Less sullen. Emily would be proud of Adam.

'I'll do the dishes,' he told them both. He wanted to try to call Emily again. William got up from the table and started putting his boots back on.

'You're not going, are you?' said Adam in dismay.

'I can't go anywhere. Your fath—I mean, I haven't been taken to get my truck yet.'

'We can do that as soon as I've finished the dishes, if you want,' said Robbie.

'But even when you've got your truck, you're going to come back here, right? I mean you're staying with us for a little while, aren't you?'

William looked from Adam to Robbie. Robbie said, 'The offer's open.'

'Please?'

Robbie saw him weighing it up. No job, no money, no home, no friends. Versus a warm house with a person he hated and a kid who clearly hero-worshipped him. Robbie thought that if William had any money for booze, he wouldn't be thinking so hard about his options.

'Maybe,' said William. He put on Robbie's coat and dug for his cigarettes in the pocket.

Adam followed him outside and frisked around him as he smoked, like a puppy.

Chapter Twelve

She walked through the sliding door at Logan arrivals and saw Robbie immediately. It was an enormous relief. A rush of warmth and happiness. Coming home.

He didn't wait for her to come around the railing to where people waited; he ran up to her and hugged her, making her drop the handle of her bag to hug him back. She breathed in his familiar scent. He kissed her once, hard on the lips, and then again, more tenderly.

'I missed you,' she said, although they'd both said it many times over the phone. 'I'm so glad to be back.'

'I'm only half here without you.' He took her suitcase and they walked, holding hands, through the lot to where he'd parked her car. New England cold was different from English cold: it was dry and crisp and breathtaking, rather than damp and insinuating. They'd had more snow since she'd been gone.

'Adam didn't want to come?'

'He wanted to stay with his brother. I was more comfortable with William having company, to be honest.'

'You don't think he'd do anything? Rob the house to get some money?'

'I don't know. I don't know him, Emily. It's like there's this huge empty space between the boy I used to know and the man he is now. I keep on thinking that if I'd been there for him, he'd have an easier life now.'

'It's as much my fault as yours.'

'He won't even mention his mother's name in front of me. I can only imagine what she's told him.' He put her suitcase in the boot. 'I can't help thinking that most of it would be true.'

She knew this expression on Robbie's face. It was the expression he always got when they discussed William: hopeless, sad, angry, full of regret. She wondered if he showed that expression to William, and if William could see what it meant.

'It's not true,' she said. 'And you've found him, now. So that's what counts. More family can only ever be a good thing.'

'It's more family for you, too.' Before they got into the car, he reached across and hugged her again. 'I'm so sorry about what happened with your dad and Polly.'

'Me too. But I'm looking forward to meeting William for the first time.'

'They've been inseparable – Adam and William. They've spent all weekend together, watching movies and kicking around a ball in the driveway. He won't say anything to me except for muffled growls, but he talks to Adam. I think they like each other.'

'It's what Adam's always wanted, and what we could never give him.'

'That part's good. The rest ...' Robbie shrugged sadly.

Darkness fell early, while they were still making their way up Route 1 to home, and when they pulled up in the drive all the lights were on in the house. Before they stepped on to the porch they could hear the music blasting out through the closed doors and windows. Emily exchanged a look with Robbie.

'Bonding session while the grown-ups are out?' she suggested.

'At least I can't object to the music.' It was one of Robbie's own AC/DC albums. The bass was loud enough to rattle the windows. When they opened the door it got exponentially louder.

'Adam?' called Emily, but her voice was drowned in the music. The kitchen was empty, though there was a pizza box on the table with a couple of cold slices of pepperoni pizza in it. She went straight through to the living room and turned the stereo down. The room smelled of cigarettes and strongly of alcohol. A red plastic cup sat on the coffee table, next to a saucer filled with cigarette butts; she picked it up and sniffed it.

'He found some money,' she said to Robbie, who'd followed her. He winced.

'He's passed out upstairs, maybe,' he said. 'His truck's still here.'

'Where's Adam, though?'

William was in the guest room at the top of the stairs, sitting on the side of the bed with his boots off and his shirt unbuttoned. His belongings were scattered all over the room, clothes puddled on the floor and draped over the furniture, a paperback book on his pillow. He had a half-burned cigarette between his fingers and another red plastic cup in his hand. When they stood in the doorway, he looked up blearily.

'Wha' happened to the music?' he slurred.

'Where's Adam?' demanded Robbie.

'I dunno. Inna bathroom?' He took a drink.

The bathroom door was locked. Robbie knocked, and then pounded when there was no response. 'Adam?'

'There were two cups,' said Emily, her heart racing. 'William had one and there was one downstairs.'

Robbie put his shoulder to the door. It took three goes to break the lock. The door swung open and Adam was lying on the bathmat. Emily rushed to him, touching his neck, feeling his pulse. His eyes were closed, his breathing slow, his skin clammy. He had been sick on the floor.

'Call 911,' she said to Robbie, and immediately checked his airways, put him in the recovery position on his side, and covered him with towels. All on automatic. The fear didn't kick in until she was holding him, his pale face near her leg, the freckles on it standing out against the stark white.

Chapter Thirteen

Robbie got home from Pen Bay Hospital about half past midnight and was dully surprised to see William's truck still in the driveway. When he got inside, William was sitting at the kitchen table with a cup of coffee. The pizza had been cleared up and the house smelled only vaguely of cigarette smoke.

William stood up immediately. 'How is he?'

Robbie couldn't look at him. He was too angry. 'They're keeping him in for the night and maybe tomorrow too. He's on a drip.'

'Is he going to be all right?'

'No thanks to you. Emily's spending the night with him. She works there at the hospital; they know her.'

'I didn't mean to—'

'Didn't mean to what? Get him drunk? Get him in trouble?' The anger was a relief, after the hours in the hospital. 'What did you mean to do then?'

'I thought . . . we were just having a good time.'

'He's fourteen. *Fourteen*. What kind of a good time was that?'

'I had my first drink when I was about that age.'

'And you want Adam to turn out just like you, do you? You've got it so good?'

William snarled. 'At least he's got a dad,' he said.

'You're blaming *me* because you got him drunk?'

'He was the one who drank it, not me.'

'How did he get it? How did you get it? I thought you were broke.'

William looked at the floor.

'Was it Adam? Did he give you the money from what he had saved? Was it his idea?' Robbie put his hands to his face. He couldn't have two sons who were strangers to him. Not this one, sobering up and sullen, and the other, pale and frail in a hospital bed.

'I bugged him for the money. We drove into town. It was like a party. It was supposed to be a party. We got pizza, and I poured him a couple of drinks. I told him it would be fun.'

'That kid idolises you! You're his hero – did you know that?'

'You're his father. *You* should be his hero.'

'I'm your father too.' Robbie's hands were fists; he banged one down on the table. 'And right now I'm ashamed of you. You're an adult – you can ruin your own life as much as you want. It's a waste, but you can do it. But you can't ruin someone else's.'

'*You* did.'

'So now you're going to take it out on my other son, are you?'

William shook his head. 'That's not what I was trying to do. I like Adam. He's a good kid. I was just . . . I didn't think he'd get sick.'

'You *didn't think* him all the way to the hospital!'

'He's not my responsibility.'

'He loves you. That makes him your responsibility.'

'*I* loved *you*.'

William looked surprised at the words that had just come out of his mouth. He'd been looking at Robbie before, but now he stared at the table again.

'And I'm trying to help you,' said Robbie. 'But you don't want any of it. And that's your decision, but don't drag Adam into whatever hell you're going through. Into however much you hate yourself.'

'I don't hate myself. I hate you.'

'You don't know anything about me.'

'I know you left. I know one day you were there and the next day you weren't and you never said goodbye.'

'And you know all the things your mother has said about me since,' Robbie spat. 'She's been fair, I'm sure.'

'Do you know what we were doing while you were living in this nice house in this nice town? We had a trailer outside Portland, Oregon. Mom worked as a waitress and I let myself in after school every day with a key I wore around my neck. We spent every Sunday all day at church talking about being saved but I never felt saved. I flunked out of school and I only started working at the marina because I couldn't figure out what else to do and every day I hated it. I hated it, because it was what you used to do. Every single boat I worked on, I pictured you sailing away on it and laughing at me. Christ, I need a drink.' William got up and went to the kitchen cabinets, opening them up as if he expected to find another bottle there. He opened one, then another, then a third, more and more quickly. 'I could have forgiven you if you freaked out because of Nam or whatever. But no, all the time you were here with your nice house and your nice doctor wife and your nice soccer-playing son.'

'Don't take it out on Adam. All he wants to do is be your brother.'

'He isn't my brother. Because you're not my father.' William slammed the cabinet door shut. 'I don't want your fucking charity. All I want is a fucking drink. Give me some money.'

'No.'

'You owe me it.'

'Not for this.'

'Jesus Christ, you're such a fucking sanctimonious bastard. Get the stick out of your ass and loosen up, will you? Give me money for some goddamn beer, I've got a headache.'

'No.'

'I *hate* you.'

'Too bad. Because you're *just like me*.'

William grabbed his cigarettes off the table and stormed out of the house.

Chapter Fourteen

When Adam was little, Emily could rarely take the day off work when he was sick. Even if she could reshuffle her appointments, women didn't choose when they had babies, and it was almost impossible in a small hospital to find someone to cover. Robbie mostly did sick-day duty.

But sometimes she was able to manage it. On those days she would open tins of Campbell's Chicken and Stars soup, and make sandwiches of Saltines and butter. She would make a nest of blankets and pillows on the sofa in the living room and she would put on *Scooby Doo* or *Muppets* videos and they would curl up together all day, ignoring the yellow bus trundling by on the way to school in the morning and on its way back in the afternoon. Robbie would find them there when he came home from work and he would climb in with them. 'Are you so sick that you can't be tickled?' he would ask Adam, gravely, and the answer was always a shriek which meant 'no'.

This time Robbie carried the television up the stairs to put in Adam's room, just for the day. Adam had blue shadows under his eyes and he was penitent.

'I'm so sorry, Mom and Dad,' he kept on saying. 'It was my own fault. Don't blame William. It was me.'

Robbie had his own opinion about that, and Emily did too, which was not exactly the same as Robbie's. When she'd come home with Adam late yesterday afternoon and settled him into his room, she'd found Robbie in his workshop out in the garage, and William on the porch, smoking cigarette after cigarette and tossing the butts outside on to the snow. She'd introduced herself to William. He'd hardly said anything, but she was still shocked at his physical resemblance to the Robbie she'd met in 1962. His denim jacket was even battered in the same places. But although William was even younger than Robbie had been then – just into his twenties, hardly more than a child, really – he had an anger worn into his face that she'd never seen in Robbie in all the time she'd known him.

She wondered why he didn't leave. In hushed tones, in the hospital café, Robbie had had told her about their argument. But she didn't ask William about it; instead she offered him coffee and a sandwich and when he refused, she told him to help himself to anything in the kitchen, and if he didn't mind excusing her, she'd go straight to bed because she hadn't slept very well in the armchair in Adam's room last night.

He'd grunted and lit another cigarette.

'It's my fault,' said Robbie when he came up to bed. She knew he hadn't meant to wake her up but she had spent too many nights without him and as soon as he crept into their bedroom she woke up and put her hand on his side of the bed, the cool side, and waited for him to join her.

'Adam's old enough to make his own decisions about what he does,' she said. 'And William's old enough to know better.'

'I told him that he should have known better. I got angry with him. But it's still my fault.'

'Like it's my fault that my mother died, and my father won't talk to me, and my sister hates me?'

'None of that is your fault.'

'And since when did we have double standards in our relationship?'

'It's different.'

'It's not different at all. If we think about it too much we'll go mad, Robbie.'

99

He moved over to her side of the bed and took her in his arms. 'I'm glad you're back.'

'I'll never go away again. Not without you.'

This morning, Adam was too old for *Scooby Doo* but they watched stupid game shows together. He was propped up on pillows in his single bed and Emily curled up at the end under his quilt. She made microwave popcorn.

'This afternoon you can go down to the yard and help your father,' she said. 'You might not be able to do much but the fresh air will do you good.'

'All right.' It was clear that Adam didn't fancy it much, but he wasn't going to argue with whatever she suggested for penitence.

'We have a lot to talk about. But let's leave it for another time.'

'I missed you, Mom. Was it good to see your family?'

'It . . . was good, in a way. I'll tell you about it later.' She reached over and ruffled his hair. 'My sweet boy.'

'Don't blame William,' he said for at least the dozenth time. 'Dad does, doesn't he?'

'Dad and William will sort it out.' She wasn't as sure as she sounded. She kissed him on the forehead and went downstairs.

It wasn't so cold today; the snow was melting off the roof of the house and dripping down the eaves. William was sitting outside on the front porch steps smoking. She had no idea where he got all of the cigarettes; maybe Adam had given him enough money for a carton, or maybe he had a stash in his truck. She sat down beside him on the step, in a place where she wouldn't be caught by the drips.

'I'm glad you're still here,' she said, though she wasn't entirely certain that she was. Robbie was tense and had barely said anything at breakfast, and William had done little more than glower over his coffee.

'I don't have much choice, do I?'

'Robbie told me you'd lost your apartment,' she said. 'And I know he's angry at you right now for what happened with you

100

and Adam, but he meant what he said about you staying here as long as you like.'

'I don't mean that. I mean my truck is running on fumes and I can't afford to fill it up.'

'Oh. Well, I don't much feel like driving. How about after lunch you give Adam a ride to the boatyard and we can fill up your truck on the way?'

'Surprised you trust me.'

'Trust has to start somewhere.'

'Your husband doesn't seem to think so. He won't even lend me ten bucks.'

'My husband – your father – doesn't want to give you money to drink. And that's nothing to do with trust, and everything to do with experience.'

'Because I fucked up with Adam.'

'Because Robbie used to be a drinker and he understands the mentality. And his father used to be a drinker, too. His father didn't stop. Robbie says it runs in the family.' She grimaced. 'I don't blame him for not wanting to finance your drinking. I want better for you than that.'

'Why should you care?'

'I'd want better than that for anyone. But I care about you in particular because Robbie loves you.'

'Like fuck he does.'

She sighed. 'Do you want to give Adam a lift, and fill up your truck? Because I was lying; I really don't mind driving at all, if you'd rather stay here and sulk.'

He grunted. She stood and turned to go back into the house, but then she glanced back at him. She remembered Robbie all those years ago, standing near a palm tree on South Beach next to his bicycle, smoking a cigarette and waiting for her as if everything depended on it, because it did. Robbie, more muted and silent than she had known him before, holding within him a silent world of pain.

'I'm going to tell you something,' she said, 'because Robbie never will, not if he's angry. Every month since you were born he's put money aside for you in an account. He didn't stop doing it when he left; he's put in part of his pay check, or his profit, every single month. He does exactly the same thing, the same amount, for Adam.'

'Fat lot of good it's done me. I've never seen a penny of it.'

'I know. We get the statements. But your mother knows about the account, William. Robbie opened it when he was still with her, and he's had a duplicate statement sent to your grandparents' address, or at least the address he knew of.'

William sucked on his cigarette. He didn't say anything.

'He does it so that you can have a down payment on a house, or a car, or to start up your business, or to go to college. Something to help you make your life better. So when you're ready to do any of those things, it's there for you.' She opened the screen door, and paused again. 'He thinks about you every day. He doesn't talk about you every day, but sometimes we don't talk about the most important things to us. Sometimes we can't.'

She left him there, smoking, on their doorstep, surrounded by melting snow.

Adam usually bounded down the stairs two or three at a time. He came down slowly, and at the bottom he looked at Emily from under his gold-blond fringe, in the way he'd been doing since he was a toddler and was in trouble for breaking a rule.

He was fine, thank God. There was no damage done, and no one had reported him to the police for underage drinking – nor William for supplying alcohol to a minor. Adam had a two-day hangover and he was a little pale, but he'd be all right. It was going to take Emily longer to get over the fear she'd felt in the ambulance, holding his hand.

'Ready to go?' she said, reaching for her car keys in the bowl. The front door opened and William came in.

'I'll drive,' he said. 'Hey, Adam.'

The two hadn't seen each other since Adam had left in the back of an ambulance. Adam's pale face flushed. 'Hey, William,' he said. He didn't quite seem able to look at his brother.

'How you doing?' William asked.

'I'm OK.'

'I'm sorry, man.'

'No, I was a lightweight.' Adam glanced at his mother and blushed a little more.

'No, I was a dick.' William put out his hand and Adam shook it. The two of them smiled at each other.

Emily swallowed, hard. She put her car keys back in the bowl. 'Well, let's get going, then.'

William's truck was battered and the ashtray was full. An exhausted pine-tree air freshener hung from the rear-view mirror. Adam sat in the middle, his long legs crowding Emily's, and Emily looked out the window while the two of them talked about soccer.

She knew from experience that this was what healed; this was what made up real life. Not the moments of drama, but all the everyday, boring stuff. The time spent together.

She thought about all the time she hadn't spent with her mother and had to bite the inside of her lip.

When they got to the gas station, she gave her credit card to Adam and he hopped out to swipe it and fill up the truck. The cab was quiet with just the two of them in it. She pressed her luck. 'Robbie would love it if you gave him a hand at the boatyard, too. I can find something to do there if you want to stay with Adam.'

William shook his head. Adam climbed back into the truck and Emily scooted to the middle seat, where she kept quiet while Adam started up the conversation he'd interrupted to pump petrol. Sitting next to William, even though she wasn't touching him, she could feel his tension and how it relaxed when Adam spoke to him. She heard him laugh: he sounded just like Robbie.

All that time never spent together. She thought of her mother's coffin and Polly, in the graveyard, smoking cigarettes as if they gave her oxygen. As a little girl, Polly had been so eager to please. She had been like Adam, that way.

Brandon's Boatyard had a white wooden sign in front of it, with the name painted in grey-blue letters the same shade as the bay. Emily felt William looking at the new workshop, the dry-docked shrink-wrapped boats, the large hydraulic lift to take boats out of the water, like a giant's doorway to the sea. He stopped the truck to let Adam out.

'Wanna come and look around?' said Adam before he opened the door. 'Dad picked up a fourteen-foot sailing dinghy and he's helping me. She needs a lot of work but she's going to be mine when we're finished. We'll probably be done by the time I'm thirty. It seems like everything needs to be sanded a hundred times before Dad's happy with it.'

'Nah.'

'OK. See you later. Later, Mom.'

'Don't forget to drink water while you work,' Emily told him. 'Don't let your father give you coffee. It's dehydrating.'

'OK.'

'Back to school tomorrow.'

'Yeah.' Adam kissed her on the cheek and then he was gone, loping around the puddles of melted snow to the workshop. William put the truck in gear and Emily slid over to the passenger seat. He turned the truck around.

'What will you do?' Emily asked him quietly.

'I'll pick up my stuff. I've got some friends in Portsmouth.'

'You don't have to go.'

'I'll send my address when I've got one so you can have those statements sent out.'

'You'll stay to say goodbye to Adam, though, won't you?'

'I don't much like goodbyes.'

He turned on the radio. Emily sighed and gazed out the window. It was beautiful in Maine when it snowed; everything white and fresh and new. But when the snow melted, it showed up the layers of dirt and sand underneath and made everything grey. The snowbanks lining the road were sad lumps of spatter. Maine didn't have a proper spring; it went straight from winter to mud to summer. Sometimes she missed English spring days: bluebells and apple blossom and crocuses poking out their tender purple and white heads from the earth. The first daisies made into a bracelets and necklaces and crowns.

She'd just left an English spring, though, and been happy to be here instead.

A woman walked along the side of the road in the dirt and muddy snow. She had slim shoulders, a cloud of curly dark hair. They passed her and Emily glimpsed a profile.

'Polly?' she said.

'What?' William was pulling a cigarette from the breast pocket of his shirt with one hand.

'Stop the truck,' she told him. 'Stop.'

He pulled over and Emily opened the door and got out. The woman was wearing winter boots and an oversized winter coat that flapped over her wrists. She had stopped walking. Her hair was the same colour and texture as Polly's, her face was the same shape, but she wasn't Polly. She looked familiar to Emily, somehow.

There weren't any houses around here, and no pavements to walk on: only a muddy, sandy verge by the side of the road. 'Are you OK?' Emily called to her.

'Yeah, yeah, I'm fine.' The woman wiped her face with the sleeve of her coat.

Emily walked closer to her and she saw that she was crying. She also saw the baby, strapped underneath the oversized coat, wearing a yellow bobble hat and resting against its mother's chest. At the sight she realised how she knew this woman: she wasn't her sister, but her patient.

'Sarah?' she said.

'Oh. Oh, Dr Brandon. Oh, hello, I didn't know it was you.' Sarah wiped her face more hurriedly. Her nose was red and chapped.

'I didn't know you lived in Clyde Bay.'

'Yeah, just . . . on Eagle Point Road.'

'That's a couple of miles from here. Do you need a lift?'

'No, I'm walking. It's . . . it's the only way that she sleeps.'

Sarah's eyes were rimmed with red. Her lips were cracked and her hands were unsteady.

'She's asleep now?' asked Emily. 'I'm sorry, I've forgotten your baby's name.'

'Dolores. I call her Dottie.'

The baby was snug under the coat, in its yellow knitted hat. Emily stood next to Sarah and looked down at the child. 'That's a pretty name.'

'It was my mom's.'

'You've been walking to get her to sleep? All this way, by the side of the road?'

'It's OK. I do it all the time.' Her voice cracked, and Emily put her hand on her shoulder. It was thin and bony beneath the stuffing of the coat. She tried to remember when she'd last seen Sarah. It was the day after she'd got the letter from her father, the day she'd decided to go to England immediately. Only a few days ago. Had Sarah looked this bad then, this worn out?

How had Emily not noticed?

'Well,' she said, 'she's asleep now. Let us give you a lift home.'

Tears were leaking from Sarah's eyes now. A drip clung to the end of her nose. She nodded and walked with Emily to the truck. The door was still open.

'This is my stepson, William,' Emily told her. 'William, can you put out that cigarette, please? Sarah's got a baby. We're going to take them home.'

William, evidently surprised, rolled down his window and dropped his cigarette out of it.

'I don't have a baby seat,' said Sarah.

'William will drive carefully.' Emily got into the truck so she would sit in the middle and put out her hand to help Sarah climb up. William waited until they'd both buckled up before he put the truck into gear.

Emily gave William directions to Eagle Point Road, all the time going through Sarah's records in her mind. First baby; single mother; father out of the picture; she'd said her mother had died. She was twenty-one. She'd needed several stitches. She'd said that Dottie cried a lot. Dottie had grizzled all through their appointment and Sarah had rocked her with an air of desperation.

How hadn't Emily noticed it? The computer system had been playing up, her mind had been on her father's letter ... but she should have noticed. She should have seen this young woman's distress.

The house was a small one, painted white, with a porch that sagged on one side. Pine trees bent over it from all sides. The drive hadn't been shovelled since the last snowfall and the car was covered with melting lumps of snow. William pulled up.

'Well, thanks,' said Sarah. During the ride she'd only spoken to tell William which house was hers. She opened the door to get out.

Emily should tell Sarah to come into the office tomorrow. She should call Yvette when she got home and get her to book Sarah in and give her a call to tell her what time. She should ask some clinical questions, weigh the baby again, weigh Sarah, examine her again, and see about a prescription to help post-natal depression.

'Do you have any coffee?' Emily asked. 'Or tea? I could do with a cup, if you've got some.'

Sarah hesitated, about to slide off the seat. 'Um. Uh, yeah. I should have some. I think.'

'Great. I won't stay long.' Emily smiled at her and Sarah's forehead creased. But she got out of the truck, and Emily followed. She turned and leaned in toward William. 'I could probably do with your help,' she told him.

William also frowned. But he turned off the ignition and got out.

Sarah was heading for the house. Her feet fitted into boot-shaped prints in the snow. While she dug in the pocket of her coat for the key, Emily spoke to William. 'Have you got a snow shovel in the back of your truck?'

'Should have.'

'She could do with her driveway cleared out, and her walkway. And the car. Come in for coffee after.'

William looked at the driveway. After a little while he nodded.

Emily followed Sarah into the kitchen and wiped her feet on the mat. The sink was full of unwashed dishes and there was an open box of Lucky Charms on the table next to a carton of milk. Sarah looked around as if the room were strange to her. 'Uh . . . I think I have coffee somewhere.'

'I'll make it,' said Emily. 'You get Dottie settled.'

Sarah began taking off her coat. 'She doesn't sleep in her crib,' she said. 'She only likes to sleep on me. And when she's not sleeping, she cries.'

'Well, you must be tired after that walk. Sit down on the sofa and put your feet up, let Dottie sleep on you, and I'll get the coffee on.'

Sarah was obviously too tired to argue. She nodded and went into the next room. Emily looked through the cabinets until she found a bag of French Vanilla coffee and some filters. She washed out the coffee pot before starting it to drip. When she glanced into the living room, Sarah was lying on the sofa, her boots and the baby sling discarded on the floor. She'd taken off Dottie's knitted cap and both of them were fast asleep. How had she not noticed before, when she'd seen Sarah, that she had Polly's hair?

Emily emptied the dishwasher and stacked it with dirty dishes and used baby bottles. She wiped down the surfaces and replaced the milk in the refrigerator, which was empty of any food except for a pack of cheese slices and a jar of pickles. The tumble dryer was full of clothes; she folded them, all the little baby clothes. Onesies embroidered with yellow ducks, tiny yellow socks. All of

108

them chosen with care, all matching and perfect. She put them in the empty laundry basket.

She hadn't even known that Sarah lived in Clyde Bay. She'd seen her only as a patient. But here in her kitchen she could see Sarah's daily life: she was alone, tired, overwhelmed, in a twilight world of crying baby and all the domestic work to be done. Infants were hard, especially an infant who wouldn't settle. And Emily had blithely told her not to turn down any help that was offered?

Who was offering Sarah any help?

The door opened and William came in, stamping wet snow off his boots. 'Coffee?' she asked him. She got down a couple of mugs and poured it.

He scratched his head. 'Why are we here?'

'Because this young woman is our neighbour, and I don't think she has anyone else. She's trying to do everything alone, and it's not possible to do everything alone.'

'I do.'

'And look at what a good job you've done of it.' She heard the baby stir and start to grizzle in the next room. When she went in, Sarah was struggling to sit up.

'Can I have a cuddle with Dottie?' she asked Sarah, who nodded. She picked up the baby, who was stiff and red-faced, and rubbed her little back. 'She's got a bit of colic, hasn't she?'

'I don't know. I don't know what's wrong with her.' Tears welled in Sarah's eyes. 'I don't know what's wrong with me.'

William was standing in the doorway, mug of coffee in hand. He looked from Emily to the baby to Sarah in bemusement. 'Put down the coffee,' Emily told him. 'You need to hold this baby and walk with her so I can talk with Sarah.'

'I don't know anything about babies.'

'The first thing you need to know about them is that they don't mix with hot liquids. Put down the coffee, and come here.'

She sniffed the baby to make sure she didn't need changing, and then arranged Dottie in William's arms, upright with her chin on his shoulder. The baby looked tiny in his arms. She had a yellow duck on the bottom of her onesie. 'Just walk with her,' she told him, 'and pat her bottom.'

'Pat her bottom?'

'Like that. Yes. Good. You're a natural.' He wasn't a natural – nobody was a natural the first time – but he would do. 'Walk around the house with her for a little while – she's soothed by movement. Talk to her a little. If she falls asleep, keep walking. If she spits up, there are some muslins in the kitchen.'

'Spits up?' said William, alarmed.

'You're washable.'

'What do I talk to her about?'

'Anything you want.' She sat down on the sofa beside Sarah, who was wiping her eyes and watching this exchange with something like wonder. William walked into the kitchen, self-consciously patting the baby on her duck-clad bottom.

'Do you sleep at all?' Emily asked her.

'Sometimes. Not much. She's up every couple of hours and sometimes she feeds and sometimes she doesn't.' She sniffed, and Emily passed her a roll of toilet paper that was on the coffee table next to a jumble of baby bottles and clothes.

'I'll give Yvette a call and get her to make you an appointment with me this week, and also with my colleague Dr Black, who's a paediatrician.'

Sarah's eyes filled with tears again. 'I'm not doing anything right.'

'You are,' said Emily. 'You're doing everything right. You love that baby and you are doing everything for her. But you have to look after yourself, too.'

'I do love her. But I don't know what to do for her. I'm a horrible mother. My mother – my mother could do anything with babies. I wish she were here.'

'I miss my mother, too.'

Her own words surprised her. She did not speak of her own

family with anyone other than Robbie and Adam. She avoided the questions, sometimes gracefully, sometimes not, when they were asked.

'Is your mother in England?'

'She's dead. I'd just heard when I saw you in my office the last time. That was why I missed seeing that you were upset. I'm sorry, Sarah.'

'Don't be sorry. That's awful. When my mom died it was the worst thing in my life.' Sarah laughed shakily. 'She would have killed me for having a baby without being married. But she would've forgiven me eventually. That's what mothers do.'

Maybe if I'd done more, thought Emily, *maybe if I'd tried harder, my mother would have forgiven me.*

'I hope so,' said Emily. 'I really do hope so.'

In the kitchen, she heard William talking to the baby – not the words, just the sound. She wondered what he was talking to her about.

'Your stepson seems nice,' said Sarah.

'I think he can be when he tries.' She smiled at Sarah. 'Listen, we'll do all the medical stuff when you come to my office. But, right now, I think you can do with some sleep. Why don't you go to bed for an hour and William and I will look after Dottie. I'll make up a feed and see if she'll take it.'

'You don't have to do that.'

'I want to. I've got a couple casseroles in the freezer; I'll drop those by later. You need to sleep and to eat, Sarah. It's no good for Dottie if you don't look after yourself.'

'Why are you helping me?'

'Do you want the real reason? The selfish reason?'

'You're not selfish.'

'You remind me of my sister. I mean, you're nothing like her in personality, but you look like her, a little bit. And I miss my sister.'

'Is . . . did she die, too?'

Emily shook her head. 'No. But it's too late for her and me. So I need to make things right with the people around me. And now that includes you and Dottie.'

In the end, Sarah slept for two hours. After some experimentation, William had discovered that Dottie liked lying stomach-down on his forearm, arms and legs dangling either side, head cradled in his big hand. After a feed she fell asleep like that. William held her and looked out the window, not saying much, glancing down at the baby every now and then, while Emily got on with doing some more laundry.

Maybe if she had tried harder. Maybe if she had brought Adam over to England to see her family, years ago, when he had been a baby. Babies healed, babies helped. At the time she had been too afraid of rejection, too afraid she wouldn't be able to bear it if they sent her away, but maybe she should have tried. Her mother and father had wanted grandchildren so badly.

It was too late now to do anything differently. All those choices had been made.

With the baby on his arm, William could rock her easily back and forth. She slept with her little lips pursed out.

'You really are a natural,' she said to him. 'I was just saying it before, but now I really mean it.'

'Nah.'

'Have you ever thought about having children one day?'

'I'd just fu—' he glanced at the baby— 'mess it up, like I mess up everything.'

'You'd be surprised how much responsibility can change you. Responsibility and connection.'

He shrugged. There was a small noise from the doorway and they both looked up to see Sarah, her hair mussed from the pillow. 'You got her to sleep,' she said to William. 'Thank you.'

William actually blushed. Emily watched it with wonder.

'Your front porch step needs shoring up if it's going to last the winter,' he said to her. 'I'll do that for you before we go. I've got some wood in my truck.'

A little later, in William's truck, Emily said, 'You're very like him, you know.'

'I wouldn't know.'

'Maybe you'll get the chance to find out.'

He grunted. She wondered, again, what he'd said to the baby.

'So, are you going to Portsmouth?' she asked.

He drove for a few minutes in silence. They passed the place where they had seen Sarah walking, where Emily had thought the young woman was Polly, a younger Polly, before all the bitterness and separation.

'I might drop you off at home,' he said, 'and then go down to the boatyard for a while. Help Adam with that dinghy.'

Robbie was in the office, on the phone with a client, when he glanced across the workshop and saw William walk in. He went straight to the corner where Adam was working. Robbie saw the smile break on Adam's face when William spoke to him.

He finished updating the client and put down the phone, watching his two sons together for a little while. He watched William pick up a piece of fine-grade sandpaper and kneel beside Adam at the little boat's hull. The two of them, dark hair and light, a grown man and a boy on his way to being grown. They sanded with the same movement, the same rhythm, stroking their fingertips over the wood to check its finish.

He joined them. 'Nice to see you, William.'

William looked up, and Robbie saw his expression change from calm to wary. And that was all right, maybe. William was here, at least. Sometimes being present was all that mattered.

'I thought I'd better help,' said William, 'if Adam's going to get this boat in the water before he turns thirty.'

What miracle had Emily wrought? He'd have to wait till he got home to find out.

'I'll help too,' said Robbie. He picked up a piece of sandpaper and began to work beside them, rubbing down the rough wood into smoothness.

PART THREE

1975-1977

Chapter Fifteen

July 1975
Miami, Florida

'You're doing so well, darling. So well. Everything's going to be all right. You just need to push now.'

Jaquinda shook her head. 'I can't. I can't push.' She gasped it out with the strength of the contraction.

'You need to,' said Emily. 'Your body is telling you to, for a good reason.'

'I'm too scared.'

Emily took off her glove. She reached for Jaquinda's hand and she held it. The other woman's grip was crushing, desperate.

'I understand why you're frightened,' Emily told her. 'Anyone would be.'

'Are *you* frightened?' Jaquinda's face was shiny and wet with the pain of labour and the effort of clenching her body tight.

'A little tiny bit,' said Emily. 'But I know that everything is going to be all right this time, Jaquinda. I'm certain of it.'

'How can you be certain?' Jaquinda wailed.

Emily couldn't. Every birth was a risk, and this one especially. Jaquinda had had two second-trimester miscarriages and a still-birth. Everything with this pregnancy, so far, had been normal. But so had her last pregnancy – and the ones that had miscarried, too. They had all been fine. Both mother and baby were healthy. Right up until the moment they weren't.

She'd been waiting for the call to say that Jaquinda was in labour for the past two weeks, both anticipating it and dreading it in equal measure. She could only imagine how Jaquinda and her husband Miguel felt.

'I'm certain,' she told Jaquinda, knowing that if anything went wrong, Jaquinda might never believe her again. Emily would have destroyed their patient/doctor trust with a single lie. And she and Jaquinda weren't merely doctor and patient any more; she had gone through some of Jaquinda's ordeals with her and, as a high-risk patient, Jaquinda had seen her for frequent antenatal appointments.

But sometimes it was better to tell a patient what they needed to hear, instead of the strict truth. Eight months ago, Jaquinda had told her, 'This is the last chance. I can't go through it any more. If this baby doesn't survive, we're going to stop trying.' So perhaps, if this went wrong, she would never see Jaquinda again anyway. Emily wasn't sure if she would have been strong enough to try for a fourth time herself, if she had lost three babies.

Jaquinda panted in between contractions, her belly heaving. Emily moved up so that she could look into her patient's eyes. They were wide, the whites bloodshot, the irises almost as dark as the pupils. Jaquinda had refused pain relief. She was afraid of losing control.

'This is going to be fine,' she said. 'You're doing really well. And you are going to hold your healthy baby in your arms. You *are*, Jaquinda. You're going to be a mum.'

Jaquinda shook her head. Her expression battled between hope and fear.

'You are. I have faith. And you're surrounded by the best people to help you. But you've got to trust, Jaquinda. I know you want to keep this baby inside you where it's safe, but you have to push now. With the next contraction. All right?'

'I don't want to.'

'You have to. Promise me, darling. Promise me, Jaquinda. It's the best thing for your baby if you push.'

Jaquinda nodded, and her face immediately contorted into the pain from the latest contraction. Emily swiftly put on a fresh glove and moved into position.

She could see the baby's head. She could see Jaquinda still clenched tight. She put her hands on Jaquinda's legs, hoping the touch would comfort her. It must be such an effort for Jaquinda to resist every instinct in her body, to try to keep the baby in when everything wanted her to push it out. It must take an enormous effort, and enormous fear.

'Push now, Jaquinda. Please push.'

Jaquinda let out a hoarse, incoherent yell as instinct overran fear and she bore down.

The baby crowned and Emily supported its head with her hand. Twenty months ago she had just started at this hospital and she had held Jaquinda's baby's head in her gloved hand and had felt the sick, impotent sensation when she saw that underneath the slick of hair, the baby's scalp was blue.

The best people hadn't been able to help Jaquinda then. Emily hadn't been able to help her.

'You're doing marvellously, Jaquinda. I think the baby's head is going to be delivered in the next contraction. You're so brave. So very brave. Miguel is going to be proud of you, and so is this little person.'

'I can't do this,' Jaquinda sobbed.

'Yes, you can. You can do it. It's the most natural thing in the world, and in a few minutes you're going to hold your baby in your arms.'

The baby was blue, its limbs floppy. As if made of rubber. The most unnatural sight in the world. Jaquinda panting, and Emily silent, the nurses silent; and over everything, quieter than them all, the baby's silence.

'Why isn't my baby crying?' Jaquinda had asked.

The contraction came. Jaquinda yelled and pushed and the baby's head was a hot slippery weight in Emily's hand.

'It's going to be all right,' Emily said. 'It's all going to be all right.'

'Please,' said Jaquinda. 'Please, God, please. Please. Please.'

Emily guided the shoulders, and the rest of the baby followed quickly on the same push. A girl, small and pink and perfect.

She didn't cry.

For a fraction of a second, Emily forgot her training and knowledge. She thought of Jaquinda's blue baby, the baby Emily had not been able to save, and the tears that Jaquinda had shed in her office, her belly still distended from the dead child she had birthed. The grief in her husband's face that had made it grey.

'Why isn't my baby crying?' asked Jaquinda, and it was twenty months ago, the same thing, except this baby was fine, she was pink and she was *fine*, there was no reason for her not to—

The baby sucked in a breath and screamed.

'It's a beautiful girl,' Emily said, and she quickly clamped and cut the cord, and put Jaquinda's daughter safely into her arms.

She managed to wait until she had locked herself into the staff restroom before she burst into tears. She sat on the toilet, eyes closed, and saw that vision behind her eyelids: Jaquinda and her healthy baby, her daughter, the baby she wanted more than anything in the world. The happiness on her face had been so intense it looked almost like pain.

And then Miguel had come in and held his daughter who had been cleaned and wrapped in a blanket. He put his finger in her tiny fist and the tiny fingers curled around it and he looked over at his wife with the most perfect awe.

Emily had thought that she wouldn't have tried again, if she had suffered the losses that Jaquinda had. But she would have. If she could, she would have. Just to live that moment.

If she could . . .

She cried a messy cry, mouth open, not wiping the tears, doubled up in pain, but she didn't cry loudly. Hospitals were places for crying, but not by the doctors.

When she was done, she washed her face and held a wet paper

towel over her eyes to reduce the swelling and redness. She left the restroom and went to change out of scrubs and to put on some make-up.

Robbie was waiting for her in the car outside: a 1956 Plymouth, which he kept going with some sort of wizardry, along with hope and, occasionally, string. He leaned over and opened the door for her.

'What's wrong?' he asked instantly.

'Nothing's wrong.' She leaned over and kissed him on the cheek. 'Everything's right. I delivered a wonderful healthy baby just now. To Jaquinda.'

The words caught in her throat. Robbie nodded, and touched her hand. 'Do you want to tell me about it?'

'Not particularly. Not right now. Maybe later.'

He nodded and started up the car. It had an old-fashioned purr. She turned on the radio, which was tuned to Robbie's favourite blues station, and leaned back in her seat, closing her eyes and focusing herself. There was no air conditioning in the car, so they had to ride with all the windows open. The air wasn't much cooler than when they stayed still.

This could be their solution. It could be the answer to the empty room in their house, to the yearning she felt every day at her job, every time she walked along their favourite beach on Biscayne Key, watching tiny chubby hands fashioning sand castles. She laid her hand on Robbie's thigh as he drove, feeling the strength of him.

Their appointment was in a new, very ugly brick building. Somehow the interior managed to look both dingy and austere. They walked up the stairs and waited on plastic chairs outside the office door, holding hands. The round industrial-looking clock on the wall at the end of the corridor ticked loudly. Robbie's hand was slightly damp. Emily wanted to say something, to offer some word of reassurance or hope, the kind of thing she'd been saying to Jaquinda not much more than an hour ago. But she couldn't. This was . . . this was a risk.

But it was a risk they were going to have to take. For that empty room. For those tiny chubby hands. For the hole in Robbie's life: not to fill it, but to help him cope with it. For the hole in her own life.

The door opened. 'Mr and Mrs Brandon?' said a woman with a perm and large glasses, a brown pinafore dress and beige flowered blouse. She was pregnant: mid-second trimester, Emily judged. Emily stood. Robbie was already smiling, that charming, friendly, confident smile. He shook the woman's hand, and then she shook Emily's. Her fingers were cold. 'I'm Donna Hernandez.'

'Great to meet you,' he said as they entered her office. Emily took in spider plants, plastic chairs, wood-effect desk, two neatly placed manila folders and three blue Bic ballpoints. There was a poster of a Keane painting pinned to the corkboard on the wall: two huge-eyed children, a boy and a girl, one holding a stick with which he had just traced a heart in the sand. It was not exactly what Emily would have chosen.

'So, Mr and Mrs Brandon,' said the woman, taking a seat behind her desk and picking up one of the Bics, 'this is your first meeting, to establish some details and for you to ask some questions.'

'Dr Brandon,' said Robbie, with his easy smile. He took Emily's hand again.

'Oh, I'm sorry, you're a doctor?'

'I'm the doctor,' Emily told her. 'I'm an OB-GYN. An obstetrician. I work at Jackson Memorial.'

'Oh. I'm having my baby there. I'm with Dr Perez.'

'Good choice. Dr Perez is excellent and we'll look after you well there. Maybe I'll see you. What are you – about twenty-six weeks?'

'That's right.' Mrs Hernandez put her hand on her swollen stomach in the universal gesture of expectant mothers. 'I've started to get terrible heartburn.'

'That's only going to continue, I'm afraid. The baby's pushing all your organs out of the way as it grows. Try small meals, more often, and an over-the-counter antacid. Some people find that peppermint tea helps. But really it's a case of mechanics, and trying not to eat too much at once.'

'Thank you,' she said.

'It will be worth the heartburn in the end.'

'You're right, it will. And you're . . . from England?'

'Yes. I live here now, though.'

'I really love your accent. That's just so beautiful. People must ask you to say things for them all the time.'

'It's nothing special where I come from, believe me. But that's nice of you to say.'

Robbie squeezed her hand, and they exchanged a look. Part of this interview was about impressing the social worker favourably.

'And Mr Brandon? You're not English.'

'No, ma'am. I come from Ohio originally, but I've lived all over. I did some travelling when I was younger, which is how I met Emily.'

Her fingers twitched on his, but he smiled at her. Mrs Hernandez had started to use her biro to write down information on a yellow legal pad.

'And what do you do for a job?'

'I'm a boat builder. I've worked at Dinner Key marina for the past seven years.'

'And before that? I'm sorry – I need to ask these things, so we can have a full record.'

Robbie hesitated. 'I was in the Navy, in Vietnam.'

Emily held her breath and hoped that the social worker hadn't been a protester.

'Well,' said Mrs Hernandez, 'thank you for your service. I certainly do appreciate it.'

'Not many people thank me, to be honest. It's kind of you.'

'My brother is in the Navy. So why do you want to adopt a baby?'

'I'm infertile,' said Emily, and although it should be an easy thing to say, after all these years, it still scraped and scratched inside to speak it aloud. There was no shame to it, but there was a shame to it.

'Premature ovarian failure,' she continued, forcing her voice to be stronger and clinical. 'I was diagnosed some years ago. Robbie and I can never have children naturally.'

'I'm sorry,' said Mrs Hernandez. 'That must be difficult for you, if you work with babies all day.'

'I chose my field because it appealed to me. Most of the time I don't even think about it.'

Except when she had to retreat to the restroom to cry. Which was happening more and more often, lately.

'Well, you can take comfort in offering a home to a child who needs one. The adoptive parents' bond with their child can be as strong as between natural parents and their own children.'

'Just as strong,' said Robbie firmly. 'We want a child very badly. Both Emily and I.'

The social worker nodded and went through more questions: their home (rented, respectable, in a nice neighbourhood), their income (comfortable). 'And your family?' she asked. 'Parents, siblings, other children?'

Robbie and Emily exchanged a glance.

'My family are all in England,' said Emily slowly. 'My mother and father, and a sister. I have uncles and aunts and cousins there, too. I . . . don't see them often. As I'm living here.'

'That's understandable. Mr Brandon?'

'My parents are both dead; my dad died when I was in Vietnam, and my mother passed away soon after. I don't have any siblings. I . . . have a son.'

Mrs Hernandez perked up. 'Oh?'

'He'll be seven years old in September. But I haven't seen him in years. His mother . . . it didn't end well between us.'

'Oh.'

'You say that as if it's a problem,' said Emily.

'Well . . . not necessarily. Have you been refused access by the court?'

He shook his head. 'No. We never had a custody hearing. She . . . just took him. I've tried to get in touch, but they move quite a lot, and her parents refuse to speak with me or pass on any information.' He frowned. 'As I said . . . it didn't end well. And I miss him.'

'The father doesn't have a lot of rights in this situation,' said Mrs Hernandez, 'but we will need documentation about him, if possible, along with your other documents.'

'Which documents are those?' asked Emily, again trying to keep her voice calm and clinical. To her ears, at least, she failed: there was a shakiness.

'Oh, just the normal ones for proof of identity and status. Your birth certificates, marriage certificate. Your Green Card, Dr Brandon. Rental agreement on your house, proof of employment, and, of course, the letters of recommendation which we'll talk about in a minute.'

Emily and Robert exchanged another look.

'We . . . don't have a marriage certificate,' said Emily.

'Well, you can obtain a copy easily. If you were married in Florida there will be a small charge and they can make a copy for you right there and then.'

'No. I mean we don't have a marriage certificate because we're not married.'

Mrs Hernandez had been holding the Bic in her right hand. Now she passed to her left, and tapped it on the desk.

'You're not married? But I thought—'

Emily's heart was pounding so hard that she was faint. It took all of her self-control and will to remain sitting in the chair, her legs crossed, her hand in Robbie's. She did not know what expression was on her face, but it felt chiselled there in stone.

'In addition to not letting me see my son,' said Robbie, 'my ex-wife also won't give me a divorce. Her family belongs to an evangelical church that doesn't believe in divorce, so maybe she's gone back to that, but I don't know for sure. She won't talk to me at all. And I don't know where she is. I've tried to serve her with papers – for her own sake as much as mine; you'd think maybe she'd want to get married again and try with someone better, if that's not a sin. But the papers come back, or disappear. Like all my requests to see William.'

It sounded rehearsed to Emily's ears. But she knew Robbie's tones so well, his normal way of speaking. The social worker would not. She might not hear anything in his words but the truth. And it was the truth. Just . . . not all of it.

Mrs Hernandez was looking stern. 'I don't think I— It's highly unusual to recommend an unmarried couple for adoption. I . . . I'll have to talk with my manager once you've put in your application.'

'But you'd still need all that documentation?' Emily asked. 'To research whether we'd be allowed to even apply?'

'Yes, I'd want all the facts possible before I presented your case to anyone.'

'I see,' said Emily. 'I . . . that makes sense.'

She couldn't look at Robbie now. It would make her truly realise what was happening.

'Yes,' said Robbie. 'Well . . . should we take these forms home? And then come back to you with all the paperwork you need?'

'All right,' said Mrs Hernandez, and handed Robbie a sheaf of paper. He thanked her and shook her hand again, but the social worker was looking at Emily. Clearly her feelings were plain on her face. Too plain. She looked down at her shoes as she stood and walked with Robbie to the door, when she forced herself to meet Mrs Hernandez's gaze.

'It was very nice to meet you,' she said. 'If this doesn't work out, maybe I'll see you anyway, when you're ready to deliver. I'll try to pop in and say hello if I'm in the hospital.'

'I— That would be nice of you.' Mrs Hernandez paused, passing the Bic from hand to hand. 'I . . . listen,' she finally said in a rush. 'I don't usually say this, but you're a really nice couple, and I can really sympathise with you. I'll try the best I can for you, but if this doesn't work out, there are other avenues, you know. You could try a private agency. Even in another state. The rules vary quite widely.'

'Thank you, ma'am,' said Robbie. 'We appreciate that.'

'But come back with all your paperwork, and we'll try hard for you.'

'Thank you,' Emily said, barely able to raise her voice above a whisper. Robbie put his hand in the small of her back, and they walked downstairs together, out of the building, to the car.

Their rented house in Coral Gables was long and low, a single storey, the same as all the houses around it. It was painted yellow with an orange tiled roof, and it was shaded by several mature palm trees in the garden. The empty room was right on the end.

Robbie sat in it sometimes, on the white tiled floor, listening to the sound of rain on the roof. He had built a window seat and put shelves on the wall. But they had kept the room empty of everything except for a small single bed, covered with a handmade quilt that Emily had bought in a craft fair.

It was supposed to be William's room, if he ever visited. If Robbie ever found him. But the years passed and the letters came back and the room remained empty.

It was a belter of a storm: one of those Florida storms where lightning and thunder seemed to come from all directions, so relentlessly that the house felt as if it were under fire. The rain fell vertically in a sheet of warm water. It battered on the roof and streamed down the windows while he was here, safe and dry, inside. Emily had once said that said babies heard things like this while they were in the womb: the rumble of their mother's body and the distant vibrations of voices and music.

When he listened to the rain, he thought about the last time he had seen William. The argument with Marie had been outside, in the yard. The neighbours overheard them, especially once Marie started yelling, but screw the neighbours: he didn't want William to hear. He had agreed with all the names she called him – there were a lot, and most of them were accurate – but he had not agreed that he was making a big mistake. She had yelled and she'd taken off her shoe and thrown it at him, and then when he'd caught it, she'd thrown her other shoe.

Finally there was only one thing left for her to say. 'Get out.'

'I'll pack my stuff,' he'd said to her, but he hadn't packed. He'd gone inside and to William's room. The boy was asleep, sprawled in Batman pyjamas, blanket kicked aside. His thumb was in his mouth.

Robbie had sat beside him and watched him. Watched him breathe, watched the small movements his eyes made under their lids, watched his long dark eyelashes on his cheeks. He smelled of Johnson's No More Tears shampoo and a faint boy grubbiness. He thought about throwing him baseballs, and teaching him to sail, and fishing, and swimming in the surf, and reading stories and adopting a dog and making box cars to race. He thought about William's first bike and his first car and his first job, the girls he'd date and lust over, the ones who would break his heart. His high school graduation. Scabbed knees and stitches and captured lizards and frogs, music his parents wouldn't understand.

He'd wanted to do so much with this boy. Instead it seemed that he was always looking at William as he slept.

He touched William's forehead, cool and a little sweaty despite the fan, and pulled the blanket up over him. He thought about leaving a note beside the bed. But William couldn't read, and Marie would just tear it up.

He hadn't known, then, that it would be the last time he'd see him. Not really; not deep inside, he hadn't known. He hadn't been able to understand the truth of it, anyway. How it would feel to live for years without his child. And if he had known, what could he have done differently? He could have woken William and talked to him while he was sleepy. He could have told him that no matter what happened, he'd always love him. But William wouldn't have understood, or remembered. He'd have forgotten by the next morning.

But maybe it would have been important for Robbie to have said it. For the words to have existed, out loud, somewhere.

Robbie lay down on the cool tiled floor of this empty room at the very end of their house and listened to the rain. He wasn't sure when this room had metamorphosed, without Emily or him saying anything, into a room that William would share with a baby. And then into the baby's room. Not *a* baby but *the* baby.

How had it even become a concept between them? When they'd both known it was impossible? But it had taken form, this idea, this baby they could never have, without them even speaking of it. In their touches and exchanged glances, in the walks they took after dinner to catch the cooling air off the bay, the rhythm of their days together. He saw it in the way that Emily glanced at and then away from pregnant women or young mothers; a look that wasn't professional curiosity. A certain weariness when she came home from work. The times when her eyes wandered from her book and she stared into the distance, not knowing he was watching her.

There was so much they didn't speak of between the two of them. That they didn't need to speak of. The cup of coffee that appeared at his elbow when he was in his workshop and tired; the reading lamp he fixed for her without her mentioning that it was broken. Often he would be on his way home from work, thinking about maybe building a barbecue on the beach, only to find when he got there that she'd already made the hamburgers.

Which was how, when she'd mentioned calling the adoption agency, he wasn't surprised. And how he knew now that she was suffering from the death of this hope that they'd hardly dared to have.

When they'd chosen to be together, on another day of rain and storms, they'd decided that the two of them would be enough. Just the two of them, alone and together. That was the bargain they'd made with themselves and the world.

And they were enough. They *were*. But there was this yearning for more. Robbie's instinct was to fix it: like he would fix a leak in his boat, a punctured tyre on his car.

But how could you fix the hole left by a child who had disappeared? Or another, who could never exist?

Robbie got up and went down the hall to the living room. She was sitting in front of the fan, also listening to the rain. Her hands were folded in her lap. She didn't look up when he entered.

He knelt on the floor by her feet, and put his arms around her waist. He bowed his head and lay it on her stomach. She threaded her fingers through his hair. They didn't need to say what they were thinking; they just sat there, holding each other, with the noise of the rain all around them.

Chapter Sixteen

December 1975
Miami, Florida

This was her fourth Christmas in Florida, and she still found it bizarre to open Christmas cards of snowy evergreens and sleighs, when outside it was seventy-two degrees and the palm trees were waving gently in the balmy wind. Robbie was at work and Emily was on call after working for the past two nights; she sat in her dressing gown by the phone and leafed through the envelopes that the postman had brought.

The cards were from her colleagues at the hospital, Robbie's friends at the boatyard, their doctor, their dentist, their bank. Yesterday she'd opened one from their local taquería where Robbie got takeout on a Friday night.

She'd thought they'd be more anonymous here, but though this was a city, the communities within it were small. During the winter months and mornings and evenings, when the sun was less fierce, her neighbours spent a lot of time outdoors. You met them, tending their gardens; you saw them fishing or taking a stroll, in the shops downtown or at the Venetian Pool.

She poured a cup of coffee and took the cards to the kitchen table. She always looked at the envelopes first, searching for a familiar handwriting. She sent her parents a card every year. This year's had a robin on it. She never quite knew what to write inside – they wouldn't want to hear news, nor answer questions – so she only ever wrote *Happy Christmas. I love you.*

They never replied. But she kept on sending the cards, in case.

Robbie sent a card to William every year as well – and also on his birthday. He sent them to Marie's parents' house in Wisconsin and sometimes they came back marked, in thick black pen, RETURN TO SENDER. And sometimes nothing came back at all.

The last envelope wasn't a card, it was a letter. The handwriting was unfamiliar, and the postmark was Miami. She opened it, drinking the last of her coffee, wondering whether to make another pot or whether that would stop her from taking a nap in the afternoon if she didn't get called in.

It was a single piece of paper, folded. On the top of the paper was an address of an attorney's office in Louisiana. Underneath it, in neat handwriting:

> *You seem like you would make good parents. Try this, if you are still looking.*
> *Donna Hernandez*
> *PS It's a girl, 7 lbs 4 oz. Named Jeannie.*

Chapter Seventeen

January 1976
New Orleans, Louisiana

It was the third week of 1976 when they drove the twelve hours up the length of Florida and along the Gulf of Mexico to New Orleans. Elliot Honeywell's office was in a gracious old brick building, the type that had shutters on the windows to be closed against the midday sun, a white wrought-iron balcony running the length of the first floor. Robbie parked the Plymouth in front and the car ticked, cooling, as he took her hand and they went up the stone steps together.

The receptionist wore what looked like a Chanel suit, and as they took a seat in leather armchairs of the waiting room Emily noticed Robbie smoothing his tie. It was one of three that he owned, all of which Emily had bought him: for weddings, funerals, special dinners, and now for appointments with social workers or attorneys. He wore one of his two suits. She could feel Robbie's slight discomfort which had nothing to do with their reason for coming here and more to do with the expensive, understated furniture, the pot of orchids on the receptionist's desk, the sedate fan whirring from the ceiling, the framed certificates on the wall.

When she'd first met him he'd been utterly unintimidated by class differences. He had spoken of the rich people he worked for, servicing their yachts, without reverence – in fact, with a certain degree of disdain. But the years, and everything that had happened, had changed him. She supposed she was changed, too.

And now, of course, both of them were waiting to be judged and found wanting.

She took his hand. She wondered how many hopeful couples had sat in these same seats, shifting and pretending to read the magazines laid out carefully on the low table.

'Dr Brandon? Mr Brandon? Mr Honeywell will see you now.' The Chanel-suited receptionist stood next to them. She led them out of the reception room, up a grand polished, curving wooden staircase, to a door with a brass plaque on it. She knocked discreetly and, at the reply, opened the door and stood aside so that Emily and Robert could enter.

Eliott Honeywell was slim and sharp, with white wings of hair and a three-piece suit in a rather gorgeous muted tartan, complete with watch chain, red silk tie and pocket handkerchief. He stood up when they entered and came round his vast mahogany desk to shake both of their hands. 'Dr Brandon, Mr Brandon, what a pleasure.'

His hands were manicured and, in addition to his wedding ring, he wore a gold signet ring on the pinkie of his right hand. His handshake was dry and firm; he gestured to the leather armchairs facing his desk and spoke to his receptionist: 'Sissy, some tea I think. Is tea all right for you folks?'

'That would be lovely,' said Emily, perching on one of the armchairs. It was big enough that she felt dwarfed, and set far enough away from Robbie's chair that she couldn't reach his hand without stretching the full length of her arm. Eliott Honeywell wore cologne, something strong and expensive-smelling, and the scent permeated the room with its striped wallpaper, bookcases lined with leather-bound books, and more certificates on the walls.

Honeywell returned to his own vast leather chair behind his desk and steepled his fingers. 'Is that an English accent I detect, Dr Brandon?' His own accent was Southern, pure honey.

'Yes, I grew up in Norfolk.'

'I've been there. It's a beautiful country. We visited the Broads on our way up to Scotland to do some golfing – eight, nine years back. You earned your medical degree there?'

'At Cambridge.'

'I see. Very nice, and impressive too. And Mr Brandon, are you a sailor or a motorboat enthusiast?'

'I work on both, but I'd rather sail.'

'Now, there I'm in complete agreement with you. We took ours to the Caribbean two summers ago. I took two months off and it wasn't nearly enough time, but then, of course, one has to earn a living. The sunsets! My wife enjoyed the beaches. I think St Lucia was our favourite. Have you been?'

'Years ago, before I met Emily, I crewed a yacht from Annapolis to St Kitts. It was a good trip. The fishing was incredible. I've never eaten so well.'

'So you know what I'm talking about. Our boat isn't quite as nimble as I'd like it to be, but at our age my wife and I like the comforts. Ah, here's Sissy with the tea. Thank you, dear.'

It was a tall, frosted glass jug of iced tea on a tray with three stemmed glasses. Sissy poured them each a glass and slipped out of the room, her high heels noiseless on the thick carpet. The tea was sweet. Even after years in this country, Emily wasn't used to drinking cold sweet tea.

'So,' said Honeywell, taking a sip of his own tea and putting the glass carefully down on a silver coaster, 'Donna Hernandez sent you to me. She's a very pleasant woman, very good at her job. I've been able to help her with several cases in the past. Arranging matters privately means that I'm able to be considerably more discreet than the state allows.'

Emily exchanged glances with Robbie. 'We . . . were hoping for discretion, yes.'

'When I meet couples, they're often at the end of their tether. They want a child to make a happy family, but they've hit roadblock after roadblock. It's my greatest satisfaction in removing those roadblocks and helping them to the baby that they want so

135

badly. I hope I can help you, too. I'm sure that I can, in fact.'

'That's quick,' said Robbie, putting down his glass of sweet tea.

'I'm a very good judge of people,' said Honeywell. 'I like you two already: a doctor, a sailor. And I can see that you've had a very sad story.'

'Can you?'

He spread his hands. 'Childlessness leaves its mark on people. It's the American dream, isn't it? A good education, a good job, the pitter-patter of little feet. No matter how happy an upbringing we've had, we always want to give our own children a better one. Isn't that so, Mr Brandon? May I call you Robert?'

'Yes,' said Robert. 'And yes, that's true.'

'And your adopted country is never going to quite feel like home until you've put down true roots here, isn't that right, Dr Brandon? Emily?'

'Yes.'

'Family is the most important thing. The most important thing in the world. It doesn't matter how much money you have, or how many material possessions, or how much respect in the community: if you don't have family, everything else is empty.' He reached for a silver-framed photo, and passed it over the big desk to Emily. 'That's Phyllis and me, and our three: Glenn, Holly and Lou-Lou.'

It was a formal family portrait. Phyllis was slender and blonde, perfectly coiffed and dressed, standing next to Eliott, and the three children ranging in age from about twelve to eight stood in front of them in height order. They were all blonde and blue-eyed, dressed as well as their parents.

'It's a beautiful family,' Emily said, handing the photo to Robbie.

'That photo's a few years old now, but you can see why I'm so proud of them. We adopted Holly, our middle child, at a few days old. Her story was very sad. Very sad. But we've been privileged to be able to give her the best home we can provide.'

'She looks just like her mother, though,' said Robbie.

'A happy coincidence, isn't it? No one would ever know she

136

was adopted, if we didn't tell them. Of course apparently a lot of family resemblance is because of environment instead of genetics. I've done some reading up on the subject – professional interest as well as personal. But we're proud of her, and we're proud of the services we can provide here for families like ours. And yours.'

He took the photo from Robbie and replaced it carefully on his desk.

'Now,' he said, folding his manicured hands, 'you mentioned discretion. That is absolutely at the heart of what we do. Adoption is a private, personal affair. And among others we have helped couples who have been turned down by state agencies or charities, for various reasons. State agencies have rather a one-size-fits-all approach, whereas we realise that every case is different. And there may be details of a couple's life that they do not wish to come to light, but yet will not be detrimental to their being good parents to an otherwise unwanted child. We're all about bringing families together, not picking over every little thing.'

'What . . . sort of detail are you talking about?' Emily asked.

'Obviously I can't tell you facts. Discretion. But we've helped conscientious objectors, for example, men who have a prison record because they refused to fight, or couples who, though sharing a deep and lasting commitment, aren't able to marry, or couples who have faced a financial mishap, for example. Most commonly, our clients are simply in a hurry to complete their family. They don't want to have to wait months and years to be given a child of their own and they find that with private adoption, the wheels move much more quickly.'

'What sort of documentation do you need from us?' said Robert.

'You already have a personal recommendation from Donna Hernandez, which is good enough for me. But for our files, another recommendation would be useful. And identification, of course: driver's licence, passport.'

'Oh. That sounds . . . easy.'

'Why should it be complicated? You want a child, and there are children out there who are desperate for a home. It's in everyone's best interest that you are brought together.'

She exchanged a glance with Robbie. Hope had been too fragile a thing to think about on the way up here; they had told themselves that they were only going to rule out another option. But this . . .

'What's your fee?' asked Robbie.

Honeywell wrote on a slip of paper and passed it to Robbie. 'That's exclusive of any additional unexpected fees that might come up, but it's a ballpark figure.'

Robbie blanched. He handed the slip to Emily. It was . . . it was not far off Robbie's annual salary.

'We're going to have to discuss this,' he said quietly.

'Of course! I wouldn't have it otherwise. We can meet again, say in a month or six weeks, or sooner if you like. The sooner we get the ball rolling, the sooner you will have your baby in your arms.' He smiled at them. 'I know it's a lot of money. But these are complicated arrangements, and my many years of experience mean that my time doesn't come cheap. And, of course, the outcome is priceless. No one could put a cost on a family.'

They packed a picnic and went out on *Little Billy* for the morning on the Bay of Biscayne. For the first hour they didn't speak; they worked together, tightening lines and raising sails and tacking, communicating with glances and experience, not setting a course but going where the wind took them. The noise of the boat cutting through water and the wind in the sails filled the silence between them and was part of their communication, part of all the times they'd done this before, in this boat and another, in this water and on the other side of the ocean.

Robbie poured them each a cup of coffee from the flask in the picnic basket and Emily pointed, wordlessly, at a pod of dolphins swimming alongside them. They watched the creatures' sleek bodies cutting through the water, pointed fins and sudden leaps into arcs of motion. They were close enough to hear the wet gasp of their breathing, mid-leap, and to see the amused expressions on their faces, ends of their mouths turned up.

'It's that same family we saw last week,' Emily said. 'I can see the scar on the big one's back.'

'He must have been nicked by a power boat.'

'It doesn't seem to bother him, at least,' said Emily. She leaned back against the side of the cockpit, her feet propped on the opposite seat. 'I don't like him.'

'Honeywell? I don't like him either. He's one of these people who flatters you while they're secretly thinking how much better they are than you.'

'But we don't have to like him, do we? We just have to hire him.'

'That sounds easier than it is.'

'Without any sort of documentation on our part, just identification and personal references,' she said. 'It seems too good to be true.'

'Then again, he has helped a lot of people. And the social worker referred us.'

'We should call those people whose numbers he gave us. Before we make any kind of a decision.'

'What are they going to say?' Robbie adjusted the sail. 'They're going to be happy with him. They wanted to adopt, and they did. They're going to say it was worth every penny.'

'We should still call. All of them.'

He nodded.

'It's all theoretical anyway at the moment,' said Emily. 'We haven't got anything like that kind of money in our savings yet. And we haven't anything we can take out a loan against.'

'Well,' said Robbie, 'I've been thinking about that. Before Christmas we had someone in who talked about making me an offer on *Little Billy*.'

Emily sat up straight. 'You can't sell this boat. You made it. You made it by hand, yourself. It took you years.'

'Her,' he corrected her. 'All boats are female. Because they take all your money and then do exactly what they want.'

'You made her,' Emily continued. 'This boat is really important to you, and to us.'

'But she's worth quite a bit of money. A handmade boat, unique. The fellow was from New York and he said he wanted something for day sails.'

'She'd only get used every now and then, in the winter.'

'She's a boat, Emily. And we'd have a child.'

'You made her for William.'

Robbie looked away, over the water. The pod of dolphins had swum off eastward.

'It's been three years,' he said quietly. 'He's seven. If he even remembers me, he won't want to see me. I can imagine what Marie's been telling him about me.'

'It could change. She could change her mind.'

'You don't know what kind of a husband I was to her.'

'If that's so, she's strangely reluctant to let go of being married to you.'

He shook his head. 'She's doing it for punishment. I never knew her well, Em, but I know her well enough to understand that. She hated that church, but not half as much as she hated me.'

Emily ran her hand over the shining teak. 'I don't like the idea of you selling this boat. It's as if . . . it feels as if you'd be giving up on William.'

'I'm not. I wouldn't. But we have to be realistic. And the boat is only a boat. It's a symbol, not a real child.'

'But all those years of work—'

'I can make another boat. You and I . . .' He hesitated, and she stiffened slightly.

'We've been in a holding pattern,' he said at last. 'We've been living in the present and trying to ignore the past.'

'What's wrong with that? That's what we wanted. It's what we decided to do.'

'Yes. It's exactly what we wanted. But I think it might be time for us to stop ignoring the past and just to let it go. Let it go. Stop letting it define us. And part of that might be to start doing things to make the future happen.'

'So you think we should go through Honeywell,' she said.

'I think we should take every chance we can.'

She gazed at him. He was forty this year; she'd spotted threads of silver in his dark hair. She had seen lines in her own face in the mirror, lines around her eyes from squinting in the sun, bracketing her mouth from smiling. Their bodies had shed cells and renewed them. In so many ways they were no longer the same people who had met all those years ago.

Who knew what they would be in the future?

'All right,' she said. She reached over and took his hand. 'I agree. Let's do it.'

He knocked on Luís Fuentes' door.

Luís was a money person. Rumour had it that he had come over from Cuba with his elderly mother in a tiny boat during the revolution, though Luís never spoke of that, and from what Robbie could see he had never actually set foot on a boat since. The marina was his investment. Luís handled the budgets and left all of the practical running of the marina to Robbie and his friend and former drinking buddy, Tom. Once upon a time, it had mostly been Tom running things. Now, it was mostly Robbie.

When Robbie went into the office, Luís was surrounded by paperwork and cigarette smoke. He wordlessly held out the pack of Camels to Robbie, who took one and sat down across from him to wait until he'd stopped punching numbers into the adding machine.

'What is it?' Luís said finally, looking up and lighting a new cigarette from the butt of the one he'd just finished.

'I need to borrow some money,' said Robbie.

Luís was obviously surprised. 'You haven't asked me that in a while.'

'I haven't needed it till now.'

'Well, it's no problem. Something to tide you over to next month?' Luís reached for his wallet, and then frowned at Robbie. 'I thought your missus was a doctor.'

'She is.'

'She must make good money. You got that nice house in Coral Gables.'

'She does. We do.'

'She know about you asking me this? It doesn't make a difference to me; I just want to know what to say and what not to say next time you have me for dinner, that's all.'

Robbie hesitated. 'She . . . doesn't. Emily knows what the money is for; she doesn't know that I'm asking you for it.'

'I see.'

'And I need to borrow a little more than something to tide me over. I need three thousand.'

Luís's only indication of surprise was the bright red flare of his cigarette as he sucked in harder than usual. 'That's a lot of money.'

'Yes, it is.'

'Can I ask what it's for?'

He thought of Emily again. 'You . . . can't. I'm sorry. If you agree to lend it to me, you can take it out of my wages every month. With interest. Or I'll write you a cheque and pay it back in a lump sum when I've got it, whatever you prefer.'

'I hear you sold your boat. That nice little hand-built wooden number.'

'That's right.'

Luís actually parked his cigarette on the edge of the ashtray and leaned forward on his desk. 'Are you in trouble, Bob?'

'No.'

'Because I remember when you were a drinking man. And that's been different for awhile now, I thought—'

'Over two years.'

'Glad to hear it. But a man can do things when he's thirsty, that he wouldn't do otherwise.'

'This has nothing to do with drinking. Or anything like that. But if you don't want to lend it to me, no hard feelings. I can understand that you'd want to know more.' He stood. The loss of hope weighed him down. There was nothing else to sell, and no one else to ask.

If Emily were with someone other than him, she wouldn't be having this problem. She would probably already have a child by now.

'Now slow down there, Bob,' said Luís. 'Have a seat.'

Robbie sat down.

'You nearly lost your job a few years back. I cut you some slack, because your work is good, and because you're a veteran. But you were becoming a liability instead of an asset. You've turned that around, now. You're the best man I've got. I don't want to think you're in trouble again.'

'I'm not in trouble, Luís.'

'Then I trust you.' Luís put his cigarette back in his mouth, reached into his desk drawer, and took out his chequebook. 'You just pay me back when you can.'

'With interest.'

'No interest. I'm considering this an investment in my business because it keeps you happy.' He tore off the cheque, cigarette dangling from his lip, and handed it to Robbie, who looked without real comprehension at the figure on it. 'You want to do something for me in return, you talk with Tom and tell him how you're managing to stay sober.'

'You see more than you let on from up here, don't you?'

Luís tapped his forehead with his finger and smiled. 'Just talk with Tom.'

'I'll try. But if someone hasn't got a reason to stay sober, it's never going to happen.'

143

'And you have a reason?'

Robbie stood up, folded the cheque carefully, and reached over Luís's desk to shake his hand. 'I have the best reason in the world.'

Chapter Eighteen

June 1976
Miami, Florida

The nurses at the station were gossiping about their husbands. Emily lingered there, going over paperwork for her rounds, letting their plans wash over her.

'Seventeen years we've been married and I've never had so much as a daisy from him. He doesn't believe in flowers. Have you ever heard it? Doesn't believe in them. Says they're dead as soon as they're cut and he doesn't want dead things in the house. I say, what about our sex life, that's dead.'

'Last year JJ gave me a box of chocolates for Valentine's Day and he ate half of them himself.'

'Andrew bought me lingerie on my birthday. I'm all, we've got three kids, when do you expect me to wear this?'

'What about you, Dr Brandon? Does your husband ever give you flowers?'

Emily looked up, smiling. 'Just one at a time.' A single rose in an empty Coke bottle and a handwritten note on her bedside table on her last birthday when she'd woken up.

'One is better than none, or half a box of chocolates. I said to my other half, I said, it's our anniversary; when I get home from work today I at least want to see a card, or you—' The phone rang and Flo picked it up without interrupting her monologue. '—you can cook your own lazy-ass dinner. Hello?'

Emily was picking up her clipboard and turning away when Flo held the phone out to her. 'It's for you. He's probably calling to tell you he loves you. Where was my hubby when the romantic genes were handed out?'

She took the phone. 'Robbie?'

'Em? Honeywell just called.'

The mixture of emotions that hit her was indefinable: joy, fear, anticipation, yearning, a kind of sickness. Similar, but not identical, to the way she had felt seeing Robbie for the second time across a crowded room of travellers.

She turned away from the others and spoke quietly. 'He . . . what does he say?'

'He says he's . . .' For the first time she realised that Robbie's voice was shaking. She clutched the receiver hard in both hands. 'He says he's found our son.'

She was water; she was stone. She was about to faint or be sick. 'Our son?' she whispered.

'He's – he's a week old. He . . .' She heard Robbie swallow, and all at once she wanted to be nowhere but by his side, holding him, seeing the mixture of emotions on his face as well. 'We can get him next month. In four weeks, he said.'

'We can take him home?'

'Yes.'

'Next month?'

'Yeah.'

'I . . .'

An orderly went past her pushing a plastic cot, a crying baby nestled inside. Emily stared. A week old. Their son. Hers and Robbie's. Not much older than that newborn, there, not yet uncurled from its foetal position, arms and legs delicate twigs, face red and screwed up in impotent baby rage.

Their son who they hadn't yet met.

'We're not ready,' she said into the phone.

'We'll get ready quick. We've got a month.'

'I thought it would take longer.'

'Apparently not. Emily, are you happy? You sound scared.'

'*You* sound scared.'

'Maybe that's how we're supposed to feel.'

'I think we're supposed to feel happy.'

'I think . . . I'll feel happy when we hold him.'

When we hold him. Emotion rose in Emily's throat and she couldn't speak.

'Come home soon, OK?' Robbie said gently, and Emily nodded, and though he couldn't see her, she knew he understood. He hung up, and Emily put the phone back in the cradle.

She stared at the wall, where the nurses had put up a corkboard for all the cards and photographs the team had been sent from grateful parents. Jaquinda was on there: a smiling triumvirate of happiness, baby Inés wrapped in a pink blanket and wearing a ridiculously large crocheted bonnet.

They needed to buy a cot – a crib, they called it a crib in America – and clothes and nappies and formula and bottles. They had nothing yet. They hadn't bought anything. It was too much like tempting fate. The empty room was still empty, except sometimes when she and Robbie sat in it, on the side of the single bed, together.

A carrycot, a pram, dummies, muslins – they all had different names in the US but she couldn't remember what they were just now, and Emily realised she had held hundreds of babies, maybe thousands by now, and she had never fed one.

'You all right, Dr Brandon? You look worried.' Flo was frowning up at her. 'Not bad news at home, is it?'

'I'm fine. Not bad news, no. It's good news. But good news I wasn't quite ready for.'

'Best kind,' said Flo, and winked at her, and went back to her charts. The other two nurses had left while Emily was on the phone.

'Flo?' she said.

'Mmm, doctor?'

'If you've got a little time today, I wonder if . . . I wonder if you

147

could show me how to change a nap— Change a diaper?'

Flo looked up, a broad smile on her face. 'I can do that, yeah.'

Afterwards, Emily could never remember precisely what the orphanage building looked like, or where in the building they went. She would think about it many times, and both wish she knew more and be glad that she didn't. She had an impression of a modern building, with glass bricks at the entrance, and a scent of floor polish and burnt toast. What caught her attention most was the corkboard near the reception desk, covered in photographs of children: drawing, playing, running some sort of race, blowing out birthday candles. It was similar to the corkboard in the maternity ward, except that the children were older. And the adults were in the periphery of the photographs. Carers, not parents.

She held tight to Robbie's hand because she thought she might drift away. Wander like an unmanned boat, sail flapping. They'd driven for hours to get here, and that morning, before dawn, she had stood in the room at the end of the house with her hands on the rail of the cot and she had looked down at the sheets, printed with Peter Rabbit, and the fluffy toy chicken that they had bought. She tried to imagine a baby sleeping there, a real baby, not an idea or a hope.

It had been impossible. But now here they were, in this building, being ushered through hazy hallways and to a waiting room furnished in brown and cream, with several chairs and a window with brown and orange drapes. An air conditioner rattled on the windowsill and there was a tall Swiss cheese plant in the corner. Elliott Honeywell was waiting for them there. He greeted them immediately with firm handshakes and a kiss on Emily's cheek.

'So, the happy day!' he said. The room was full of his cologne and another scent, like maple syrup. 'How do you feel?'

'We've been getting ready,' she said. She wanted to wipe Honeywell's kiss off her cheek but instead her hand found Robbie's again. 'We thought it would take longer, the whole process.'

'I told you that finding your family was my first priority,' said Honeywell, looking pleased with himself. 'As soon as I received the phone call I knew that I had found your son.'

Your son. Emily swallowed. 'May we . . .?'

'Yes, Alice has gone to get him. I thought you would want to meet him before we—' He held up a thick folder. 'Paperwork. Tedious.'

She couldn't sit down. She held tight to Robbie's hand and tried not to float away. Tried to stay here and now, in this room which could be anywhere with its drapes and its plants, with the scent of Honeywell's cologne. Robbie was beside her. He was solid and real beside her, the only real thing there was.

'We're doing this together,' he whispered into her ear, and then the door opened and a woman walked in with their son.

He was wrapped in a white waffle blanket and all she could see at first was his tiny outline and a bit of fluffy blond hair. The woman who held him was wearing a nurse's outfit but to Emily she was a blur. Emily went to step forward, and then she checked herself. Staring and hungry.

Babies. She had seen hundreds of babies. Thousands of babies. This one could be hers.

'It's all right, you can hold him,' said Honeywell. Robbie let go of her hand. Slowly, she held out her arms and the nurse put the baby into them.

He was a warm, sweet weight. He was awake; his eyes were blue and they looked up into hers with that serious, intent expression that babies had sometimes. His hair was longer in front and formed a sort of soft quiff. His breathing was quick, like a bird's.

'He's small,' she said, surprised to find her voice sounding almost normal. 'I've held newborns who were this weight.'

'He's lost some weight since birth,' said the nurse, 'but he's started putting it back on again. Two ounces since his last weighing.'

She touched his cheek. It was soft as thistledown and he turned his head towards her finger. It was instinctive rooting behaviour but it felt like a gesture of trust and she had to blink back sudden tears.

'He's beautiful,' murmured Robbie, behind her. 'Look at him, he's looking at you like he knows you.'

'He does know,' said the nurse. 'We often see it. Babies seem to know their parents.'

She couldn't take her gaze from him. 'What about his – his birth parents?' she asked. Though she had been told the facts already, she wanted to hear them again. She wanted to check that this could possibly be real.

'She was an unwed mother,' said Honeywell from the side of the room. 'She knew she couldn't raise a child on her own and decided to give him a better chance. It's a hard decision, but the kindest one.'

'Do you know . . . how old she was?'

'She was very young. She was no more than a child herself. Not old enough to be a mother.'

Emily had seen these girls. These young girls with swollen bellies and varying expressions of fear. They came to see her because they had to. Consuela Diaz, she thought, because she always saw Consuela Diaz in these girls. But Consuela had not been frightened, and these girls were. The babies went to grandparents, mostly, or aunts or older siblings, but she knew that some were adopted. She rarely saw the girls again. If post-natal care was required, they avoided her eye.

She could have delivered this baby herself, to a young girl who knew she could not keep it. The girl could have been seemingly indifferent through labour, or crying with grief. She'd seen both. The mother might have asked to hold the baby, or requested that it was sent away immediately. She'd seen both of those, too.

In all of these cases she had been focused on the present, not the future. Working for a safe delivery and a healthy baby. She had never thought that perhaps the future of one of these children might rest with her.

150

'I know your mother didn't want to give you up,' she whispered to the baby, who looked back at her with those grave blue eyes. 'Who would want to give you up? She had to.'

'He's got a new mother now,' murmured Robbie, close to her. 'He's got you.'

'He's got us.' Hardly able to believe it was true, she raised the baby and kissed him on his forehead. He smelled of baby powder and milk and when she lowered him he squirmed, screwed up his little face, and began to cry.

'It's nearly time for his feed,' said the nurse. 'I'll go get it.'

Emily put the baby on to her shoulder and rocked her body back and forth, patting his bottom. His crying settled to a grizzle.

'You're a natural,' said Honeywell.

'He knows,' said Robbie. 'He knows who his mommy is.'

His voice was awed. Emily caught his eye and she almost burst into tears again.

The nurse returned with a bottle and a square of muslin and Emily sat in one of the chairs, cradling the baby in the crook of her left elbow. She touched the nipple to the baby's lips and he immediately began to suck.

'See, he's a good feeder now,' said the nurse. 'It took a little while. Sometimes it does. Put the bottle farther in; that's it.'

'What's his name?'

'He doesn't have an official name,' said Honeywell. 'You'll decide that yourselves.'

'You've got to have called him something, though.' She tore her gaze away from the baby to look at the nurse.

'We call him Adam,' the nurse said. 'We go through the alphabet, and we were back to A again.'

Again. How many children came here nameless?

'I like Adam,' said Robbie. 'What do you think, Emily?'

'I think that names are important,' said Emily. 'And if he's heard himself called Adam for the past five weeks, then we should keep on calling him Adam. And I like that name, too.'

'Perfect,' said Honeywell heartily. 'Well, I'll go and make out the paperwork and leave you two alone with your son.' Emily heard the door swing, and then it was just the three of them in the room.

'Your son,' repeated Robbie softly, and he sat on the chair beside Emily. He put his arm around her; he held out his finger to the baby. Adam curled his tiny hand around Robbie's finger and Emily saw the awe on the face of the man who she loved.

'He's *our* son,' she said.

Chapter Nineteen

Robbie had one photograph of William, the one in his wallet. The edges were soft and the print was scratched. William James Brandon, forever four years old, squinting at the camera and smiling a gap-toothed, crooked smile. His teeth would have come in by now, his hair grown and cut dozens of times. Every time Robbie looked at the photograph he was reminded that William, unseen, was becoming different from the person captured in it.

He bought a Polaroid camera. Each photograph, pulled out and shaken in air, developed instantly. The clothes had no time to date, the sunny weather had no time to fade. Each moment was experienced and almost immediately captured, magically appearing in a square of gloss, framed in white.

He captured Emily bending over baby Adam so that her loose hair formed a veil around his face: Madonna and child. Emily, sleepless and feeding Adam in their bed at 3.30 a.m., half-lit by the bedside lamp. Adam in a high chair: his first taste of mashed banana. His first taste of mashed avocado. His first taste of ice cream, his eyes wide in shock.

Adam crawling across the coarse grass of their lawn. Adam dwarfed by a stuffed Mickey Mouse that Robbie won for him shooting ducks at a carnival. Adam and Emily both asleep on the sofa mid-afternoon, the electric fan trained on their flushed faces. Adam had his hand on Emily's cheek.

Emily took the photographs too: Robbie giving Adam a ride

on his shoulders as the little boy shrieked with delight. Adam sitting beside Robbie at the helm of a borrowed boat, his life preserver nearly as large as he was. Adam walking towards his father's outstretched hands. Robbie pulling Adam in a red Philadelphia Flyer wagon, up and down the street in front of their house, up and down, up and down, over and over and over again until he was soaked in sweat and still laughing.

On weekends and holidays, neighbourhood barbecues and picnics with their colleagues or boat trips with Robbie's friends, they asked other people to take their pictures. The three of them sat or stood together, their arms around each other, shading their eyes against the sun or smiling in the shade. Adam had blue eyes like Emily's. He liked to hold Robbie's hand. He had a laugh that could stop your world.

The laughter wasn't in the photographs, of course. But Robbie could hear it when he looked at them.

Chapter Twenty

September 1977
Miami, Florida

He was building a swing in the yard when Emily came home from work. He heard her car pull up in front and he yelled cheerfully, 'We're in the back!'

Emily came around the side and instantly he could tell there was something wrong. He put down his tools. Adam, who had been digging under the hibiscus, got to his feet and toddled over to Emily. 'Mummy!' he gurgled, holding out tiny hands caked with soil.

She bent and picked him up. His hands made black marks on her white blouse. 'You need a bath, little man,' she said, and caught Robbie's eye over Adam's blond head.

'What is it?' he asked.

'Have you seen the news today? Or heard it on the radio?'

'No. Why?'

'Newspaper in my briefcase. Wait till I'm done?' She handed him her leather case, and nuzzled Adam's cheek. 'Let's get you clean, sweetheart.'

Robbie took her briefcase into the kitchen while Emily carried Adam into the bathroom. He could hear his toddler-babble: only a few words were comprehensible as yet, but 'Mummy' was clear, and 'Daddy'. He smiled, washed his hands at the sink, and poured a couple of glasses of lemonade. He got out the cookies for Adam to have as a snack when he was finished with his bath.

Usually bath time was drawn out with games and splashing

and bubbles. This time Emily was finished within fifteen minutes. Adam was in his pyjamas, his damp hair sticking up in spikes, his eyes sleepy. Robbie leaned over and kissed his sweet-smelling cheek on their way through the kitchen, and then Emily settled him in front of *Sesame Street* with his cookies.

Then she returned to the kitchen and got *The Miami Herald* out of her briefcase. She sat down beside him at the table and she passed it over to him. It was folded over; the headline was on the bottom half of the page.

LAWYER STOLE CHILDREN TO ORDER

The photograph was of Elliott Honeywell. It was a professional headshot, the kind you would use in an advertisement: he looked slick and prosperous with his pressed handkerchief and styled hair.

Horror gripped him, iron-cold. 'What is this?' he asked through numb lips.

'One of my antenatal patients mentioned it. She'd heard it on the radio and she was nearly hysterical, thinking that it could happen to her, that her baby could be stolen. So I bought a paper. I tried ringing you, but you didn't answer.'

'We've been outside all afternoon.'

He glanced towards the living room, where there was the distinct sound of Bert, Ernie and a rubber duck.

'Read it,' she said quietly.

He did, but he could only take in some of the words. *Wealthy couples. Paid adoptions. False death certificates. Co-conspirators.*

He looked up from the paper, the article only half-read. 'They told the mothers that their babies were dead?'

'But not always,' she said. 'Not always. It says that some of them were orphans. It says he did legitimate adoptions as well.'

'But some of them were stolen. He stole babies and gave them to someone else.'

'It says he paid some of the mothers. Young mothers, unmarried ones. He had – he had doctors helping him. Nurses. Social workers. Do you think that one who recommended us . . .?'

He scanned. 'There aren't any names besides his.'

'But the police will be following up.'

They stared at each other.

'What are we going to do?' she whispered.

He couldn't answer.

'I know mothers whose babies have died,' she said. 'I know how – Robbie, it's awful. You can't . . . the heartbreak. I see it again and again. Imagine it hadn't really happened. Imagine that baby was growing up with another couple, and you didn't know it.'

'Imagine the baby was happy,' he said. 'And the parents were happy.'

'Robbie—'

'And the baby maybe had a better life because of it.'

'That's not for someone else to decide. How could a doctor even do that? Or a nurse? How could they? For money? What?'

'He said he wanted to help families,' Robbie said softly. 'He wanted to help families get together. He helped us with ours.'

'Robbie, you don't think that . . .'

In the other room, the Cookie Monster began to sing about cookies starting with C. Adam laughed.

Emily had fallen asleep, somehow. It had been a twelve-hour shift for her, with another day on call before that, but Robbie didn't think he would have been able to sleep after this news. He remembered long nights sailing the Atlantic when it was his shift to stay awake at the helm. He'd liked that feeling of being the only person awake for miles, the other crew asleep below him. It was up to him to keep everyone safe.

His wife slept in her bed and his son slept in his. He got up and went to the kitchen and opened the back door so he could hear the cicadas humming to each other. They stayed under the ground for years: seven years, or fourteen, some for longer; some for an entire human lifetime. And when it was their time they came up to sing and mate with each other then they died.

He remembered a night like this, years before, with a different wife and child. How he'd been thirsty and gone to the fridge for another beer and there had been none left. So he'd gone out and changed everything forever.

He was thirsty now. It came on him: the thirst. Out of the blue, sometimes. He could be happy, doing something else, driving his car or doing the shopping or working on a boat, and he'd want a drink. Or at least, he'd want a drink more than he always wanted a drink. Which was to say, he'd want a drink very badly.

Just one, his mind would tell him. The dark, shadowy corner of his mind where the secrets lived. *Remember the bite in the back of your throat? Remember the warmth spreading through your veins? Wouldn't it feel good? Just to have one?*

When you felt that bite in your throat, everything else was taken out of your hands. You only had to make one decision: whether to have another drink or not. And that was an easy decision.

Everything became very easy after that first drink.

Robert poured himself a glass of water. He added a handful of ice cubes. Very cold water helped. It wasn't the right kind of bite, but it bit. He went outside again, closing the screen door behind him, and sat on the back step, listening to the cicadas singing and looking at the black outline frame of the swing he'd started building. He drank the water when it was cold enough to make his teeth ache.

He was the only one awake. He was the one making sure that everyone was safe.

They had gone through it and gone through it. They had read the article and analysed every word. They had thought of every possibility, every permutation.

Adam had fallen asleep in front of *The Electric Company* and Robbie had carried him upstairs to his crib. He'd laid him down and tucked him in and Emily had stood behind him, her hand on his shoulder.

And now he was outside in the back yard again in the middle

of the night again, thirsty and on the verge of a change that would mean losing another child. And, if that happened, quite possibly losing Emily as well.

He knew if that happened, that he would only have one decision to make. One easy decision, over and over and over.

He drained his glass. The bite of cold wasn't enough to reduce the thirst.

The screen door banged and Emily joined him on the step. In her white nightgown, her hair floating loose, she looked like a ghost.

'Do you want a refill?' she asked him. He nodded, and in a few minutes she came back with glasses for both of them, both clinking with fresh ice. She sat beside him.

'I thought you were asleep,' he said.

'I had a nightmare.' She leaned against him and he put his arm around her. 'I'm frightened.'

'So am I.'

'And thirsty?'

He knew he didn't have to answer; if she asked, she knew. She put her hand in the small of his back.

'I keep thinking about that family photograph he showed us,' she said, after a little while. 'Remember how we were so surprised that his middle child was adopted? Because she looked just like the other two? And he said that family resemblance was down to environment rather than genetics.'

He squeezed her tighter and took a drink. The ice bite was different from the bourbon bite.

'I keep thinking,' she said again. 'What if he stole that child because she looked like the one he already had? Told the birth mother she was dead, and took her away? What if that child's mother wanted her?'

'But what good would it be for that little girl to know that?' he asked. 'How old is she now – eleven or twelve? After all her life with one family, suddenly to find out that she belonged to someone else and that the people she thought were her parents were never supposed to be her parents at all? That they'd stolen her? And the mother – she would have come to terms with losing her baby, after all these years. Suddenly the past would come back. I don't . . . I don't know how the truth could do any good.'

'But it's the truth,' Emily said.

'Sometimes the truth doesn't do anyone any good.'

'Does that mean that you can ignore it?'

'We have,' he said, very quietly, the words coming from the dark, shadowy corner of his mind.

She didn't have to answer that, just as he hadn't had to answer her question about his thirst. They both knew the answer.

'They've asked people to come forward,' she said, eventually. 'Anyone who knows anything.'

'What would happen?' he asked her. 'If we came forward, and told the police about how we got Adam? Either they'd find out that the adoption was illegal, that he was taken under false pretences. In which case, we might lose him. Or, if he really was given up by his mother for adoption, like Honeywell told us, they'd find out why we went to Honeywell in the first place. In which case, we might also lose him.'

'But we acted in good faith.'

'It could be in the papers. *We'd* be in the papers. All your patients, all your colleagues, all our neighbours. Everyone we *know*, will know what we did. They might ask why we did it.'

In the light from the house and the streetlight beyond their fence, her face was pale with terror.

'I can't just think about us, Robbie. I don't want that to happen – I can't bear to think about it – but it's not just about us. If it happened, we could leave. We could start new somewhere else.'

'And Adam – what would happen to him? Would he go into foster care? Would his real mother even want him, or be able to take him? What if he ended up back in that orphanage?'

'I don't know.'

'We're his parents, Emily. We're the only parents he knows.'

'Yes. We are. But I can't stop thinking about that mother, Robbie. His mother. How much she might miss him.'

'She doesn't know him. We do.'

She pulled away from him and put her face in her hands. 'I want to think that you're right,' she said, muffled by her palms. 'I want to know that we're making the right decision by keeping quiet. I want to know that we haven't done anything so terrible. Because I was that mother, Robbie. And you were that father. I was that mother who never had her child, and you are that father whose child was taken away from him.'

The glass of water in his hands, the biteless and powerless water. He wound back his arm and threw it as hard as he could. It disappeared into the darkness and he heard it shatter on the fence. Heard the water and broken glass and ice falling to the ground.

'I'm not going to lose another child,' he said. 'I'm not going to lose him.'

And as soon as he said it, he knew this was the only possible decision. All the permutations and possibilities had to be gone through, but this was the decision he was going to make all along. It was the decision he'd made as soon as the infant Adam had wrapped his hand around Robbie's finger; just like the decision he'd made the first time he had caught sight of the woman who'd then been known as Emily Greaves.

Emily raised her head and looked at him. She was crying; he could see the shine of tears. He took her hand and traced his thumb over the ring she wore on the fourth finger of her left hand. Two hands, male and female, clasped together.

'I don't want to lose him,' she said. 'I love him. He's our son.'

'Then we won't lose him,' he said.

'But what if they find out? Who knows? That social worker – what if they trace back to her, and she gives our names? Our names would be on file with Honeywell, too, wouldn't they? They might be looking for us right now. Or what if someone around here figures it out for themselves? We haven't made any secret of the fact that we adopted Adam. We never told anyone how, but what if people start asking questions?'

'We'd just have to . . .' He took a deep breath. 'I borrowed the money we needed from Luís. He might . . . he could figure it out. If he sees the news, and puts two and two together.'

'We would have to leave,' said Emily. 'We'd have to move some-where else, somewhere far away, the three of us. Somewhere that no one would know that Adam is adopted, where there would be no reason to connect us with any of this. But Robbie, if we did that – would William be able to find you?'

'He's not going to look,' Robbie said, dully. 'We can't stay here forever, hoping that one day he'll come back. I'll keep on trying; I'll send new addresses. But . . . he's not going to look.'

'We couldn't tell Adam,' said Emily. 'If we're going to start again and pretend this never happened, we can't tell him anything about it at all. Never even tell him he's adopted, because what if he grows up and decides to find out the truth? How would he feel about himself? About us?'

'Another thing never to talk about,' Robbie said, and he felt Emily flinching beside him. 'We can add it to the list.'

'Is this what we're going to do?' she asked. 'Move on, when things get tough? For the rest of our lives?'

'If necessary, yes.' His jaw was set. 'Places aren't important. You and Adam are important. You're *all* that's important.'

'But we're not, Robbie. You have a son. Adam . . . he might have other parents.'

'It's the three of us.' Robbie put his arm around her shoulders and held her tight. He was still thirsty; he'd always be thirsty. But when he held Emily, it didn't matter.

'I don't know,' said Emily. 'I don't think it's just the three of us. I think it's lots of people, all of them involved. We could be hurting someone by going.'

'But we'd hurt us by staying.'

'I don't know,' she said again. She leaned against him, but her eyes were looking out into the dark night. As if she could see something if she tried hard enough.

Chapter Twenty-One

In the morning they went to the beach on Key Biscayne. Emily packed a picnic and Robbie packed the toys and towels. Sometimes they borrowed a boat for the day but today they didn't.

Robbie had made up his mind, she knew. Maybe it was simpler for him: he'd lost a child already, and he didn't want to go through that again. For Robbie, love was always enough of an answer. But for Emily, things were more complicated. She saw the way their decisions reached out to affect other people. How a chance encounter – in an airport, a train station, a gust of wind from nowhere – could create rippling circles all around them. Change everything forever.

They spread a blanket out on the sand. School was back in session and, on a weekday morning, the beach was nearly deserted. There was a woman walking along the shoreline in the distance and a group of teenagers, presumably skipping school, lounging and smoking on the sand near the car park.

Adam sat on her lap to eat his peanut butter sandwiches. He laughed and pointed with a sandy finger at a pelican standing with its legs in the surf. She bent her head to smell his hair, which was still sweet from the shampoo she'd used last night.

He might not, by any rights, be hers.

She thought about the orphanage where they'd first met their son: all the photos on the walls of children and no parents. Where they assigned names to children according to the alphabet. She'd always been grateful that Adam would never remember that place. What if he'd only been placed there because he'd been stolen from his real parents? What if Robbie and she had done him an enormous wrong, just because they loved him?

Her eyes filled with tears and she felt Robbie touch her arm. 'Why don't you take a little walk,' he said to her. 'Adam and I are going to build a sand castle, aren't we Adam?'

She nodded, not trusting her voice, and set Adam on his feet. He immediately toddled over to Robbie, who gave him a plastic bucket and spade. Before either of them could see her tears fall, she turned and walked quickly towards the sea. The pelican spread its wings and flapped off with its strange prehistoric grace. When she reached the water, it was warm on her bare feet, hardly colder than the tears she wiped from her face with her sleeve.

How was she supposed to decide what to do? Every choice she could possibly make was wrong.

'Dr Brandon?'

A woman had approached her and was standing a few feet away, up to her ankles in the water. Emily thought it was maybe the one who'd been walking by herself. Her hair was scraped back from her face; she wore rolled-up jeans that hung off her skinny frame.

Emily quickly pulled down her sunglasses from the top of her head and put them on. 'Hi,' she said.

'You don't recognise me,' said the woman. 'I'm sorry. I shouldn't disturb you.'

'Not at all. How do we know each other?'

'I was one of your patients. Back in May? Bev Schulman? With the twins. Born at twenty-four weeks.'

She said it matter-of-factly, but as soon as Emily heard the word 'twins' she knew who this was. Mrs Schulman had given birth to fraternal twins, a boy and a girl, prematurely. Emily had seen her as an emergency.

Both children had been born alive: tiny, curled up, too small for their wrinkled skin. Each of them could fit into the palm of one of

165

Emily's hands. She was able to give Mrs Schulman only a glimpse of them before they were rushed away from their mother to the tubes and machines of the neonatal ICU.

The boy died within twenty-four hours. The girl hung on for two days.

'Oh,' said Emily, instinctively stepping forward and holding out her hand to the other woman. 'Mrs Schulman. I'm so sorry I didn't recognise you.'

'That's OK. I've changed a lot.' The hand she gave to Emily was thin and cold. 'I'm Bev Hirsch now. Back to my maiden name. Jonny and I split up.'

'I'm sorry.'

Bev tilted her head so that she could look out at the water. 'We weren't strong enough to last after we lost Matthew and Miriam. He blamed me, and I blamed him. But I've been walking on this beach every day since he left, and I'm coming to see that it wasn't anyone's fault. It was just the way it happened.'

'Loss can split up families,' said Emily. 'We see it all the time as doctors. I'm sorry it happened to you.'

The other woman nodded. 'You were kind to me. I was really scared, and you were kind. I meant to send a letter to the hospital after I got home, but I couldn't. It was too hard. So when I saw you, I just wanted to say thank you.'

Behind them, there was a roar and a child's shriek. The two of them instinctively turned to see what had happened: Robbie was lying on his back on the beach, with piles of sand on top of him. Adam held an empty bucket and Robbie was laughing and brushing sand out of his eyes and hair.

'They're your family?'

'Yes.'

Emily remembered how she used to feel, walking along this beach before Adam and seeing all the children playing. How she used to feel around pregnant women, despite her job. The way she hated herself for being envious of them, for having to turn away sometimes. But Bev, who had lost so much, didn't turn away.

'You're lucky,' she said to Emily. 'Hold on tight to them, OK?'

She squeezed Emily's hand again and went on her way, along the tide line in her bare feet.

Emily went back to where they'd spread out the blanket. Adam was digging up a spadeful of sand to dump on to his father. The child looked up as she approached and she saw the simple gladness on his face.

'We should go,' Emily said. She ruffled Adam's hair and sat beside Robbie, who looped his arm around her waist and pulled her down on to the sand with him.

'You want to go home?' he asked her.

'No. I'm talking about *going*. Living somewhere new. It doesn't matter where, as long as it has a coast and a hospital, right? We can make anywhere our home, as long as we're together.'

She looked along the beach, to where her former patient was walking along the edge of the turquoise water, alone.

PART FOUR

1972

Chapter Twenty-Two

August 1972
Miami, Florida

Miami was hot. After the thin air at La Paz's high altitude, the atmosphere felt almost solid and soupy. Sweat sprang out on to Emily's skin, dampening her shirt as soon as she stepped out of the plane on to the stairs leading down to the tarmac. The surface, ablaze with heat, penetrated the soles of her shoes soon after she stepped off the stairs.

Christopher carried their coats and their smallest suitcase as they walked to the waiting bus. Even so, he touched her elbow as she stepped up into the vehicle, as if she needed steadying.

In less than an hour they would be meeting her family at the holiday villa they'd rented in Miami Beach. Emily hadn't seen any of them for over a year; she'd hadn't even spoken to them on the phone for weeks, as service was patchy in Bolivia at the best of times. But as the bus motored its way to the terminal, she wasn't thinking about her father and her mother and Polly She was thinking about Consuela Diaz.

Consuela Diaz was fourteen years old and a street child. She lived under a bridge in La Paz with a loose group of other orphans who lived by stealing, begging, scavenging and selling themselves. She had thick black hair that was tied tightly in plaits around her head. She was eight and a half months pregnant and her belly protruded from her skinny body.

She also had a suppurating foot, blackened and swollen, the result of a rat bite that had gone untreated.

When Consuela had come into Emily's antenatal clinic early yesterday morning, Emily had seen Consuela's smile first, and then her elaborately plaited hair, and then she had smelled the rot.

'How much of her foot did you need to take?' she asked Christopher, now, as they embarked from the bus. The terminal was air-conditioned and it chilled her skin.

'Whose foot?' Christopher was busy looking for the signs pointing them to passport control.

'Consuela Diaz.'

'The young girl with gangrene?' He shook his head. 'You saw how far advanced it was. We couldn't risk the baby as well as her. I had to take it off mid-shin.'

Emily stopped walking on the polished floor. The other passengers streamed around and past them. 'Mid-shin?'

She had held Consuela's hand and told her: 'I'm sending you to my husband, Mr Knight. He's a good surgeon, and a good man; he'll do everything for you that he can.' And Consuela had nodded trustingly and her baby had kicked, and a beautiful smile had blossomed on her face. She had a gap between her two front teeth, which made her look even younger than she was.

'Mid-shin?' Emily repeated. 'How is she going to survive, where she is, without half her leg? How is she going to cope with having a baby?'

'With any luck, she'll get a prosthesis. I spoke with Randall.'

'I don't think we should have left.'

Christopher put down their suitcase. He touched her chin, tilted up her head. 'Darling. We did a lot of good, but our time there is over.'

'We could have stayed. They're not even getting a replacement OB/GYN for two months, at earliest.'

'Our visas ran out. We can discuss going back. We have plenty of time to talk it over, once we go back to England. But this is our holiday, now. It's time for us to relax. We've earned it.'

'It's difficult for me to think of us having a nice holiday in

Florida while all of that is still going on back there without us to help.'

'We can only do so much,' he said, gently. 'We have to think about ourselves, as well.'

She gazed at her husband's kind, narrow face; his blue eyes behind his spectacles. His time had been worse than hers. Post-operative care in La Paz could be dire, and she knew that he often operated knowing that even if the surgery was a success, the patient might well die anyway. At least she had the compensation of delivering healthy babies.

He deserved a rest. He deserved a successful, lucrative career, and to make a name for himself as a surgeon. There was no reason why Christopher should have to share her dread at going back to England, to a normal life. An empty life.

'I just can't stop thinking about Consuela,' she said.

'I understand.' He kissed her forehead and they continued on to passport control, where Christopher explained to the immigration official why they were in Miami, and had a polite few minutes' chat about their work in Bolivia. In the luggage hall, Emily grabbed her own suitcase off the belt. It was light: hardly heavy enough to contain everything she'd lived with for two years. But then, all the important things she'd lived with in Bolivia couldn't be carried in a bag.

Every day there had been a new emergency, a new problem, new lives. The clinic was over-used and under-staffed. For two years she had barely slept for more than four hours at a time. She worked closely with a number of Bolivian midwives but there were endless complications, and programmes to be developed for antenatal and postnatal care, for disseminating and educating about contraception when possible, for SDT testing and treatment. Christopher could help individual patients, but the changes she could help to make in this desperately poor area could help the next generation, and the one after that.

It had been inspirational and heartbreaking and exhilarating and depressing, and for two years she had barely had enough time to think about herself.

Whenever she thought about two weeks' holiday with nothing to do, her mind shied away from it.

Christopher fetched a trolley and put their suitcases on it. He stowed their passports safely away in the breast pocket of his jacket, smoothed back his neat sandy hair. He smiled at her.

'I can't wait to get to the villa,' he said. 'I feel as if I could sleep for a week.'

Emily thought about Consuela Diaz, fourteen years old, pregnant, penniless, missing a family and half her leg, lying in the clinic, feeling her baby kicking beneath her hands.

Emily didn't know if she was going to sleep at all, and if she did, what dreams would come.

She followed her husband through customs, out to the arrivals hall.

Robbie tucked his flask back in his pocket and popped a Wint O Green Life Saver. If his breath smelled of Jim Beam he wouldn't have five minutes of peace before they got home and he could escape to his shed. And he didn't want to have to escape; he wanted to play Hot Wheels with William and tuck him into bed. While William and Marie had been gone he'd set up the kid's bedroom with an elaborate track for the cars to go on, hills and curves and loops.

Marie was going to go crazy, of course. She'd been gone a week and Bob had made another mess she would have to clean up. But he couldn't resist making the track bigger and bigger until it reached from the bed to the door and covered nearly the entire room in an orange plastic tangle. And William wouldn't see it as a mess. He'd see it as heaven: something that his daddy had magically created for him.

Robbie couldn't wait to see his face. The two of them would spend a long, happy time zooming the cars around, racing, adjusting the track so the cars could go faster. *Two peas in a pod*, Marie would say, in a disapproving tone, and Robbie would try not to think about the times that his own mother had said exactly the same thing about him and his father.

He pulled out the flask and unscrewed it before he remembered his resolution not to smell of bourbon, and put it back into his pocket. He lit a cigarette instead.

Their plane should have arrived already, but the lady at the counter had said it had been delayed in Chicago by bad weather. So he stood at the arrivals gate with the crowd of people waiting, and watched the people coming through the doors. All the little dramas going on around him, with people flying from all over the world and arriving home. A family came through, mother and father and a toddler and a baby, and the elderly Latino couple standing next to him cried out in joy. The toddler wobbled over to them to be scooped up and fussed over. A slender young man with an Afro emerged, looking anxious, until he spotted a tall young woman in the crowd and the two of them ran to each other and hugged so hard they looked as if they were going to meld together. A grey-haired woman in a flowing caftan wafted through the door and the expression on her face when she scanned the crowd was almost angry. It set into grim resolution as she approached another grey-haired woman, in a pants suit, and the two of them leaned forward to kiss each other on the cheek with the minimal possible contact.

He'd used to love this. Arrivals and departures showed you what you really needed to know about people. He used to pause when he was travelling and notice these hellos and goodbyes around him.

Recently, not so much.

He remembered his own arrival at this airport six years ago, unshaven and covered with mosquito bites, in civilian clothes that didn't fit him any more, looking for sunshine and quiet, and his brain skipped ahead and his hand automatically reached for the flask again.

175

He was midway through his sip, the liquor's bite a welcome taste, when she came through the door.

Ten years had done nothing to her. She was the girl he had seen on the station concourse, the girl he had kissed in the rain, the girl who had said goodbye to him in her father's car. Robbie's heart paused and then it thumped two beats at once and happiness rushed through him, a physical presence more than an emotion, grabbing hold of him and stopping his movements and his breathing, the bourbon pooled in his mouth waiting to be swallowed.

Her hair was pulled back into a neat ponytail. Her face was tanned. She had small gold earrings in her ears and she was wearing a white blouse and khaki trousers and flat shoes. The way she moved was the same. Even if he could not have seen her face he would have recognised her from her walk. She emerged whole, from his memory, into the arrivals area of Miami airport, the girl he tried never to think of, the girl he thought about all the time.

Emily.

His body came unstuck. He gulped down the whiskey, dropped his cigarette and shoved the flask back in his pocket, stepping forward to greet her, to touch her.

She looked in his direction, met his gaze, and stopped. He saw her freeze, as he had done. Her tanned face turned suddenly pale. Her eyes widened and her lips parted.

And then he remembered. He remembered what his body had not remembered, in its explosion of joy at seeing her.

Emily flushed violently. She looked down at the floor. The man next to her touched her arm, said her name, and Robbie noticed him for the first time. He was tall and slender, with horn-rimmed glasses, white shirt, a khaki jacket the same shade as her trousers. He pushed a cart stacked with luggage. The hand that touched Emily's arm had a gold wedding band on its fourth finger.

Emily looked up at this man as if he'd woken her from a dream.

She shook her head, and then nodded, and she made as if to glance in Robbie's direction again and instead put her hands on the luggage cart next to the man's. They veered off to the right, in the opposite direction to where Robbie stood.

Robbie pushed through the crowd to follow her. To intercept her before she could disappear from his life again. He had no idea what to say to her; his mind was a mass of emotion, not words – the need to touch her, to look at her, to hear her voice again. The happy grandparents were in his way and he barged past them, not hearing their protests in vehement Spanish. He could see Emily's back retreating. The man with her placed his hand in the small of her back as they walked. It was a casual gesture of affection and intimacy.

Robbie was through the crowd, now, could catch up with them easily if he ran, but this gesture made him stop.

'Emily,' he said instead, the name in his head that he hadn't said aloud for ten years. It came out rough and unaccustomed, and the second time he shouted it. 'Emily!'

She paused. Didn't look around. For an infinite second and a half he watched the back of her head, the neat ponytail, light hair kissed by the sun. Then she started walking again.

The man with her turned around and looked back. He spotted Robbie, frowned, and spoke to Emily. She shook her head vehemently and he walked off with her, glancing once more over his shoulder.

It wasn't until they'd gone through the glass doors, outside, that Robbie could move again. He ran to the doors and out into the steaming heat in time to see them getting into a cab. Emily first, and then the man shutting her door for her and going around to the other side, while the driver put their bags into the trunk of the car.

Then the driver got in and drove away. He couldn't even catch another glimpse of Emily before she was gone.

He stood there staring at the space where the cab had been as other cabs pulled up and drove away, as people walked past, as everyone else's lives moved forwards without him. Remembering ten years before. The way they had said goodbye.

A sharp tap on his shoulder. 'What are you doing out here? We've been looking for you all over the place.'

Marie stood beside him, holding William's hand. She was frowning. William was wide-eyed under his shock of dark hair, thumb in his mouth.

'Hey,' he said. 'Sorry.' He kissed Marie's cheek and knelt down to hug William. 'You've grown in a week, buddy. You look about ten years old now.'

'I'm *four*,' said William through his thumb.

'I know.' He kissed his son's head. 'You're gonna love what I built for you at home.'

'Gramps gave me ten dollars for saying my prayers right.'

'Twenty,' corrected Marie. 'What are you doing out here, Bob? I thought you were going to meet us at the gate.'

'Yeah,' he said, straightening up. 'I just saw someone I used to know, that's all. Walked them to their taxi.'

'Well, you took a long time of it. We waited half an hour at least before we started looking. I was going to try the airport lounge next.'

'They said your flight was delayed out of Chicago.' He picked up their suitcase, a big battered grey thing like an elderly elephant, and began to walk towards the parking lot. Marie didn't move, though.

'You've been drinking?' she said.

'A beer with lunch. Hours ago.'

'Doesn't smell like beer.'

With his free hand, he pulled the Life Savers out of his jeans and popped one into his mouth. 'Want one, buddy?' he asked, passing the roll to William, who took three.

'I know what beer smells like, Robert.'

'How are Gloria and Les? You gave them my love, right?' Out

of habit he slipped his arm around Marie's waist, his hand on her hip to placate her.

'Oh, Mom's sciatica is bothering her again, and Dad gives her no sympathy as usual. He says—'

He walked to where he'd parked the car, family unit, nodding and making noises in the right place, carrying the suitcase, watching the dark head of his child as he walked in front of them.

His mind was in the cab that had driven away, carrying Emily.

Chapter Twenty-Three

Christopher waited until they were alone in their room to ask her. Her parents were in bed, and Polly had gone out with some young people she'd met on the beach the day before. Emily came out of the bathroom in her dressing gown, her hair tucked under a towel, her skin still damp and cooling in the air conditioning, and Christopher, stretched on the bed, looked up from the journal he was reading.

'Darling,' he said, sounding carefully nonchalant, 'who was that man who called your name in the airport this afternoon?'

She couldn't look at him. Instead she went to the dressing table and sat down, unwinding the towel from her hair. 'I can't get used to having so much space. And carpets.'

Christopher didn't reply. She knew him well; she knew he wouldn't ask again, but she also knew that he wouldn't stop thinking about it. Christopher hated confrontation. In all their time together, she had only seen him truly angry once. And that had been ten years ago.

She brushed her hair and glanced at him in the mirror. He'd put his journal down, and was looking up at the ceiling where a fan rotated.

'It's someone I used to know,' she said at last. 'Someone I didn't want to talk with.'

'You seemed . . . it really affected you, to see him. I thought you were going to faint.'

'I haven't seen him for a long time, that's all. Or thought about him.'

She felt a pang of guilt at the lie. Christopher didn't deserve to be lied to; he was a good man, a good husband. He was kind. A skilled, careful surgeon. He helped people; healed them. He had helped to heal her.

Except she had been lying to him for years, by omission at least. And she was not yet healed. The way she felt right now proved that: she was raw, unprotected flesh. The sight of Robbie had driven a barb into her and she had thought of nothing but him since she'd glimpsed him. Seeing his eyes, his dark green shirt, his unshaven chin. The way he stood in the airport – the way he stood anywhere – as if he owned it, comfortable in his own skin.

The utter shock of seeing him, as if ten years had never passed at all.

Earlier, with her family, she'd been preoccupied, hardly able to answer their questions about what her and Christopher's life had been like in La Paz, only able to summon the faintest of interest at her mother's gossip about what was going on in Blickley or Polly's funny stories about the male-dominated advertising agency where she worked. She had been aware of her father watching her.

'You look pale,' he'd said to her, quietly, in the kitchen when they were clearing the plates after supper.

'I'm tanned, Daddy, I can't be pale.'

He laid his palm on her forehead. 'You're not ill, are you?'

'No, I'm fine.'

'Or expecting? If you are, you should be seen by a doctor here straight away. You've been working amongst a lot of communicable—'

'I'm not pregnant either,' she said, swallowing hard, not expecting how difficult it would be to say this. Her father had never asked her before.

'You're not my normal Emily.'

'I've seen a lot of difficult things, Daddy,' she'd said. 'It's going to take me a little while to get over them. Right now, I just want to go back there.'

Her father merely opened his arms and she went into them, resting her head on his chest, smelling his familiar odour of pipe tobacco, the comfort from her childhood.

But she had been lying to her father, too.

Now, she put her brush down.

'It was nothing,' she said to Christopher's reflection in the mirror. 'A chance encounter with someone I didn't expect to see, and didn't want to see. It rattled me, that's all. I'll be fine tomorrow.'

Christopher didn't say anything. She got up, hung her dressing gown on the back of the chair, and got into bed beside him, sitting up against the pillows.

'Daddy asked whether I was pregnant.'

He looked at her with quick understanding. 'What did you say?'

'I said no. Mum's been asking for ages, but this is the first time he has.'

He nodded.

'I'll tell them eventually,' she said. 'Maybe this holiday would be a good time.'

'It will be fine.'

'Daddy will understand. I'm not sure how my mother will react to Polly being her only chance of grandchildren, especially as it doesn't look as if she's going to get to it any time soon.'

Christopher took off his glasses and put them on the bedside table. 'We have other options. We could adopt.'

'We have other things to think about first: our careers, where we want to settle – whether we're going back to La Paz.'

Whether it was fair to bring a child into a marriage that could be disturbed by a single glance of a stranger in an airport arrivals hall.

He settled on his side of the bed and turned off his light. 'You're still thinking about Consuela, aren't you?'

She turned out her own light and lay on her side, facing away from him, her eyes open in the darkness.

'Yes,' she said.

She hadn't been thinking about Consuela at all. Not since seeing Robbie.

Robbie awoke to darkness and the *thip-thip-thip* of the bedroom fan. One of the blades had come loose and it put the whole thing out of synch. He'd meant to fix it yesterday before Marie came back.

Marie slept beside him. She was the soundest sleeper Robbie had ever known. One time, the smoke alarm had gone off at midnight, Robbie staggering out of bed, half hung-over, searching for flames, checking on William, stumbling over a toy truck left on the floor and bashing his hip on William's chest of drawers, waking up his son, who cried. It had been caused by the battery in the alarm running out. Marie slept through it all.

He got up, pulled on his jeans, and went into William's room. The little boy was fast asleep with his thumb in his mouth. Robbie gently pulled his thumb out and William's mouth made soft sucking noises at the air, like a hungry baby's. He smoothed his son's dark hair back from his forehead and went to the kitchen.

The whole house was hot. The fans only stirred the hot air around. He opened the refrigerator and stuck his head into it for a few cool seconds. Then he took a beer, opened the back door and stood in the doorway drinking, looking at the low shadow of the house behind theirs, listening to distant thunder and the cicadas declaring love for each other in the trees.

If someone were to walk into his back yard right now and ask him why he was there at one in the morning, in this small rented pink stucco house in Coconut Grove, Florida, barefoot in his jeans and no shirt, drinking a Michelob, he wouldn't know how to answer. He could tell them the facts but there would be no thread to it, no way for it to make sense. He wouldn't be able to explain

183

the past few years, the son sleeping inside whom he loved and the wife sleeping inside whom he didn't.

The only way he could think to describe it was as the path of least resistance. The destiny that seemed to require the least effort. Something he could slide into without thinking, cushioned by a few beers or some bourbon, maybe both ... usually both. Something that didn't require him to think too deeply about who he was or what he had done.

He had sleepwalked here. He had been asleep for years, as deeply as Marie was now.

He hadn't remembered what it was like to be awake until he saw Emily yesterday.

He finished his beer and went to the refrigerator for another, but they were all gone. He'd bought a twelve pack yesterday, or was it the day before? It must have been the day before.

It had been yesterday. He thought of his father suddenly and scowled.

The thirst itched in his throat and he knew what it was. He knew why it was there. It was the destiny that required the least effort.

He knew that the smart thing to do would be to go back to bed and sleep next to Marie and get up sober in the morning and go to work at the marina at Dinner Key. To make the best of what he'd been given, to take his joy in William and his work, to try to be happy. To stop using the booze to anaesthetise himself. He'd seen what it did to his father, and what it did to his mother. Marie deserved better than that, and so did William.

But he'd seen Emily today. Emily Greaves. And she'd walked past him without speaking, without meeting his eye again, as if she wished that he didn't exist.

He wanted another drink.

Coconut Grove at night was music and lights, small bars spilling out on to the sidewalks, guitars and pot smoke and rum.

In JB's, he ordered a beer and a chaser, lit a cigarette, and gazed around the crowded room to see if there was anyone he recognised. He saw a couple of familiar faces, but none of his usual drinking buddies. A few tourists had made their way here, judging from the clothes and the sunburns. In the corner, two Cuban guitarists improvised a fast, complicated melody.

He'd just have one. Maybe two. And then go home. Marie would be none the wiser.

Except she would be. And William didn't know yet about his father's drinking, but he would soon. He had to know it, deep inside, in that childish part that picked up on adult complications. William had to know that his mother and father argued, that sometimes his father spoke too loud, laughed too long, had trouble keeping his balance. How old had Robbie been when he'd realised that about his own father? Seven? Eight?

He raised his glass to his lips.

A voice caught his attention over the talk and music, made him swivel his head quickly in its direction. The accent, the tones . . .

'Emily?' he said, half off the stool to go to her, his eyes scanning the crowd for the source.

'But where can we see a crocodile?' demanded the voice, English and clear, and Robbie saw it came from a young woman in a red and orange sundress. She stood with a group of other young people with several empty pitchers of beer on the high table in front of them. She had dark curly hair and hoop earrings, red lipstick, nose and cheeks stained pink from the sun. As he watched, she tossed her head and grinned in a way that he knew. 'Or OK, are they alligators? What's the difference, anyway?'

It was a bad idea. He picked up his bourbon and walked over to her table anyway. 'Paulina?' he said.

She was still half-laughing from her conversation, and he saw her take him in. She was drunk enough and he was sober enough so that he could almost read her thoughts: *He's a bit old, but cute . . . why not?*

'Oh, hi,' she said, moderating her smile to a flirtatious one. 'Have we met?'

'Are you Emily's sister? Emily Greaves?'

'Yes! Yes, we're on holiday together in Miami Beach. Do you know my sister? And why did you call me Paulina?'

'Polly. I'm sorry. You asked me to call you Paulina once.'

'We've met?' She scrunched up her nose and eyes in an exaggeration of remembering.

'A couple of times, though you were much younger. I'm Robert Brandon.'

She frowned, and then she remembered and her eyes got wide and angry. 'Wait. You're Robert? You're *that* Robert? I thought you looked familiar.'

'It's nice to see you again.'

'It's not nice to see you. You broke my sister's heart! You're a wanker.' She turned to her friends. 'This is the bloke who broke my sister's heart. He got engaged to her and then he left her. Like *that*.' She wheeled on him again, to the tune of general disapproving muttering from her friends. 'What are you doing here?'

'I live here, in Coconut Grove. Listen, Polly, I saw Emily in the airport today – yesterday. I only recognised you because I knew she was in Miami. Can I . . . let me buy you a drink and talk to you for a few minutes.'

'No! You're a creep.'

'It was a long time ago. Please, I just want to know how she's doing. As an old friend.'

She was clearly not happy about it, but she nodded. He bought them each another beer and they went to a corner booth together, still in sight of her friends.

He could see the resemblance to her sister. When she'd been twelve, it hadn't been so apparent: he remembered her as skinny and a bit wild, all mouth and wide eyes. But she had the same nose and almost the same lips as Emily, and the same shape face. He caught himself staring, trying to trace

Emily in her, and looked down at his beer instead.

'How is she?' he asked her.

'She's fine.'

'What is she . . . what is she doing? Is she a doctor?'

'She's an obstetrician. She's *amazing*. She's been working in South America with poor people, helping them. With her husband, Christopher.'

He'd known she was married. He'd known that man was her husband as soon as he'd seen him. The confirmation was still a stab in the gut.

'I *liked* you,' she said, suddenly and vehemently. 'I thought you were a really nice bloke. God, I remember telling Em that she should marry you.'

'I wanted her to.'

'Well, it's a good thing she didn't.'

'Maybe it was,' he mumbled, and drank his beer.

'She doesn't even talk about you. She never mentioned you again. She burned all your letters and everything. I saw her doing it one night. God, how long ago was this?'

'Ten years. It was ten years ago.'

'Wow. Well, whatever you did, you fucked it up.'

'You don't know?' he asked involuntarily. 'She didn't tell you?'

'I told you, she never mentioned you again. Believe me, I asked her.' She regarded him over the rim of her beer glass. 'What *did* you do?'

He shook his head.

'It must've been something bad. I remember my parents sent me to my friend's house for a couple of days, and when I came back it was like you'd never existed. Except Emily was miserable. Did you cheat on her?'

'It was something like that. Yeah.'

'Dickhead.' She took a drink of her beer.

'I need to see her,' he told her urgently.

'I don't think she'd be keen on that.'

'I need to know she's all right. That's all, Polly.'

'You want to apologise to her for being an ass, ten years ago?'

'I . . .' He bit his lip. 'Yes.'

'I don't know. What did she say to you at the airport when you saw her?'

'We didn't get a chance to talk. Please, Polly. Can you give me the address of where she's staying, or a phone number, or something?'

'I'm not sure she'd want to hear from you. I should ask her first.'

If she asked Emily, she'd refuse.

'Polly, it was a long time ago, as you say. A lot of water under the bridge. I just want to get in touch with her, for one last time, to see how she's doing. And to say sorry.'

'She's happily married now.'

'I'm married too. I've got a little boy. I'll just call her, once, and then that will be it. For old times' sake.'

'Well . . .' She screwed up her mouth, thinking, and in that moment, despite the make-up and the beer in her hand, she looked like a kid again. 'I suppose it can't do any harm. She can always hang up on you.' Polly pulled out a pen from her handbag and paused. 'Are you going to promise not to be a wanker?'

'I promise.'

'Say it. "I won't be a wanker".'

'I won't be a wanker.'

'Cross your heart.'

He did.

'All right. Wait, there's nothing to write on.'

He held out his hand, fingers curled, palm down. She scowled, but she wrote the number on the back of his hand.

'Thank you, Polly.'

'Don't make me regret it.' She drank the rest of her beer and stood up. 'She's happy, now. She's really happy. Don't mess it up for her.'

'I won't,' he said. 'I want her to be happy. That's what I want, more than anything.'

Chapter Twenty-Four

Even at nine o'clock in the morning it was too hot and humid to go outside. The minute you did, sweat sprang out under your arms, between your breasts, on your upper lip. Your lipstick melted off and your mouth tasted of salt. Emily hovered in the air-conditioned living room, looking out the window to the pool, where her father was swimming laps. There was a long-legged white bird standing on the concrete near the pool, absolutely still. It looked like a crane, though Emily didn't know what it could possibly be looking for in the clear, sterile pool water. It tilted its head slightly as her father swam past.

Her mother, incredibly, was cooking a full English breakfast for Christopher, after he'd made a chance remark yesterday that he hadn't had one for years. Heat and the scent of bacon radiated out from the kitchen.

The telephone rang across the room. She abandoned her window and the crane and picked it up.

'Hello?'

'Hello, can I speak to Emily?'

She knew his voice at once; would have known it even if she hadn't heard it the day before calling her name.

'Robbie,' she said, in a whisper, before she realised that the right thing to do would have been to hang up immediately.

'Emily,' he said, his voice full of relief. 'Oh my God, it's so wonderful to hear your voice. Don't hang up.'

'Why are you calling me?'

'I had to speak with you. I had to – I couldn't believe it was you, yesterday.'

She looked around, though she knew no one could hear her: her father was swimming, her mother and Christopher were in the kitchen, and Polly, who'd been out till very late, was asleep and wouldn't be up for hours yet. Still, she cupped her hands around the phone, and lowered her voice. 'How did you get this number?'

'Polly gave it to me. I ran into her by chance.'

'Why are you in Miami?'

'I live here. Listen, Emily, I never expected to see you again. I know you said we couldn't see each other again. But now we have, and I can't stop thinking about you.'

'I . . .' *I can't stop thinking about you either.* 'Don't. Don't think about me.'

'I need to meet you. Please? Please meet with me?'

'I can't. I'm with my husband.' As soon as she said it she knew it was a mistake: she shouldn't have given him any reasons to argue with. She shouldn't be talking with him at all.

But his voice. She heard his voice when she slept, sometimes. It hadn't changed at all.

'Bring your husband with you. It's just an innocent meeting, Emily. Old friends.'

'We're not old friends.'

'Old . . . acquaintances, then. Please, Emily. A lot has changed.'

How can it have changed, when I remember you like this? She didn't say it. That would be a real mistake.

'When can you get away?' he asked. 'Tonight?'

'Not tonight,' she said without thinking.

'Tomorrow morning, before I go to work? Are you in Miami Beach?'

'Yes. I'm—'

'What about on South Beach? Say six o'clock? Right on the south end.'

'I don't know. It's not a good idea.'

'I'll be there, waiting. If not tomorrow, then I'll wait the next day too.'

'It's . . . Robbie, we agreed never to—'

'Please come, Emily. Please.'

When she put down the phone, her hands were shaking. Her father slid open the patio doors and walked in, towelling off his hair. 'Did you see that bird?' he said. 'Who rang?'

'It was a wrong number,' she told him.

She slipped out of the house as the sun was rising, but he was still there before her. He stood straight and tall, smoking a cigarette. A light blue bicycle was propped against the trunk of the palm beside him. She remembered him standing on a station concourse and she nearly turned around.

But then he spotted her and she forgot all about running away. His presence pulled her to him as he dropped his cigarette and ground it out.

'Emily,' he said.

She couldn't say his name. Instead, unwillingly, she drank him in: the length of his dark hair, grown out since the last time she'd seen him. He was unshaven and wore a white T-shirt and shorts made of cut-off jeans, and his eyes had dark circles under them, as if he hadn't slept for a while, or not slept properly. His eyes were the same as she remembered. His mouth was the same. He was more filled out now, more muscular, his forearms tanned and corded.

Even this early, it was too hot to breathe.

'Should we – should we take a walk?' he asked her, and she nodded.

They walked down across the fine white sand to where the surf kissed the beach. She remembered the other beach they had walked on, with shingle mixed in with the sand. The water had been a different colour. There had been no palm trees, just buildings, and it had been a spring afternoon, cool enough to have to wear a jacket.

The beach was nearly deserted. Her sandals filled with sand and she bent down and slipped them off. Robbie put his hands in his pockets as they walked. She couldn't bear to look at him. Instead she gazed out at the sea, where the sunrise was colouring the water with pink and yellow. But she still felt him beside her. Still saw him in her peripheral vision, like she'd seen him in the periphery of her memory for ten years. Her body fell into rhythm with his as they walked.

'You didn't bring your husband with you,' he said.

She'd forgotten he'd suggested it. She'd not said a word to Christopher. He'd been still sleeping when she'd left.

'Why did you want to see me?' she asked him.

'I want to know if you're happy.'

'Yes,' she said quickly. 'Of course I'm happy.'

'Good. I only wanted you to be happy. Polly said you're an ob-stetrician, and you're working in South America.'

'Yes. We're on our way back to England after this holiday.'

'How long have you been married?' he asked her. There was a forced casualness in his voice.

'Seven years. Christopher didn't want to wait until we'd quali-fied. It made sense for us to be in married accommodation.'

'Christopher . . . that's . . .' He took a breath. 'You told me about him.'

'Yes. He's a good husband. Are you – are you married?'

'Yeah. Five years. I've got a little boy.'

It choked her. Her hands flew to her throat before she caught herself and made them return to her sides.

'Oh, that's wonderful. What's he called?'

'William.' He took out his wallet and held out a photograph to her. She took it: a skinny scrap of a boy, with Robbie's dark hair and eyes. He wore a striped shirt and dungarees and was holding a toy car by one wheel. He smiled, revealing a gap in his teeth.

His beauty burned. She couldn't look away from it. She had to look at the photo and look at it and burn. She wondered what his mother was like.

'He's lovely,' she managed. 'The spit of you.'

'Chip off the old block.'

She gave back the photograph. Her fingers had left smears on its glossy surface, near the child's dark head.

'Do you have children?' Robbie asked, replacing the photograph in his wallet.

'No.'

'You're probably too busy.'

She didn't answer that. Her diagnosis seemed too clinical; too much of an excuse for her failure, the failure of her marriage. Just kept walking along the beach. The wet sand was cooler than the air. In the distance, palm trees hung their fronds like limp scarves. They could be on a different planet from the one they'd been on the last time they had spoken, the last time they'd really spoken, on the silty bank of the river, with mist rising up from the water because of the rain.

'What else have you been doing?' she asked at last. 'How are Dennis and Art?'

'I don't know. I haven't spoken with them in years.'

'What did you do after – after we said goodbye, the last time?'

'I got on a boat out of Bristol to New York. I travelled around a little while and then joined the Navy.'

'Did you go to Vietnam?'

He nodded.

'You ... you never seemed like the armed forces type to me.'

'I didn't know what else to do. I had to do something.' From studied nonchalance, his voice had gone curt. 'I was there for two years. Took some shrapnel in the thigh, so they sent me home.'

'Robbie.' She stopped walking, and he did too. 'You were hurt?'

'It's fine. I was one of the lucky ones. Then down to Florida, got a job in a marina here. Marie's a snowbird from Wisconsin.

Nobody in Miami is originally from here.'

'I can see why they come here,' she said automatically. 'It's beautiful, though too hot for me.'

'Are you happy, Emily? Are you really happy?'

'Yes.'

'I want you to be happy,' he said. 'It's all I've ever wanted. You were right. I had to keep thinking about that, after I left. You were right. We hardly knew each other after all.'

'Are you happy?' she burst out.

'No.'

He bent down and scooped up a handful of wet sand and threw it at the pink and yellow surf. It dissolved from a lump to a scattering of pieces and didn't make a single ripple at all.

'No,' she repeated. 'No, me neither.'

'Why did we do it, then?'

'Robbie, please don't ask me that.'

'You're the only person who calls me Robbie.'

'Please,' she said, though she didn't know what she was asking him to do, or not to do.

He touched her cheek with a sandy finger. She breathed in sharply.

'Please,' she said again.

'This isn't enough, is it?' he whispered. 'It isn't what either of us wants.'

'I don't know what I want. Yes, I do. I want everything to be the same as it was before I saw you again.'

'I don't. That moment when I saw you in the airport was the most alive I've felt for ten years.'

She touched his lips with her fingers. She couldn't help it. She didn't want to and she knew she shouldn't but her fingers, his mouth. His lips were firm and warm and she remembered what it was like to kiss them. She remembered them on the back of her sunburned neck and how they had tasted in the Cambridge rain.

'We can't do this,' she whispered.

He nodded. 'But we're going to anyway.'

She didn't trust herself to speak. She nodded.

Chapter Twenty-Five

After he watched her walk away through the dunes, he didn't go to work. He rode his bike back over the causeway and rode around until he found a liquor store that was open. He bought a fifth of Beam, took it to the waterfront, and sat, watching the waves, drinking.

Water always ran in the path of least resistance first. It would take the easiest way. But then when the easiest way was full, when the water pressure was too great, when it had to flow, water would eat through rock. It would push aside mountains to get where it needed to go. It would break apart the earth into sand.

It just needed time, and sufficient pressure.

He thought of her face when he had told her about being wounded.

When JB's opened, he went there for a beer.

They had cocktails by the pool before they went to dinner: Christopher was very good at making dry martinis, and Polly had a bottle of Cuban rum and wanted to make a cocktail she'd had at one of the bars she'd visited. She'd also procured several Cuban cigars, probably highly illegal. One of them was clenched between her teeth, emitting puffs of smoke as she filled four glasses with rapidly melting ice. Christopher and her father were sitting at the patio table, chatting about cricket, each with their own cigar, although Christopher was only holding his, not smoking it. Emily perched on the edge of a sunlounger.

No one had noticed. They hadn't noticed she'd been gone that morning, and they hadn't noticed the seismic change in her since she had agreed to see Robbie again. As far as her family knew, everything was normal.

Robbie had been the same and yet so different. He was sadder. He had a quietness to him that he'd never had before. He spoke less quickly and smiled less often.

She had done that to him. She had done at least some of that to him.

Her mother joined her, stretching out on a neighbouring sunlounger. She had a martini glass in her hand. 'It's a bit cooler, at least.'

'Maybe people get used to the heat,' Emily said. 'When they live here for a while.'

'The palm trees, though,' said her mother. 'With real coconuts. It's like being on a film set. I have to pinch myself to believe I'm here. Oh, Emily, look!'

She pointed at a small dun-coloured lizard on the cement near the pool. It paused, absolutely still, in a ray of sunshine, long enough for them to see its pinpoint black eyes and its legs parallel to the ground, and then it darted off, fast as thought.

'In La Paz we knew a man who'd trained a tegu. They're these big black-and-white lizards. He would ride on a bicycle, and it would ride on his shoulder, like a parrot.'

Her mother nodded, and this was normal, too. As long as she could remember, Emily had been offering her little interesting facts, conversational gifts. Hoping to please her. Impress her. As a child, she used to read the encyclopaedia in her father's study, starting from the middle of the alphabet, and she would memorise lines and find her mother in the kitchen and recite them. Watching her nod, hoping for a smile or a 'Well done,' the kind of easy praise that her father could always give her and that her mother never did.

The habit was difficult to break.

'Well,' Emily said, starting to get up, 'I'd better powder my nose before—'

'Look at you,' said her mother suddenly. 'Look at you, Emily. A doctor, married to a surgeon. Helping the poor in a foreign country. I never thought . . .' She trailed off and took a sip of her drink. Christopher's martinis were quite potent, and she was on her second one, though she never normally had anything stronger than a single sherry.

'I'm very proud of you,' her mother said. 'Very proud indeed. There was a time when I was worried. But I shouldn't have been. You always knew how to find your way.'

'Oh,' she said. She'd half got up, but now she sat back down. 'Thank you.'

There was a hammering sound from Polly's direction. 'How do you muddle mint?' she asked no one in particular.

'Muddle?' asked her mother. 'As in confuse?'

Polly grunted and poked mint into the glasses. She poured rum and soda and tried a sip. 'This just tastes of rum. How come they tasted so good in the bar? Maybe they need sugar, do you think?'

'Don't ask me,' said Emily. 'I've never had one.'

'I'll go get the sugar bowl. But then the ice is going to melt. Oh, bother.'

'Put the glasses in the freezer,' suggested Emily.

Polly snapped her finger. 'My genius sister.' Balancing four glasses in her two hands, she went into the house.

'Do you think your sister will ever settle down?' her mother asked. 'You were married at her age.'

'She'll be fine,' said Emily, wondering at this idea: her mother asking her for advice or reassurance.

'I suppose she hasn't met a Christopher yet.'

'Perhaps she doesn't want a Christopher.'

Emily glanced at her husband: tall, lean, his legs pale in his shorts. She hardly ever really looked at him; he had been a fixture of her life for so long. Here by the side of the pool, holding a Cuban cigar he had no intention of smoking, he looked so very English. Much more English than he'd ever looked in Bolivia, where he'd always had a purpose and didn't wear things like shorts. He laughed at something that her father said: his polite English chuckle.

He adored her. She knew that he did, although he never said anything of the sort. She caught him looking at her, sometimes, late at night when she was lying beside him in bed reading a book, when he thought she wasn't paying attention. He loved her so very much and had loved her since they had met when they were students together at Cambridge, although he had gone for a long time without telling her. Bolivia had been her idea, not his.

And yet he didn't know what was in the corners of her mind. The way she could still feel Robbie's lips under the pads of her fingers.

Christopher didn't know. He was going on loving her, without knowing. He had gone on not knowing for ten years.

'Will you speak with her?' her mother asked her.

'With who?' she asked, surprised.

'Your sister. She won't listen to me, or your father. I worry that she's so . . . frivolous.'

'That's Polly.'

'She admires you so much though. She's always hero-worshipped you. You could have a word.'

Polly came back outside with the bottle of rum and an empty glass. 'I can't make it taste good,' she announced. 'We might as well drink it straight.'

'All right,' said Emily. 'I'll speak with her.'

'You what?'

Polly leaned on the sink, peering in the mirror as she applied a thick swoop of black eyeliner.

Emily shut the bathroom door behind her, speaking quietly. 'I told Mum and Dad and Christopher that I'm going out with you tonight.'

'You are?' She grinned and started on the other eye. 'That's fantastic! All you've wanted to do since we've got here is sleep in the evenings. I was beginning to think that Bolivia had sucked all the fun out of you.'

'Are you . . . you're thinking of staying out quite late, aren't you?'

'It's not a night out unless you're on the beach when the sun rises. I'm excited you're coming with me!'

'The thing is, Polly, I'm not.'

Polly put down her eyeliner. She reached for the cigarette she'd left burning on the side of the sink and took a puff from it. 'You're not coming out with me? Then why did you say—'

'I need you to cover for me.'

'*Cover* for you?'

'You don't have to say anything if you don't want. I've already told Mum and Dad and Christopher. You don't even have to agree. We'll go out together, and I'll call a cab to pick me up on the corner.'

'Em, why do you have to—' Understanding dawned in Polly's eyes. 'Oh no, you're not seeing *him*, are you?'

Emily didn't reply. But her cheeks flushed bright red.

'You can't. You can't! He's . . . what about Christopher?'

'Christopher will never know,' she whispered. 'You can't tell him. It would make him very upset.'

'Don't do it, then! Emily, this man is bad news. You've been fine without him for ten years.'

'You don't understand.'

'I do understand. I understand completely!' She ground out her cigarette in the sink. 'Bloody hell, Em, he told me he just wanted to see you to apologise. I shouldn't have given him the phone number.'

'It's not your fault. It has nothing to do with you, Poll. I just need to see him.'

Polly looked hard at her. Emily did her best to look steadily back.

'You've seen him already, haven't you?'

'You don't understand. I need to see him again. I need to, Polly. Only once, I swear.'

'I'm not going to lie for you.'

'You don't have to lie. You don't have to say anything at all. Just go out and have a good time. I'll be back home before you are.'

'But *Christopher*,' Polly said. 'He's a bit of a bore but he loves you, Em. He really *really* loves you.'

'He will never know,' Emily repeated. 'Not unless you tell him. And even if you won't help me, I'm going out tonight. I've made my mind up. All you're doing by agreeing is helping Christopher not to get hurt.'

Polly frowned at her. 'This doesn't even *sound* like you. You're not manipulative, or secretive. You're not like this.'

Emily thought of the love for Robbie she'd kept secret in her heart, every day for ten years. Secret, most of the time, even from herself.

'I'm like this now,' she said.

Chapter Twenty-Six

The hotel was out near the airport: a newly built box, squat and ugly. They signed the register as Mr and Mrs Smith and they took the lift to the top floor. There was an elderly couple in it with them, not saying anything, and Emily shifted from foot to foot, certain that the couple knew that they weren't married to each other, that they should not be together, that they were here to do something wrong. It was in the way the man of the couple stared at the closed doors, careful not to catch their eye. The lift stopped on the third floor and the couple got out before them and Emily walked beside Robbie in the other direction, glancing back over her shoulder to see if the other couple was watching them. They weren't.

Her skin itched, her heart pounded. She couldn't catch her breath. It was the way she had first felt at altitude in La Paz, arriving from a place where the air was normal to a place where it was rare and thin.

She'd got used to that eventually. Would she get used to this?

This was against everything she believed in. She had worked so hard to make her life a good one.

Robert held the hotel room door open for her and she went in first. Ten years ago they had done this. A different country, a different decade, an old hotel with a pink ruffled bedspread and the sound of seagulls outside the window. Back when there had been no one else, just the two of them. They had joked with the desk clerk and used Robbie's real name. Her cheeks had tingled with sunburn and excitement.

This hotel was new and the only sound was of planes overhead, going somewhere else. Her fingers were numb.

He shut the door behind them. They stood, several feet apart, looking at each other.

'What did you tell him?' he asked her.

'That I was out with my sister. What did you tell her?'

'I didn't tell her anything. I'm . . . often out.'

'This is wrong,' she said. 'It's wrong for us to do this.'

'We've done it before.'

'That was different.'

'But you want to. Or else you wouldn't have come.'

She nodded.

He reached out and touched the tips of her fingers. She shivered.

'Emily,' he murmured. 'I love you. I still love you, all this time, since the first moment I met you. Nothing else can matter, can it?'

'Please. Please don't say anything.' She stepped forward; close enough so that she could feel the heat from his body. 'Please just kiss me.'

That last time in that hotel in Lowestoft, ten years ago, she had made him promise not to promise anything. She had not known if she was ever going to see him again. She had taken refuge in not thinking, only feeling. Living right here, now in the moment. Robbie was the only one who could make her feel that way.

He looked down at her. In the dark brown of his eyes she saw the decision that they had made, and that could not be unmade.

Then he bowed his head and kissed her.

It happened instantly. As soon as his lips touched hers, as soon as his breath touched her face, she was aflame, eager, desperate. She clenched her hands in his shirt and pulled him closer, as close as he could get, and he wrapped his arms around her waist and pulled her closer too. It had never been like this with Christopher, never like this. She didn't have to close her eyes and she didn't have to try to feel anything she didn't. She felt Robbie's body against hers and she tasted him with her tongue and touched him with her hands and everything felt monstrously, hideously, perfect and right.

She was clumsy with desire and could hardly negotiate the buttons of his shirt, but when she did and touched his chest and shoulders, his skin was hot and smooth and so entirely familiar and she remembered how she had dreamed about it, and woken herself up to try to forget. The memory of his skin had never left her, even though she had tried to make it disappear.

'Emily,' Robbie murmured against her lips.

They were hurting others. They were hurting themselves. He was close enough so that he was a blur of darkness and light, hair and eyes and skin, the scent of salt and tobacco. He smelled and he felt exactly as he had been ten years before, when they hadn't hurt anyone, when all of the pain had lain in their future.

She tugged at his clothes and her fingers touched an unfamiliar patch of skin. Something she didn't remember, something new. It was pitted and tight, at the top of his thigh, and when she drew back a little bit to look at him, he pulled her closer to kiss him again. He grasped her hand gently and put it on his chest, away from his scars.

Later, when they were naked, when they had made love and were lying side by side on the bed, the air conditioning cooling their skin, Emily ran her fingers over his scar again: the shrapnel wound from Vietnam. He never looked at it, made sure his shorts were long enough to cover it, but when she touched it, he glanced down. It was a burn and a puckered puncture and a smooth white line: the outward signs of everything that had happened to them while they were apart.

This time he let her touch it. He watched her face as she touched him and he felt her fingertips on the skin that was strangely both sensitive and dead, as if there were a thin and brittle sheet of glass laid over his raw nerve endings.

'Did it hurt?' she whispered.

'They gave me a lot of morphine.' It was his standard answer for when he talked about it, which was never.

'But it must have hurt.'

'It felt like a punishment that I deserved.'

She looked into his face, and he saw there were tears in her eyes. 'Robbie, you could have died and I would never have known. I never would have found out.'

'I was mostly numb,' he told her. 'I was numb my whole time over there. I had to be, to see what I saw. And do what I did.'

'I can't imagine you numb. You've always been the most alive person I know.' Her touch on his scar was like a balm, warming and softening the tightened skin.

'We were going up the Mekong River to rescue a patrol boat that had run aground. We stopped a sampan, a routine check. There were children in it. The man had a grenade. I tried not to ... you couldn't ... if I felt the truth of everything that I saw then I would have ...' He swallowed. 'I don't talk about it. There are no words, anyway. Just a ... noise. And a scent.'

A peppery scent, heavy, catching the back of his throat, making his tongue clumsy. Hammering of guns, the giant footsteps of shells exploding. Screams.

'There's a scent to the slums in La Paz,' she said quietly. 'There are all the normal human scents, cooking and sweat and urine and faeces, and another scent. Like rotting flowers left too long in a vase. Rotting funeral flowers. There was a girl ... a pregnant girl with a rat-bitten foot. I couldn't help her.'

Her sigh feathered on his skin. He put his hand over hers, both of their palms together covering the twisted skin on his leg.

'I can still smell it now,' she told him. 'Even though I've left. Sometimes I can taste it.'

He nodded.

'Bourbon drowns out the taste,' he said. 'For a little while.'

'And what about the noise?'

'I sail. When I can. It's quiet on the water.'

'Is it quiet now?'

'Yes.' He rolled on to his side, and kissed her. 'With you, it is.'

'You could have died,' she said again, 'and I would have never known.'

'You would have known,' he told her. 'We'll always know.'

Chapter Twenty-Seven

Christopher was asleep when she returned. It wasn't late, hardly past midnight. Polly was still out. She had showered in the hotel, but she showered again before she went to bed.

Her husband didn't stir as she climbed in beside him and turned her back on his sleeping form. Without moving, her hands rehearsed the way she had touched Robbie; her lips remembered their kisses.

She was exhausted, but she didn't fall asleep for a very long time.

Marie was sitting at the kitchen table when he got home. She had a cup of coffee and a full ashtray. 'Hey,' he greeted her as he walked in and got a glass down from the cupboard to fill at the sink.

'There isn't any beer,' she said.

'That's OK, I'm good with water.' He took a drink and Marie lit another cigarette. She was staring at the wall, a line dug between her eyebrows.

'Well, guess I'll give him a kiss and turn in,' he said, heading for the door.

'I can't do this any more,' she said.

He paused.

'Do what?' Though he knew.

'I can't sit here and wait for you to come home, not knowing what state you'll be in.'

'I'm not drunk.'

'You're not drunk tonight, maybe. But you usually are. When you even come home at all.'

'I didn't know you waited for me,' he said, knowing he was changing the subject unfairly. 'I thought usually you were asleep.'

'You don't know anything half the time. I know why you do it.'

He thought of Emily, thought about lying beside her on top of the sheets in the hotel room. The way she had touched him and made years disappear as if they had never been. Made his scarred skin feel whole again.

'Do you believe in God?'

He was surprised by the question, and a little relieved. He thought she'd been going to ask him if he loved her.

'You know I've never been one for religious stuff,' he said.

'But you believe in sin.'

Emily believed in sin. She thought they had done wrong.

'I . . . don't know,' he said. 'Anyway, I thought you'd decided you were done with all this, Marie.'

'Everything that you do is dragging us down with you,' she said. 'You don't care that you're putting William and me in danger.'

He sighed. 'This is from your parents, isn't it? They never liked me.'

'I'm the mother of your child. I'm your wife. And you have no respect for me at all.'

'That's not true.'

'Then why are you out every night? Down at JB's or wherever you go? And the nights you're here, even if you're not drinking, you don't look at me. You don't talk to me. I might as well not exist.'

There was no answer he could give her that wasn't either cowardly or hurtful. So he said nothing.

She stabbed out her cigarette half-smoked, next to the other cigarette butts, each imprinted with the coral of her lipstick.

'I'm through with it,' she said. 'I'm finished. I can't live like this any more.'

'It's not your fault,' he said to her. 'It really isn't your fault at all, Marie.'

'I *know*. It's yours.'

He nodded.

This was a relief, really. To have it spoken out loud, everything he had been thinking, that he wasn't sure that she had noticed. But of course she'd noticed.

'But it's over,' she continued. 'It's over. I can't put up with this any more. I don't deserve to be treated like this.'

'No, you don't,' he said, honestly.

'So I've made a decision. Either you're here with us, Bob, or you're not. If you want to be a family, be a family.'

'I want to be William's father,' he said. Wishing he had a beer in his hand.

'That's the thing, Bob. William comes with me. We're a package deal.'

'What are you saying?'

'I'm saying that either you start acting like a real husband, or William and I are leaving.' She knocked another Winston out of the package and struck a match. He noticed that her hands were jittery, but her face was closed. Chin out. Eyes hard.

He remembered when he had first met her. It had been Fourth of July weekend in Peacock Park, with picnic blankets spread out everywhere, radios blasting out competing music. They'd both been drunk. Her hair was longer, long enough for her to sit on, and it had been in Pocahontas braids with coloured ribbons on the ends. 'Catch this!' she'd yelled to him in her Midwestern accent and she'd tossed him a beach ball and he'd bounced it off his head. His leg still hurt back then, but he'd forgotten it for a little while when she'd laughed.

They'd both been running away from something. She was trying to escape her closed-in evangelical family; he was trying to escape the memory of Emily and what he'd done in the war. All their running hadn't done anything, in the end.

'And if we're leaving,' she said, 'we're leaving. William and I. We're leaving for good.'

'I understand,' he said.

'No, I don't think you do. You need to stop this, this . . . whatever you're doing. The drinking, the avoiding us. Or you won't be seeing William again.'

'You can't do that.'

'I think you'll find that I can. And I will.'

'He's my son.'

'You don't love him.'

'Of course I do!'

'If you loved him, you wouldn't be dragging him down.'

'I'm not dragging him anywhere.'

Marie stood up abruptly, scraping the chair on the linoleum. 'You've got another woman, haven't you?'

He hesitated.

'You are! You're having an affair, you bastard!'

'Keep your voice down, Marie. You'll wake him up.'

'You don't care about waking him up when you come in dead drunk!'

'Calm down, please. Please, Marie.'

She pointed at him, with a shaking hand that held her smoking cigarette. 'He's innocent. I'll do anything to protect him, Bob. Even if that means taking him away from you forever.'

Emily took a bath the next morning, washing for the third time to counteract the fact that she didn't want to wash Robbie from her skin. The bubbles were cloying, hibiscus-scented, and the bathroom was aggressively pink: pink bath, pink sink, pink toilet, pink tiles on wall and floor, pink-tinted lights around the vanity mirror. She made the water as hot as she could stand and climbed in, stretching her body in the bath.

A soft double knock on the door, and Christopher leaned his head in. 'May I come in? I brought you a cup of tea.'

She didn't want a cup of tea; she wanted time alone, to think. Even though thinking was painful.

All she could do was think about Robbie, and when she was going to see him again. But she was here, with her family. Polly wasn't going to lie for her. She would have to invent excuses herself, with Polly watching her and knowing.

She knew now that for the last ten years she'd been deceiving herself about her true feelings. But that was very different from consciously deceiving the people she loved, and who loved her. It was the difference between suffering, and making other suffer. She thought of the icons of the bleeding, torn Jesus on the cross that hung from the walls of the clinic in La Paz, dabbed in lurid red paint; so different from the austere, restrained cross in the church where she'd accompanied her parents to service every Sunday as a child. But the message was the same in both.

This was not what good people did.

'Thank you,' she said. He came in, closing the door softly behind him, and set the cup on the side of the bath. Then he sat down on the side of the bath, too. He was neat, controlled, but the bathroom tinted his hair and skin pink.

'I'll say this once,' he said. He stared at the pink tiles on the wall above her head. 'I know who you've seen.'

She started, violently enough for the water to slop over the side of the bath. 'I—'

He held up a hand. 'Please, don't say anything. You want to reassure me, but I don't want you to lie for me. Just listen.'

But he didn't say anything for several moments, and the only sound was Emily's quick breathing and the dripping of the tap into the bath.

'It's that man at the airport,' he said at last. 'He's the man you never talk about. You've been thinking about him for ten years.'

'I haven't—'

'Don't lie, Emily. Please, don't lie.'

She swallowed. 'I didn't know that I'd been thinking about him.'

At that he did glance at her, as if surprised, but then he focused on the tiles again.

'How did you know?' she asked, at last.

'You haven't been yourself since we arrived – not since he called your name. You've been different.'

'But that could have been about anything.'

'I love you. I *know*. You'd know the same, if it happened to me.' He smiled, sadly, at the tiles. 'It wouldn't happen, but if it did, you'd know.'

She didn't think she would know. When did she look at Christopher closely? When had she ever had to? He was always there, always Christopher, lean and tall, wearing glasses and a tie, even in the heat. He had a haircut every three weeks; he shaved every morning – once, even, after an earthquake. He worked with extraordinary care and could face even the most daunting surgical conditions with equanimity. He did not change; had never changed.

But he watched her closely enough, loved her enough, to see right through her.

'I remember when you told me about first meeting him,' he said. 'At Cambridge. For six months, you were walking on air, and I had nothing to do with it.'

He sounded sad.

'And then you were . . . Emily, that September when you came back up, you were a shadow of yourself. No matter what I did, I couldn't reach you. It was awful to see you like that, and not be able to help you.'

'I'm sorry.'

'I thought that when you started loving me, we could forget all that. I thought I'd helped you.'

'I thought so too.' She had to whisper it. 'I thought it was over.'

'I do – I do believe that you don't want to hurt me, Emily.

Maybe I'm a fool. I am probably a fool. But I love you enough to think that you wouldn't intentionally hurt me.'

'I don't want to hurt you.'

But I have.

That hung in the air between them, heavy as the scent from the bath oil.

'We're here in Miami for another ten days,' Christopher said at last, and now his voice was brisk. 'Then we go back to England. And once we're home, Emily, this is finished. Forever. And we shan't speak of it again.'

Emily stared at him, unable to believe what he was saying.

'So do what you feel you must. And then, when we're home, it will be over.' He nodded as if reassuring himself. 'I can trust you. Can't I?'

'I . . .'

He waited.

'Yes,' she said. 'Yes, you can trust me.'

'Fine.' He stood up, brushed down his trousers. 'I won't ask any questions, and I trust you to invent plausible enough excuses for your family. I have no desire to be an object of pity.'

His voice broke on the last word. He turned and left the bathroom.

It wasn't much of a workshop; more like a ramshackle shed, built from bits of fencing and corrugated iron that Robbie had managed to salvage from around the neighbourhood. But it had a neat pegboard of tools, and a scarred workbench (also salvaged), and it smelled of sawdust and glue and varnish, and William had his own little stool in the corner.

Robbie sat, an opened beer on the workbench in front of him, and watched William rubbing sandpaper over the head of the dolphin that Robbie had carved for him out of a piece of driftwood.

'I'm gonna make it real smooth,' said William. His chubby fingers gripped the sandpaper. 'Then I can take it to bed with me.'

'As soon as your mother says you're old enough to use a knife, you can carve your own. I'll teach you.'

'I'm going to carve dogs. A lot of dogs. I'll carve a dog for you, Daddy.' He gave the head of the dolphin a last rub, and put down the sandpaper. He considered the other pieces of sandpaper spread out beside him, and carefully chose a finer grade. Just as Robbie had taught him, to work from coarse to fine, to take care to get into the corners, not to rub too hard, to let the grain of the wood be your guide.

It hurt Robbie's heart to watch him. William's movements were so similar to his own. He reached for his beer, thought better of it, and pulled his hand back. He picked up a screwdriver and began work on the bilge pump he'd been repairing.

'If we had a real dog,' said William, concentrating on his sanding, 'he could look out for Mommy and me when you're away. He could bark at bad guys.'

'You don't have to worry about bad guys.'

'I have dreams about bad guys sometimes. But if I had a dog, I wouldn't have to worry.' He rubbed the fine paper over the bear's belly. 'I like Duke.'

Duke was Marie's father's dog. He had bitten Robbie on the one and only time he had visited them on the farm in Wisconsin. Les had seemed to think this was funny.

'Mommy says that if you ever go away, we would go live with Pop-pop and Nana and Duke.'

So she'd talked about it with William. She was serious about what she said.

The proof made the air heavier, made it difficult for him to breathe. She'd mentioned it to their child. She'd made plans.

'Would you . . . like that?' he asked. 'Living with Pop-pop and Nana, instead of with me?'

'I like Duke.'

'Would you miss me?'

William nodded. 'I'd miss my room too.'

Robbie put down the screwdriver. He went to his son and put his arms around him. Buried his face in his hair and breathed in the scent of sandpaper and strawberry milk and child. This small being, in every way perfect, who he'd loved from the first moment he'd seen, still slimy from birth. Who he loved more than any other person in the world except for one.

'I'd miss you,' he whispered. 'I'd miss you so much. I won't go away. I promise.'

'OK,' said William.

'I promise you.' He held him tightly, tightly enough so that William struggled and he had to let him go.

'So does that mean we can get a dog?' William asked.

Chapter Twenty-Eight

The air was heavy, thick with moisture. Emily found the weather in Florida oppressive at the best of times but this was like a blanket around her shoulders. 'Is there even going to be enough wind?' she asked Robbie as she followed him down on to the dock where he kept his boat – not near the ranks of sleek white yachts, but on the side of the marina near the public boat launch, next to a row of fishing boats which reeked faintly of fish. It was a small sailboat, with a tiny cabin. The hull was painted blue, the decks white, its name painted in black on the stern: *Little Billy*.

'It'll pick up. There'll be a storm before sunset.' He held out his hand to help her aboard and she caught a whiff of alcohol on his breath. *Bourbon drowns out the taste*, he had told her. She frowned, but said nothing. His hand didn't linger on hers. He merely helped her aboard, and then he was untying lines from cleats and springing on to deck himself.

'It's not going to storm soon, is it?' There were puddles on the walkway and pontoon from earlier rainfall; she could almost see them evaporating away in the sunshine. In the distance, the clouds towered, stacked on top of each other. After La Paz the horizon here in Miami seemed so vast and flat. And the rain here was nothing like the rain in England: it was heavy and absolute, and often over as soon as it had begun. Emily had seen a rainbow almost every day. It was so casual a miracle here that people didn't even bother to look up.

'We'll be back long before the storm,' Robbie said. He pointed to a bench in the cockpit of the boat and busied himself around her, loosening and tightening lines and lowering a small outboard motor on the stern. He moved with quick competence; he'd done this a million times before.

He'd built this boat. He hadn't said so, but she could feel Robbie in the curve of the bow, the blunt end of the stern. And the name, she realised with a pang, was obviously for his son, William. He'd spent hours making this boat and thinking of his son.

He did not touch her. No slight, almost accidental, meeting of hand and hand; no stolen caress as he went about the business of getting the boat ready to set off. He hadn't kissed her on the dock, but she hadn't expected him to. They were being discreet. But here they were almost alone. No one else was on the dock except for a pair of long-billed, shaggy grey and black birds perched on the roof of one of the fishing boats.

Every inch of her burned to touch him. Just thinking about him made her skin heat and her stomach feel queasy with desire. Her pulse quickened from being close to him. But he worked around her, almost studious in his avoidance. The only contact was the scent of bourbon that followed him like a shadow.

He'd suggested a sail instead of a hotel. And she'd thought of their first sail together. How he'd put his hand over hers on the tiller. Lightly kissed her ear as he taught her how to tighten the line, how to keep the wind in the sail, how to tack to change direction.

If Robbie touched her now, if he kissed her, she would at least be able to feel as if she had no choice. That she was being carried away by passion, that she had an excuse, however wrong, for her actions. Instead, she watched him start the motor and navigate the boat away from the dock, past some little scrubby islands out into open water.

Yesterday she had told her mother that she wanted to do a little bit of shopping for her and Christopher's birthdays, which were both next month. They'd rented a car and gone down to Key West for the day, and were having dinner at a beachfront restaurant under a palm canopy. The surf washed the beach in a steady heart-beat and between waves little birds ran back and forth searching for prey. Emily had sat between Christopher and Polly, which at least hid the fact that both of them were conspicuously not look-ing at her. She could feel the hostility emanating from her sister. Polly's movements were jerky and angry.

Christopher was hardly different at all from the way he nor-mally was. Their conversation in the bathroom might as well have never happened. He had been as courteous as ever, as solicitous of her comfort; he'd been full of genial conversation with her family and when they'd gone to bed that night he had made sure to be in his side of the bed with his eyes closed and the light turned out before she emerged from the bathroom.

They often didn't touch at night, but the gap between them had seemed very cold. Very large.

In the restaurant on Key West, the blazing orange of the sunset had reflected off her mother's glasses. She wore a wide-brimmed hat and hadn't tanned in the way both Polly and Emily had, but the colour of the sky gave her skin a tinge of pink. Charlotte Greaves had lifted her Mai Tai and said, 'This is heaven. This is utter heaven. I've been so worried about you, Emily and Christo-pher. It's such a relief to have you safe and happy with us.'

'I'm just happy the whole family is together,' her father had said. 'Polly has been busy with work, and with the two of you away, it's been lonely. I'm so very proud of you, all three of you.'

'It's all I've wanted,' said her mother. 'All five of us together. I just wish you could find someone to settle down with, Polly, who will make you as happy as Christopher makes Emily.'

And she had tried very hard not to look at Christopher and instead she had tried to look away at all the little hunting birds and caught Polly's eye instead, and her sister was glaring at her with such anger that she had dropped her fork on the floor to give herself an excuse to hide her face under the table for a moment.

She had always been a role model for Polly. Her younger sister had always looked up to her, copied her, stolen her clothes, asked her advice, even though Polly was much more stylish and cool than Emily ever was, even though she was more fun-loving and less serious. She had been used to being Polly's idol.

Seeing the contempt in her face made her feel sick. She barely touched her meal, and passed on dessert.

Robbie turned off the engine as soon as they were in open water and he began to unfurl the mainsail. 'Can I help you?' she asked him.

'No, I can do it more quickly on my own.'

She watched him hoisting the sail and tightening the lines. The muscles in his arms flexing, his hands sure and strong. Two nights ago, he had touched her. He had breathed his secret sadness into her ear.

In the hotel room, she had known it was wrong but she had been too thrilled, too reckless to truly care. She had wanted him too much. But was wanting a good enough reason to ruin everything?

Surely this wanting would stop one day, and then what would she be left with?

Perhaps it had stopped for him already.

One moment the boat was clumsy, fragile, tossed by the waves. The next, the sail had caught the wind and it was powerful and sleek, moving so quickly, with the waves, that the movement was almost undetectable. The sea seemed to be motionless beneath them. And it was silent: nearly silent. Only a splash and a snapping of the sail.

This was like them. Caught up by the forces between them. Moving so fast that they hardly noticed that the rest of the world was stopping still.

'Robbie,' she said.

He was standing by the tiller, eyes on the horizon. When she spoke he looked at her at last. He sat down and held out his arm for her and she slid under it, nestling against his body.

'Do you love me?' he asked her.

She had not said it, not to him. Not since they had first parted, ten years ago.

She nodded.

'Tell me. Say it. Please.'

'I love you.'

His arm tightened around her, or maybe he was just trimming the sail. The scent of alcohol was stronger, here, close to him.

'You've been drinking,' she said.

'I'm always drinking.' He said it in a matter-of-fact voice. 'It drowns out the taste of what I've done and what I am now. I'm not proud of it, but there it is. I'm just like Dad. Just like Dad, in almost every way. Except he liked planes, and I like boats.'

'You don't have to be like him,' Emily said.

'You're a doctor. You know how powerful genetics are.'

'Biology is just biology. It's not destiny.'

'Isn't it?'

He pointed the boat out to sea, away from the shore.

'And William is just like me,' he said. 'He looks like me, talks like me. He uses goddamn sandpaper like me.'

'I wish I could meet him.'

'I wish you could meet him. You'd like him. Right now he thinks I'm his hero.'

'I'm sure you are.'

'I'm not. I'm not anyone's hero.'

'Polly doesn't like me much, either. Not since she found out about us.'

'Tacking,' he said, and she ducked as the boom swung around over her head to the other side of the boat. There was a moment where the boat wavered, unsure of where to go, but then it picked up the wind and they were moving swiftly again, towards land in the distance.

'So that's Key Biscayne,' he said. 'We'll go out there and round

Cape Florida Lighthouse. Have you seen Stiltsville?'

'No,' she said. She didn't want a tour guide.

'It's something to see. A little village of houses in the sea. Built by shipwreckers, gamblers and rum-runners.' Robbie reached into his jacket pocket and took out a flask. He offered it to her, and she shook her head.

'You shouldn't be drinking while you're sailing,' she told him.

'I can sail this boat in my sleep.'

'You still shouldn't be drinking. You just said that you shouldn't.'

'I just said that I drink, and I know I shouldn't, but I do it anyway.' He took a drink from the flask and put it back in his pocket. 'Like you know you shouldn't be here, but you are.'

'Robbie,' she said desperately, 'we only have a little while. Let's not spoil it.'

'A little while today? Or forever?'

'I'm leaving the country next week.'

'So this is it. Then it's back to being unhappy, for both of us.' He jerked the tiller, and the sail flapped.

'What's the alternative? This is wrong. All the reasons why we parted back then, they're still there. And now there are too many people, Robbie. We'd hurt too many people.'

He didn't answer, or look at her. He took another drink.

'Christopher knows I've met you again,' she told him. 'He's said that he'll look the other way while we're here, but it has to end when we get back to England.'

'And you . . . agree with that?'

'I don't see what other choice I have. It's not just him. It's Polly, my father, my mother—'

'Your mother hates everything about me. Your father too, I imagine.'

'We'd hurt everyone, Robbie, if we stayed together. Everyone we're supposed to love.'

'What you're saying is that you don't love me more than everyone else.'

'How can anyone even begin to make a decision like that? Love isn't a finite thing that you can measure. It's my family. And I've known Christopher for a very long time.'

'Do you love him?'

'Of course I do.'

'The same way you love me?'

She swallowed. She looked away from Robbie, to the coast they'd come from: the trees and the white masts and the buildings of white and pink, like a city made of candy floss.

'Not the same way,' she said quietly. 'But I love him. Very much. He's a good man. He doesn't deserve any of this.'

'He's a better man than I am. I can't look the other way. I can't forget that you're with another man who isn't me.'

'He's not forgetting. He's . . . giving me time.'

'I'm not a good man,' said Robbie. 'I'm not good without you, and I don't know if I could be good with you, either. I drink. I'm a horrible husband. I'm probably a horrible father. I don't know why I think that being with you would change anything.'

'Robbie,' she said, and put her hand on his knee.

'I don't love Marie. I shouldn't have married her. But I'm responsible for her now. And I love my son. I love William.'

'Of course you do.'

'She's going to take him away from me.'

She wasn't prepared for the cold that seized her – the horror that another woman, someone she'd never met, could know their secret, that it could have spiralled so far out of control, that this woman, Robbie's wife, could take such calculated revenge.

'She knows too? About us?'

He shook his head. 'She knows that I'm not committed to her. She knows that I don't love her as I should. She knows I come home late every night and I make every excuse not to touch her. She knows I've never told her about what I did in the war, and I don't tell her what I really feel and what I really want. She deserves better. She deserves for me to be a better person, but I can't.

222

Or she deserves someone better than me, but then I won't see my son again.'

'She couldn't take him away from you. He's your son.'

'She could. She's got steel in her. She could do it, if she wanted to. She could move away and stop me from seeing him. If her family closed ranks, I wouldn't have a chance.'

'But legally—'

'Emily, I'm a drunk. A court would choose Marie.'

'You're not a drunk. You could stop drinking.'

He didn't reply.

'I'm not a good person,' she said. 'When I came here, all I could think about was my patients. And now all I can think about is you.'

He took his eyes off the horizon for the first time to look at her. 'We can't do it, can we? We can't have anything but this.'

'No.'

'And this used to be enough. When I first met you, all I wanted was to live in the present. To spend as much time with you as I could and savour every moment. But this isn't enough. I want our past back. I want a future.'

'But neither of these can happen. Now is all we've got. Today, and the next few days.'

'It isn't good enough.'

He put out his hand for hers. His hands were so different from hers, from Christopher's: tanned, weather-beaten, calloused. She held on to him tightly. Something rumbled in the distance, from the towering clouds.

'So this is the last time,' he said softly.

She nodded.

'It doesn't seem fair to have to do this twice in a lifetime,' he said.

'But nothing has really changed. We still can't be together. We have even more reasons not to be together now.'

'I love you,' he said.

'I love you,' she said.

Where was the sun? The sea had gone as dark as the sky. Even the white sail was muted and grey. Emily took her hand from Robbie's. When she'd said goodbye ten years before, she'd tried her best not to look at him. She didn't want to see his face, see his pain, in case it tempted her to touch him and to prevent him from leaving.

This time she knew what it was like to hold someone for years in your memory instead of in your arms. She knew how features blurred, voices faded, touches dissolved. So she looked at Robbie and tried to imprint him on her memory, to be able to take him out when she was alone and felt strong enough. When she was safe, and able to think about this moment when she had been perfectly loved and perfectly alone.

'Emily. Please.' Robbie stood and reached for her, leaning forward, and several things happened at once. A wave hit the boat and he stumbled. His hand let go of the tiller. The wind gusted, bringing the boat round. The mainsail flapped, the boom swung, striking Robbie on the head and sweeping him over the side of the boat.

She heard the splash before she understood what had made it. The boom kept going, though slower than it had been, and she fended it off with her hands and then twisted to look over the side of the boat.

'Robbie!'

She could see him, a dark shape in the dark water. He wasn't moving.

There was a life preserver near the tiller, attached to the boat with a rope. Emily grabbed it and threw herself over the side of the boat into the water. It was nearly as warm as her blood and she struck forward, swimming frantically to reach Robbie. Her clothes weighed her down, her shoes. She was not a good swimmer. She couldn't see him any more. Salt water stung her eyes and the waves had come up with the wind.

Her foot struck something and frantically she reached down into the water, diving, to find it: material, his jacket. She grabbed hold and kicked her legs hard to pull Robbie up to the surface. So heavy.

Thirteen years old, in the pool in Norwich with the other Girl Guides . . . She tried to remember her lifesaving lessons but the water there had been calm and tame. She kicked and kicked, got herself on her back with Robbie's head leaning back against her shoulder, her arm around his chest, the other looped through the preserver. He was a dead weight in the water. His eyes were closed.

'Robbie,' she gasped, salt water in her mouth. She looked over her shoulder and the boat was several feet away. The rope anchoring the mainsail had come loose and the sail was flapping back and forth, useless for the moment, until it caught the wind by chance.

Emily kicked her legs, trying to get them closer to the boat. Robbie might be dead already: the blow might have been hard enough to kill him. He might have inhaled water and be drowning even now, even though she had his face out of the water. Dry drowning they called it. She couldn't check for breathing or feel for a pulse: she was too busy swimming, and she didn't dare. His mouth was open, his eyes closed, his skin pale. His hands floated just below the surface.

She kicked and kicked, holding him tight. Her shoes were stopping her so she toed them off, letting them fall away into the deep sea. Her skirt tangled around her legs. She wished she'd worn trousers. She thought about reaching the boat only not to be able to haul Robbie's body aboard. What would she do? Cling on to the side, cling on to him, praying someone would come and rescue them? Had there been other boats out? She hadn't noticed. But this was a busy place – surely someone would come by.

But when? Could she hold on to Robbie until then?

They could die here. They could both die. Not to embrace and to part, but to embrace and to sink, together, to wash up on the shore days or weeks from now. Their bodies returned to the families whom they had decided not to leave.

But they'd never know that. Christopher, and her parents, Polly, Robbie's wife and son. They'd never know that Robbie and Emily had chosen them over their own happiness. They'd see this death as a betrayal: the two of them had died in illicit, snatched hours.

And if that didn't happen? If she lived and he didn't, if he was dead already and she had to live the rest of her life knowing she hadn't saved him? Who, or what, would that be a betrayal of?

'Please,' she sobbed, kicking and kicking and getting nowhere, 'please wake up, Robbie. Please. Don't leave me alone.'

Water in her eyes, in her nose, in her mouth. Burning salt and his body wanting to drift away. Lightning flashed and thunder boomed, incredibly close. Her muscles ached and burned, her fingers clenched in the cloth of his jacket. His hair was a dark slick on his head. A wave hit them and her face went under.

She felt his arm tighten around her.

He was awake – he was alive.

The boat loomed blue and white out of the water. The hull was impossibly high. 'Hold on,' said Robbie, and she held tight to the rope while he hauled himself up on to the boat and turned to pull her up. Banging her ribs on the boat, knocking the breath out of her, scraping her legs, but then she was there. Safe. Gasping for air, shivering, holding tight to Robbie. He clung to her. His breath came in short gasps. It was raining now, hard, warm rain that made the air nearly as liquid as the ocean. The boat rocked.

'I can't do it,' she said. Her teeth chattered. 'I can't do it.'

'You can, you can do anything, you will be all right,' he said, smoothing her wet hair back, kissing her wet cheeks with his wet lips. Thunder crashed. 'You are OK. You are safe. I'm so sorry.'

She kissed him and tasted salt. She was shaking badly now. 'I can't leave you. I can't – I thought you were dead.'

'I'm not dead. I'm stupid. I'm all right.' But she saw blood flowing down his face now, from where the boom had hit him. She touched it, wondering at its colour on her fingers, before instinct kicked back in and she pulled his head down so she could look for the wound. Her hands shook as she put pressure on it. She seemed to have no strength.

'I thought you were dead and I'd lost you and it was the most terrifying thing I've ever felt,' she told him through chattering teeth. 'I thought about what it would be like going on living with you dead and I don't want to do it.'

'I'm not dead. I'm not dead. It's all right.' He soothed hands down her back.

'I don't want to live without you. I never want to live without you.'

He pulled back. There was blood on his face, and he was shaking now, too. Shock. Hypothermia, maybe, even in this warm water. They should get a blanket.

Lightning so close, it left an after-image on her retinas: Robbie's silhouette in black and red. Thunder.

'What are you saying?' he asked.

'I'm saying we've already betrayed them. We betrayed them from the minute we met each other. I can't love him as I should, and you can't love her as you should. If we'd died together, no one would know that we'd decided never to see each other again. We belong together. I can't love anyone as much as I love you, Robbie. I can't do it. I've tried and I can't.'

'What are you saying?' he asked again, except this time he whispered it.

'I can't lose you again. It's all hollow in the centre of things without you.'

He swallowed. Staring, pale, into her face.

'I can't lose you either,' he said.

And he held her tight up against him, boat wandering free in the storm.

*

227

There were dry clothes in Robbie's locker below. She rolled up the sleeves of his shirt and the hems of his trousers. He had only one rain slicker and she stayed below, shivering, wrapped in the only blanket, as he piloted the boat to shore. The cabin was tiny and steamed up immediately. She watched him through the hatch and thought about concussion and shock but her thoughts kept returning over and over to what they'd said. What they had done.

It was decided now, whatever would happen. She tried to summon something: joy, guilt, even fear. But she couldn't seem to. That would come later. Right now she could only think: it was decided.

When they reached the marina, Robbie pulled the slicker over both of them to shelter them from the rain and they walked in step to a little hut with a palm canopy, with a rickety wooden picnic table underneath it.

'¿Recibió mojado, Bob?' called the woman in the window of the hut.

'Sí. Cafecito, Analena.'

They sat at the picnic table and in a few minutes, the woman brought them two tiny cups of coffee. Emily drank hers down immediately: it was incredibly sweet and incredibly strong. '¿Podemos por favor tener otro?' she asked the woman, who nodded. The rain drummed on the canopy and dripped from the palm fronds.

'I can't stop thinking of that piece of music,' she said to Robbie. 'The Bach we listened to, that night we met. It's stuck in my head.'

'The music that begins where it ends.'

'And that ring. That ring you gave me, that I gave back to you.'

'I still have it. It's in a drawer at home.'

Her knee touched Robbie's under the table.

'We don't have a choice,' she said. 'We've made the decision and it's over. The ending is the same as the beginning. Isn't it?'

He nodded. 'I don't know if we ever really had a choice.'

'Do you think she'll really take your boy away from you?'

'I don't know. I hope not.'

'I don't think I can do that to you,' she said softly. 'Or to him.'

He sighed. 'The thing is that she's going to leave me. Now, or ten years from now. I can't be who she needs me to be. Even if I stopped drinking, if I were home every night. I still couldn't be that person. Not for her. It's better to be honest.'

'We've betrayed them anyway. I betrayed Christopher before I even married him, because I knew he'd always be second best. But your son shouldn't get caught up in it.'

'I'll try. I might not have a choice.'

'We'll both try, together.'

Analena brought them two more tiny coffees. As Emily lifted hers to drink it, her eyes caught on the flash of her diamond ring, the gold band beneath it. She put down her coffee and slid the rings off her finger.

On the rough, weather-beaten table, they looked like the relics of a life that had been unmade. Another country, another time, another set of decisions, a different ending.

Robbie slid off his own ring and put it with hers. A bigger circle, also made of gold. There was a band of pale skin beneath it and when Emily looked at her own bare finger, she had a matching band.

'I'll never leave you again,' he told her.

PART FIVE

1962

Chapter Twenty-Nine

13 April 1962
Cambridge, England

She was rushing across the station concourse, late to meet Polly's train, searching for a glimpse of curly hair, when she saw him.

He was wearing a denim jacket and he had a rucksack slung over his shoulder, and he had paused, bowing his head to light his cigarette with a match cupped in his hands, when he glanced up – and he saw her too. Even at a distance, even across a crowded station, she could see his eyes were dark.

She couldn't breathe. He stared at her as she was staring at him, and this was completely not something you did, you didn't stare at strange men in stations, but the side of his mouth quirked up in a smile. It wasn't a flirtatious smile, not exactly – it was more like . . .

. . . more like wonder.

She looked away, then looked back. He was still staring at her. He seemed to have forgotten about his cigarette. He raised his hand, as if to wave, and she raised hers, as if to wave back.

Hello, she thought.

The tannoy spoke. 'The train arriving on platform three is the delayed eleven fifty-five train from Norwich.'

Delayed. Platform three. She turned away from the man and saw the train pulling in on the platform. Automatically, she hurried towards it.

But when she glanced back over her shoulder, he was still there, still watching her. It was almost as if they knew each other already.

'Em!' Polly's voice, and the sound of running footsteps. She collided with Emily in a tangle of skinny arms and legs. 'I am so excited,' she began right away. 'I sat on the train next to this group of boys and they kept on looking at me but I didn't look back, I just looked out the window but I watched them out of the corner of my eye. Do you think they thought I was older because I was travelling by myself?'

Emily regarded Polly's untidy hair, her skinny frame, her freckles and her crooked-toothed smile. If anything, she looked younger than twelve.

'They thought you were a sophisticated, independent woman,' said Emily. 'They probably thought you were a student here.'

Polly punched her arm and giggled. 'I'll never even get into Cambridge. I'm not as clever as you.'

'Keep studying,' said Emily, taking Polly's suitcase. 'Oof. What have you got in here, rocks?'

Polly leaned close and whispered. 'Make-up. Don't tell Mum!'

'Where did you get make-up?'

'Woolworths. I've been saving my pocket money and hiding it in my wardrobe. I wanted to put some on while I was on the train but the lavatory was occupied the whole time. Also, I brought some records to play. I wanted to bring my record player but it wouldn't fit and you have one anyway, right?'

Emily began to walk them down the platform, Polly skipping beside her. Her hands were shaking a bit. She gripped the suitcase more tightly to stop them. 'I've got my portable, but there's a better one in the JCR. I mean, the Junior Common Room.'

Polly inhaled in rapture. 'The Junior Common Room. I'm going to hang out in *the Junior Common Room*.'

Emily suppressed a smile. 'Have you eaten?'

'Mum gave me sandwiches.' She held up a squashed paper bag with some grease stains on it. 'But I was too excited to eat on the train. Also, they were egg. Who eats egg sandwiches on a train? Everyone would smell them.' She theatrically tossed the bag into a bin as they passed. 'Goodbye, stinky sandwiches. Don't tell Mum.'

'I have a feeling that's going to be a continued refrain this weekend.'

'But you won't tell her, will you?'

'Do you think I'm likely to tell Mum anything, after everything I had to do to get her to let you stay with me overnight? I'd be in just as much trouble as you. More, because I'm supposed to be the responsible adult.'

They crossed the concourse and Emily hesitated by the exit, searching the people waiting.

'What are you looking for?' Polly asked.

'No one. I mean, nothing.' She looked around again briefly, though she was chastising herself even as she did it. She wouldn't recognise him again even if she did see him. And he was long gone, anyway.

She linked her arm through her younger sister's. 'I'm glad you didn't eat the stinky sandwiches, because we're meeting Christopher for lunch.'

'At a *student pub*?' She said it with the same reverence she'd pronounced 'Junior Common Room'.

'In Fitzbillies.'

'Can I have a real coffee?'

Emily rolled her eyes in the way expected of an elder sister. 'If this is what you're like without caffeine, I can't imagine you with a coffee under your belt.'

'But can I?'

'Oh, all right. If only in the spirit of scientific enquiry.'

'Don't—'

'I won't tell Mum.'

She took a last look around outside the station before starting down Station Road towards the centre of town.

Polly kept up a running commentary on everything they passed and saw. She'd been to Cambridge more than once, but everything seemed to be new this time, without their parents with her. She mentioned students on bicycles, the buildings, the shops, even the trees, and Emily tried her best to be attentive and not look up and down the pavements, peer through the windows of cafés and shops, looking for dark hair and a denim jacket. She caught a flash of faded blue in the window of a used-book shop and paused, staring. Polly proceeded several paces before realising she was alone.

'What's wrong with you?' she demanded, returning to where Emily was transfixed on the pavement. The flash of blue was gone, disappeared between the bookshelves.

'Nothing,' said Emily quickly. 'Can we – do you mind if we pop in here for a minute?'

'Books?' said Polly doubtfully. 'Can't we go in a record shop instead?'

'I just need to look for something.' Her heart was in her throat as she pushed open the door. Emily loved this shop but she hardly noticed the warm scent of books, the colourful spines. She hurried to the end of the first bookshelf and peered around it. There was no one there.

What am I going to say? Am I going to say anything? What could I possibly say?

I'll say – I'll say 'Hello'. That's a start.

She swallowed and went deeper into the shop. It was nearly deserted on this sunny day, and she passed shelves and aisles, from Fiction (General, Alphabetical) to Poetry to Art History to Chemistry until she heard a male cough in the row next to her.

Emily closed her eyes for a moment. She bit her lip.

Just say 'Hello'.

She walked deliberately to the end of Divinity and rounded the corner.

'Hell—' she began and the man standing there, in a light blue jacket with an open book in his hand, turned around and he was in his forties with hardly any hair at all.

'Sorry,' she said, and retreated quickly to where Polly was

standing by the door, gazing sulkily at a small selection of science fiction paperbacks.

'I didn't find what I was looking for. Sorry. Let's go to lunch.'

Christopher was already in Fitzbillies, shoved into a corner table in the busy café. He stood when they entered. 'Hullo Poll,' he said, ruffling her hair. Polly pulled a face at him at the little-girl treatment.

'Paulina,' she announced. 'I want to be called Paulina while I'm here.'

'But that's not your name, is it? I thought you were a proper Polly.' Christopher smiled at Emily and took the suitcase from her, placing it carefully near the side of their table. 'What would you like, Poll? An orange squash?'

'A coffee.'

'I promised her one,' Emily told him. 'Do you want to go up and get it, Polly? You can get one for each of us.'

'Paulina,' corrected her sister.

'Paulina. And do you want to order our food as well? I'll have a cheese toastie, and Christopher will have Welsh rarebit. And order what you like for yourself?'

'Welsh rarebit, ugh.'

She wrinkled her nose and stuck her tongue out at Christopher, who looked sternly at her. Emily fished the money out of her purse and gave it to Polly quickly before Christopher could argue about whose turn it was to pay. Polly went to the counter. There was quite a long queue, which she joined with an air of happy importance.

'She got here all right then,' Christopher said, pulling out a chair for Emily and sitting back down. 'Sorry I couldn't go to the station with you.'

'She's convinced all the boys on the train were flirting with her.'

'She's a child!'

'In her own mind, she's twenty at least.' Emily smiled fondly at

237

her sister, who was studying the menu on the wall as if she were making a grave decision. 'Mum didn't want her to come, but Dad convinced her.'

She didn't have to explain any more than that to Christopher, who had met her family, and been home with her on several occasions. She'd met his parents too. He had an overprotective mother who made even her hypercritical mother look like an amateur when it came to nagging.

'Here.' Christopher pushed a pound note across the table at her, and she shook her head and pushed it back to him.

'I can afford it,' she said.

'I can better afford it.'

'I've saved up, and I like to give my sister a treat.'

He didn't put the note back in his pocket, but began folding it into a tight rectangle.

'Did you get your essay done?' she asked.

He shook his head, a movement that made his glasses slide down his nose, but his hands were too busy folding and refolding the pound to push them back up. 'It's in on Monday morning. I've got to do more work on it today and tomorrow, so I can't spend the weekend with the two of you. I'm sorry, Emily.'

'Oh, that's too bad,' said Emily, though she had to admit to a small speck of relief that she wouldn't spend the weekend mediating between her sister, who wanted to act grown-up, and her best friend, who wanted to act like Polly's indulgent uncle. 'Can you join us in Hall for dinner? You have to eat, even if you've got a lot of work to do. I can have another guest.'

'I'll do that. Emily—' He glanced at Polly, who still had several people ahead of her in the queue. He unfolded the note, and rolled it into a narrow cylinder with his long fingers. 'I need to ask you something.'

'Oh yes, sorry, you were about to say something when I had to run for the station?' She'd completely forgotten about it in the rush to meet her sister in time, and then those split seconds as she'd entered the station, when she'd seen . . . whoever it was.

Her throat tightened a bit at the thought of whoever it was. His eyes had been so intense, so direct.

She didn't think she had ever been looked at that way before, with so much naked desire. Out of nowhere, from a stranger.

Christopher had twisted the pound note tighter, into a thin roll.

'Chris, what did that poor money ever do to you?' She laid her hand on top of his for a second to stop him from tearing it and he looked up so sharply that she pulled her hand away.

'What is it?' she asked.

'On Monday night – I mean, any night is fine, but I say Monday because I'll have my essay done and Poll will have gone home. So, on Monday night, do you – will you have dinner with me?'

'All right,' replied Emily, wondering what all the money folding and babbling was about. Christopher and she ate together several times a week, alternating Formal Halls between their two colleges and other times grabbing a sandwich between lectures. 'Why Monday?' she asked, sweeping a bit of spilled sugar off the table and on to the floor. 'Is there something on the menu you don't like?'

'I mean, have dinner. Properly. In a restaurant.'

It was her turn to look up sharply. 'A restaurant? You mean not in college?'

'I just . . . I've been wanting to ask you for ages, and my sister said it would be best if I – if I asked you on a date. Somewhere nice.'

She stared at Christopher's familiar face: pale, with his shock of sandy hair falling over his forehead, his horn-rimmed glasses slipping down his nose. The same face she'd been looking at since they'd first become friends, in between Professor McAvoy's anatomy lectures in the first month of their first year. He'd been one of the few medics who *hadn't* tried to ask her out. She hadn't had any illusions that the invitations to drinks and films and late-night revision sessions had been out of any intrinsic attractiveness on her part. It was pure curiosity, and a point of male honour, for the other medics to proposition the very few female students on their course. She'd turned them all down, and now, midway through their second year, they'd stopped asking.

But Christopher had never tried. Christopher had always been her safe, easy, no-expectations friend, her brilliant friend who inspired her, her thoughtful friend who helped her and noticed when she was struggling or sad. Some of the other medics in their year and people at their respective colleges thought they were a couple because they spent so much time together. She and Christopher had laughed about it.

Had she been the only one who was actually laughing?

'Christopher . . .'

'I know,' he said fervently. There was a spot of pink on each of his cheeks. 'I know, you've never thought of me that way, but I can't – I can't carry on as we have been without at least trying.'

His hand was less than an inch from hers on the table. She could feel the warmth from it. His blue eyes were wide and almost . . . fearful?

'Can we try?' he asked. 'If it doesn't work, we can go back to how we were. We can pretend it never happened. But can we please try, Emily? Please?'

This was Christopher. Christopher who had gone with her to choose a new second-hand bike when hers was stolen, Christopher of the late-night revision sessions in the library, reciting Latin names together, Christopher who liked to line up his scalpels during dissections so that the bottoms of the handles were perfectly even, Christopher who knew just how she liked her tea with half a sugar in it, on whose safe chest she had rested her head on lazy summer term afternoons on the Backs, listening to his heart beating whilst she made daisy chains and drilled him on neurobiology.

He was handsome, when you thought about it. He had a narrow face, blue eyes, a straight nose, a strong chin to offset his glasses. He was always smartly dressed. He was public school to her grammar school, and unlike most men she knew, he didn't resent the fact that Emily was better at their subject than he was. Her friend Laura had had a crush on him this autumn, though nothing had ever come of it.

Perhaps this was why.

Polly arrived at their table, a little breathless. 'I need more money,' she demanded.

Emily turned to her, glad of the interruption. 'I gave you plenty.'

'Yes, but I wanted a Chelsea bun too.'

'Polly, don't be—'

'Use this.' Christopher handed Polly the tortured pound note. 'And order a bun for me too, will you? Do you want one, Emily?'

She shook her head.

'I might have another coffee after,' said Polly in triumph, bearing away the money. Emily watched her go and wondered how to answer Christopher.

'Well?' he asked her.

Emily looked at his mouth. She'd seen his mouth eating, talking, chewing on a pencil, smiling, pursed in worry. She'd never particularly thought about it as a mouth in its own right. He had smooth lips and his teeth were a little crooked, but in an endearing way.

She tried to imagine kissing that mouth, where their noses would go, how Christopher would look that close up. Where they would put their hands, which were used to not touching each other.

She didn't have a lot of experience to base it on; she'd only been kissed once before, in sixth form, by Edward Norris, and as he'd been eating pickled onions it wasn't particularly pleasant. Despite all the propositioning from the male medics, Emily wasn't really the kind of girl that boys thought about kissing. She was too studious, too serious. She didn't spend much time thinking about kissing.

241

Though she hadn't had to imagine kissing that man at the station, the one in the blue jacket. His gaze had felt like a kiss in itself.

But that was a single glance from a stranger. That was silliness, a bit of fantasy, hormones running wild, too many times watching *Brief Encounter*. A little bit of madness that sent her running into book shops after a glimpse of blue.

Real love wasn't like that. She'd seen her mother and her father; she'd studied biology and psychology. Real love was based on mutual respect and trust, on shared goals, things in common. Real love lasted a lifetime, not a split second.

'All right,' she said to Christopher. 'Let's try.'

'Let's try it,' he said to the girl with him. 'I'll push if you pay.'

The shadows were getting long, later than they would where he was from; they were fifteen or so degrees further north here. Robbie liked how the buildings were all scrunched tight together and how they seemed to grow bigger as the day progressed. They had an hour or two till sunset, and the weather was warm enough that Robbie had abandoned his jacket on the grass as he lay here beside the girl, enjoying the sunshine, relaxed and a little sleepy from the beer.

The girl screwed up her face. 'I paid in the pub.'

'So you did. OK then, it's my turn.' He jumped up and helped her up, too. She was cute, blonde with an hourglass figure, wearing a flowery dress, worked mornings in the newsagents on St Andrew's Street and hadn't taken much persuasion to join him for half a pint of bitter shandy, and then a few more halves, while she told him about how much she hated her job and that she lived in a flat on the Huntingdon Road with two other girls and that she had her own room.

The room of her own was the key, of course.

She clung on to his hand, a little unsteady on her feet, and giggled. Her name was . . . it was . . .

'Cynthia,' he said, and he knew he'd got it right, mostly because she didn't slap him. 'Don't fall over. I need you to talk to the guy watching the boats.'

'Talk to him?' She wrinkled up her nose. It was a common thing with her; she'd have wrinkles one day if she wasn't careful.

'Flirt with him. You're good at that.' He nudged her and she giggled. 'I only need five minutes and then I'll meet you—' he pointed upstream, under the bridge— 'that way. OK?'

'Kiss me first.'

He checked to make sure the boy with the punts wasn't watching and then kissed her swiftly on her lips. They tasted of lipstick and beer. 'Now go. Turn on the charm, will you?'

She wiggled her hips in an exaggerated fashion as she went down the bank to the place where the punts were moored. He watched as she approached the boy. He couldn't hear her from here, but he knew what she was saying: she was asking him for a cigarette, which was exactly the same line he'd used on her earlier this afternoon. It worked, because the boy got a hopeful look on his face and dug into his breast pocket for a pack.

While he was bent over her, lighting the cigarette with matches that kept going out, Rob slipped behind them and around to the bank. The punts were moored to each other, side by side. He jumped on to the first one lightly enough so that it hardly rocked and swiftly made his way across them like stepping stones until he'd reached the one on the end. He stashed his duffel back in the bottom, threw the line off and pushed away downstream, free. He waited until he was several yards away to get up on the back and use the pole, ducking under the bridge. Glancing back over his shoulder, he saw that Cynthia was still deep in conversation with the boy, who hadn't noticed a thing.

He'd never been on this particular type of boat, but he pushed the punt with efficient jabs of the pole, getting into the rhythm immediately: into the water, push away, use the pole to steer the craft like a rudder. The punt was simple, shallow and wide-bottomed.

It was sturdily made, which it had to be; although the river was shallow here, the current subtle, the prow and sides of the boat were covered in dents and scrapes from poor handling. It was well enough looked after, though, probably re-varnished earlier this spring.

Robbie steered it past colleges made of warm red brick and yellow sandstone, windows, under a willow and a mullioned medieval-looking bridge. Everything here was so *old*. And the buildings . . . he'd never seen anything like it. Seen from the river, they seemed even taller but more like human dwellings, with moss growing on them and windows open to the air.

When he got to a place where the river opened out a bit, with grass on either side of the bank and buildings rising in the near distance like wedding cakes, he slowed down and lingered until Cynthia appeared. He held out a hand and helped her on to the boat, though she made it rock and wobble as she got in.

'He's going to be angry when he sees a boat missing!' she said.

'We'll have it back before he even notices.' He launched them away from the bank with a strong push.

'Watch out!' Another punt, full of what looked like students with their jackets of tweed, lay directly in their path. Robbie knew their type: the idle rich who bought the boats Robbie made and owned the boats Robbie sailed and who paid him to ferry them back and forth in his dinghy and to haul their boats out of the water every winter and sand and repair and varnish and paint. Sometimes they paid him to give them sailing lessons, though Robbie tried to avoid that when he could – unless they had a pretty daughter.

The man on the back of the other boat held up his punting pole as if he were going to fend Robbie's boat off. The action made his boat wobble, and the passengers held on to the sides, even though there was little chance of such a wide-bottomed boat capsizing in totally calm waters.

Robbie put some strength into his steering and they veered

safely to the side, missing the other boat by inches.

'Tosser!' yelled one of the tweed jackets and Robbie laughed. They were soon far ahead, gliding easily along the smooth, green river between smooth, green banks.

Cynthia had settled back into the boat, facing him so she was riding backward. 'Do you like my nails?' She waved her fingers at him. The nails were painted pink.

'Great.'

'I got lipstick the same colour but you can't really tell unless you hold them together.' She put her fingers on her lips, pouting as if she were kissing them, and waited for him to appreciate her.

'Perfect,' said Robbie.

'It's the same one was in *Vogue* last week.'

'Nice.'

She lowered her hand and looked around. 'This is quite boring, though, isn't it? Just sitting in a boat.'

'It's good practice for when I go to Venice.' And he liked it: the green, almost ripe, scent of the water, the stately pace of the punt, the liquid dip of the pole and the ripple the drops made when he lifted it out of the water. It had a nice rhythm to it.

'This doesn't even go fast,' Cynthia said.

'Oh, I can make it go faster.' He put more arms into it, pushed harder, enjoying the burn in his muscles.

Cynthia yawned. She trailed her fingers in the water, then evidently remembered her manicure and took them out again, wiping them on her dress.

They passed under another willow that caressed Robbie's face with soft narrow leaves. He was just going to suggest they stopped the punt somewhere secluded for a little while so he could possibly show her something that wasn't so boring, when he heard a female yelp of alarm.

Ahead of them, a punter had got her pole stuck in the mud and she'd held on while the boat went on without her. She clung to the pole in the centre of the river, her feet dabbling in the water.

The shriek hadn't come from her; it was a young girl in the boat she'd left, kneeling in the bottom with her arms outstretched towards her suspended pilot. 'Emily!' she cried, drifting in slow motion with momentum and the current.

Robbie didn't stop to think. 'Try to catch the boat with the girl,' he said to Cynthia, laying the pole down in the punt and immediately jumping off the back and into the river.

The water wasn't cold, nor was it deep; he'd guess three and a half feet at the most, but it was quicker to swim. He reached the stranded girl on the pole in seconds and stood up, laughing, his arms outstretched and dripping. 'Jump,' he said, and she looked at him.

It was the girl from the station. The one with the blue eyes.

She stared at him as if she was trying to figure out if he were a figure of her imagination.

'Jump,' he told her again, 'or you'll get wet.'

She let go of the pole and slid into his arms. She was light; the fabric of her blouse was soft in his hand. Her body was warm and slender.

'It's you,' she said.

'It's you.'

'What are you doing here?'

'Rescuing you.' He began wading towards the bank. The bottom of the river was very muddy; it crawled into his shoes and made walking difficult. He couldn't have cared less.

'The pole got stuck,' she said.

'I'm glad it did.' Her eyes were deeper blue than he'd thought, or maybe it was the sunshine that made them seem so. The same colour the ocean had been the first time he'd ever seen it, aged sixteen, and never having been anywhere but Ohio in his life: a few shades darker than the bluest of cloudless skies. She had fair skin, freckles on her nose, a white parting, straight, light brown hair tucked behind one ear and escaping the other.

'Put your arm around my neck,' he told her, and she did. It

brought her face closer to his. She smelled of daffodils and sunshine. He could feel her heart beating against his chest.

He reached the bank far too soon and set her down gently on the grass. She scrambled to her feet as he climbed up beside her.

'You're sopping wet.'

'But you're almost dry, so it's worth it.' He stared at her again. She had a waist like a willow branch. She wore a white blouse, tucked into a blue skirt. And those eyes, like every freedom he'd ever tasted. 'What's your name?'

'I'm Emily.'

'I'm Robert.' He held out his hand to her, a silly formality, but he wanted to touch her again. Touch her bare skin.

She put her hand in his and he curved his fingers round it.

The world didn't stop. Not exactly. He still felt his soaked clothes clinging to his body, still felt the sunshine on his shoulders and the top of his head; he still breathed and dripped water on to the grass but all of that had become more, somehow. Bigger and brighter. Louder and wetter and warmer. And the feeling of her little hand in his, like it belonged there.

'Wow,' he said, and she took a step closer to him, just one, enough so he could smell her hair.

'Robert!'

'Emily!'

Oh. Yeah.

They turned at the same time, hands still joined, to look at the river. The young girl in Emily's boat was holding on to the punt that Robbie had abandoned, which had obviously been carried by momentum. Cynthia sat in the back, her arms folded against her chest, the punt pole lying on the bottom of the boat, untouched.

'Useless,' muttered Robbie, but he couldn't wipe the smile off his face. 'Who is that? Your sister?'

'Help!' cried Polly. 'We're going to drift into the sea!'

'My melodramatic little sister Polly,' confirmed Emily. She hadn't removed her hand from his. 'Who's that in your boat?'

'My date.'

'Oh.' She tried to withdraw her hand, then, but Robbie kept it.

'What are you doing later tonight?' he asked her.

'I'm entertaining my little sister. And you've got a date.' She managed to pull her hand away from his.

'I don't have to have a date.'

She screwed up her eyes. 'Really? You did this very nice thing by rescuing me and now you have to ruin it by being an utter bounder?'

'*Bounder*?' he repeated, amused. 'Do you really say that?'

'Robert! I'm waiting!'

'I'll go and fetch them.' Emily stepped towards the bank, but Robbie caught her by the wrist.

'And get all wet? That would mean I'd rescued you for nothing.' He called, 'Cynthia, tie the boats together with that line. And you've got a pole there. Try pushing yourself towards the bank with it.'

Cynthia continued frowning, her arms folded, making no move towards the pole, as the boats continued to drift slowly downstream. They were quite a distance away from Robbie and Emily now.

'I'll do it!' yelled Polly. She grabbed the line trailing from the bow of her punt and scrambled up and over the side of her boat into Cynthia's. She tied the two bowlines together and then reached for the pole.

'Your little sister is something,' Robbie told Emily. 'Does that run in the family?'

Polly nearly whacked Cynthia in the face with the pole, getting it into the river.

'She's never been punting before,' said Emily.

'Have you?'

'Only as a passenger.'

'I'm not sure she's going to manage,' said Robbie. He couldn't seem to make himself let go of Emily's wrist. He thought about slipping his arm around her waist and wondered if she'd slap him, considering he'd admitted he had a date currently drifting away from them down the river. On balance, he thought it was worth the risk.

She didn't slap him.

Polly pushed, grunting, and the boat wavered very slightly towards the bank. 'How was that?' she yelled. 'Should I do it again?'

'I'd better go after them.' Reluctantly, he released Emily's waist and jumped back into the water.

It only took a few minutes for him to reach them. Polly was pulling the pole up to have another try. She narrowly missed his head as he stood up next to the punt.

'Whoa,' he said. 'Don't kill me, please.'

'Oh, sorry,' said Polly. 'Thank you for rescuing us.'

'No problem.' Cynthia was staring daggers at him, but he smiled at her and began pulling the linked punts towards the bank.

'It's very romantic,' said Polly. 'My name is Paulina Greaves, what's yours?'

'Robert Brandon the Second.'

'Are you *American*?'

'Yes, ma'am.'

'Wow.'

Having the punts tied side by side was a little awkward and the boat full of snooty students glided past them, taunting, but Robbie managed to get his boats to the bank without too much trouble. Once there, Polly hopped out immediately and Cynthia stayed in the boat, on her high horse. Standing waist-deep in the water, Robbie lashed the boats together more efficiently and then climbed out on to the bank to moor them to a pole sunk in the bank for this purpose.

Emily had walked the short distance along the bank to meet them and her sister was chattering a mile a minute to her.

'Did you see how I jumped from our boat to the other one? I think I could have steered it to the bank if Robert hadn't come back. Did you notice he's American? That girl he's with is snotty, though, isn't she?'

'Polly,' Emily said, warningly.

'Do you want to get out?' Robbie asked, holding out his hand to Cynthia, who merely glared. Shrugging, he went to Emily.

'You were doing a fine job, Paulina,' he told her. 'You would have got the hang of it eventually. I can show you some tricks, if you want.'

'Yes! That would be—'

'No,' said Emily. 'Robert isn't free to spend time with us. He's got a prior commitment.'

'But Em—'

'His date is waiting for him. Isn't that right, Robbie?'

There was a loud 'harumph' from the punt.

'At least let me get your pole for you,' Robbie said. He jumped in the river a third time and the boat full of toffs jeered. He cheerfully treated them to a rude hand signal before swimming to the stranded pole and retrieving it.

By the time he'd returned, Cynthia had disappeared.

'She stormed off,' Polly told him.

'Oh.' Robbie heaved the pole into Emily and Polly's boat. 'Well then, that solves one problem, doesn't it? I've officially got no plans.'

He grinned at Emily, who tightened her lips and looked down at the grass.

'Paulina,' he said, not taking his gaze from Emily, the way her hair slipped out from behind her ear to fall around her face, 'you can practise your pole placement right here on the bank, if you want to. Practise twisting it when you pull it up. That way it won't get stuck and you won't get stranded, like your sister did.'

'Good idea!' said Polly and she bounced away to the punt.

'Her name is Polly, really,' Emily said to the grass. 'It's not Paulina.'

'Paulina suits her.' Robbie stepped closer. 'Meet me tonight, Emily.'

'I've got plans with Polly.'

'Can I tag along?'

'No. You can't.'

She shook her head and a strand of hair fell into her eyes. He tucked it behind her ear for her. Her hair was like silk.

She swallowed. 'You're supposed to be with another woman.'

'But right now, you and me. We saw each other at the station, and I wanted to talk to you, but you were running in the other direction. I thought you were getting on a train. If I'd known you weren't I would have stuck around.'

'I was meeting my sister.'

'I don't think I've ever felt this way before.' He made to touch the side of her face, the softness of her cheek, but she inhaled sharply again and stepped back.

'That doesn't matter,' she said. 'You've been incredibly rude.'

'OK,' he said. 'OK, I'll go after her and apologise. You're right – I've behaved badly. But I couldn't resist. You were just . . . hanging there. Like an apple on a tree.' He laughed, and he saw her mouth curve slightly into an answering smile.

'Go and apologise,' she told him.

'I'm already gone.' He took a step backwards, another, watching her face. 'But only if you promise you'll meet me. If not tonight, then tomorrow.'

'I don't think it's a good idea.'

'It's a great idea. It's a wonderful idea. Meet me at – when are you free?'

'My sister's train goes at four,' she said reluctantly.

'Meet me at five. Right here, in this very spot. Five o'clock.'

'I might not make it.'

'I'll be waiting anyway.'

He walked backwards for as long as he could, so he didn't have to stop looking at her. Then his shoulder hit a tree and he rubbed it ruefully and turned around.

He found Cynthia not far down the path, sitting on a low wall smoking a cigarette. Although she made a show of not looking at him, it was obvious that she'd waited on purpose.

He sat beside her. 'Sorry. That was rude. I shouldn't have let you drift down the river on your own.'

'Anything could have happened. I could have tipped over.'

'Well, no, that couldn't have happened. You were perfectly safe, and anyway, the river was only a few feet deep.'

'That *other* girl's dress was worth saving.'

There wasn't much he could say to that, that wouldn't also be rude, so he didn't say anything. Water ran from his clothes and dripped on to the path under his feet. He wanted a cigarette, and the ones in his pocket were ruined, but he didn't quite feel able to ask her for one.

She stubbed out her own cigarette on the wall. 'Well, you can make up for it by buying me a drink.'

He shook his head. 'Sorry, Cynthia.'

She huffed. 'What, you don't have *any* money? I'm supposed to be impressed by your nicking a boat?'

'I have some money,' he told her, 'though it's pretty wet right now. I mean that it wouldn't be a very nice thing to do.'

'What wouldn't be a very nice thing to do?'

'For me to spend any more time with you while I'm thinking about someone else.'

'You mean *her*? That girl?'

'Yes.'

'But you've just met her!'

'To be absolutely fair, Cynthia, I've only just met you, too.'

She jumped off the wall with a swish of skirts. 'You are such a bastard,' she said, and stormed off as fast as her heels would allow her.

'I prefer "bounder",' he said to her back.

Chapter Thirty

She waved Polly off on her train at ten past four on Sunday, making her promise to ring the college and leave a message that she'd got home safely. Then Emily dawdled. She took far too long to walk back to Newnham, and still more time tidying her room. Polly was like a whirlwind – everything in Emily's room was subtly misplaced because of her presence.

She definitely wasn't going to meet Robbie. It was a bad idea. She should check through her essay before she gave it in tomorrow, anyway. She'd tried to plan ahead and get all of her work done early because of Polly's visit, but a whole weekend was a lot to spend without doing any revision at all.

She sat on her bed with her copy of her biology textbook and her lecture notes and stared at her own handwriting as if it were that of a stranger.

I don't think I've ever felt this way before.

He had a deep voice but his accent was soft, not so hard on the Rs as other Americans she had heard. There was something relaxed about it. Something that made her want to smile.

He probably wouldn't even be there on the riverbank. He'd probably have found another girl to pursue by now. One he rescued from a tree or something.

And she had a date with Christopher tomorrow. A real date, which she'd hardly had any time to think about. That wasn't something she could do unprepared; it would require a whole consideration of tone, a whole adjustment of feelings.

A whole lot of forgetting how it had felt when Robbie had tucked her hair behind her ear.

She threw the book on to her bed and walked around her room. Christopher had twisted and tortured that pound note when he'd asked her out. It had been a real effort for him; he'd been afraid of her answer. He cared so much about her that he was willing to risk their friendship. Not like the way Robbie had tossed out an invitation, urged her to meet him as if it were the easiest and simplest thing in the whole world, as if he was so cocksure that she would do it, as if any objection she could make was laughable.

'He's an arrogant sod,' she muttered.

But he was so beautiful.

She checked her watch. It was ten past five.

She ran down the staircase and across the quad and out past the porter, who called after her, 'Careful as you go!'

He was waiting for her on the backs not far from Clare Bridge; he'd rolled his trousers up and his feet were in the river. She remembered his confidence in the water yesterday, and then he looked up as she approached and she didn't think about anything, not about his swimming or the fact that this was a bad idea.

She felt simply glad to see him.

His face lit up entirely, as if someone had turned on a switch. He jumped up and ran to her, putting his hands on her shoulders. For a dizzy moment she thought he was going to pull her into his arms and kiss her and she didn't think she would be able to help herself from kissing him back, but he just grinned at her and looked at her, drinking in her face.

She drank in his. His eyes were dark, dark brown, with thick dark brows above them. His hair was a little long, uncombed and untidy. He had a wide, generous mouth, a straight nose that turned up a little bit at the end. His skin was tanned and he hadn't shaved for a couple of days.

'I'm so glad you came,' he said to her.

'Where's your . . . date?' she asked.

He had the grace to look slightly sheepish, but only slightly. 'That's over, Emily. She wasn't pleased with me. But I'd only met her yesterday afternoon.'

'You only met me yesterday afternoon.'

'You're different.' He slid his hands down her arms and clasped her hands in his. 'God, you're beautiful.'

Emily felt her cheeks flushing. 'You say that to everyone, I'm sure.'

'Not like I mean it.' He regarded her for a few more moments; Emily gazed at his shirt. It was wrinkled, and unless she was mistaken, it was the same one he'd been wearing yesterday.

'So is this what you'd planned when you asked me to meet you?' she asked his shirt. 'We could stand here and look at each other?'

'I'd be happy with that,' he said, 'but maybe you'd like to sit on the bank and talk with me for a while. I brought a little picnic.'

The little picnic was a punnet of strawberries and a bottle of red wine. Emily slipped off her shoes and dangled her feet in the water while he pulled an impressive-looking penknife from his pocket and uncorked the wine.

'I don't have any glasses,' he said, holding the bottle out to her. Emily shrugged; she was already doing something foolish, why not drink wine straight out of the bottle on a Sunday afternoon? It warmed her throat and her belly. She passed it back to him and he took a drink, tilting his head back so that she could see his throat as he swallowed.

She wanted to touch it: the cords of his neck, the dark stubble, the tanned skin.

'So who are you, Emily?' he asked, handing her back the bottle. 'Tell me about yourself.'

'I'm a medic,' she said, and then clarified, 'A medical student. In my second year at Newnham.'

'Newnham, is that part of the university? I'm not exactly up on all this college stuff.'

'It's a women's college.'

He whistled. 'You're a med student at Cambridge?' He regarded her with such frank admiration that she blushed again.

'Don't.'

'Don't what?'

'Look at me like that. It's so . . . American. And you don't mean it.'

'I do mean it. I've never met a medical student at a women's college in Cambridge before, even one who doesn't know how to punt.' He splashed his foot in the water. 'And besides, I *am* American.'

'Why are you here?'

'Other than because I was fated to meet you?'

She couldn't help but laugh at that, but she said, 'Stop it.'

'Why? Why should I stop it?'

'Because it's . . . silly. We weren't fated to meet each other.'

'How do you know? We might be. We could be. This might be the first day of a very, very long life together, did you ever think that?'

'No, I did not,' she said. 'Because you are a charmer, and I can tell that these are lines that you use on every poor unsuspecting girl whom you meet.'

'*Whom*. I love it. I've never met anyone who says "whom".' He lay back on the grass, his feet dabbling in the water, his arms folded behind his head, and he looked so delicious and carefree that she took another gulp of wine.

'I can't talk with you if you do that,' she said.

'Do what?'

'Flirt with me so much. I can't take you seriously.'

'OK,' he said. 'I won't flirt with you at all.' He stretched his arms out as if he wanted to embrace the world. 'In fact, I'll pretend that I'm not even slightly attracted to you and we can talk like two entirely genderless human beings, on a spiritual level. Is that better?'

'Yes.'

'You're missing out, though. I'm better at flirting.'

'I don't mind.'

'So, what made you want to be a doctor?' he asked.

'My father's a doctor.'

'That's lucky. My father's a drunk.'

'I'm sorry.'

Robbie shrugged. 'It's OK. He's a happy drunk. He spends all his wages in the local bar buying rounds, and everyone loves him. Except for my mother. They say I'm a chip off the old block.' He closed his eyes for a moment, a line appearing between his brows. 'Are you sure I can't talk about how beautiful you are?'

'Yes.'

'That's too bad, because I'd much rather talk about that than my parents.' He opened his eyes. 'Actually, I'm here because of Dad. He was here in the war, an American volunteer pilot in an RAF Eagle Squadron. He flew missions over France. He was stationed at Duxford at first.'

'That's interesting.'

'I think it's the reason he drinks. Or one of them. It can't be easy living your early life in constant fear.' He shrugged. 'Anyway, he doesn't talk about the war, or what he did in it, and I was curious, so I hitchhiked up to the base.'

'Did you discover anything?'

'It's closed. So no, not really.' He propped himself up. 'I'll trade you the wine for a strawberry.'

He pulled the stem off a berry for her, and put the fruit in her hand. It was warm from the sun and when she put it in her mouth, it burst into sweet juice.

'Look at that,' he said.

She swallowed. 'Look at what?'

'You. I can tell how delicious that strawberry is just from the expression on your face. And now you're blushing.'

'Stop it!'

'I'm not flirting. I'm stating facts. You have a very expressive face. Saying that isn't flirting.'

She punched him on the arm, and he laughed and took a swig of wine.

'You're about a hundred times more clever than me,' he said, 'and you're resorting to violence to prove a point?'

'Shall we talk about the weather?'

'Is this what English people do?'

'It's what we say to subtly insinuate that the topic of conversation should be changed. When we don't want to resort to violence.'

Was it the wine that was loosening her tongue, or was it him? She'd never been any good at witty banter. At flirting. Maybe he was contagious. She felt fizzy, as if she were drinking champagne instead of warm red wine.

'The weather,' he said. 'Skies are mostly clear, visibility good, it's about forty-nine degrees Fahrenheit, high pressure with a light wind from the south-east. A low should come through in the next six hours and there'll be rain.'

'What are you, a meteorologist?' she asked, impressed. Of course, he could be making it all up.

'I'm a sailor. That's how I got to England.'

He looked like a sailor. That tanned skin, his whipcord-thin, strong, agile body, and his hands were capable. She could picture him shinning up a mast, or whatever it was that sailors did.

'You're a long way from the sea here.'

'I can't help noticing the prevailing conditions, even as far inland as this.'

'You can really tell the temperature without a thermometer?'

'I'll admit I may have been a little bit too precise to impress you. It could be fifty degrees.' Absently, he hulled two more strawberries for her. 'Anyway, Emily. Tell me about you. I know hardly anything about you, except for the things I'm not supposed to mention. I keep on asking, and you keep on changing the subject.'

'Actually, I think *you* keep on changing the subject.'

He thought. 'Yes, you're right. OK, I'll shut up. Tell me about yourself. How long have you wanted to be a doctor, what's your favourite colour, what's your favourite film?'

She counted off the answers on her fingers. 'All my life, blue, *Brief Encounter*.' She met his eyes when she said that, startled at herself, because her real favourite film was *The Wizard of Oz*. She'd seen it with Christopher last month.

'A romantic,' he said. 'Good. And I like blue, too. For example, the colour of your – but I'm not allowed to mention that. Favourite book? Let me guess – *Romeo and Juliet*?'

'*Romeo and Juliet* isn't all that romantic, actually, and it's a play. It's mostly about two foolish people being in the wrong place at the wrong time.'

'Isn't that what romance is? Being foolish at the wrong time?'

'My favourite book is *Watership Down*,' she said firmly. 'It's about rabbits. It has no romance in it whatsoever.'

'I like rabbits. I'll read it.'

'What's yours?'

'*Moby Dick*.' He reached for his bag, which was lying beside him on the riverbank, and took out a thick, battered paperback, which he handed to her. 'It's about whales and obsession.'

She turned it over. It was soft from handling, with a creased cover, and bits of paper stuck between the leaves. 'It's a big book.'

He held his hands to his chest, feigning heartbreak. 'You seem so surprised. There's a lot of time to read on a boat, and there's only so much Jack Kerouac. Have you read it?'

'No.'

'Keep that one, then. I can pick up another.'

She reached for the wine, and when she drank from it she was surprised to find that it was nearly all gone. And the sun had gone behind Clare College, making it suddenly significantly cooler than forty-nine-or-fifty degrees. She rubbed her arms, which were bare in her short-sleeved blouse, and Robbie immediately sat up, took off his jacket and put it over her shoulders.

It smelled of him. Up till that moment she couldn't have said what he smelled like, but this was him. Hair oil, an undertone of sweat, beer, cigarettes, grass, mint, teak. A hint of salt and sea air. It was the same scent she had breathed in when he had carried her across the river.

If you had asked Emily what her favourite smell was – if Robbie had included it in the questions that he'd asked her ten minutes ago – she would have said lilac, or a cake fresh from the oven. She would not have said: a jacket warm from a man's body, a jacket that had not been washed for a week at least and probably much longer, with a worn collar and cuffs.

She couldn't speak for a moment. It was exciting, this smell, and at the same time comforting. She hunched her shoulders to bring it closer, wrap it around her, buried her nose in the collar.

Then she realised what she was doing and she straightened up. 'Thanks,' she said.

'Want to go for a walk?' Robbie asked her. 'You can show me your Cambridge; tell me about all your favourite places. I'd like to be able to picture you here. And it'll be much easier for me not to flirt with you if we're walking.'

But he held out his arm for her as they started walking, and she took it. Holding on to him, wearing his jacket, she felt a little bit as if she were floating.

The streets were quiet, and Emily kept her arm linked with Robbie's as they walked. She was a little bit drunk but his arm was strong and steady, and he kept hers pressed close to his side. As they passed King's College, Robbie paused.

'Do you know this song?' he asked her. He whistled a clear, pitch-perfect melody. Emily tilted her head, listening.

'Bach?' she said.

'I don't know. I heard someone playing it last night as I walked past here. I think it was some sort of concert.'

'Do it again.'

He whistled it for her again.

'The aria from the *Goldberg Variations*, I think,' she said. 'Was it on the piano?'

'You're a marvel.' He smiled down at her and she had to catch her breath. She couldn't ever remember wanting to be kissed so badly in her life.

'I'm mad,' she said to him. 'I've got to be mad, walking around talking about Bach when I should be studying. I've got an essay due tomorrow.'

He brushed her hair back from her forehead, tucked a strand behind her ear. 'Some things are more important than essays.'

'Not to a student, they're not.'

'This is more important,' he told her. 'Don't you think? Can't you tell?'

He ran his thumb along her cheek, so gently, as if she were delicate and could be broken. Emily shivered.

'It *is* fate,' he said to her. 'I know you don't believe in it and you said you don't want me to flirt with you but since I saw you in the station, you're all I've been able to think about.'

'And that's why you went immediately and met another woman.'

'I thought you were gone. I thought you'd got on a train and I'd never see you again ...'

His face was in shadow and she had no basis for believing him, but she did.

'I don't know you at all,' she said. 'This is all so quick.'

'It has to be quick.' He touched her bottom lip with his index finger and the longing threatened to knock her over.

'Why?' she asked.

He hesitated, furrowing his forehead in an expression that looked like he expected to be slapped.

'What is it?' she asked.

'I've got to leave tomorrow.'

Her eyes widened. She stepped back.

'Tomorrow? Why?'

'I'm captain on a ketch to the Med.'

'I don't even know what that means.'

'I'm working on a sailboat that's leaving Lowestoft on Tuesday, to go to Italy.'

She stepped back. 'Why didn't you tell me?'

'I've been trying to ignore it. And I didn't want you to be angry at me?'

'I'm not angry at you.' Though she was. She was angry with him for showing up and making her feel this way, if only for a few hours, and then disappearing. A raindrop hit her cheek, and she wiped it away. 'Are you coming back to England?'

'That wasn't the plan.'

'Then why did you insist on seeing me again, if you knew you were just going to leave?'

He caught her hand. 'Because any time together is better than none? We have tonight, at least.'

'I'm not spending the night with you! I hardly know you.'

'That's not what I meant. Well, I did mean it if that's what you wanted, but if you don't, then this is fine. Walking and talking with you. I just want to get to know you, Emily.'

'But what's the point, if you're leaving tomorrow?'

'*This* is the point,' he said, and he pulled her to him and kissed her on the mouth.

His lips on hers, the roughness of his chin, the taste of red wine. Emily wrapped her arms around his neck without meaning to and she stood on tiptoes, pushing up towards him, pressing her lips to his.

This is what it feels like to be properly kissed, she thought. She closed her hand in the hair at the back of his head and he pulled her tighter to him. She felt not just his lips but all of him, his breathing, his heartbeat, his arms around her, the lean strength of his body.

She hadn't known it would be so wonderful, or that she would crave to be even closer, or that nothing else would matter at all.

'Wow,' he whispered against her lips, and then kissed her harder.

The rain began with a sudden fall, instantly drenching their hair and shoulders. Robbie looked up, still holding her tight, and laughed.

'Guess I'm not as good at the weather as I thought.'

'Let's get to shelter,' she said. He wrapped his jacket more tightly around her and they ran for a shop doorway. By the time they'd reached it, her shoes were soaked and water was running down the back of her neck.

'There, that's better,' he said, and settled himself back against the wall, with her pulled close to him. Raindrops rolled down his cheeks, dripping from his hair; she brushed them away with her own wet hand and he kissed her palm. 'You look even better wet.'

Then he kissed her again, this time with his mouth open, and the heat of it warmed her through. Outside their shelter the rain fell and fell. It drummed on the roof and ran down the cobbles outside their shelter in a sheet. They kissed and kissed until Emily had to break away, breathless.

'This was worth coming to England for,' he murmured, his lips brushing her cheek and then the hair beside her ear.

'We can't stay here,' she said, rationality asserting itself, despite the feeling of his breath in her ear and the shiver it sent down her spine.

'Why not?'

'Because it's raining and we'll catch our death, if a policeman doesn't come along and turf us out first.'

'I'd like to see him try.' He began kissing her neck and she shivered again because it felt so exciting. She had never been pressed this close to a man before. Her chest up against his, her hips against his thighs.

'So you want to kiss in this doorway all night until you have to leave in the morning?'

'Sounds perfect.' He tilted her chin up to kiss her again, but she shook her head.

'Where are you staying?' she asked.

'Right here, I told you.' He inclined his head to hers.

'No, I mean, where did you stay last night?'

'In a park not far from here.'

'You slept *outside*?'

'It was a nice night, and hotels are expensive.'

'So what were you planning to do tonight?'

He shrugged. 'I hadn't thought much further than meeting up with you.'

'How can you not even—' Something struck her. 'You'd been planning to spend last night with that woman you were with yesterday, weren't you?'

'Um ...' He looked sheepish. 'Can I refuse to answer that question on the ground that it might incriminate me?'

'And did you think that you were going to spend the night with me, tonight?'

'I hadn't planned anything. And as I said, this, right here, is absolutely fine with me.' He kissed her and although Emily was beginning to get cross with him, she couldn't resist kissing him back. Losing herself for a few more minutes in a world where the rain didn't matter, other people didn't matter, tomorrow didn't matter either.

'In my defence,' he said when they had finished, 'I *didn't* spend the night with Cynthia. As soon as I saw you again, all I could think of was you.'

'So you spent the night in a park.'

'Thinking of you.'

'Robbie, you can't spend the night in a park again.'

'It doesn't matter. I've spent the night in worse places. A little rain doesn't bother me.'

Emily looked at the rain sheeting it down. As she made the decision, she was aware that it was probably the only rash one she'd made in her life so far.

'Right,' she said. 'Come with me.'

She grabbed his hand and pulled him out into the rain. They

ran together, through the empty streets, across the bridge and down Sidgwick Street until she saw the light above the porter's lodge at Newnham. Then she stopped him and drew him into the shadows.

'Can you climb?' she asked him breathlessly.

'Sure.'

'All right. Go past the college, turn left, hop over the first wall you see into the gardens.' She pointed along the side of the college. 'Go right round to the back of the college, and wait. In a few minutes I'll turn on my light and open the window and you'll see which room is mine. It's on the first floor.'

Robert grinned. 'We're doing a Romeo and Juliet, are we?'

'We're doing something bloody foolish and if I get caught I'll most likely be sent down, so you have to be careful, Robbie.'

'I will.' He crossed his heart. 'Swear it.'

'I'm serious.'

'So am I.'

'Somehow I doubt you're ever fully serious.' Yet he appeared to mean it, and he couldn't stay out here in the rain, so what else could she do? She kissed him swiftly on the lips and then ran to the lodge to sign in.

'Got caught in the rain?' asked Howard the porter, jovially.

'The weatherman said it wouldn't start till morning,' Emily replied, and it was that exact moment that she realised she was still wearing Robbie's jacket. 'Goodnight, then.'

'Miss Greaves!' called the porter after her, and she turned around in dismay. 'Almost forgot. Telephone message for you.' He held up the slip of paper and Emily, hardly able to breathe, went back to retrieve it. *Your mother rang to say your sister was home safe and sound and she hopes you have not fallen behind on work.*

'Could have told her myself, you're never behind on work,' said Howard, winking at her. She managed a smile in return and hurried out, towards her room

What was she doing? She was risking her education and her

265

career for a man she'd only just met? A man who slept rough and picked up women on a whim?

A man who kissed like an angel. But then again, he'd probably had quite a lot of practice.

She let herself into her first-floor room and turned on the light. Her essay was where she'd left it, on the bed. She could leave her window closed. She could pick up her essay and go through it one more time, as she'd planned to do. She could let Robbie take care of himself. He'd said he didn't mind the rain, and he was leaving tomorrow, forever.

Emily went to the window. She couldn't see Robbie outside, only darkness. Maybe he'd left anyway. Maybe he couldn't get into the gardens. Maybe he'd had a better offer between the front and the back of the college – another student on the ground floor, maybe, with a more convenient window.

She opened the tall window and leaned out, into the rain, and he was there in the light cast by her lamp. 'Romeo, O Romeo,' he mouthed to her. She shook her head and pointed at the old lead drainpipe bolted to the wall. It was roughly halfway between her room and her neighbour Adrienne's; she didn't speak much with Adrienne, who was studying art history, but rumour had it that Adrienne had let in a boy last term.

Robbie slung his bag over his shoulder and began climbing immediately, hand over hand, like he'd been shimmying up drain-pipes all his life. Perhaps he had. Emily assessed the drainpipe, wondering how he'd get from it to her window, but before she could consider it properly, he'd scrambled across using the ivy and was holding out his bag for her. She took it and pulled it in, and Robbie grabbed the sill with one of his hands and swung his leg over it.

Then he was in her room, dripping wet and smiling and hardly breathing heavily at all from his climb.

And oh dear, what was she going to do with him now?

She shut the window, drew the curtains, and put her finger to

266

her lips. 'You have to be very quiet,' she whispered to him. 'No one can hear you.'

He nodded. She took her towel from her peg and handed it to him, but he shook his head and pointed to her hair. She dried herself off first and then he took it. 'Do you have any dry clothes?' she whispered.

'The stuff in my bag shouldn't be too bad.' He knelt and began to open it. Emily took off his sodden jacket and hung it from the back of her chair. She glanced down at herself and saw that her wet white blouse was stuck to her skin, revealing her white bra and the shape of her body.

Robbie's shirt was stuck to him, too. He had broad shoulders and a dark shadow on his chest where there was hair.

She swallowed, for the first time really understanding what it meant that she'd done.

'I'll get changed in the bathroom,' she said, grabbing pyjamas and a jumper from her chest of drawers. 'There's a spare tooth-brush on the sink.'

She fled the room. The corridor was empty; she ducked into the bathroom she shared with four other girls and locked the door behind her.

In the mirror over the sink, her eyes were bright, her cheeks red. Her chin was pink from rubbing against Robbie's beard stubble as they kissed. Her hair hung in damp rats' tails around her face. She looked panicked and bedraggled, and . . .

Happy.

'Kissing in the rain,' she whispered to her reflection. It was a thing that Emily Greaves did not do. Emily Greaves who was so busy studying, always trying to please her exacting mother and her admirable father. She'd never had time or opportunity to kiss in the rain. She'd never met a man whom she wanted to kiss in the rain.

What was she going to do with him?

She stripped off her sodden clothing; she was wet to the skin.

Robbie must be too – he hadn't even had his jacket – but he'd seemed happy to stay in that doorway with her all night, until he had to leave in the morning.

She changed hurriedly, the pyjamas sticking to her wet skin as she pulled them on. A slip of paper fell out of her skirt pocket: the telephone message from her mother.

Her mother. Her mother would kill her if she knew Emily had a strange man in her room at night. The depths of her mother's disappointment would know no bounds.

Emily was surprised to hear herself giggle.

She tiptoed down the corridor and had her hand on the door-knob about to rejoin Robbie when she thought, *What if he's not finished changing yet and he's naked?*

Cold and hot flushed through her all at once.

She listened at the door, but didn't hear anything. But the thought of Robbie naked had started a whole new chain of thought. Would he expect her to have changed her mind about sleeping with him, since she'd invited him in? He was obviously experienced with women. He might expect her to be sophisticated, someone who'd had lovers; after all, she'd known exactly how a man could climb up to her bedroom.

Or worse. What if he knew she wasn't? What if he'd been able to tell, by kissing her, that she was utterly inexperienced?

She knocked lightly on the door, heart in her mouth, and when there was no answer, opened it and peered in. Robbie had turned off the overhead light and turned on the desk light near her bed, filling the room with cosy shadows. He sat on the floor next to her bookcase. He was wearing a very rumpled white T-shirt and undershorts. Cautiously, she entered the room.

'I like the PJs,' he said.

They were flannelette, with tiny forget-me-nots on them; she'd had them since she was in school and they were a little too small around the bust. Emily entered the room, hugging herself, and decided that in this situation, with a strange, beautiful man half-naked in her bedroom, her best weapon was to be brisk.

'I'm not going to sleep with you,' she said.

'That's not why I gave you the compliment. You really do look adorable.'

'I'm still not going to sleep with you.'

'That's all right.' He turned his attention back to the books. 'Have you really read all of these?'

'Yes. Several times.'

He pulled her histology textbook off the shelf and began to leaf through it. Apparently she was completely safe. Perversely, the realisation made her frown.

'Aren't you *disappointed* that I'm not going to sleep with you?' she asked.

He got up and came over to her. Her room seemed very small all of a sudden. When he kissed her, it was with so much passion and desire that she had to put her hand against the wall to steady herself.

'I'm very disappointed,' he said. 'But it's your choice.'

Robbie returned to the bookcase and sat cross-legged on the floor, perusing the shelves.

Emily stood there for a long moment, her hand on her lips. He wasn't looking at her, but she could see rather a lot of him: his arms and legs, lean and muscular and covered with dark hair. The sole of his bare foot was presented to her – the skin there was darker than the skin on his legs, probably from walking around without shoes – and something about the underside of his toes, the way they curled into soft pads, was unbearably vulnerable and naked.

There was no pressure to sleep with him. Only temptation.

She straightened her shoulders. 'You can sleep on the floor,' she told him, taking a blanket and a pillow off her bed. She spread the blanket out on the floor, right next to her bed. There was nowhere else to spread it.

'It should be better than a park, anyway,' she said.

'Much better. Thank you.'

He was looking at her now. He made no move to lie down on the blanket.

'Well,' she said. 'It's getting late, and I have a tutorial tomorrow.'

'Yes. It's late.'

How on earth was she going to sleep next to him? Knowing she could reach her hand down and touch him?

She needed a distraction, something to stop her from listening to his breathing.

'Oh,' she said. 'You might like this.'

She had to kneel quite close to him to pull out the portable record player and the LP, and even closer to plug it into the wall socket. She put on the record, lowered the needle, and retreated to her bed before the first soft notes of the piano began.

Robbie recognised it immediately. 'This is it. That music I heard yesterday. Something variations?'

'*Goldberg*. It's Bach.'

Quietly, listening to the music, Robbie lay down on the blanket. Emily arranged herself under her own and she reached over to turn off the light. In the darkness, the music filled the room, but she could still feel him beside her. Listening fiercely, with the same concentration he had given to her when he kissed her.

When she ventured her hand over the side of the bed, he found it and clasped it in his own. He held it until the record ended, and afterwards.

Chapter Thirty-One

Emily awoke to see Robbie gazing at her in the morning light that filtered through the curtains. It was such a seamless transition from her dream that for a moment she wasn't sure she was awake. But in her dream he'd been in bed with her, and in reality, he was still lying on the blanket on the floor.

'Morning,' he said to her, in a voice full of sleep and warmth and sexiness. He was lying on his side, his head propped up on his arm. It would be so easy to stretch out her hand to him, lift her own blanket and invite him in next to her.

In her dreams, his hands had been on her skin, unbuttoning her pyjamas, his lips pressing kisses in the hollow between her breasts.

She sat up. 'Did you sleep well?'

'Not particularly. It seemed like a waste of time.'

He'd been watching her while she slept? Could he see what had been going on inside her dreams? Had she said anything in her sleep?

'You're leaving today,' she said.

'My train leaves at eight thirty.'

Her clock said quarter to seven. 'I suppose ... I suppose we have enough time to listen to the other side of that record. It ends with the same aria it began with. It's a hello, and then a goodbye.'

The word caused an unexpected lump in her throat.

'Come with me,' he said.

'What? On the boat to Italy?'

He grimaced. 'No, I doubt there's room, unfortunately, unless you can sail.'

'I can't sail.'

'I meant to Lowestoft. We don't sail until tomorrow morning. I have to check in with the others today but I have the rest of the day free – we could spend some more time together.'

'I don't think I—'

He sat up and took her hand, the same hand he'd been holding as she fell asleep. 'We might never see each other again, Emily. I can try to come back to England but I don't know when that will be. You might have met someone else by then.'

'I'm not looking for anyone.'

'You weren't looking for me, but you found me. I can't bear the thought that I might come back to find you with another man.'

'This is all a bit . . . quick, isn't it?'

'Looking at you makes me feel happier than I've been in years, maybe ever. I've been thinking about it all night and it's been driving me crazy. You feel it too, don't you? Just a little bit?'

'I . . .' She whispered it. 'Yes.'

He seized her other hand. 'Then come with me. Just for a day – you can get a train back tomorrow. I just want to spend more time with you, another twenty-four hours. We have to see if this means anything.'

'Even if it does mean anything, you're still leaving.'

'I know,' he said. 'I know. It's crazy. It's ridiculous.'

'It can't be real,' she said. 'Things like this don't happen. I'm attracted to you, that's all.'

'Then be attracted to me enough to come to Lowestoft with me. It's one day out of your life, Emily.'

'I have a tutorial at ten. And . . .' There was something else, but she couldn't remember it with Robbie kneeling beside her bed, holding both her hands and looking entreatingly at her.

'You'll be back tomorrow,' he said. 'It'll be as if none of this ever happened.'

'It's not the sort of thing I do.'

'All the more reason to do it, I would have thought.' He squeezed her hands. 'We won't be young forever, Emily Greaves. And we only have one day. Let's make the most of it.'

She wavered.

Looking at you makes me feel happier than I've been in years, maybe ever.

He might be lying. But he didn't look as if he were.

'I'll have to find someone to give in my essay for me,' she said. 'And I'll need to leave a note for my tutor.'

His smile made her heart turn over.

'Oh, you beauty,' he said, and kissed her.

'You'll have to leave the same way you got in,' she said, pushing him gently away from her. 'I'll be dressed in ten minutes. Meet me by the front.'

She scurried out to the bathroom, giving a false, bright smile to her neighbour Adrienne whom she met coming out, and by the time she came back the window was open and Robbie and his bag were gone. The blanket had been folded neatly on the bottom of her bed.

After she dressed she scribbled a note to Dr Madison and was reaching for another piece of paper to write a note to Christopher, to drop in his pigeonhole on her way to the station along with her essay, when she stopped.

Christopher. She'd completely forgotten.

The blood rushed to her face as she recalled how shy he'd been, how difficult it had been for him to ask her for a date. The date that was supposed to be tonight. Being with Robbie had driven it utterly out of her mind.

She should stay. She had promised Christopher.

If she could feel this strongly attracted to a man after less than a day – ten thousand times more strongly attracted than she was to Christopher, after having known him for two years – wasn't that a sign that it wasn't right to date Christopher?

I'm sorry, she scribbled on the paper, before she could let herself think about it too much. *I've had to go away for the day. I'll be back tomorrow and I'll explain it then. Can you please give in my essay to Dr M? So sorry, Christopher.*

She began to write *Love* but thought better of it and just signed it *Em.*

She shoved some clothes and her toothbrush into an overnight case, gave her hair a brush and hurried down her staircase, already rehearsing her excuse to the porter about an emergency at home.

Emily stared out the train window, chewing on a fingernail. She checked her watch: two minutes till the train left, and there was no sign of Robbie since he'd left her on the platform, asking her to find them a couple of seats.

What was she doing? She didn't know this man. He could be anyone. He could be lying to her about the boat. He could be lying to her about everything. He could have some sort of nefarious plan to lure her somewhere. He could have a wife, children, be a murderer. He could have changed his mind and decided he didn't want to spend his last day with her after all.

She heard the guard's whistle and the doors slamming up and down the train. He wasn't coming, and she didn't have a ticket. Emily stood up to leave and through the window she saw Robbie running along the platform outside, carrying a paper parcel.

He burst on to the train, breathing hard, and smiled widely when he saw her. 'Provisions,' he said, holding up the bundle.

He'd bought sweets, crisps, biscuits and bottles of Coca-Cola which he opened using the penknife from his pocket. They spread everything out on the table in front of them and Emily ate what was probably the unhealthiest breakfast of her life and she couldn't stop smiling.

Somewhere past Thetford, the guard came into the end of their compartment. 'Tickets to Norwich,' he announced, and began to make his way down towards them.

Robbie swept up their picnic, shoved it under his seat, and seized her hand. 'We've got to go,' he whispered to her, and pulled her out of her seat and up the aisle away from the conductor.

'Go where?'

'To the bathroom.' He reached the loo at the end of the carriage and tugged her into it, shutting the door behind them.

It was rather unpleasant smelling and so tiny that Emily was pressed right up against Robbie, her stomach against his hip and her face close to his. The train lurched over points, and he wrapped his arm around her waist to keep her steady. He was very warm and very solid.

'What on earth are we doing?' she asked.

He put his finger on her lips and whispered. 'Quiet. If we're caught without tickets we'll be thrown off the train.'

'You didn't buy *tickets*? I thought that was what you were doing while I found the seats.'

He shrugged. 'I was too busy getting our picnic.'

'So—'

He put his palm over her mouth. 'Shh. The conductor will be walking by any minute now.'

Emily kept quiet, her eyes wide, looking up at Robbie. He seemed to think this was an enormous joke. He held her easily and close and the motion of the train made her body vibrate against his, rubbing her even warmer. She felt herself beginning to sweat. Her nostrils were filled with the scent of his skin. If she stuck her tongue out and touched his palm, she would taste salt.

Long moments later, he removed his hand from her mouth and reached behind her to unlock the door. 'I'll follow you in a minute,' he murmured, pushing her out and closing the door again.

She was more than a little unsteady walking back to their seats.

He joined her, sliding into the seat next to hers, whistling a snatch of the music they'd listened to the night before.

'Why didn't you get tickets?' she asked in a low voice.

'I thought there were better things to spend money on.'

'Robbie, you have to buy tickets if you're going to ride a train.'

'Why?'

The question was so ridiculous she sputtered. 'Because – because that's what you do. I could have given you the money if you'd told me.'

'I had enough money. I just like to keep it for important things.' He reached under the seat and retrieved the parcel. 'We can split the last Coke.'

'Did you pay for that?'

'Of course.'

'The snacks for the train journey were more important in your mind than the actual train journey?'

He popped open the bottle. A small wisp of fizz appeared at its mouth. 'I don't like having to pay for travel; travel should be free. We should all be able to go wherever we want to. That's the point of being alive.'

'But what about the guards who have to make a living? And the drivers? And the signalmen, and the people who build the trains and the track and—'

'Emily Greaves, you're going to give me a conscience if you keep on like that.'

He tried to kiss her, but she pulled back. 'We're buying tickets in Norwich for the rest of the journey.'

'I love it when you get all strict.'

'Robbie, I mean it.'

'All right, all right. Point taken. You're right, I'm wrong. Can you forgive me?'

He widened his eyes in such a puppy-dog penitent expression that she couldn't help but laugh.

'Yes,' she said. 'But that last Coke is mine.'

And she took it.

They emerged from the station in Lowestoft to a deserted street in strangely muted light. Grey clouds rolled between the buildings;

Emily instinctively breathed in but smelled nothing, and it still took a moment or two for her to realise that it was fog, not smoke.

'It'll burn off within a couple of hours,' said Robbie, taking her hand.

'And I'm supposed to believe your weather predictions now?' But she clung to his hand; the town felt empty, as if they were the only two people in it. Their footsteps were muted and Emily felt a film of damp settling on her face, her clothes, her hair; her eyelashes felt heavy and moist. 'It's like being inside a cloud,' she said.

'I should really say something about you being an angel at this point, but I'm scared you're getting tired of my lines.'

'They're very well practised.'

'Well, then you won't be surprised when I say I'd like to introduce you to a lady that I've been spending a lot of time with.'

She shot him a look but he was smiling. He'd been so sure of himself, from the moment she'd met him. She wasn't usually attracted to arrogance; quite the opposite. And the thing about his lines was that even though she knew they couldn't be, they sounded totally sincere.

The buildings opened out to an esplanade, presumably fronting the sea, but all Emily could see was a wall of grey, with fog billowing in. She shivered and Robbie took off his jacket and put it over her shoulders.

He led her down a set of steps to a wooden walkway. The scent of the sea was stronger here: she could see greyish-green water lapping at the walkway, and sense large ghostly shapes around them. Every now and then, the splash of a wave or the clink of metal against metal.

'She's here,' he said, and as he said it the boat loomed out of the fog, suddenly solid and real.

It had a red hull, two masts; it was wide and long with a spotlessly clean deck and hundreds of incomprehensible ropes everywhere. Robbie put his hand on the side of it, as if he were fond. 'Emily Greaves, meet *Nora Mae*,' he said. 'This is the lady I was telling you about.'

'The boat?'

'She's a sixty-foot ketch, made in Annapolis, Maryland about six years ago. I've known her all her life.' He patted the hull again. 'I put this paint on myself.'

'You built this boat?'

'Parts of her. We're very fond of each other.'

She tried to imagine building something as big and intricate as a boat by hand, and couldn't. 'Do you own it?'

'Her,' corrected Robbie. 'No, she's owned by a oil magnate from Texas called Bud Walker. Before that, she was owned by a New York banker called Chad Lund.'

'But you sail her? This Texas owner hires you to sail his boat for him?'

'He pays me to crew sometimes, yes. When he's on the Chesapeake, which is about four weekends a summer. Bud can sail, just about, but he likes to have yacht parties more than he likes to do any of the actual work on board. I look after her when he's not around, and do the overwintering work on her, and this year he wants to spend the summer in Italy, so I'm sailing her to the Med.'

'By yourself?'

'We're a crew of three. Come and meet them.' He led her to the back of the boat, where the hull dipped enough so that he could climb on. He put down his hand to help her up.

It felt somehow different from being on land. The water was calm in the marina, and the movement of the craft was very subtle, but the boat felt alive.

'I've never been on a boat before.'

'You were on a punt two days ago.'

'I mean a real boat, a big boat.' She peered upwards at the masts, which were tall enough to disappear in the fog. An undetectable breeze made the ropes flap slightly. 'What do you even do with all of these ropes? There are so many of them.'

'Not so many, when you know what they're for.'

'I can't imagine knowing.'

'Don't you know all the names of all the veins in a human body? It's easier than that.'

'Not to me.' Gazing up at the ropes, she felt for the first time exactly how much of a stranger Robbie was. Not just his past, or his motivations: there was this whole world of knowledge and competence inside his head – knowledge about a thing that she'd never even given any thought to.

A head popped up through the door leading below deck. 'Thought I heard you up here, Bob. I was expecting you last night.'

The man wore a blue baseball cap with a red B on it and a dirty grey shirt. He was older than Robbie, his face was weather-beaten and sunburned. His accent was similar to Robbie's, but with softer r's, flatter vowels, a slower way of speaking. He regarded Emily with distinct surprise.

'Something happened. Emily, this is Dennis, my first mate.'

'*You're* the first mate. I've been the captain since you didn't come back last night.'

'Dennis, this is Emily.'

He stretched his hand up for her to shake. His skin was rough and calloused, like tree bark. 'You any good at cooking, Emily?'

'Don't be a chauvinist,' said Robbie. 'She's going to be a doctor.'

'I can also cook,' said Emily.

'If you're on board, you have to be useful. I have a dozen eggs to use up before Art gets back with the supplies and Bob's omelettes are like rubber.' Dennis went back down below.

'You don't have to cook,' Robbie told her.

'I don't mind. And I'm hungry. We haven't had anything proper to eat since yesterday.' She followed Dennis down the hatch. The stairs were more like a ladder; she had to hold on tight to the handholds not to slip. She couldn't imagine what it would be like at sea, with the boat rolling all over the place.

The ladder led down into the kitchen area, which had cabinets, a cooker, a sink. Beyond it there was a seating area, with benches and a table, lamps, a bookshelf. All of it gleamed with polished teak and brass; the seats were upholstered in leather. Between the portholes, or whatever the windows were called, there were actual oil paintings of horses on the walls. Compared to her Spartan room in college it was a mansion. 'Wow,' she said.

'Bud had the whole thing refitted when he bought it,' Robbie told her, swinging down the ladder with ease. 'It's a nice home for a few months. Nicer than my actual home. Here, I'll show you around.'

He put his arm around her waist and gave her a tour of the boat: the radio, sonar and charts hidden in a teak cabinet set into the wall; the way the dining table pulled out to seat at least ten; the compact bathroom with a toilet, sink and shower; the cabins, with beds neatly made and a sink in each room. There was no clutter anywhere. You would hardly know that three men had lived on this boat for weeks.

'Which one is your room?' she asked him.

'This one. The aft cabin.'

She went further into it, looking for a sign of Robbie, something to tell her more about him. He'd slept in this bed while he sailed across the entire Atlantic ocean; he must have dreamed in it.

There were several paperbacks on the shelf beside the bed: three thick mystery novels, a well-thumbed guide to Italy. A photograph had been Sellotaped to the lampshade. It was battered, like something precious that had been carried around in a pocket. Emily lifted up a corner of it so she could see it better. It was a black-and-white snap of a pretty dark-haired woman and Robbie; he had his arms around her and was gazing at her with open adoration.

His expression was exactly the same as it had been when he'd gazed at her this morning, when she'd awoken near to him.

She pulled her hand away as if she'd been burnt. She'd been

right; Robbie was a charmer who'd been feeding her lines.

'Does your girlfriend back home know what you're up to whilst you're away?' she asked, not bothering to keep the crossness out of her voice.

'My girlfriend?'

'Forgot about her already, despite the picture you keep by your bed?'

'I haven't – oh, that.' He sounded relieved as he joined her by the bedside. 'That's my mom and dad. Before he volunteered as a pilot and went off to Europe to fight.'

She lifted it again, unsticking the Sellotape so she could hold it closer to her face. Though the expression was the same, there were a few subtle differences between the man in the photo and the man who stood beside her. The man in the photo had a cleft in his chin; his face was rounder, his hair Brylcreemed back. Now that she looked, she saw the wedding ring.

'Oh,' she said, relieved. 'You – you look a great deal like him.'

'I told you: I'm a chip off the old block,' he said, though he sounded not entirely pleased about it. 'I'm even a Robert Junior.'

She remembered what he'd said about his father being a drunk. 'Your parents look happy in this photograph.'

'I suppose they were, once.'

'Do you have any brothers or sisters?'

'Just me. I was born before he went to Europe, and when he came back, he was different. That's what Mom says, anyway.' He took the photograph from her and stuck it back on the lampshade. 'I'm not even sure why I keep it.'

'Because they look happy?'

'Yeah. I sort of think – maybe this is crazy – that one moment of pure happiness like that, might make everything else worth it.'

He looked sad, and she'd never seen him sad, so she kissed him on the cheek.

'Whatever you're doing in there,' called Dennis from the main cabin, in his flat drawl, 'it's not getting these eggs cooked. Also,

Bob, I saved bilge in the engine room for you to clean out since you've been gone for the past three days.'

'He always likes to spoil my fun,' Robbie muttered, kissing Emily swiftly on the cheek in return and disappearing back up the ladder.

'I've never cooked on a boat before,' she told Dennis, who was leaning against the worktop with a box of eggs in his hand, waiting for her. 'This kitchen is pretty impressive, though.'

'It's called a galley. And the bathroom's called a head. You can find all the stuff you need for cooking in the cabinets. Bud has the thing tricked out like a gourmet's dream, though we rarely eat anything fancier than Boston baked beans on board.'

She opened cabinets, revealing pots and pans and cooking implements, all held in place by wooden dowels and mesh nets, presumably so they wouldn't rattle around in rough seas. She found a bowl and began to crack eggs. Dennis settled into a seat and watched her with the air of someone who wanted to make sure he was getting his money's worth.

'Does Robbie often bring girls on board?' she asked, tentatively.

'Bob? Never. He's got a girl in every port, if you don't mind my saying – sometimes two or three – but you're the first he's ever brought on board.' He pronounced the last word as 'boar-award'.

'That's because I'm going to marry this one, Dennis,' called Robbie from above. His face appeared in the hatch, backlit, grinning.

'I don't give a tinker's cuss who you marry as long as you fix that pump and I don't float away in my sleep,' replied Dennis, making himself more comfortable in his seat.

Art returned before she'd actually started cooking, with a wheelbarrow full of boxes of supplies, and like Dennis, he accepted Emily's presence without much comment. He was ridiculously slender, looked about twelve, with red hair and a face that was more or less one big freckle from the sun. Emily helped him stow

282

away the food he'd brought, following his instructions: everything had its place, and was arranged for ease of access according to frequency of use. As Dennis had said, the pantry's contents were skewed rather radically towards baked beans, but there was fresh food too, to be packed carefully in the icebox.

She managed to make cheese omelettes, toasting bread under the gas salamander, and they all ate lunch together below, around the polished table on plates that had rubber attached to the bottom to make them less slippery. Robbie opened a bottle of beer for each of them and the three men performed like a triple act, teasing each other and regaling Emily with stories about their sailing trips that were sometimes incomprehensible because of the amount of jargon in them. Sometimes they finished each other's sentences. When they were through eating Dennis got up to make coffee and Art started doing the washing up as though this were their habit after every meal.

Robbie held out his hand to her. 'Now, since Dennis and Art have volunteered to the rest of the prep for tomorrow, you and I can go have some fun.'

'I didn't volunteer—' Art began, but Dennis elbowed him, slopping water out of the sink.

'She cooked for you, now hush,' he said. He held out his hand to her again. 'It's been a pleasure meeting you, Emily. I hope to see you again.'

'You will,' said Robbie, and after she had also shaken Art's distinctly wet hand, they climbed the ladder on to the deck.

The sunlight dazzled her for a moment. As Robbie had predicted, all the fog had burned away, leaving her with a view of boats clustered around wooden pontoons. *Nora Mae* was one of the largest, but there were sailboats and motorboats, some with people working on them.

'They liked you,' Robbie said, helping her off the deck and on to the pontoon.

'I liked them.'

'You can see why I can't leave them in the lurch. They could manage with two of them, but it's easier with three.'

'Yes.' And she liked him better for it. She liked that he was the type of person not to let his mates down. 'You're all good friends.'

'It helps.'

'Even in such a big boat, you still must be on top of each other all the time.'

He shrugged. 'You get used to it. You learn to be aware of each other so you can work together, sometimes without talking about it. But you learn to ignore each other, too, when you need some space.'

'Dennis said ... he said you'd never brought a girl on board before.'

'Nope.'

'And you said it was because you were going to marry me.'

'Yup.' His eyes twinkled in the sunshine.

'You should probably ask me before you start telling your friends.'

'Oh, I will. But we have to sort out a few things first.'

'Such as?'

She was flirting hard, in a very uncharacteristic way, and her heart was pounding like crazy. And of course she had no intention of marrying him. She'd known him for no time, and he was going away tomorrow. But Robbie had something that made her feel as if she had stepped slightly out of her real world, into a world where things were sharper and riskier.

'Well, for one thing,' he said, 'it doesn't matter how clever and beautiful she is; I could never marry a girl who didn't know how to sail.'

They'd stopped walking, because they were at the end of the pontoon, and Emily started to turn around, but he stopped her and pointed to the boat moored on the end. It was a little sailboat, toy-sized, compared to the yachts around it, wooden, with two seats, a tiller, a single mast. The name painted on the bow was *Serendipity*.

'I've borrowed her for the afternoon,' he told her.

'You're going to take me on a sail?'

'No, you're going to take me on a sail. I'm going to teach you. I told you, I can't marry you unless you know how.'

'You can't marry me anyway, Robert.'

'If you don't learn how to sail, we'll never find out, will we?' He hopped lightly into the boat, which hardly rocked as he landed in it. 'Come aboard.'

It tilted when she stepped on, and she would have stumbled if he hadn't been holding on to her. 'I can't sail this.'

'I'm going to teach you.'

'I don't even know what all the ropes are called.'

'They're called lines, not ropes. And this is a catboat so there are only two: the main sheet and the mooring line.' He pointed to each in turn. 'You only have to worry about the main sheet. This is the mast, this is the boom, this is the tiller. The front is the bow and the back is the stern, left is port, right is starboard. That's pretty much it.'

'I can't be in charge of a sailboat, Robbie.'

'Of course you can. I'm going to show you exactly what to do.'

'I'll run us aground, or into a container ship or something. I'll sink us.'

'No, you won't. I have complete faith.'

'When we met I was dangling from a punting pole!'

'And you looked adorable.' He kissed her forehead. 'Don't worry, Em. I'll get us out of the harbour, and once we're in open water there's nothing you can hit.' Deftly, he unwrapped the line tethering the boat to the pontoon. 'Help me raise the sail, and then you'll learn how to do it.'

Raising the sail, at least, was easy. But Emily had time to get nervous as Robbie navigated the little boat with ease out of the marina, up the narrow strip of water into the manmade harbour, formed by a jetty made of stone blocks. The air had been still and foggy this morning, but now, with the sunshine, there was a breeze even in the shelter of the harbour. A fishing boat passed them coming in, its engine loud, stinking of fish and followed by a cacophony of gulls. Robbie waved to the captain who waved back.

'What if I crash into one of those?' she asked.

'You won't. And anyway, for your information, a craft under sail has right of way over a motor craft.'

'What if they don't know that?'

'They do.' Robbie handled the line, sail and tiller as if they were extensions of his own body. As if he'd been born to do it. And she liked this about him, too: his self-assurance here was well earned. He built boats, he sailed them, he lived on them. This was his world, as, she supposed, hers had been Cambridge and Bach and heavy textbooks. When you met a person you only saw the flat edges of them, their appearance and the scant facts you could glean from conversation. You never really knew them until you'd entered the sphere where they lived and been surrounded by it.

And this was her chance to touch Robbie's world, the whole rounded swell of it, if only for an afternoon.

Outside the jetty, the wind was stronger, and the water dipped and waved the little boat. Her hair whipped around her face and she wished she'd brought a scarf. Looking towards shore, she could see the sandy beach with its layer of shingle on top, and the buildings of Lowestoft behind in colours of brick red and white. It looked very far away.

'Ready?' Robbie asked her.

'We're in open water. I don't think this is a good idea. Maybe we should go back to the harbour, where it's safer.'

'It's safer out here. There's less to hit. And the wind won't be swirling so much.'

'Don't you think it's a little windy for a beginner?'

'I think it's perfect for a beginner. Come here.'

He scooted back on the bench a little bit and patted the seat in front of him, between his legs. Reluctantly, holding on to the side of the boat, she staggered to the back. She meant to sit down daintily, leaving space between her body and his, but the movement of the boat ruined her balance and she ended up practically falling into his lap. Robbie laughed and put his arms around her.

'You'll get your sea legs soon,' he said into her ear. He took her right hand and put the rope into it, and then put her left hand on the tiller handle. 'We'll do it together until you get the hang of it.'

She kept her hands loose and let Robbie do the work. 'OK,' he said to her. 'We want to tack now. That means we're going to turn the boat. Ready about?'

'What?'

'That's what I say to warn you I'm going to tack. So that you don't get hit by the boom as it swings around. Loosen up the main sheet – keep it around that cleat just once so it doesn't fly out of your hand, that's right – and steer the boat into the wind.'

'Where's the wind?'

'Look at the sail. See the way it's bellied out now?'

'I think so.'

'Then the wind's coming from the direction to fill it. Go ahead and do it. Hard a-lee.'

'What?' she said, half-panicked, but she pushed the tiller anyway in the direction Robbie had told her. The sail flapped, losing the wind.

'Take the line off the cleat now,' he said. 'Watch out for the boom, sweetheart. Lean back to let it pass. Good. Now – see how it's catching the wind on the other side? Tighten up the sheet again on that side. Here.' He helped her tighten the rope and secure it to the cleat. They were now going more or less at a right angle to their course before.

'Good work.' He beamed at her.

'But what if I want to go that way?' She pointed along the coast. 'Can't I?'

'You can, eventually. But in sailing, the distance between two points is rarely a straight line.'

'What do I look at? The sail, or around us, to make sure we don't hit anything?'

'You watch the sail to learn how it behaves. I'll keep a look-out where we're going, though it's not like driving. We have all the space in the world. Just keep it nice and loose, feel the boat and where she wants to go.' He kissed her cheek and she became aware of what she'd been too panicked to notice before: his thighs on either side of hers, his arms embracing her. The strength of his body behind her. Protecting and guiding her.

She'd have thought that sailing would be windy and noisy, but it was almost entirely silent. She heard the liquid sound of the bow cutting through the waves, the flap of the sail, a distant gull, Robbie's calm, quiet explanations of what they were doing. They tacked twice, each time her movements getting smoother. Despite the flimsy boat, the vastness of the ocean, the mystery of the wind, Emily felt herself relaxing back into Robbie's arms. She felt . . . safe.

'Very good,' said Robbie. 'You're doing great. Now it's your turn. Keep it nice and loose, just like that. Let the boat tell you what she wants to do.'

He released her hands and scooted out from behind her, nimbly resetting himself in the passenger seat.

Emily's hands tightened up on the line and jerked the tiller. The sail flapped loose, windless.

'What do I do?' she cried. 'Robbie? What's it doing?'

He leaned on the side of the boat, unconcerned. 'Let her show you, Em. Trust the way she makes you feel.'

The boom swung towards her head and she ducked, but then it swung back to where it had been. 'How do I get the wind back?'

'It hasn't gone. It's waiting for you. Just find it, sweetheart.'

She watched the sail. And all it once, it happened. The sail bellied out in a perfect taut white curve and the tiller steadied, she tightened the sheet and they were flying over the blue water, flying faster than the sun sparkling on the waves. The boat was alive beneath her, the tiller an obedient animal.

Emily laughed. She felt the wind in her body. The sea was vast and endless, all possibility and freedom.

She caught Robert's gaze and he was laughing, too.

And, just like that, she was in love.

Later, hours later, they returned the boat and sat on the beach with their shoes off, eating ice creams.

'I can't write you a poem,' he said to her, 'but I'll build you a boat. Something small that you can sail yourself, but big enough to sleep on for a night or two. And I'll write the name of it in gold.'

Emily wiggled her toes in the sand. She could feel that her nose and cheeks were burnt by the sun and the wind, and her hair was pretty much a snarl. The ice cream melted on her tongue and she thought, *This moment can't last, but that doesn't make it any less real.*

'Don't promise anything,' she said to Robbie. 'I don't need promises. This is enough, right here.'

Robbie finished his ice cream and licked a drop off his hand. 'That's what I was saying to you last night, wasn't it?'

'I didn't understand it then.' She tipped the last melted bit of vanilla into her mouth, crunched the tip of the cornet, and leaned against him. In front of them, the sea stretched endlessly. Tomorrow Robbie would sail across it towards Italy and away from her, possibly forever.

He lay back with her on the sand and she rested her head on his chest. He ran his fingers through her hair and his heartbeat sounded as familiar as her own name.

'I want to stay with you tonight,' she said to the cloudless sky.

They checked into a hotel on the seafront: an Edwardian brick building with wide, tall windows. Emily kept her left hand tucked in her skirt pocket as Robert signed the register *Mr and Mrs R Brandon, Cambridge.*

'Only visiting for one night?' asked the desk clerk, and Emily was uncomfortably aware of their lack of suitcases, her tangled hair and sunburnt cheeks.

'I'm sailing out tomorrow; early start,' said Robbie, insouciant. 'We thought the extra hours together were worth the price of the hotel. Newlyweds,' he confided, winking.

'You'll want an en suite, then? We have one, sea view. It's often used by honeymooners.'

'We want the best,' said Robbie.

He paid for it and they went up the stairs together, Robbie holding the key. Emily's heart was pounding, her hands damp. *This is 1962*, she reminded herself, *no one is going to force you to wear a scarlet A for being unmarried and checking into a hotel with a man.*

Then she thought of what her mother would say, and thought she would probably prefer the scarlet letter.

The corridor was long and silent, lined with doors. 'You're a worryingly good liar,' she whispered to Robbie.

'It's not a lie. It's the truth, only told too early.'

He unlocked the door to room number eleven and opened it for her. Emily had to take a deep breath before she went in.

But once he'd shut it behind them, and they were alone in the room with the double bed, the pink ruffled bedspread, and the view through the window of the sea, she turned to him. 'You have to stop talking about marrying me,' she told him.

'Why?'

'Because you don't mean it.'

'I do mean it.'

'Nobody decides to marry someone else after only just meeting them.'

But then she remembered that feeling on the sea, her heart lifting with love, keen and dizzying.

'I mean,' she amended, 'people do, but it's not a good idea. I can't get married anyway; I have to finish my degree and my training before I can even think about something like that. It'll be years. And that's not why I'm here, Robbie. You don't have to promise me anything.'

'Emily,' he said, and took her into his arms. 'I don't have to promise it to you. I'm going to prove it. There's something special about you. I never thought that I would ever want to get marr—'

'Stop,' she said. She put her hand on his mouth. 'Stop it. I told you, I don't want promises or the future or anything. I can't worry about your sincerity or whether you mean what you say right now and that you might change your mind later. And I don't want to marry you, anyway. I just want right now, the two of us, here.'

She stood on tiptoes to kiss him on the mouth.

Afterwards, he filled up the bathtub with hot water and they climbed in together. He took the tap end and she leaned against the other end and they faced each other, their legs bent. Emily wet a flannel and ran it over his chest and shoulders. He was slender but strong, and he had dark hair in the centre of his chest. She had never seen a grown man's body so closely: the play of muscles underneath the skin, the frank shape of his shoulders and the hair under his arms.

He had touched her with such tenderness and eagerness. He had whispered her name in her ear.

She scooped up water in her hands and dribbled it on to his hair, slicking it to his head. Wet, it was glossy as one of the dark pieces of black flint on the Lowestoft beach. She massaged shampoo through it, feeling the soft strands in her fingers, the hard shape of his skull. He bent his head so she could reach him better and she saw the nape of his neck. There was a white line of skin where his hair had stopped him from tanning as much as the rest of his neck and face. It was vulnerable, somehow: secret.

'That feels great,' Robbie murmured. 'Nobody's washed my hair for me since I was a child.'

She lathered white foam through all of it, and then rinsed it with water scooped in her hands. She wondered if the future held a child with dark hair, who she would wash in warm water like Robbie's mother had washed him. The slender, pure back of a child's neck, untouched by the sun.

He raised his head and wiped water out of his eyes. 'Your turn. Come round here.'

She manoeuvred herself around, splashing water over the side of the bath, so that her back was resting against his chest.

Nakedness was surprisingly easy. Any self-consciousness she'd had was erased by how Robbie appreciated her body, how he made room for her in his arms and against him. He was comfortable in his own skin and made her feel comfortable in hers. He wet her hair the same way she'd wet his and she felt his fingers rubbing in the shampoo. He teased out the tangles that the wind and the pillows had made.

'I've never washed a girl's hair before,' he said. Drowsy with warm water and his skin and pleasure, she thought of asking him how many girls he had taken to bed before her. He was clearly experienced. But the thought didn't bother her as much as it could have, not nearly as much as it had bothered her when she'd first met him. She'd had no desire for her first time to be with someone clumsy and awkward.

It would have been that way with Christopher, she thought, and the idea was uncomfortable enough that she bit her lip. They both would have known the mechanics, and none of the reality.

'What are you thinking?' Robbie asked her.

'I was supposed to be on a date tonight,' she told him. 'My best friend Christopher wanted to take me to dinner.'

He twisted her clean hair into a soft rope and laid it on her shoulder. 'Oh no. I'm sorry.'

'It's all right. I'd rather be here.'

'I wasn't really sorry.' He kissed her cheek and settled her back against him. 'Is he in love with you?'

'No, he's . . .'

But was he? Why would he ask her out, why risk their friendship, if he wasn't?

'It doesn't matter,' she said. 'I'm here with you.'

'What's he like?'

'He's sweet and kind. He's studying medicine, too.'

'Sounds like I'll have to fight him when I get back from Italy.'
She laughed. 'No. Please don't.'

'What was he like when he asked you out? Was he all cool and casual, or was he nervous?'

'He was nervous. Unlike you, when you asked me to come here with you.'

'I was nervous when I asked you. I'm just really good at hiding it.'

She hit his arm, splashing water. 'You weren't nervous at all. You're a cocky sod.'

'Cocky sod,' he repeated, imitating her accent, badly. Then he kissed her ear. 'I was nervous,' he whispered.

Desire filled her, melting and new and clean. She leaned back against him as his hands smoothed down her body.

When she awoke she knew she was alone before she opened her eyes or stretched out her hand. They had fallen asleep wrapped around each other, his breath in her hair and his heartbeat in her ears, and he had become entwined in her dreams: bright sea, kind wind, warm skin, the soft touch of his mouth.

Sun leaked through the crack in the curtains. She sat up. His clothes were gone from the chair, his shoes from the floor. But there was an emptiness in the room that told her anyway. She reached for her watch on the bedside table to see what time it was, whether she could go after him to say goodbye before he sailed, and saw the piece of paper, carefully folded, beside it.

It was hotel stationery, written in biro. She'd never seen his handwriting before but she would have recognised it anywhere as belonging to him: it was neat and confident, with bold down-strokes and full stops that dented the page.

Emily, my sweetheart,
You are a beautiful sleeper. I didn't want to wake you. And it's better to leave this way anyway – this way I get to set off remembering you in this bed, with that sleeping smile on your face. Instead of watching you disappear behind me in the distance.

I've left some money on the dresser for your ticket back to Cambridge. I don't think you'll have as much fun hiding in the lavatory without me. Besides, in only two days, you've made me into a reformed character.

This isn't goodbye, though. I'll be back. I know you don't want promises but this is one. I am not going to say goodbye to you, Emily. Don't forget me.
I love you.
Robbie

Chapter Thirty-two

August had rained and rained. Emily hung up her hat and shook the flowers she'd cut in the garden out the front door, to get rid of the worst of the water. In the kitchen, her mother was sitting at the table frowning at the crossword. She glanced up when Emily entered.

'Men don't care about flowers,' she said. 'You're wasting your efforts, and my dahlias.'

'You always put a bud vase in the spare room when Christopher comes to visit.' Emily went to the sink to fill a vase.

'Christopher is different. He appreciates the finer things.' Mum put down her pencil. 'You don't even know this boy, Emily.'

'I know him well enough. He's only coming for a visit, anyway.'

'You're too young to throw yourself away on someone. All that work you did to get into Cambridge—'

'I have no intention of throwing myself away. It's a visit, Mother. He's been in Italy and Malta and the Maldives and he's coming to England for a little while.'

'You don't even know how long. He didn't say, did he?'

Her cheeks flushed at this. 'He won't be any inconvenience to you. I'll do all the extra housework.'

'You're dropping everything for him already. You have work to do, don't you? For your medical degree that you're so proud of? If you're going to be a doctor, the summer isn't meant to be gadding away with boys. Your father has been very generous—'

'I'm not gadding. I'm not running away with him. He's coming to visit. I've plenty of time to study.'

'Because women get trapped, Emily. If they're not careful. You can find all of your dreams disappearing, just from making one mistake.'

'Mother.' Her cheeks flushed harder. 'I'm not an actual fool.'

'Well. I hope not. Because it's not just your career that's at stake, it's your entire future. You could throw away your reputation – everything. You hardly know this man, and after he's gone you could find that no decent man would want to—'

Her father came into the kitchen, whistling, and Charlotte broke off. She picked up her pencil and went back to her crossword.

Emily wished that she'd stayed in Cambridge for the summer. Some of the other girls from her college had rented flats and found jobs. She could be preparing her own room for Robbie's visit, purely happy, instead of arguing with her mother about it. But Polly had wanted her home for the summer, and her father had offered to let her sit in with him on his practice.

He filled a glass of water from the tap. 'Two o'clock, is it, the train?' he asked Emily.

'Yes, two.'

'I'll be ready with the car.' He glanced at the crossword over Charlotte's shoulder, and left the room again. Emily, rearranging the flowers, didn't dare say anything to her mother. She finished and picked up the vase to leave.

'It's that you hardly know him,' her mother said suddenly. 'You know nothing about him. Whereas Christopher—'

'Christopher is my friend. A very good friend, but nothing more.'

'You're both going to be doctors. You have so much in common. And he's got wonderful connections, which—'

'I don't care about *connections*.'

'You may not, but people do. He could make everything so

296

much easier for you. It's not something to be underestimated, Emily.'

'I could never marry Christopher. Not even to please you.'

'Oh well,' said her mother, 'perhaps all of this is for nothing, and this Robbie won't even show up. From what you've told me, he doesn't seem horribly reliable.'

Emily left the kitchen with her heart pounding and her fingers slick on the vase.

Emily huddled in her mac on the platform. The train was late. He might not have caught this one; his letter had been sent from France three days ago. Were winds predictable in the English Channel? Could you get lost there? Were the trains running properly from Portsmouth? Why hadn't he rung her when he'd arrived in England? Maybe he wasn't here yet. Maybe she'd spent three days in a frenzy of nerves for nothing; maybe she'd had her hair cut and bought a new lipstick and a new dress for no reason. Maybe it had all been a waste: all the careful preparation of the spare room, the flowers in the vase, the endless assurances to her mother that there wouldn't be any extra trouble, that she didn't know how long he was staying but it was going to be fine, that she was sure that he liked whatever she cared to cook, that yes, perhaps it was odd to have a strange man to stay but he had been writing to her for *months,* Mother.

She had not told her parents about how he told her in his letters that he loved her and he was going to marry her. She couldn't quite believe those parts, anyway. They seemed a bit too much. She read the parts about Robert's journey over and over again, picturing them in her mind. But the declarations of love she skimmed through, almost embarrassed, and then a sort of hunger would seize her minutes later and she had to reread them and murmur the words to herself, over and over again, until they were lodged in her mind. *My sweetheart my darling my beautiful girl my love my only my treasured. Mine. I love you.*

She touched the words with the tip of her finger and smudged the pencil and then saw how the smudge stayed on her finger. Words from his hand transferred to her skin.

Forty-eight hours, they had spent together.

Maybe he wasn't coming. Maybe her mother was right.

She turned up her collar.

Polly was convinced that Robbie was coming. The letters came in packets, posted from whatever port Robbie happened to be at, and since Emily had been down for the summer holidays, Polly insisted that Emily read them to her as soon as they arrived. 'From that man who rescued you in the river? That's so romantic, Em. He was so swoony.'

Emily read Polly the descriptions of the journey and the places Robbie was visiting. She left out the words of love, even though Polly kept on pestering her to read out 'the smooshy stuff'. She strongly suspected that if she hadn't hidden the letters, Polly would have read every one. She had to make sure she intercepted the postman, or else Polly was liable to open them herself.

Emily checked her watch and then peered down the track. The train was fifteen minutes late and there was no sign of it.

Her father was in the car outside the station, waiting. He would have lit his pipe and be reading the paper. Would he like Robbie? He *had* to like Robbie. Dad liked everyone; he was a popular GP. He could hardly walk down the High Street without him being hailed by half a dozen people, at least, eager to talk to him, pass on news, chat about the weather. Sometimes they thanked him. When Emily was by his side, she felt, by proximity, that glow of being liked, of having well-earned respect. You didn't get that by not liking people.

But she had never brought a boyfriend home before. Well, Christopher. Her father and mother both adored Christopher. But Christopher hadn't visited this holiday. He had gone to the south of France with his family and she had only received very cautious letters. Very polite.

Polly hadn't clamoured to read those.

Faintly, the sound of a train. Emily's heart thumped and she started forward, leaning, desperate for the sight of the train. It was there, a black shape in the rain, growing too slowly bigger.

She stood on tiptoes and searched the windows as it pulled up to the platform. Where was he? The pause between the train stopping and the doors opening was years long, unbearable. An elderly couple alighted, tugging luggage: a mother with a child held by the hand, three men in suits, a woman carrying a small dog and then, at last, sure-footed, easy in movement, dark-haired, wearing the same battered jacket, same bag slung over his shoulder. It was him.

He spotted her at the same moment and they ran towards each other and then she was in his arms.

Why was this so familiar? When she'd spent so much more time away from him than with him? Two days, two nights, and he was imprinted on her forever?

He kissed her and all that rain fell on them and neither one of them noticed.

Her father got out of the car when they approached, Robbie's arm around Emily's waist. He knocked the plug out of his pipe.

'Dr Greaves,' said Robbie, holding out his hand. 'I'm pleased to meet you, sir. I'm Robert Brandon.'

They shook hands heartily and Emily was relieved to see that her father's smile was genuine. 'Emily didn't tell us you were American.'

'Didn't she? Afraid that you wouldn't open your doors to a Yank?'

'Not at all,' said Emily's father. 'Let me take that bag for you.'

'Wouldn't consider it.' Robbie stowed it in the back seat and made to get in after it, but Emily shook her head and pointed to the front seat.

Sitting behind him, not dizzied by his gaze or his touch, she could see that he was more tanned than he'd been the last time she'd seen him, and he'd had a haircut recently. Perhaps even since he'd come to England, in order to meet her.

He turned around and grinned at her as her father started up the car and she smiled back at him, her whole body beaming.

'So you're a sailor?' her father asked, pulling away from the station.

'A sailor and a boat builder, sir. I'm not good enough for your daughter. I'm sorry about that.'

'Well, I think she can decide that for herself. You met her in landlocked Cambridge, I gather?'

'Yes, sir. I was a tourist. We had a stop off in Suffolk on our way to Italy to deliver a yacht.'

'And what are your plans for the future?'

'That very much depends on Emily.'

She half-listened to their words as they chatted in the front seat about Robbie's journey, the places he'd seen, recognising names from his letters. Her eyes were drinking in glimpses of Robbie, and her mind was listening to the tone of their voices, rather than what they said. She was her own woman; she was going to be a doctor; she should not care whether her father approved of her choice in boyfriends. But she did, a great deal. And her father was so habitually polite and friendly to everyone that it was impossible to tell whether he really approved of Robbie, or whether he was just being himself.

Her mouth still burned from his kisses. She wanted to reach over the seat to sink her fingers in his hair, trace the outline of his ear. She woke sometimes thinking he was beside her in bed. She was glad she was riding in the back seat, so her father couldn't see this desire lighting her up from within. She had no idea how she was going to hide it from her family.

She wondered if she'd be able to sneak into his room during the night. It was next to hers, at the end of the corridor. But the floor squeaked; she'd tried it already.

'What a beautiful home,' Robbie said from the front seat and she came back to her surroundings. They'd pulled up in front of their house, a Victorian flint and brick building with white-painted sash windows and a glossy green front door. She looked at it from Robbie's point of view. It must seem boxy to him, clumsy, maybe, after spending months on board a sleek, elegant sailboat.

Polly came rushing out of the house, hair flying. 'Hello hello hello hello hello do you remember me?' she cried as soon as they got out of the car.

'Of course I do, Paulina,' said Robbie, and Polly squealed and gave him a hug.

'Come on, come out of the rain, and I will give you a tour of the house. Mummy has a headache and she says she won't be up before teatime, so we have to be quiet as mice.'

Robbie winked at Emily as he retrieved his bag from the back seat. Polly immediately grabbed his hand and tugged him into the house. As they followed, Emily restrained herself from asking her father what he thought. He didn't speak until they'd gone through the front door. 'Very cordial young man, isn't he? He seems excited to be seeing the world.'

She didn't quite trust herself to answer one way or another; she knew she'd give away how much it mattered to her. The fact that her mother had gone up to bed with a headache didn't bode well, but if her father liked Robbie, he might be able to sway her . . .

'You like him very much, don't you?' her father asked. She nodded. 'Then I hope we shall all like him, too.'

'Polly already does,' said Emily, wincing as a blast of Petula Clark came from upstairs.

It took some doing to manage to escape Polly's clutches and go for a walk, just the two of them, together under an umbrella, holding hands. They wandered down the muddy and dripping lanes, hidden by hedgerows, and Robbie stole kisses every few steps.

Emily had never felt so incandescently happy.

'Your family are nice,' Robbie said.

'You haven't met my mother yet. She's being ... difficult.'

'Well, she hasn't met me yet. I'll win her over with my Yankee charm.'

'Not to doubt your Yankee charm, but Mum is very good at not changing her mind. We have an interesting relationship, where she tells me everything that's wrong with me and I'm not allowed to return the favour.'

'Your father seems great, though. And Polly's a peach.'

'Polly doesn't have the same problems with Mum that I do. It's easier between them, for some reason. But Dad is great, yes.'

'I see why you admire him so much.'

'I want to be just like him. Except a quiet country practice doesn't really appeal to me; I'd rather be somewhere that I can really help people. In a hospital, or maybe abroad.'

'If you keep practising, you can be a sailing doctor. Going from port to port, helping all that are in need.'

'Wearing a swimming costume and a tiara like Wonder Woman.'

'Well, I wouldn't complain.' He stopped them and kissed her, thoroughly. 'I'm so very glad to see you, sweetheart. I thought about you every day.'

'I know,' she murmured. 'I've had your letters.'

'And I've had yours at every port. You can't imagine how long that made every journey, knowing I had a letter from you waiting for me when I got there.'

'I'm sorry.'

'You shouldn't be.'

She kissed his forehead, his cheeks, his eyebrows. He didn't feel like a stranger at all. 'This is crazy, you know.'

'It's a good kind of crazy.' He wrapped his arms round her waist and lifted her up. 'I think it's the kind of crazy that only happens once in a lifetime.'

'I hope so. I couldn't deal with the stress, otherwise.'

He put her down. 'I've had a lot of time to think while we've been apart.'

'Dennis and Art must have loved that.'

'They laugh at me and call me a changed man. Art is convinced it's his chance to become the boat Casanova. By the time I'd left Italy, I think he was engaged to seven different girls.'

'Maybe he'll stay and marry them all.'

'More likely he'll be forced out of the country by Italian grand-mothers carrying pitchforks and flaming torches.' He smiled. 'They were planning to go on to Greece, and then maybe North Africa, if they could get work. Bring the *Nora Mae* back next spring.'

'You've missed that. That's what you wanted to do – travel and see the world. You should have gone with them.'

'Nah. I wanted to see you more.' He hugged her tight. 'Anyway, this is a nice part of the world to see, too. England is so ridicu-lously green.'

'That would be all the rain.'

'I'd rather be in the rain with you, than in the bright sunshine with a dozen grandmotherless Italian girls. Speaking of which . . .' He dug into his pocket and pulled out something. It was a small leather box. He put it into Emily's hand.

It was red, with gold edging. Emily stared at it. 'This had better not be what I think it might be.'

'Open it and see.'

Slowly, she opened it. Nestled on white velvet was a gold ring. It was fashioned into the shape of two clasped hands, smaller female inside larger male. She caught her breath.

She had never seen it before, but it was perfect. Two equal hands clasped, together, captured in gold, forever.

'I couldn't afford a diamond,' Robbie was saying, 'but this is a traditional Italian ring. It's not new, either, so if you don't like it, I can find something—'

Tears brimming, she raised her eyes to his. He stopped talking. For the first time since she had met him, he looked less than entirely confident. The realisation made her swallow, hard.

'It's beautiful,' she managed. 'It's . . .' She wiped a tear from her eye. 'Robbie, we can't.'

'We can.'

'We're not even from the same country. And you want to travel, and I . . . I have four years left before I qualify, and then all the training. We can't get married.'

'Sweetheart, we can do anything we want to do.'

She shook her head. 'Where would we live? How could we be together? You have dreams and I have dreams too.'

'From the minute I met you, I haven't had any dreams that didn't include you somehow.'

'But how?'

'I don't know. I can stay in England for a while, working in boatyards. Maybe we'll just have to write to each other until you've finished your degree. Whatever we have to do, we can do it. I don't mind waiting, Emily. I don't mind waiting years.'

'We hardly know each other.'

'We know everything that matters. Don't we?'

She gazed up at him through a haze of tears. Robbie was crazy – impulsive, risk-taking, brave, able to change his entire life on a chance encounter. She . . . was not. She planned, made goals, took baby steps, worked hard.

She loved him. She had no idea how it had happened, but she did. He had lodged himself inside her heart and changed every single thing about her.

Robbie hit himself on the forehead. 'Oh wait, I'm doing this totally wrong. Let's try this.' He took the ring box, gave her the umbrella, and knelt down in the lane in front of her. His knees were in muddy puddles. The rain immediately began to run down his face.

'Emily Greaves, I love you. However it happens, whatever it takes, I want to spend my life with you. Whatever life throws our way, I promise you, we will find a way through it as long as we're together.' He took the ring out of the box and held it up, a perfect gold circle, two clasped hands.

'Will you marry me?'

'Robbie . . .'

A fat drop of water rolled off the umbrella and hit him on the forehead. He didn't move: just held the ring up, gazed steadily into her face.

'Oh for goodness' sake, get up out of the mud. This is silly. If we're still together in a year, then maybe we can talk about it, but . . . Can't we just be happy in the time that we have?'

'We can do that, too. But we'll be happier if you promise to marry me. Please, Emily?'

His dark brown eyes, his mouth that was often smiling but now was serious. The haircut he'd got especially for her, the way the rain had soaked his shirt collar. The way he saw life as an adventure. The ring he'd bought for her many hundreds of miles away that she had never seen before but she had recognised, straight away, as the right one, the only one.

'All right,' she said. 'Yes, Robbie. Yes, I will.'

Wonder broke over his face. Cleared the sky of clouds.

He slipped the ring on her finger and it fitted perfectly as she knew somehow that it would. Then he stood and held her and kissed her and it was some time before either of them realised that they had dropped the umbrella.

Robbie went up to the guest room to change his wet and muddy trousers, and Emily went into the kitchen. There was an aroma of cooking, which either meant that her mother was up, or that Polly had started on the supper herself. Either circumstance was cause for worry.

They were both there. Her mother was putting the lid on a pot of potatoes, and Polly was peeling carrots. 'Are you feeling better?' she asked her mother, beginning to wash the salad leaves.

'A little. But it's getting late, and people are hungry.'

'You should have stayed in bed. I would have done all this.'

Polly came over to wash the carrots. 'What is that?' she squealed, staring fixedly at Emily's hand. 'Did he give you that?'

Emily curled her hand around the head of lettuce. She was tempted to slip off the ring, pretend that Polly hadn't seen anything and swear her to secrecy later. But the ring was beautiful. And she had nothing to be ashamed of.

Her mother joined them at the sink. 'Emily, is that a ring on your finger?'

'Yes. It's from Italy.'

'Oh, it's so romantic,' swooned Polly.

'Did you not listen to a single thing I told you, Emily?'

She lifted her chin. 'It's my life, Mother. I'm a grown adult.'

'You're twenty. You know nothing. You think the world's arranged for your pleasure.'

'Is it an engagement ring? It's on that finger, is that what it is?' asked Polly.

'We're not going to get married until we're ready. I've got to finish my degree, and my training, and—'

'So why even talk about it?' her mother demanded.

'Mother, I love him.'

'Oh Mummy,' said Polly, 'they're so *sweet* together, his letters, you wouldn't *believe*—'

'Polly,' said their mother, 'I would like you to leave the room please.'

Polly shut her mouth. Eyes wide, she left the kitchen, glancing over her shoulder at them. Emily heard her footsteps running upstairs.

On the cooker, the potatoes began to boil and rattle the pot lid.

Emily put the salad aside. 'It's my decision to make,' she said.

Her mother clenched her jaw. 'You are twenty years old. Some girls are grown up at that age but you are not. You're still a girl. Everything, all your life, has been done for you. Your father and I have bent over backwards to make sure you've had an easy life.

So you think everything will just work out. You want something, and it happens.'

'Mother, that's not true. I'm grateful. And I've worked very hard.'

'But you've known him for five minutes. He's written you some letters. And you expect to jump right into some sort of happy ever after? You expect him to wait?'

'Yes, I do.'

'Men aren't like that, Emily.'

'Daddy is.'

'Your father is . . . you can't expect to meet a man like James every day.'

'I don't. I expect to meet *one*, and fall in love with him, and marry him. In a few years, Mother, when we're ready.'

'How do you know he'll wait? How do you know he'll come back?'

'He says he will.'

'But how do you *know*?'

'How do we know anything?' she asked, exasperated. 'I trust him and I'm willing to take the risk.'

'You don't know what can happen. You've been kept so safe you have no idea.'

'Mother, you haven't even met Robbie yet.'

'Um . . . is this a bad time? It's a bad time, isn't it?'

She whirled round. Robbie stood in the doorway, a sheepish, appealing smile on his face, and she marvelled at his cheekiness. He fully expected to charm her mother into liking him, even though he must have heard at least part of their conversation.

And she loved him for that. Chancer, full of sunshine and self-belief.

'Can I help with the dinner?' he asked. 'I'm a decent cook as long as you tell me what to do.'

Emily smiled at him and was about to reach out to take his hand when his expression changed rapidly to surprise and concern.

'Mrs Greaves? Ma'am? Are you all right?'

He started forward, and Emily turned to see her mother, who was standing with her back to the cooker. All of the colour had fallen out of her face. As Emily watched, she dropped the spoon she'd been holding and it clattered to the flagstone floor.

Chapter Thirty-Three

'Mummy?'

Her mother's face was a ghastly mask, white with holes for eyes and mouth. Behind her, the potatoes boiled over with a hiss, spilled on to the cooker and put out the gas flame. Her mother continued to stare at Robbie.

'Get out of my house,' she said. Her voice a rasp.

'Mummy?'

Emily touched her mother's arm. She shook her off.

'Get out,' she said to Robbie. 'Get out of my home. Don't come back.'

'Mrs Greaves, I—'

'*Get out!*'

She shouted it, screamed it, with her face that mask of horror. A fury Emily had never seen before.

James rushed into the room. 'Charlotte, what's wrong?'

'Get him out. Get him out of here. Get him—'

Robbie backed quickly away. Emily heard the front door close. She stared, wide-eyed, at her mother and her father, who had put his arm around her. Then she ran after Robbie.

He was outside on the drive, in the rain. He looked terrified, which matched how she felt. 'What just happened?' he asked.

'I don't know.'

'Why did she tell me to leave? Did I say something wrong?'

'If you did, I don't know what it was. She wasn't . . . she didn't like the idea of our getting engaged, but this seems . . .'

'Is she well? You said she had a headache.'

'My father's with her. He'll look after her. Robbie . . .'

She stepped into his arms and clung to him. Her mother had been an entirely different person. Completely out of control of herself, gripped by some strong hatred that Emily couldn't begin to explain.

'It seemed to happen as soon as she saw me,' he said. 'She was looking cross, but when I came in, she just . . . I thought she was going to faint.'

'She almost seemed to know you. You haven't met my mother before, have you?'

'Not that I know of.' He shook his head. 'No, I don't think so. I'd think I'd remember meeting someone who hated me so much.'

'It's got to be a mistake. She must think you're someone else. Or maybe she's angrier than I thought about our getting engaged.' She looked up at him. 'What are we going to do?'

'I don't know.'

'You can't just stand outside. I need to talk with her.'

'Do you think I should go stay somewhere else?'

'Robbie, I can't think of what's got into her. I'm so sorry.'

'It's all right, I don't mind. I'll wait till she calms down. Is there a hotel somewhere nearby?'

'The pub has rooms.' She hesitated. 'Maybe it's best if you don't go back in the house. I'll get your bags and borrow Daddy's car keys. Wait in the car?'

Inside the house, she took the keys from the bowl near the front door, then went to the kitchen and peered in. Mother was sitting at the table now, her head in her hands, her father with his arms around her, stroking her back gently. He'd poured her a glass of water.

'Mummy?' she said. Her mother flinched but didn't look up. She met her father's eyes, though, and he shook his head slightly.

Polly was hovering at the top of the stairs. 'What happened?' she demanded. 'Why was Mummy screaming? I tried to find out but Daddy sent me away. Who was she shouting at?'

'I don't know what's happening,' Emily told her. 'I'm going to take Robbie to the Royal Oak and see if we can get him a room there.'

'Are you going to stay there with him?'

'I . . . don't know.'

'Is there something wrong with Mummy? Or does she just not like Robbie?'

'I don't know, Polly. I don't know any more than you do. Just . . . don't bother them for a little while, OK? I'll see you later.'

They drove to the pub in silence. Emily felt as if something had shattered. The ring on her finger was an unfamiliar weight. She kept glancing at the two hands, clasped together in gold.

At the Royal Oak, Colin Farmer was behind the bar and told them there was an available room. 'Are you visiting the Greaveses?' he asked Robbie. 'They're wonderful people. My brother would have died if Dr Greaves hadn't diagnosed his appendix and sent him to hospital. It was this close to bursting.' He held his fingers an eighth of an inch apart.

'Yes,' said Robbie. 'They're a great family. Mind pouring me one of those beers? Emily, what will you drink?'

'A lemonade, please,' she said.

Colin passed the room key over with Robbie's change. 'It's up the stairs in the lounge bar, first door on your right. I can show you in a minute, after I've served these customers.'

'No need, I'll find it.' They took their drinks to a table in the corner. The pub wasn't that busy, but there were several people whom Emily knew. She nodded faintly to them and returned their greetings, feeling as if she were in some parallel universe where nothing strange had happened.

Robbie downed practically half his pint in one. 'So what's the plan?' he asked her. 'Are we going to lie low until your mother tells us what's wrong?'

'We can't talk about this here. Most of the people in this pub know my family.'

'Let's go upstairs then, where we can talk in private.'

She shook her head. 'I can't go up to your room with you.'

'Of course you can. You can do whatever you like.'

'You don't know how quickly word travels around here.'

'We're engaged, Emily. And who cares what people think?'

She just sipped her lemonade. The bubbles pricked her tongue and lips.

'I guess that answers my question about whether you're going back to the house or staying with me,' he said.

'I have to check whether my mother is all right, and find out what's going on.'

Robbie nodded. He reached over and touched the ring she wore with his index finger. 'Whatever's wrong, we'll get through it together. That's the deal.'

She swallowed, and tried not to picture a situation where she would have to choose between her mother and Robbie. Having to make a decision between the woman who'd given her life and the man she'd known only for a few hours, but whom she loved.

Surely that wouldn't happen. This was strange, but there must be an explanation. Her family weren't given to histrionics. Aside from Polly's enthusiasm over pop music and romance, no one in their house ever raised their voice. Her mother usually showed disapproval with criticism or with withdrawal, not with shouting.

It would all be a misunderstanding. She wouldn't have to choose between her mother and Robbie. That was the sort of thing that happened in Greek tragedies or soap operas, not in real life. Not in a village like Blickley, with locals chatting happily in the pub, with the most dramatic event being a narrowly avoided burst appendix.

But if she had to choose . . .

She would have to choose Robbie, wouldn't she? Wasn't that

what she had agreed when she promised to marry him?

And if it wasn't, what *had* she promised? Had she been as foolish, as impulsive, as her mother had accused her of being?

'Emily?'

She'd been staring at the ring, and Robbie's finger touching the clasped hands. She looked up, startled.

'We'll get through it together,' he repeated. 'Whatever happens. This is meant to be, the two of us.'

She nodded. Two days, she'd known him for. Two days and two nights. And then all those months of letters, longing written in every line. And this ring: so real on her finger.

He squeezed her hand. 'I need another drink. Do you want one?'

'No, thank you.'

He went to the bar and she felt the glances of the other customers. They could be a normal couple, out for a drink before dinner with her happy, normal family. There was no reason to suppose that anyone could tell that anything was wrong.

Robbie returned with another pint, which he immediately took a long draught from.

'You're not . . .' she began.

He wiped his mouth with the back of his hand. 'I'm not what?'

'I've got to leave you here. You're not going to drink lots, are you? I might need you.'

He frowned. 'I don't plan on getting plastered, if that's what you mean.'

'That just seems to be going down rather quickly.'

'It's been a strange afternoon. I can use a drink. I'm not my father, Emily. I'm not a drunk.'

'I wasn't saying you were. I don't even know your father. I was just saying . . .'

'This will be my last beer.'

'All right.'

'I'll wait for you. Ring the pub and I'll meet you.'

He leaned over the table and kissed her cheek, and Emily blushed, knowing they were being watched.

The house was silent. In the kitchen, the pot of potatoes still sat on the cooker, cool now. 'Mum?' called Emily. 'Daddy?'

'Here, Emily.'

Emily followed her father's voice to the sitting room, where both her parents were on the sofa. They were holding hands. Their faces were grim, and Emily felt a heavy weight of dread in her stomach. She twisted her ring around on her finger.

'Where's Poll?' she asked.

'She's gone to Margaret's house,' said her father. 'She doesn't need to be part of any of this.'

'Part of what?'

They didn't answer, only exchanged a long glance.

'Part of what?' she repeated. 'Mum, you kicked Robbie out of the house for no reason. He's at the Royal Oak wondering what on earth he did wrong. I understand that you didn't want me to get engaged to him, but this is ... inexplicable. You don't even know him.'

'I do,' said her mother, quietly. 'I do know him.'

'How?'

'Emily, you'd better sit down,' said her father.

She perched on the chintz armchair. For the first time, she noticed that her mother held a long white envelope. Emily stared at it.

Whatever was about to happen, whatever the explanation, that envelope held it.

All at once Emily felt sick. Heart beating fast, gorge rising. She wished she could go backwards in time, back to the lane and the raindrops and the mud, back to the wet railway platform. Back to Lowestoft and to Cambridge and to the first time she had seen Robbie, dark eyes and denim jacket.

'What is it?' she asked, though she didn't want to. Didn't want to move forward in any way.

'Emily,' said her father, 'you know that I love you very much. Both your mother and I do. And we are so proud of you. I couldn't have asked for a better daughter than you are.'

'Thank you,' she said automatically. This praise made her even more anxious.

'But,' said Mum, 'James isn't your real father.'

'What?'

'He's not your father. He's your stepfather.'

'You were a year old when Charlotte and I married,' said Daddy.

'A year old? But I don't . . .'

'James took us both on. An unmarried woman with a daughter. There weren't many men who would have done that.'

'And I have always, always considered you my own daughter, just as much as Polly is.'

'But . . .' She looked from her mother to her father. She took after her father. She got her medical brain from him, her interest in science, her meticulousness, her care. Everyone in the family said it over and over again: Emily looked like her mother, but in personality and mind she was the spit of James.

She had never wanted anything but to be just like him.

'But – but if you're not my father, who is?'

'I was a fool,' said her mother, eyes narrowed, teeth gritted. 'I was twenty years old and I believed every promise he made. There was a war on. I hardly knew him, but I thought I was in love. I thought he loved me. He said he'd come back for me. But he never did.'

'Why didn't you tell me?'

'I was an unmarried mother! I want to forget all about that time in my life. I never want to think about it. He was transferred. I waited for him. And then one day, when you were a few months old, he wrote to me to tell me he was already married and had a child. He'd been married all along, and never told me.'

'Who was he?' she asked again, touching the clasped hands on her finger, warmed by her skin. An old ring, worn by other

315

fiancées and brides, who knew how many of them, through the years from love to death.

Her mother swallowed hard, shook her head, and so her father took over.

'He was an American pilot, a volunteer with the RAF. Based at Duxford. It wasn't . . . there were a lot of war babies at that time. You can't blame your mother.'

Emily stared at her mother. She felt more than sick, now. She felt as if she were falling.

'What was his name?' she asked.

Her mother held out the envelope.

As if she were watching herself, Emily took the white envelope. She saw her hands opening it. Taking out a folded piece of paper.

It was her birth certificate, long and printed with red ink, with the details handwritten in fountain pen. Emily Ann, a girl born on 15 June 1942. Mother's name: Charlotte Atwell.

Father's name: Robert Edward Brandon. Occupation: Pilot.

Chapter Thirty-Four

When she arrived to pick him up at the pub, she was white-faced, tight-lipped. She would not look him in the eyes.

Robbie had had two more pints after she left, but he was far from drunk. The alcohol had barely touched the sides. He'd been pacing in his room since then, round and round the little bedroom with the slanted walls and the low ceiling and paned glass windows. He'd have found it quaint, if he hadn't had other things on his mind. When he'd seen her car pulling up below, he didn't wait for her to come into the pub; he'd run straight down and got into the passenger seat beside her.

'What's wrong?' he asked her immediately, and tried to take her hand. But she pulled it away.

'Let's go somewhere else,' she said quietly. And didn't say a word as she drove.

It had stopped raining, but the trees were still dripping. She drove out of the village and down an empty lane, finally pulling off into a muddy parking lot.

He'd been rehearsing arguments. Things he could say to convince her that her mother was wrong. That for every example she could come up with of people getting engaged too quickly, he could come up with a better example of love at first sight lasting forever. Or maybe it was that her mother didn't like Americans. Or people with brown eyes. Or men in general.

The thing was, he had no idea what he was arguing against,

really. He had never seen anyone react so violently to anything as Mrs Greaves had reacted to him. The closest he could think of was his mother's reaction the time his dad had been brought home by the police, still drunk and with his head split open forehead to ear, but even that had been more resignation than shock.

Or when he himself had seen Emily for the first time and that bolt of recognition had struck him, the knowledge that he didn't just want her, but *needed* her.

'Emily?' he said, but she just shook her head and got out of the car. He followed her.

Down a grassy bank, there was a wide, flat river, grey in the grey afternoon, choked with reeds at its margins. Emily walked down to stand beside it. It had a green, muddy smell after the rain, and insects danced up and down on its surface. He realised that she had chosen this spot because there were no other people here to see them or hear them.

He was more afraid than he'd ever been in his life.

'Emily, you have to tell me what's going on or I'm going to go crazy.'

She still didn't meet his eyes. She reached into the pocket of her coat and pulled out an envelope, which she gave to him.

He saw it straight away, like how you could instantly recognise a boat you'd worked on yourself, even from a distance. His own name glared up at him from Emily's birth certificate and yet he didn't understand the significance of it, and he was about to ask why he was listed as her father when he wanted to be her husband, and then . . .

'No,' he said.

'Daddy isn't my real father,' she said, so quietly he could hardly hear her.

'It's not true,' he said. 'It's got to be . . . some other . . .'

'He was an American volunteer pilot stationed here, she said. She said . . .' Emily swallowed hard. 'She said he looked exactly like you, at your age. She said that when you walked into the kitchen she thought for a minute that he'd come back.'

He was never the same after he came back from the war, said his mother's voice in his head, and the truth hit Robbie like a sledge-hammer between the shoulder blades. He nearly staggered with it.

'It doesn't have to matter,' he heard himself saying. 'Why does it matter? Why should anybody care?'

'Robbie . . . we're . . . you're my brother. We have the same father.' She said it with revulsion, and it made him speak more quickly. 'I don't believe it.'

'It's on the birth certificate.'

'It's a lie. Your mother doesn't like me. She wants to keep us apart.'

'She hasn't faked this.' Emily pointed to the paper he still held. 'It's evidence, Robbie. It's the truth.'

'We don't look alike, at all.'

'I look like my mother. You look like your – like *our* father.'

'You're very quick to accept this.'

She choked on a sob. 'I haven't . . . I haven't accepted it at all. I'm just trying to understand what we've done.'

'We've fallen in love.'

She turned her back on him and started walking rapidly down the bank. Robbie followed her. 'Don't,' she said.

'We didn't know.'

'We know now. My parents know. Your father would know. It's on my birth certificate.'

'I love you,' he said desperately. 'I refuse to believe that this is true.'

'It's true. We're related. It's illegal, it's immoral.'

'It doesn't feel immoral. It feels like the best thing I've ever known.'

'Robbie,' she said, 'don't you think that's *why* we fell so quickly? There have been studies – I've read about them. Siblings separat-ed at birth, they encounter each other years later, as adults, and there's a-an affinity. Suddenly. Like they're . . .' She choked, but forced the words out. 'Like they're meant to be together.'

'We didn't know. We've done nothing wrong.'

'Yes, we have,' she whispered.

'We can go somewhere no one will know us. Somewhere far away, just the two of us.' He reached out to touch her cheek and she stepped back quickly.

'No. We can't. Maybe it's not our fault, what happened, but we can't continue. Not now that we know. It's wrong.'

He felt as though he couldn't breathe. 'Please, Emily.'

She shook her head. Deliberately, her mouth firm, she slid the ring he had given her off her hand. She held it out to him.

'No,' he said. 'I gave it to you. I won't take it back.'

'I can't wear it.'

'Maybe we can never get married. But we can still be together. We're – we only have one life. We're not responsible for where we came from or what our parents did. We have to do what we feel is the right thing, no matter what anyone else says.'

'But this is wrong. Robbie, the shame on my mother's face . . .' She sobbed, suddenly, and a tear fell from her eye. 'If we stay together, that is how we are going to feel. All the time. Even if we go away, even if I give up all of my dreams to be with you, and you give up all of yours to be with me, even if no one knows, *we* are going to know. It's going to poison everything we do.'

'It doesn't have to.'

'Please. *Please.* Take back your ring.'

'No.'

'Then I'll throw it in the river.' She drew back her hand to throw, and he caught her wrist.

'Don't do that. I'll keep it.' He took the ring from her hand. It felt small and warm in his palm. 'But I won't . . . I'll only be holding it for you. Until you decide you can wear it.'

She pulled her arm away from him. 'Robbie, don't you see? We can't ever meet again. Not ever. After this conversation, I need to take you to the train station and we need to say goodbye forever.'

'No.'

'Yes. It's the only thing we can do.'

'I could never, ever feel ashamed of being with you.'

She only bowed her head. Another tear ran down her cheek and Robbie wanted nothing more, had never wanted anything more, than to wipe it away. To take her in his arms and whisper that everything was going to be all right.

'I don't care who we are,' he told her.

'I do,' she said.

She drove him to the pub to pick up his bag, and then to the railway station, in silence. Emily was still, every movement deliberate. Tears were in her eyes but very few of them fell. Robbie was restless, hand-clenched furious. The ring he had taken from her was in the pocket of his shirt and he felt it there like a red-hot coal.

He wanted to find the words to make this right. He wanted to talk and talk and explain everything away. He wanted to run, to punch something, to jump into water and swim, some sort of physical struggle that he could win.

He couldn't do anything. Without meaning to or wanting to, they had become something shameful.

The car pulled up outside the station. He'd only arrived six hours ago, and he'd felt the happiest he'd ever been in his life. He'd thought he was finally sure of his purpose and his direction. Finally with some sort of meaning to his life other than the passing joy of the moments on the sea.

'There's a train every half hour,' she said. Her voice was scratchy with unshed tears. She sat behind the wheel of her father's big car, gazing down at her bare hands, waiting for him to leave.

He wanted to run, wanted to swim. Wanted to wrestle the facts into some sort of shape that made sense, harness the wind in a sail, control the uncontrollable, do something that meant that they could be together.

'Emily . . . Will you please kiss me? One last time.'

She shook her head.

'Then look at me, at least.'

Her eyes, that shade of ocean blue. Troubled and beautiful. He remembered the first time he'd seen her, hurrying across the station in Cambridge. How as soon as he'd seen her, he felt as if he'd known her forever.

He looked into her eyes for as long as he could, committing them to memory, until she looked away.

Then he opened the car door, got out, and retrieved his bag from the back. He bent and looked at her one last time. She was fragile and small and much, much stronger than he was.

'I'll never forget you,' he said.

And then he walked away.

Postscript

October 2016
Clyde Bay, Maine

I often think about the first time we met.

Sometimes we don't know the moments that are going to be significant to us, not until later when we look back and reflect. But when I first saw you I knew, even though I didn't want to, that my life had changed.

Today is a glorious autumn day, one of those days when the sky is so blue it nearly blinds you. I went out sailing this morning, to Monhegan Island and back. I met the lobster boats coming back into harbour, each one surrounded by a cloud of gulls. Some wheeled away up into the sky, and I watched them. The other sailors call them rats with wings but you always looked up at them, tilted your hat back and squinted into the sun to watch the way they circled and flew in spread-out Ms, like a child's drawings of birds.

From below, you can't see the spots on their beaks, red as drops of blood. You told me a long time ago that gull chicks were programmed to peck on those spots, to prompt their parents to feed them. You told me that baby gulls who pecked the red spots were more likely to survive than those who didn't. It was a classic case of nature versus nurture. A scientist had won a Nobel Prize for his work on these red dots.

This morning I heard you saying this to me, in my head. And I held a single point of sail and I watched the gulls until I felt the sun beginning to burn my nose and cheeks. I had forgotten my

323

hat. I forget these things, sometimes, now that you're gone.

I never forget you.

Robbie, I was angry with you. So angry that, for days after you did it, I couldn't unclench my teeth. I could hardly talk, let alone eat, and my jaw sent a fierce ache up the side of my head and down my neck to my shoulders. I was angry enough to welcome the pain because I thought somehow it would punish you.

I'm not angry any more. I'm empty.

I miss you. When I wake up I put my hand out and touch your uncreased pillow. A hundred times a day, a thousand, I turn to say something to you and you are not there. After all these years I had almost failed to notice any more how you made my life more solid, how I only truly knew things when I had shared them with you. Even small things, even the shape of a pebble or a spot on a gull. When I showed you, when we spoke of them, they became true and real and part of us.

And the large things we shared . . . there was so much we never spoke of, and perhaps that was a mistake, but we both knew those secrets. All we'd given up and lost, and all we'd found together. I saw the knowledge of them under your surface, like the currents under the ocean, stronger than any force on earth.

The days go on without you as you said they would, and the waves strike the shore and wear the rocks into sand. William has gone home, though he calls every Sunday, now, the way he never did when you were here. I have Adam and Shelley and the grandchildren, I have Tybalt and Rocco, I have everyone here in Clyde Bay. I have the ocean and the sky and the taste of salt and the view of sails from the shore, our house you built for us, the boat you built for me, all the memories of our life, well lived, together.

I have the letter you wrote to me. The words that you ended it with, before you walked across the yard and down into the sea away from me.

I love you. You're my beginning and my ending, Emily, and every day in between.

You always used to say that you and I were free, if we were brave enough to take that freedom. I knew different. We were bound together, tangled up in exquisite complication.

But now, for the first time since I met you, I *am* free. Freedom was the last gift you gave to me.

And I would gladly give up that freedom, Robbie, to go back to the day we met and do it all again.

Acknowledgements

Teresa Chris, my agent, has been both loyal and fierce in her dedication to this story and to me. In twelve years of being my agent, she has never steered me wrong, and she is always, always, on my side.

Harriet Bourton is an extraordinary editor: sensitive, talented, and with the most marvellous instincts for story. It's an utter privilege to be her literary partner in crime.

Thank you so much, Teresa and Harriet. You are strong, incredible women. This book is dedicated, with so much gratefulness, to you both.

Thank you to David Shelley, Katie Espiner, Sarah Benton, Rebecca Gray, Lauren Woosey, Lynsey Sutherland, Jen Breslin, Bethan Jones, and all at Orion who have made me so welcome. Thanks too to copy editor Kati Nicholl for saving me from an embarrassing error in military history.

Regine Smith has been my summer neighbour all my life, and she and I had an extremely enjoyable and useful conversation about her experience as an adoptive parent in 1970s America. I'm also indebted to the book *The Baby Thief* by Barbara Bisantz Raymond, about the Tennessee Children's Home Society crimes which inspired the character of Elliot Honeywell.

My lifelong friend Captain Dennis Gallant, of Windjammer *Angelique* based in Camden, Maine, helped considerably with details of boatbuilding, boat maintenance, and sailing. (We'll gloss over the story of how he successfully navigated across the Atlantic in a sailboat and then, on land, promptly got on the wrong bus.)

My parents, Jerry and Jennifer Cohen, also helped with sailing terms and explanations, and with choosing the perfect location on the Maine coast for Emily and Robbie's house. It has been such a pleasure writing about the state that they and I love so much and will always call home. They also looked after my son while I went to Miami for research and then closeted myself away to finish this novel.

Captain Matt, of Ocean Force Adventures in Miami, Florida, answered questions about sailing the Bay of Biscayne and gave me a memorable tour of Miami from the water.

Pierre L'Allier made a generous donation to children's cancer charity CLIC Sargent to have his name and the name of his daughter in law, Sarah, given to characters in this novel, as part of the 'Get in Character' campaign.

Midwife Harriet Greaves gave me help with the childbirth and antenatal aspects of this story, and also kept me running. I stole her maiden name for Emily's maiden name.

Rowan Coleman, Miranda Dickinson, Kate Harrison, Tamsyn Murray and Cally Taylor give me daily inspiration and support. Brigid Coady is a constant source of sanity. Lizi Owens rang me up, having read this manuscript, in floods of tears to tell me how much she loved Emily and Robbie. My dear friends: I love you.

Bhavya Singh, Patricia Lee, CT Gallagher, Liz Carbone, and Sierra Chittenden provided creative distraction when I needed it most, and sometimes when I really needed to be working instead.

I wrote a good chunk of this book nurtured and inspired by Janie Millman, Mickey Wilson and Rory at Chez Castillon, France.

Thank you to everyone, too many to name, who helped me with encouragement, booze, and listening to me complain how bloody difficult it is to write a book backwards. Also to my dog who is awesome.

I listened to two albums while writing this novel, hundreds of times on repeat: Glenn Gould's 1955 and 1981 recordings of Bach's *The Goldberg Variations*, and Sufjan Steven's *Carrie and Lowell*. These artists inspired me more than I can say, and the rhythm of their music is in every line of this book.

Finally, always and ever, thanks to my husband and to my son.

together

Reader's Notes

In Conversation with Julie Cohen

Q The structure of the novel is so special; it immerses you instantly in the story and makes you invest so completely in Emily and Robbie's love for one another. Did you have the idea to write the novel in this way first or was it more a means for you to make their secret more shocking? And did you always know that that was going to be what they were hiding?

A I came up with the secret first, and the characters of Emily and Robbie soon followed, but it took me nearly a year to come up with the idea of telling the story backwards. I needed a way of making the reader believe in the couple's love first, before they knew the real reason why Emily and Robbie should be apart. I didn't write the story backwards to make it more shocking; it was more so you could see the truly good life they had together, so you could understand that their love transcended their circumstances.

I remember the moment I came up with the backwards idea. It was like a flash of light, and the story assembled itself into my head, almost fully-formed. Those moments don't come often as an author, but when they do, they're incredible.

Q There is an overarching idea of fate pulling two people together that really shines through the novel – is this an important concept to you?

A Actually, I'm not a great believer in fate in real life. I'm more of a believer in free will. But the idea of fate is powerful and compelling in fiction, and I am an absolute sucker for stories about people who are meant to be together despite the odds, or who are meant to be together but can't be. I am still crying over the endings of *Casablanca* and *A Tale of Two Cities*. I wanted to capture some of that bittersweet emotion in my story. (As an aside, there is a recognised phenomenon of genetic attraction, when close relatives who have been separated from birth experience a strong sexual attraction when they meet. I suppose our genetic code is as close to destiny as we get, though the characters fight against that in the story. The most uncomplicated main character in the book is Adam, who's genetically related to no one else.)

Q What are your thoughts on their secret generally? Obviously, as the author, you will have had this in the back of your mind when writing – but did it affect how you viewed them as characters and their relationship/feelings towards each other?

A One of the reasons why I love reading historical or classic novels is that the stakes are higher, and there's such a thing as impossible love. Anna Karenina can never truly be with Vronksy, whom she loves, because society sees her as an adulteress. Class separates Anne and Wentworth in Jane Austen's *Persuasion* for years. But in the world where I live, divorce is commonplace, and – thankfully – homosexual marriage is legal, and racial and religious and class differences aren't as important. One of the only things that can truly keep a couple apart is taboo. I wanted Robbie and Emily to be forced apart by circumstances beyond their control, which they didn't choose. I wanted them to have to give up nearly everything they care about in order to be together. And I wanted the reader, discovering their secret, to question what they think they know about morality and love.

I have enormous sympathy towards Robbie and Emily. If they had met as children, introduced by their parents, their relationship would have been very different. If they'd never discovered the circumstances of Emily's birth, their marriage would have been very different. They've committed a crime, according to almost everyone's sense of morality; they've broken one of the oldest and strongest rules of civilised society; but I don't feel that they're guilty.

Q How did you tackle the actual writing of the book? Did you start at the beginning of Emily and Robbie's meeting and work forward from there, or did you start from the story's beginning? Did you enjoy writing in this structure?

A I wrote the postscript first, the very last pages of the finished book; and then I wrote the first chapter where Robbie walks into the sea. I needed to know where my characters were heading. After I'd written those two parts, I wrote the book chronologically, starting in 1962 and working my way forward to 2016. I'd already planned what was going to happen in each section, and what would be revealed, so I could foreshadow as well as refer to backstory, but it was easier for me as the writer to build the characters organically over time. For example, the reader first encounters Emily's wedding ring in 2016, but I didn't know Robbie was going to buy her that particular ring until I'd written him doing it in 1962. Then I reassembled it into the order of the finished book, starting with 2016 and going backwards to 1962.

It was fun to write this way but I'll admit it was pretty brain-twisting. Each section has its own revelations and I had to be careful not to spoil them in parts that were set later, but read earlier. Also because the reader sees the effects before the cause, it was tricky to keep suspense in some areas – for example, if the reader already knows that Emily and Robbie have a child and grandchildren, how do you write about their real pain at losing William and at being unable to have a child? It was very challenging to write.

Q You mention in your acknowledgements that there were two albums in particular that you played while writing *Together* – how important is music to you? Do you always play something when you sit down to write? And what was it about these albums in particular that inspired you?

A I always listen to music as I write, usually the same songs over and over again. Hearing the songs puts me into the world of the book. With this book, though, it became much more obsessive and focused on two pieces. *The Goldberg Variations* became a powerful symbol of this story for me. It begins and ends the same way – an aria which is both hello and goodbye – and in between these two arias it takes in an incredible range of emotion and beauty. It's a metaphor of a full life, well lived, and the connection between birth and death.

Carrie and Lowell by Sufjan Stevens is an incredible album. He wrote it about the death of his mother, who had abandoned him as a child, and every song is infused with the beauty of sorrow and hope. It's profoundly compassionate and emotional. I listened to that album literally hundreds of times while I was writing this book, and after I'd delivered the final draft to my editor, I saw Stevens perform the songs live at the Royal Festival Hall in London. I cried for the entire show, for the songs and for my characters.

Q Maine is described as the most beautiful place. Do you think you will ever move back there or is England just as much a home for you now? And there is so much passion and love for sailing in this book – does this come directly from you?

A I can't sail at all. I seem to be missing the part of my brain that would help me understand basic stuff like how a sail works and how to tie a knot. But my parents owned a sailboat on the coast of Maine for many years, and my aunt and her ex-husband had one in Chesapeake Bay, and I've spent many very happy hours on those boats. There's magic in being in a boat under sail. You're moving and apart from the rest of the world, and yet you're connected with the planet in a fundamental way, tapping into the huge forces of the wind and the water and the tides.

Maine is, truly, a beautiful place. It made me very happy to write about it. My parents, my husband, my son and I went on a quest to find Emily and Robbie's house, which really does stand as described, surrounded by pink roses, very close to Marshall Point Lighthouse in Port Clyde. I visited the coast in Maine, in Miami and in Lowestoft for this book, and the quality of the light was so very different in each place. I don't think I could quite capture that in words.

There's a scene in the book where Emily stands on the beach in Lowestoft, and wonders where she truly belongs – England, where she was born, or America, where she lives now. I feel a lot like her: my heart is in two places, but home is wherever my husband and child are. And my dog, of course.

Questions to Readers

- The structure of this novel sets it apart from your 'traditional' love story – it establishes a deep connection to the characters before we discover that, perhaps, their love should not have existed in the first place. Did you enjoy the way the story was told? How do you think the backwards structure impacted your reaction to the secret?

- How does the author foreshadow the secret that Emily and Robbie are hiding? Did you see it coming?

- *'You always used to say that you and I were free, if we were brave enough to take that freedom. I knew different. We were bound together, tangled up in exquisite complication.'*

  What did you think of the secret itself? How did it make you feel and in what ways did it affect your view of Robbie and Emily? In your opinion, were they right to stay together?

- How did you feel about the opening moments of the novel? Did you sympathise with Robbie's decision to die to save Emily, or do you think he was wrong?

- How does the author use the ocean throughout the novel almost as a character in its own right?

- Opening of chapter six:

  'Emily was dreaming about a crowd. She was rushing through it, pulling a heavy, clumsy suitcase behind her, bumping into people. She had to get a train, it was about to leave and she was going to miss it and she couldn't find the platform, she'd forgotten the tickets. Heavy voices boomed from the tannoy, announcing departures and arrivals in words she couldn't understand.'

  Discuss Emily's dream and where it falls in the novel – what does it signify, for you?

- One of the most difficult decisions for Emily and Robbie in the novel is whether to tell anyone about the adoption of their son, Adam. How did you feel about this choice and did you see it in a different light once you knew all of their reasons for making it?

- The concept of life being cyclical and fate pulling us back towards our destinies is a key theme of the novel – discuss the different ways that the author explores this through setting, plot, character and objects.

Suggested Further Reading

FOR THE STRUCTURE . . .

One Day by David Nicholls
The Time Traveller's Wife by Audrey Niffenegger
House of Leaves by Mark Z. Danielewski
The Versions of Us by Laura Barnett
The Summer of Impossible Things by Rowan Coleman
Life After Life by Kate Atkinson

FOR THE EPIC LOVE STORY . . .

The Notebook by Nicholas Sparks
The End of the Affair by Graham Greene
The Light Between Oceans by M. L. Stedman
Hold Back the Stars by Katie Khan
Me Before You by Jojo Moyes
Persuasion by Jane Austen
Romeo & Juliet by William Shakespeare

LISTENING SUGGESTIONS . . .

The Goldberg Variations by Bach, played by Glenn Gould
Carrie and Lowell by Sufjan Stevens